CHOICES OF HONOR

GODDESS'S HONOR
BOOK FOUR

JOYCE REYNOLDS-WARD

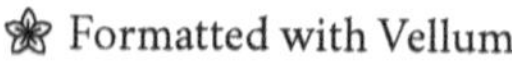 Formatted with Vellum

THE FIRST VISION

And what was worse, she couldn't identify whatever it was.

Rekaré Kinslayer scowled into the tiny warming fire of dried grasses, dead sagebrush, and juniper twigs, looking for wisdom in the flickers of flame and finding none.

Maybe it was the season that caused her worry as spring and winter fought for supremacy, the weather unsettled and raw, warm one day, bitter cold the next, all abrupt transitions that made the hair on her forearms prickle with uneasiness.

Except that today was a nice day.

The fires that her two tens of Mer Galad riders had kindled in this bare spot were for the purpose of drying out gloves and preparing a hot drink for the noon meal more than the need for warmth. While scattered clouds occasionally diffused the early spring sun's rays, that soft chill was momentary. The short interruptions in sunlight didn't pause the tiny rivulets of snowmelt trickling from under the knee-high snowbanks under the rimrocks. Mud and not ice squished under her heels. The trill of a bluebird swooping overhead testified to the presence of enough bugs for it to feed.

So just another lovely early spring day on the sagebrush plateau. Except that worrisome tingle, which had grown to a cool tightness in her gut.

Rekaré raised her head, tired of not finding answers in the flames. She inhaled deeply, savoring the fragrant smoke, working her fingers open and closed to help banish the chill. Nothing revealed itself in the clouds as she watched the sky, either.

There was nothing unusual about this trip, save that it was earlier in the season than she and Katerin usually met.

So why did she have this nagging sense of *wrongness* that had been tugging at her all day? The land would not be talking to her. It wasn't hers.

Maybe it was something amongst her people.

Except she *knew* how that discord felt from past experience. That wasn't the source of her uneasiness. Senth and Deta would have sensed any dissonance as well and moved to deal with it before her fretfulness escalated this far. So not amongst her riders.

No. Whatever this was affected her and her alone. But what could it be?

She looked away from the fire to check the Mer Galad anyway, even though Senth and Deta were moving from fire to fire talking to their tens, joking and chuckling, and would report any issues to her soon. Brown-skinned peoples from the nations of Larij, Medvara, Keratil, the Two Nations of Keldara and Clenda, and Saubral mixed with the gray-skinned Saubral Shadowwalkers without worry. Twenty riders, male and female, in equal numbers. All wore the blood-red cap and cowl of the Mer Galad as they warmed themselves by the fires, some squatting like her, others standing.

Nothing out of line, certainly nothing that would fuel her uneasiness, not like it had been in the early days when it took her, Detaluna, and Sesenth to smooth out fights between riders of different nations. Their tens had ridden together without change for two years, had worked out collaborations and disagreements.

Was what bothered her something that awaited in Chellni?

Normally they wouldn't be riding this far north during the mucky transition from winter to spring. But her cousin Katerin, who now led Medvara, had summoned her to the Chellni Spring Trade Fair, to report on her work monitoring the alliances between the nations of Varen.

Chellni.

Was that why she was nervous? Katerin had summoned her much sooner than she expected. Did this same dread haunt her cousin? She hadn't alluded to it in her message, not using any of the codes that implied problems. The earliness of this meeting was due to Katerin's official schedule, not anything untoward.

What was fueling her worry? Rekaré sighed. She studied the gray-white clouds lingering high above them, returning to the weather as a cause for uneasiness. The Gods Karnoi and Cirdel could use sorcerers dedicated to them to spell up hard storms unexpectedly.

But that sort of magic was hard to hide. She would feel it if someone attempted such a working close enough to affect them. By the Goddess's golden tits, even Garlat, the least magically sensitive of her riders, would be uneasy if someone was meddling with the weather. Certainly, it would have interfered with the daily divinations that Kovi, Staul's priest, performed.

Rekaré shook her head as the anxious tingles intensified.

What was wrong?

Deta joined her, reaching her hands out to the flame.

"All is well?" Rekaré asked.

Deta nodded, rubbing her hands together vigorously. "Mostly. Quertal's warming up after falling through the ice at the Deer Jump ford. No frostbite, thanks be to the Lady Dovré." Her fingers traced that Goddess's sigil in the air. "He's down to his last pair of warm pants through sheer wear, though—and he's not the only rider running short of clothes. Good thing we're going to Chellni. We can restock."

"This has been a tough winter."

"The melt and icing over and over hasn't helped. Sesenth is checking the horses."

"Shouldn't be a problem. Basnen didn't know of any issues."

Horses were the least of her worries. Rekaré had mind-spoken with her mare, Basnen, one of the magic-gifted horses called daranvelii. Basnen was also the lead mare amongst the riding stock. She had reported minor scrapes from breaking through ice-encrusted snow and some strained muscles, but mostly just fatigue that would ease from this midday break.

Fortunately, the troop all rode daranvelii, not ordinary horses, and their pack stock were daranval-bred mules. Expensive, but it wasn't a cost that Rekaré begrudged. She wanted her riders well mounted.

"You know Sesenth. She wants to see for herself."

"I do, indeed." Rekaré exhaled.

Attention to detail had helped the Mer Galad many times over during the past few years. The worry became a pounding in her ears. Something was happening somewhere. But what?

Maybe the land would tell her what was wrong. And maybe it would not. Tapping into its magic was iffy. She hadn't had the land's magic ever since she renounced the Leadership of Medvara. And this land was Saubral, which had never been hers to draw upon.

Her personal magic had taken her down different paths than earth magic since she walked away from Medvara. The Gods rode her with ease ever since the Hidden One who led Saubral had pronounced Rekaré as *benghaalph,* The One Spoken Of, the prophet meant to lead the Saubral to glory instead of the curse they had become amongst the nations.

Well, two of the Gods rode her. One was Dovré, her mother's patron, who had been one of Rekaré's guides. The other was Staul of the Balance, and his voice had grown stronger as the visions that accompanied her role as *benghaalph* came more frequently.

Artel and Terat were occasional visitors. The other three of the Seven Crowned Gods knew better than to disturb her.

She would destroy them if she could.

If she was going to tap the land's magic, she needed to get on with it instead of brooding. Rekaré reached down and fingered the damp soil in front of her, tentative, delicate, to sample magic's flow. She dared not be as aggressive as her Heartfather Heinmyets, who was the strongest earth sorcerer she knew. Heinmyets would press both hands hard against the ground, summoning power with ease. She wasn't comfortable with that sort of working, never had been, and even though she was *benghaalph* this Saubral land was not hers.

She extended her awareness into the earth as a slender, gentle probe, seeking a thread of the land's magic.

Damp. Cold. The soil frozen about a hand's width under the surface.

Rekaré closed her eyes to focus further. Tingles needled her fingertips, the magic in the land rousing, a different sensation from the worry haunting her.

There.

Something stirred beneath her touch, becoming aware of her presence. The sharp little barbs against her fingertips jabbed instead of pricking, intensifying and burning, small fiery sparks of pain lancing up her arms. The flow of magic capriciously danced against her hands. The land felt a danger—but she was not the threat, else those tiny jabs would be akin to hammer blows.

And there it was. Her answer. She wasn't imagining her apprehension. The land shared it, almost as if it held its breath in anticipation of something dire happening.

Power washed over Rekaré and a vision took her.

She was back in her wintertime childhood home of Dera, a silent observer in her Secondmother Inharise's bedchamber. Inharise lay immobile, skin grayish under brown, her breath coming slower and slower as Healer Yevtin held one hand, taking her pulse, frowning. Heinmyets sat on the bed, face twisted with anguish as he held Inharise's other hand. Behind him stood Rekaré's former husband, Cenarth, the son of Heinmyets and Inharise.

But the son Rekaré had borne for Cenarth, Linyet, wasn't there—*must be riding for Chellni, to meet me—oh Gods, she's dying and he isn't there.*

Agony twisted through her. Rekaré wanted to reach for them as she realized what was happening. Comfort—for them or herself, she wasn't certain.

Inharise is dying. Why didn't anyone tell me before now?

She screamed, trying to make them hear her across the distance. Nothing. No one looked at her. No one acknowledged her voice. Her shrieks grew lower, head pounding, black spots bobbing in her vision, the black spreading until the vision snapped away.

No. No.

She reached out. Wet. Cold. She drew ragged breaths, gasping, head pounding, suddenly aware she lay on her right side as the land's magic still jangled through her body. The damp cold of the earth felt good against her freshly shaven head. Rekaré blinked to clear her vision, but black spots still pulsed in front of her eyes. Her legs and arms trembled, a rebuke against exerting this much power. She delicately placed her left hand on the ground to push herself up.

"Ow!" Sharp prods zapped her palm and she yanked it away, shaking her hand. Why could she lie on her side and not be hurt, but try to use her hand to get up and this happened?

Inharise....

She tried again to raise her awareness, reach for Cenarth, for Heinmyets, someone in that chamber. But her magic stubbornly stayed silent, refusing to let her see more than this ridge tip.

Sometimes magic has no logic.

She lay there quivering as dampness formed in her eyes. The cool earth felt good to her pounding head, but she was chilling. She had to get up.

"Rekaré." Sesenth's touch eased the trembling.

Rekaré grasped Sesenth's forearm. Sesenth's grip steadied Rekaré as she pulled herself up and wobbled to her knees. She brushed the damp and dirt off of Rekaré's side. Then she reached for the blood-red cap and cowl Rekaré had pulled off sometime during her vision, shaking off the crumbs of dirt and dry grass on them, then deftly replaced first cap, then cowl on Rekaré's head. The post-vision quivers eased as Sesenth held her steady, banishing the discord of her vision and the land's magic. Rekaré still gasped for breath but it was easier, much easier than it had been moments ago.

"Thank you," she whispered.

Sesenth took Rekaré's face in her gray, scaly hands. They had been brown but were changing as part of the Shadowwalker transformation Sesenth was undergoing.

Once Rekaré would have found a Shadowwalker's touch fearful and frightening. Now it was familiar and friendly. Sesenth pressed her forehead to Rekaré's, humming a soothing tune. Rekaré closed her eyes, focusing on that familiar contact.

Fool. You know better than to idly reach for the land's magic without preparation, she chided herself. *What happens if Sesenth is not here? Think. Don't react.*

Sesenth pulled back, taking Rekaré's hands. Their eyes met. Rekaré shivered again as she met Sesenth's yellow-flecked green eyes—*Shadowwalker eyes, the eyes of an old foe.*

No. This was Sesenth. Sworn to serve Rekaré as *quixnafal.* Sesenth was a part of her Mer Galad, one of the Shadowwalkers who followed Rekaré. They were no longer enemies. Rekaré stared deep into that yellow-flecked green, centering herself on Sesenth's eyes as her breathing steadied.

Magic withdrew until she was once again aware of damp on her knees, clouds scurrying overhead, the small warmth from the tiny fire, the shuddering weakness that came over her after a vision like this one. She chuckled but it sounded faint and tinny to her ears.

"At least I didn't fall into the fire this time," she rasped.

Sesenth dropped her hands and rocked back on her heels, eyes still boring deep into Rekaré. "What did you see?"

Rekaré sniffled and dabbed at her eyes, sorrow washing over her again.

"Inharise is dying."

Sesenth's brows shot up as she inhaled. "Then—then the time foretold is upon us," she whispered.

Rekaré seized Sesenth's hand.

"Yes." She rose, pulling Sesenth up with her. "Mer Galad. To me!"

She shuddered. Seven years ago, the time had not been right to punish the Witches of Waykemin for their role in the attack that had crippled Inharise. But now—

We must wait until we are certain, else we risk Artel's condemnation.

She didn't want to attract the wrath of Artel the Judge. And yet—earth magic was reliable, not as quixotic as air or fire. Could she trust her vision, justify it to that stern God? She thought so.

Time to act.

She waited to speak until all twenty-two riders, counting Deta and Senth, stood around her, considering what to say. Surveyed her riders. Shadowwalkers. Saubral. Medvaran. Keldaran. Larij. A microcosm of almost all of the peoples of Varen on this side of the Barrier, save the Waykemese.

How many of their kin could they summon for what lay before them? How hard would it be to integrate outsiders into more tens like this? She dared not ask the Hidden One for any more Shadowwalkers, and the Saubral Houndriders lacked the discipline needed for the task ahead. But the others—they would need more than two or even five tens to attack Waykemin. And not all would be warriors. They needed shamans. Priests. Magicians.

But that task of raising warriors would also fall to her cousin. Inharise's kindred.

Katerin will raise Medvara, and Cenarth will raise Keldara and Clenda.

Especially Clenda, Inharise's home. Many people thought of the Clendans as peaceful pastoralists. But Rekaré had spent too many childhood winters by the story fires listening to the tales of Clendan past glories in battle to believe that assumption. Had learned battle from Clendan warriors. Had fought alongside Tletset and Mnenit of her Mer Galad, from Inharise's own clan.

It would have to be enough. It *would* be enough. She and Katerin had discussed this possibility over the past seven years, itching to be released—but now the time had arrived.

And this was the first step. Waykemin was but a tool of Chatain, Emperor of Daran-over-Sea. Before Rekaré could take any action of her deferred vengeance against Chatain, she had to secure Varen. Otherwise, she risked Waykemin rising up to conquer Varen in Chatain's name.

It was time that the Ralsem family that ruled the Darani Empire—also cousins of Katerin and Rekaré—met the fate which should have been theirs thirty-six years ago.

But first steps first. She had to share her vision with her riders.

"The Lady Inharise of the Two Nations is dying," she said. "That was what I saw in my vision."

Shocked expressions met her news.

Kovi's lips tightened. "Staul has been warning me that we approached a cusp. Now I understand."

"Yes." Rekaré gave herself a moment to inhale, exhale. "I created the Mer Galad seven years ago to be the defenders of Varen against Daran's colonial ambitions. Chatain's machinations murdered my mother and daughter. His allies the Witches have brought this fate to my Secondmother. It ends now!"

"It ends now!" Sesenth and Detaluna echoed, followed by their tens.

"So what next?" Deta asked.

Rekaré took another deep breath. "We meet Katerin in Chellni. Then we ride upon Waykemin. It is time for vengeance. I vow it as Rekaré Kinslayer. The Mer Galad will fulfill its purpose! We will make the world right!"

"Rekaré Kinslayer!" Kovi, Sesenth and Detaluna roared, thrusting their left fists into the air while holding their right hands over their hearts. "Mer Galad!"

The others chimed in. "Rekaré Kinslayer! Mer Galad! We ride for vengeance!"

She studied her riders as they repeated the chant, searching for any signs of doubt or fear.

None.

The feeling of dread faded from her. She finally had a clear path and—her riders were with her.

Waykemin was just the first step toward her ultimate goal. A faint smile quirked her lips.

First Waykemin, for daring to support He-Who-Sits-in-Daran.

Then he will pay. Then will I truly be Rekaré Kinslayer.

One more thing remained. She spread her arms wide and

raised her face to the sky, closing her eyes as she concentrated on this summoning, this time carefully *not* reaching for the land's magic.

Katerin, Katerin. It is time. We must ride.

Her right index finger traced a sigil into the open air, one that would only have meaning for her cousin.

THE SECOND VISION

KATERIN LEADER FELT THE LAND'S ICY TEETH PULLING AT HER AS they rode along the slick river trail, almost as if the icicles dangling from the cliffs and rock faces bit into her torso and grabbed at her arms to keep her from crossing the Dry Line and leaving Medvara. It added to the growing irritation and fretfulness she had been feeling all morning.

she thought to the spirit of Medvara, annoyed.

The sharp icy bite faded somewhat at her reprimand, though the land's uncertainty still remained.

Katerin sighed. Even after almost seven years of Leadership, Medvara's magic clung to her like a small child fearful of a parent disappearing. The eleven years of Rekaré and Cenarth's rule had not been enough to heal the damage done by their predecessors over the course of twenty-five years. She had to endure the land's clinginess every time she left Medvara.

But today the dread projected from the land stuck hard in her throat and sunk chill needles in her gut, as if she were facing the reddest of red opponents.

It could be worse.

Rekaré had never been able to leave Medvara until her abdication of the Leadership. At least the land let Katerin leave.

Still, this was the worst fussing Medvara had done at her leaving since her first year as Leader.

Katerin's daranval Rainin snorted, sending her an image of an over-dependent weanling, followed by pictures of a mare driving away the timid foal to join the others of its age. Katerin laughed as Rainin's deliberate distraction brought relief from the land's fretting, and patted her mare's neck.

Gods, what would she do without Rainin? Fortunately, daranvelii were longer-lived than regular horses.

"You would know, dear one!"

Rainin's boldest and most magically talented foal, Daro, now proudly trotted beside them as an adult, carrying Witmara, Katerin's daughter, as his bonded rider. While he had never clung to his dam, two of his older siblings had been shy and anxious, requiring Rainin to chase them away when it was time to be weaned.

Rainin shook her head and snorted, pulling a little against Katerin's hold on her reins, then settled back into her ground-eating travel jog, hooves crunching through the thin skiff of ice over puddles in the road. Satisfaction radiated from the mare's thoughts with every crack of ice. Medvara was never quite as cold as the upland plateaus of Keldara where Rainin had been raised. This arid chill near the Dry Line felt like returning home to both Rainin and Katerin. Especially after the clammy cool damp and dark of a Medvaran winter.

"The land is fussing again?" Witmara asked.

"Yes," Katerin sighed. "I keep hoping it will reconcile itself to my coming and going."

Her daughter quirked one eyebrow, an expression reminiscent of her late father Metkyi. It sent a pang through Katerin. "Mother, it will take many years before the land is healed. Until then, it's going to fuss whenever you are gone."

"Alas, yes," Katerin agreed. "But once you become Leader, perhaps the land will settle."

Witmara winced. "And perhaps your attitude is why the land doesn't calm, Mother. It needs a committed leader, not someone temporary. You have been good for Medvara. Of course it clings to you."

"It will have that leader soon. I still plan to leave my regency in six months, when you come of age."

Witmara's lips tightened and she stared straight ahead. "That might be why the land is unsettled."

"I am no Leader, but a simple Healer."

Oh really? something whispered deep inside of Katerin. *You, the daughter of Terani-the-God-Killer? Katerin ea Miteal? She who is the Banisher of Shadows? It has been a long time since you were anything but a simple healer.*

Witmara shook her head, scowling, and turned Daro to join the riders behind them.

Katerin sighed. She had only accepted the Leadership when Rekaré resigned on the terms that she held it as regent for Witmara. She hadn't been raised to lead. Hadn't been trained in the nuances of Leadership, and had spent the last seven years wrestling with the responsibilities and details that came along with serving the people. The people of Medvara had confirmed Katerin in her position, with Witmara as her successor.

The land insisted she was its true Leader, however.

But it deserved someone whose entire heart was dedicated to mending its ills and making it whole again. Someone who wanted to lead its people, not an unwanted bastard child born to the head witch of Waykemin and an exiled scion of the Miteal family. Not a former circuit healer who missed those healing tasks and at times wished that the Gods had not called her to be more than Katerin Healer.

Witmara is yet young. And even the Goddess says she is born to rule.

She had made every effort to train her daughter in what was needed in a Leader.

You cannot run away.

The sword sheathed at her side stirred, purring as it mind-spoke to Katerin.

I am not a Healer's tool.

True,

Katerin acknowledged.

But she still hoped to be able to pass the shapechanging, sentient Spear of War and Unmaking now wearing the guise of a sword to someone else's custody. She had not asked to become the Banisher of Shadows, had not asked to become embroiled in the wars between the Seven Crowned Gods, had *certainly* not asked to become the Spear's custodian.

That destiny had just managed to find her.

Witmara's laughter rang out from the group of riders behind Katerin. Toran must have made a joke. The Mershaunten of Larij's youngest son was able to distract Witmara from her brooding moments. Fostering him over the past three years had been a good choice. He had become Witmara's closest confidant, something both Katerin and the Mershaunten had hoped for.

Perhaps she should talk to Toran privately about why

Witmara didn't want to ascend to Leadership. Worry? Feeling inadequate? Medvara's Leadership was supposed to be Witmara's destiny, was something she had been training for over the past seven years.

Meanwhile, she gained nothing from brooding and arguing with Witmara. She knew better, but everything irritated her today. Why? The land's fretfulness and demand for attention? It usually didn't bleed over into her like this when she rode to Chellni—nearby, safe, almost Medvara.

Katerin shook her head. Maybe a good gallop would shake off her worry and distract her from the land's disquiet.

She urged Rainin forward to join the lead riders. Another annoyance that came with Leadership. She couldn't just ride, but needed to consult with the Captain of her guard before she could do something as simple as gallop along this road. She hadn't been this constrained when she had been Alicira's personal Healer. Heinmyets and Inharise resisted being limited, and this degree of security hadn't been necessary in the Two Nations.

But Medvara was not the Two Nations. Not in its histories, not in its customs, not in what it expected from its Leader.

"Jeralte," she called to her Captain. "Let's gallop. This next stretch is flat and the ice isn't too bad."

"Are you sure?" Jeralte guided his black gelding around the others to ride next to her. "It's still slick underfoot."

Katerin rolled her eyes. "I've galloped on much worse in the Two Nations. This next stretch ahead is sandy and there's no ice covering the ground. An easy hand gallop. Rainin could use it."

Not just Rainin.

Jeralte nodded. Katerin touched Rainin's right side with her heel and the mare broke into a gallop. Katerin rose in her stirrups, taking a soft feel of the reins as Rainin extended into the gait, snorting with each stride. The mare's joy at being able to run instead of jog was infectious, sending a thrill through

Katerin. They outdistanced the other riders easily, though Daro's hoofbeats drew closer as Witmara urged him to catch them.

Easy now,

she thought to the mare.

Remember, not all these riders and horses have our experience.

Rainin eased back on her speed, though her ears flattened and she shook her head, then bared her teeth as Daro came up to her flanks. Katerin laughed as Daro yielded to his dam. She took a firmer hold on the reins as the trail narrowed to wind through rock spires.

"Easy, girl," she said out loud, straightening up and dropping back into the saddle. Rainin reluctantly slowed her strides. Katerin grinned at Witmara. "She still won't let Daro run by her!"

"And he still listens to her," Witmara laughed back, smiling.

Then the land screamed around them.

Roiling sorrow struck Katerin as if she had been punched in the gut, doubling her over Rainin's neck as the mare half-reared. She gasped for breath as *sorrow, loss, pain, sorrow* rolled over her, clutching Rainin's neck as a quick image of *Inharise in bed, Heinmyets screaming, Cenarth trying to comfort him, Yevtin trying to resuscitate Inharise* appeared before her.

Had it not been for Rainin's steadying presence under her and in her mind, she might have fallen. As it were, she needed to bury her face deep into Rainin's mane and cling hard as the vision played out, grateful that the mare stood stock-still, not twitching a muscle.

It faded, leaving that overwhelming sense of sorrow and devastation.

"No. Oh no," Katerin breathed into Rainin's mane.

Part of her hoped that vision wasn't real, wasn't true, but she knew better.

"No."

She blinked back tears, remembering the summers in Clenda's canyon country riding with Heinmyets, Alicira, and Inharise as they traveled with the sheepherders grazing the Leaders' flocks on the sunlit golden grasses of the high country.

"No," she whispered again, now a protest rather than denial.

Inharise dead. That just leaves Heinmyets—oh Gods.

At least Cenarth and Linyet were in Dera with him. But still —oh Gods.

This death changed everything. Would launch events she had hoped would not come to pass for some time yet.

Enough. Katerin Healer might continue to mourn. But Katerin ea Miteal, Katerin the Leader of Medvara, Katerin the Banisher of Shadows, did not have that luxury. Katerin sniffled and pushed herself up from Rainin's neck slowly, aching in every joint as if she had been beaten. She shuddered and drew a deep breath.

Metkyi, Metkyi, speak to me! Please!

she called to the ghost of Witmara's father. Sometimes he would come to her during a crisis like this.

Silence from the shade of her beloved. His manifestations had become fewer and fewer over the past few years.

But I had hoped....

Still, Metkyi's lack of response was but another signal that the time foretold was upon them.

A wisp of cloud separated from the higher ones, descending until it twisted over the next ridge and shaped itself into Rekaré's summoning sigil. Katerin gulped at the sight while Rekaré's voice whispered into her mind.

Katerin, Katerin. It is time. We must ride.

"Of course, cousin," she whispered, dashing her tears away with her sleeve—sleeve of finest Eastern silk smuggled from Daran by the magic ships sailed by the Sorcerer-Captains, nicer than anything she had owned before she became Leader. "Of course, cousin," she repeated louder.

The world had changed again.

Katerin drew a deep breath and dropped her reins.

Rainin, protect me,

she thought to the bay mare. Waited until she felt the warmth of Rainin's shielding surrounding her, the small projection of a bay mare on the edge of Katerin's awareness.

Then she reached for Medvara's magic. The land, still quivering from Heinmyets' anguished projection, seized at her presence with icy teeth, snapping and chewing in its worry. Rainin's image stomped a foot and flicked her ears back. The intensity of the land's projection softened, the icy teeth changing to a colt nuzzling her hand.

This news means I must leave for longer than planned,

she told the land flatly, shaping her thoughts and projections with an aura of stern determination to forestall any outcry or objection.

Witmara will care for you in my absence. I need to do this to keep you—and all Varen—safe. The time has come.

She waited. Medvara's colt-like projection clapped its short stubby teeth at her submissively. Good. The land was taking the news better than she had hoped—then again, it had been nearly as roiled by Heinmyets's anguish as she had.

Lend me strength for the time ahead. Please.

Medvara changed shape from young colt to a young, wounded warrior in leather armor leaning on a spear for support. He staggered forward and pressed his forehead to Katerin's projection, his free right hand grasping for hers. She tightened her fingers on his as he fed power into her. At last he pulled back from her, younger and stronger but mute, staring at her with milky-white eyes.

Witmara will care for you. I will pass the Light of Medvara to her so she can do that.

Medvara nodded. The projection faded, and she felt the land around her calming, waiting.

Katerin blinked at the sigil. Rekaré couldn't be too far away. After all, they had planned to meet on the edges of Chellni this evening so that Rekaré didn't need to enter the town. But if she angled to meet Rekaré on the road instead of riding to Chellni first, they could speak sooner. She could split her troop, send part on to Chellni with Witmara, and ride with the rest to meet her cousin.

Yes. They needed time to talk and plan privately. To mourn quietly together before they had to do what was needed.

Katerin spread her arms wide, closing her eyes as she summoned the sigil to her. Then she opened them, reached for the wisp of cloud, and traced her response into it.

I ride to meet you on the road, cousin.

She tossed the sigil into the gray sky overhead.

Thank you, dear Rainin,

she thought to the bay mare's projection. The small shape shoved her nuzzle hard against Katerin, then faded.

Katerin blinked. Time to switch magics, though this next one was easier and less draining. Depending on how far Rekaré had come on the Southern Road, she could meet her by early afternoon. Best to figure that out now. She rested her fingertips on the hilt of her sword and traced a circle, then wavy lines on its hilt.

Show me where Rekaré is,

she commanded, visualizing a map of the Southern Road. This spell didn't always work through the Sword. Sometimes it was more effective in its Spear shape.

For once working through the Sword succeeded.

The map unrolled in her mind's eye. Her small figure hovered on the River Road. Rekare's shape appeared, not on the Southern Road yet, but not far from it. It looked like she and her Mer Galad had cut across ridges and canyons after crossing the Nixyin River—probably following trails known to the Shadowwalker members of Rekaré's Mer Galad riders.

Katerin and her riders weren't far from a trail that split off from this river path to bypass Chellni, connecting with the Southern Road not far from where Rekaré would eventually reach it. It would take hard riding but nothing out of her ability, especially if she took the faster riders of her troop. That would move their meeting up from evening to late afternoon.

Katerin traced the route. It split off from their current road after they crossed this ridge. She had ridden it before. Doable.

She dismissed the map with a snap and shook her head, refocusing on the world about her. It took a moment to come back from the map, the vision, all of it and realize she was still on the River Road, still within the bounds of Medvara—and the land had calmed, was less anxious. But she quivered from the intensity of her magical exertions.

She untied the smaller leather flask from her saddle horn and took a swig. The Coos berry wine's richness burned pleasantly down her throat, warmth spreading from the magic within it, giving her further strength.

"Mother?" Witmara's voice brought her back the rest of the way. "We're here. Are you back from the vision?"

She and Daro were on Katerin's right side, Toran on her left, ready to offer support if she required it. "Yes. Thank you. We need to change plans. Jeralte."

"Yes?"

"I need to meet Rekaré before she reaches Chellni. I want you and ten other riders to come with me. The rest go on to Chellni with Witmara and Toran."

"Mother, what's happening? I felt the land's reaction but—not why."

Katerin took a deep, ragged breath. "Inharise has died."

Witmara's eyes opened wide with shock. "Oh, *no*."

Katerin nodded. "I can't wait until tonight to talk to Rekaré. We need to plan. This changes things. I need you to go to Chellni and prepare things there. Speak to Headwoman Mohanisha. Send messages to Medvare for troops to come by sternwheeler. I'm not certain how quickly we'll be riding on Waykemin, but...." Katerin swallowed hard, suddenly unable to speak.

Witmara grasped her shoulder, all business, dark brown eyes firm with determination. "I will prepare the way for you and Rekaré, Mother. I'll organize riders and sternwheelers, get your magical supplies. Glimmer dust?"

Relief poured through Katerin. "As pure as you can find. Neutralizing paste for healing. I'll restock the rest of my supplies from the Healing House in Keldara. Chellni won't have everything I need."

"I will gather as much as I can," Witmara said.

"I'll contact my father," Toran said.

"Thank you, Toran, but I don't know if he can get forces shifted in time to help with Waykemin."

"Uncle Haran and Orlanden are currently in Nixyin," Toran said. "There's a brigade with them. Both would take it poorly if they did not have the opportunity to take vengeance on Waykemin for Inharise's death."

Oh Gods, Haran and Orlanden were getting to be old. She didn't think she could face the possibility of losing them in Waykemin. But Toran was right about their desire to be a part of avenging Inharise's death—wait.

There was another important role they could play without going to Waykemin. Another power to consider, and one reason why Witmara needed to be in Medvara. Waykemin's allies were Medvara's foes—the primary one being Chatain, Emperor of Daran-over-Sea. Chatain, their distant cousin, had struck at Medvara once before through his spy Chiral, bringing about Rekaré's abdication. Chatain might well have a role in Inharise's death. He would not hesitate to support Waykemin. And *his* Gods had not constrained him as Artel the Judge did Katerin and Rekaré.

"Medvara will need a defense to call upon," she said after a moment's consideration. "While we've not heard of Chatain preparing an immediate attack on Medvara and Varen, it doesn't mean that's not possible once we strike at Waykemin. This would give him an opportunity. Ask them to help you set up Medvara's defenses."

Witmara nodded. "If Chatain wanted to attack—it's a seven-day sail from the Ourigny Islands for the Sorcerer-Captains. Two more days than that for traditional ships, according to Setkin."

Nine days before Chatain could respond to an attack on Waykemin or the reports of their preparations to attack Waykemin, then. Perhaps fewer than that if this *were* a coordinated attack between Waykemin and Daran. Inharise's failing health wasn't a secret, after all, and neither was the knowledge that the God Artel had restrained both Katerin and Rekaré from attacking Waykemin until her death.

Katerin chewed her lip thoughtfully. "What are the odds that they've already launched?"

"I would think that one of the Sorcerer-Captains could warn us before now."

"True," Katerin conceded. "Send five tens with me. The rest you keep for Medvara's defense." Katerin scanned the riders. "Jeralte. Pick the riders to come with us. The rest ride with Witmara. We'll cross the ridge and turn off on the trail there."

Jeralte nodded. As he selected riders, Katerin turned back to Witmara and Toran. "Rekaré and I will ride into Chellni tonight. I want to supply in Chellni. It's the end of winter and the Two Nations won't be able to meet the demand. Figure two days before we leave. It will take you that long to organize sternwheeler traffic." She winced at the thought. Water traffic was not pleasant for magicians or daranvelii—but it couldn't be helped. Sternwheelers upriver were faster than riding across the land, and even with water's detrimental effect on those with magic, boat travel was still less draining than a hard ride cross-country.

"I will send messages to my father as well as Haran and Orlanden," Toran said. "Once we strike at Waykemin, then Chatain will know that we plan an invasion for certain."

"Agreed," Katerin said. Even though four of the Seven Crowned Gods supported them—the other three Gods were behind Waykemin and Chatain. Artel, Terat, Dovré, and Staul had scruples. But Karnoi, Cirdel, and Nitel were bloody, vengeful Gods with a desire to walk the reddest of blood roads.

Jeralte rode back to Katerin. "We are ready."

"Good. I will lead. I know the pathways we need to take."

"We will follow."

Katerin reached under her tunic and pulled off the Light of Medvara, the citrine pendant worn by the Leaders of Medvara. "Witmara. Wear this while I am gone. I pronounce you as my Regent-Designate." She tugged the Regent's ring off of her left finger and held it and the Light to Witmara. "Wear this, too."

"Thank you," Witmara murmured as she placed the chain that held the Light of Medvara around her neck, then slid the ring onto her finger. "Ride safely, Mother."

"I will." Katerin turned Rainin away from her daughter and urged the mare into a fast trot toward the intersection with their trail.

It took longer than Katerin wanted to negotiate the rocky point. But at last they dropped down into the next draw, and she saw the path leading south.

"Ride carefully and fast!" Witmara called to her. "I will have things ready in Chellni!"

"Ride safe!" Katerin answered.

She urged Rainin into a canter. The bay mare happily extended her stride, her hoofbeats a counterpoint to the buzzing of Katerin's thoughts.

A part of her felt relieved that at last the time had come. No more waiting for Chatain to make a move on Medvara from the west while Waykemin festered to their east.

But oh Gods, what a price they had to pay for this to happen. Her fear had been that the first attack would come from the west, and then Waykemin would move from the East.

She just wished that the Gods would make things clearer. That her late beloved Metkyi would speak to ease her mind. She could use a little of his support and strength right now. Gods, she needed him to help boost her courage before returning to

Waykemin. Just thinking about going back to her birthplace made her shudder.

CHOICES

"Well," Toran said to Witmara as her mother cantered away from them, Jeralte and half their entourage riding after her. "It looks like we are in for it now. Attacking Waykemin."

"Yes. The timing is—interesting." Witmara looked over who was left as her escort as Daro pranced impatiently. She stroked the Light of Medvara. The gem didn't glow like it did when her mother wore it. Still, her sense of the land's presence was stronger than it had been before she put it on.

I am here,

she sent to the land, as she had learned to do from her mother.

I assume title as Regent. I will guard you.

The Light of Medvara pulsed gently against her chest and hand, quietly accepting her as caretaker.

"Six months more and you would be Leader, not your mother," Toran said as she dropped her hand from the pendant.

"I think she hoped for that outcome," Witmara grumbled. "This gives her an excuse to make it happen."

"What are you going to do?"

"Do? I am Regent for her right now. Someone has to keep Medvara safe—and that is me. I can't walk away from this responsibility."

"I'd be the last one to suggest you do that." Toran rested his hand on hers. "Are you going to change your mind about permanently becoming Medvara's leader?"

She shook her head. "The land will speak for itself if that happens. But—" she drew a deep breath— "it will not come to that. I sense that I will not become Medvara's Leader. Not if what we hear from Daran is true."

"*If* it is true. That's the problem." He squeezed her hand, then pulled it away. "Nonetheless, I will support whatever you choose. You know that."

"Thank you."

At least she had Toran's backing. He might be the youngest son of the Mershaunten and unlikely to become Mershaunten himself—but his aid and what he had learned growing up in his father's court meant more than she wanted to admit.

Witmara studied her escort again. Ten more riders, mostly young and less experienced, as well as a string of three pack mules and their handler. She didn't foresee any problems.

"Let's ride for Chellni," she called, projecting her voice. "Elenari, I'll lead," she said to the ranking rider. "You keep an eye on what's happening behind us. We should be good, but who knows what will happen once we cross the Dry Line and drop into Chellni. Shouldn't run into any problems with raiders but I still want you watching behind us."

Elenari saluted Witmara and turned her daranval back to ride with the pack string. Witmara tucked the Light underneath her tunic. Despite its exposure to the cold air, Medvara's sigil was warm against her bare skin, another sign that all was well and that the land accepted her as caretaker.

It wasn't a burden she really wanted to acquire. And yet—right now there were no options but for her to step up and lead. After Waykemin—

After Waykemin Rekaré will drag Mother to Daran. Chatain waits, and Rekaré yearns for vengeance. And you?

That was the question. She had known for years that her future did not lie with Medvara. But getting her mother to consider that option…. Empire was something one did not bring up lightly, and the nations of Varen did not have the resources to back an offensive against the might of Daran. But if Chatain brought the fight to her….

Not yet time.

For now, she needed to think about Medvara. Witmara nodded to Toran and raised her rein hand, squeezing her calves against Daro's side to send him ahead. Daro lunged into a half-trot, half-canter, reluctantly coming back to Witmara's command as she tightened her gut and squeezed her left hand on the reins until he picked up a jog again. She opened her hand slightly to ease the pressure on his mouth. Daro mouthed his bit in protest at their slowing, chomping on the bar and flicking the roller mounted in the curb's port, sending her impatient pictures of cantering off like his dam had done.

We must wait for the others,

she sent to him, thinking privately that perhaps she could find a place to let him gallop. Daro enjoyed a rousing hard run, just like his dam, and that little stretch before the land had roiled wasn't enough for him.

Daro sent back pure annoyance, no pictures. She eased her hand on the reins more to let him extend the trot a little bit, posting to the faster pace. A period of long trot wouldn't hurt any of the riders with her, or even the pack string. He fussed a little then settled into the quicker trot.

Once Daro was trotting smoothly, she felt the *presence* of the God Staul, a faint smoky scent in her nose, the squeeze of bony fingers on her right shoulder.

> This temporary leadership of Medvara is the final test of your worthiness for the fate ahead of you.

Witmara tightened her lips, catching her breath, grateful that at least the God had waited for Daro to settle before demanding her attention.

> What does that mean, Lord Staul?

> You and your mother are right to be concerned about the possibility of attack from Daran while she deals with Waykemin—as Betsona has warned you.

Chills ran down Witmara's back. She knew the likelihood of invasion from Daran was strong, more than her mother admitted. One of Chatain's bastard sisters had approached them to warn of this possibility two years ago, sending a letter via Setkin's smuggler connections.

> Cousins,
>
> I am Betsona ea Ralsem ei Vespla, and I want you to know that not all your Darani kin think ill of our distant relatives. Some of us even admire those women of our family who follow in the path of our ancestress Elithtra.
>
> Know that I am no Chiral ea Ralsem to seek your confidence and betray you. I abhor and condemn that

branch of the family. I have also been told that you seek information about our family's history in Daran and Varen. I can send manuscripts to you via Sorcerer-Captain Setkin.

He will vouch for who I am and can establish secure linkages. It is unlikely we will ever meet due to my poor health, but I would have my distant kin be aware of events here in Daran for your own good.

Best,

Betsona

Lanivar, Ourigny Islands

Neither Katerin nor Rekaré had wanted to respond, fearing another Chiral. But something about the letter—perhaps the offer to share manuscripts—had attracted Witmara's attention, enough to consult first Staul and then Setkin.

She is dedicated to Dovré and is the youngest daughter of the late Emperor, the God had told her. Dunaran wanted her to become Empress. But a magical accident caused by Chatain left her crippled and unable to rule. She is scorned by Chatain and his followers because her mother was one of Dunaran's body slaves. She and Chatain are Dunaran's only survivors. Chatain has murdered his other siblings, but Betsona survives thanks to her wits and magic skills. She is trustworthy.

Setkin added more. "The common people love Betsona. Chatain keeps her in exile, bringing her out once a year to be seen at the Commemoration of his crowning, but does not move against her."

"Then why does she not supplant Chatain and rule Daran herself?" Witmara asked.

Setkin shook his head sorrowfully. "She has the heart to rule but not the health and strength. Chatain only needs to wait for her to die to be rid of her threat."

Witmara had taken both Staul and Setkin's information to her mother. After exchanging letters with Rekaré, Katerin had approved Witmara's careful correspondence with Betsona. They had written to each other regularly over the past two years. Witmara had a better idea of what life in Daran was like, especially in the artistic circles that Betsona patronized. One of her few outlets was a regular visit to the great Festival of Plays in Adalane. She sent copies of the winning plays to Witmara.

Literary and artistic references also proved to be an effective cipher, especially as Witmara read more works from Daran.

But still—could she trust Betsona? Was Betsona was intended to lull her suspicions, distract her from the real challenges?

> There are times when I wonder what Betsona's real purpose was in contacting us,

she said now to the God.

The God laughed, a mixture of humor and menace in his tone.

> Do you not trust the source I sent you?

> One must always question what comes from Daran! Chiral came from Daran and look what ill fate she brought. Betsona has been reliable— so far. But I have not met her face-to-face and she is his sister, even though he's exiled her.

> True, true about Chiral. Still, Betsona does not deceive you in this. I confirm the veracity of what she says so far. I vow this to you who is the daughter of the Banisher of Shadows and my most beloved left hand, Metkyi.

Can you tell me more?

Not without angering Artel the Judge. I press my limits already. He draws near. I must go.

Her sense of the God's immediate presence faded, though she could tell he lingered nearby.

Toran rode quietly beside Witmara as she brooded about what lay ahead of her. Preparations to enable her mother and Rekaré to lead the battle against Waykemin. Securing Medvara against possible attack. Physical or magical? The more things she considered necessary to do, the longer the list of tasks became.

"Gods," she said finally. "So much to do in so little time."

"I have the latest records in my saddlebags."

"Good." Not that she expected any less. They were supposed to do an audit of the Medvaran tens assigned as part of Chellni's multinational protective forces. Six months ago, her mother had delegated the supervision of military preparedness and provisions to Witmara while she focused on trade agreements. She had recruited Toran to help. "Let's run through the list. Magical supplies. I should have your uncle obtain them for us."

"He does have leads on the best sources," Toran said.

"Communications."

"I don't know if we have enough express riders."

"Messenger birds. Mother and Rekaré will use some magic but we can't depend on them for everything. We need to send a full complement of messenger birds. Where should we get them, Chellni or Nixyin?"

"Chellni."

And so they continued to plan. It was almost a surprise when they topped the last hill and dropped down into the wide plain below the stark rimrock cliffs that was Chellni. She had lost track of where they were.

"Will you go back to your father or return to Medvare with me?" she asked as they rode toward the mass of tents and long-houses that was Chellni during the Spring Fair.

"Do you think he'd reject the opportunity to have me riding by your side as a close advisor? My father would be a fool to recall me, especially since he already has Aldan to succeed him and Neath after him—and he is no fool." He grinned at her. "I expect you'll still want to keep seeing my reports before I send them on?"

"I'd be a fool not to know what you're telling my fellow Leader."

Toran laughed. "You're not a fool." He sobered. "Who's riding toward us?"

Witmara squinted to identify the five riders. The lead rider seemed small and young.

Linyet?

She hadn't known that her cousin was coming to Chellni for Spring Festival.

Daro pricked up his ears and snorted. He danced sideways, then nickered.

A familiar nicker answered Daro—Yaranei, Linyet's daranval.

Dread tightened Witmara's gut at that confirmation.

Linyet.

Did he already know? She couldn't imagine her cousin not being aware of his grandmother's death—not when it had roiled the lands so much. As they drew closer, she noticed that his face was tight and hard, and that his braid had been roughly shorn.

He knows.

When they were three strides away, he waved at those riding with him to stay back. Witmara also signaled her riders to remain behind as she and Toran rode on ahead. She approached Linyet in the way of Inharise's people, riding Daro up to Yaranei. Yaranei dropped his head submissively without squealing or striking after the two stallions touched noses, acknowledging Daro's high rank amongst the daranvelii. Daro snorted in acknowledgement.

Witmara moved him forward so that the two stallions stood right-side to right-side, nose-to-flank, both quiet since rank had been established. She extended her right hand and clasped arms with Linyet. Linyet's hand closed hard on Witmara's arm as he blinked back unshed tears, looking younger than ever.

"I am sorry for your grandmother's passing," Witmara said.

His fingers tightened even harder on her arm, then released. "Thank you. Where is your mother?"

"She rides to meet Rekaré. They plan to come into Chellni together later this evening." She was careful to refer to Rekaré by name instead of "your mother" to Linyet. As far as she knew, he still denied the relationship.

Linyet nodded sharply. "That is good. Rumors run wild in Chellni. I—Grandfather had sent me with messages for Rekaré, and a bracelet linked to him for quick communication. Not necessary now."

"So your grandmother was ill before you left?"

"Fading, but not in immediate danger. Nonetheless, Father did not expect her to last until winter." His lips tightened. "What has happened is far too similar to what happened—*that* summer. You know which one I mean."

Witmara nodded, remembering the summer when every-thing changed. When first Alicira, then Melarae died. When Chiral as Chatain's tool, along with the support of Waykemin, brought about the attack that weakened Inharise.

"I remember," she said, her voice low and choked. "How bad was she?"

"Just like Alicira that last month. Failing but not dying. Father and Grandfather both thought it safe for me to come with the Wickmasa riders, to see Mo—Rekaré, to bring her messages. That Grandmother would still be alive when I returned. And then—" he released her arm to gesture about them— "*this*. No word that she was in danger of dying this soon. No indication of trouble. Just gone."

He drew a deep, shuddering breath and Witmara reminded herself that for all his apparent maturity he was still barely fifteen, even though he rode on his own authority in the name of the Two Nations.

And yet—some nerve on her part to judge him for being young, she who was only six months away from her eighteenth birthday. True, he had attained the age of magical majority. Was older than his parents had been when they were on the run, hiding from the wrath of Rekaré's father Zauril, the then-Leader of Medvara. But still—Linyet was young.

Rekaré was my age when she became Leader of Medvara.

"My mother plans to ride for Dera as soon as she can," Witmara said. "Rekaré sent her a sign after the land roiled. I have tasks to prepare for them riding out. I am to guard Medvara. But for now—I am here, cousin. If you have no other duties, it would be a pleasure to have your company and advice while I go about my duties."

"Thank you." Another deep, shuddering sigh from Linyet.

"Who rides with you?"

"Traders from Wickmasa, mostly. Yetklet and his kin. We rode sternwheelers downriver."

"All right. The sooner I get to my tasks, the sooner I can finish them, and we can talk," Witmara said. "Let's ride."

Linyet nodded and waved to his riders. They fell in with hers as the three of them led the way toward the main part of Chellni.

"I would ask to ride with your mother back to Dera," Linyet said. "I don't see the need for the traders to come back with me. Do you?"

"I wouldn't think so." Witmara swallowed hard. "But I won't be there. One of us needs to hold Medvara. The land is—needy."

"That is too bad. I wish you were coming with us."

"So do I. But someone has to hold Medvara, and that has to be me." She sighed, deciding not to tell him about the possibility of attack from Chatain's forces. Though he was vowed to eventually lead the Two Nations, Linyet had been born in Medvara after all, and might feel the need to join her in its protection. "Tell me about Keldara and Clenda, the grasslands, the canyons, the mountains," she said instead. "I miss them horribly."

And I fear I will never see them again, if my fate holds true.

Gods, she would miss the land where she had grown up. As Linyet spoke of the last summer he had spent with his father and grandparents in the high ridges over the great canyons where she had been born, the longing became more tangible.

Farewell, the high ridges over deep canyons of Clenda.

Farewell, great mountains surrounding the round valley of Keldara.

Farewell, grasslands of the Two Nations.

Who knew what her future would bring?

THE LAND'S GIFT

Gods, even after seven years of Leadership the *always knowing* exactly where she was in Medvara still shocked Katerin. After visualizing the map, she recognized every twist and turn of the path they rode, although it had been at least a year since she had ridden in this area. Last spring, she had met Rekaré along the Southern Road at the edge of the Dry Line, had spent a long night talking and planning, but her cousin had not come into Chellni. That had become their routine, to meet near Chellni in the spring and Cooscol further south in the fall, right on the border of Medvara but never inside of it.

Rekaré had crossed the line—once. The land's angry reaction to her presence made it clear she was not welcome to return.

That will have to change if this truly is the beginning of our challenge to Chatain.

The trail wound through oak highlands, rising into the tall green firs before dropping down into first the pinelands, then grasslands along the Chellni River. Katerin steeled herself as they approached the edge of the pinelands, anticipating the land grabbing at her as she crossed the Dry Line and entered the open grassland. Even though the Light of Medvara was with Witmara and the land had accepted her custody, she still didn't think it would let her go very lightly. Not after the events earlier.

Icy tug at her hand as the trees thinned.

Don't go.

Witmara is caring for you now. I must go.

She is gone from me too.

Sadness radiated from the land.

She will return. I must avenge my friend.

You go to your birth land?

Yes.

It will be jealous of me. It will not want you to remember me.

Nonetheless I must go. It is a greater duty than Leader.

STOP.

The intensity of the land's voice startled Katerin into halting Rainin.

I must go.

You leave the Light with Witmara. So you must still carry a token of me. It will keep you safe even when Waykemin would strike against you.

A token?

Dismount.

Bemused, Katerin followed Medvara's instruction. What *could* the land want her to carry?

"What is it?" Jeralte rode up beside her.

"The land wants me to do something—see!" She pointed as steam started to twist in a small wisp above the damp earth about ten strides in front of her. The haze intensified and the ground parted, greenish bubbles boiling through the crack. Then the fracture snapped shut, leaving a chunk of palm-sized gray rock with small green globules sitting on top of the recently disturbed earth.

It is hot. Drop it into a snowbank,

the land instructed.

Still mystified, Katerin followed its instructions, snatching a cloth from her saddlebag to scope the rock up and drop it in the nearest, iciest-looking, snowbank. More steam arose as cloth and rock sank into the snow.

It should be safe to handle now. Pick it up,

the land said after the last misty wisps faded.

Katerin delicately used the cloth to pull the rock from the snowbank. Ice surrounded the small stone. She brushed it off.

What am I to do with this?

Keep it with you at all times. It is a part of myself and will give you added protection, though not as strong as the Light. It will let Waykemin know that you are vowed to me. Should you need to draw upon my magic, hold it in your hand.

"Thank you," she said out loud, turning the rock in her fingers. She closed her hand around the stone to test it. Immediately a sense of Medvara's *presence* filled her.

And more.

Vision took her, transporting her from the pine forest to the dank stone cavern in the city of Forsim where the Witches Council of Waykemin met and held ceremonies.

Truth or memory?

Katerin looked for the stone altar. Did her mother's senseless body lie there in the endless sleep? That would mean this was memory and not a true vision.

No. Three poppets were mounted on the altar, two upright, one fallen.

Waykemin's Chief Priestess laughed as she pounded a drum around the Great Council chambers, chanting, "We have prevailed! We have prevailed! Inharise has fallen, and the others will succumb soon!"

The other members of the Witches Council joined her, keening in exultation.

Who were the figures on the altar?

Dread gripped Katerin. Moving closer to the altar felt like slogging through deep mud—testimonial to the power of the spells that protected this most sacred site in Waykemin. Ever since babyhood her mother had drilled into her that the chambers of the Witches Council were impenetrable, impossible for any outsider to breach.

Well, she had learned a lot about magic since that time.

And I am not an outsider but the daughter of Terani-the-God-Killer. If anyone not of the Council can break through, it would be me. Dovré give me strength!

No response directly from the Goddess, but Katerin's spirit found it easier to approach the heavily shielded altar. None of the witches noticed her presence—*thank you, Goddess!* The fallen figure was a rough representation of Inharise. And the other two—Heinmyets, knees buckling. Herself. The hairs on the back of Katerin's neck stood up.

Her hand closed tighter around the rock Medvara had given her. She had seen enough of these workings before leaving Waykemin as a child to know what it meant. The Witches *had* struck against Inharise. Their success now emboldened them to plot against her and Heinmyets.

This cannot happen.

But knowing this meant yet another thing to be wary of. Somehow—during the attack seven years ago?—the witches had acquired tokens which gave them power over Heinmyets and Inharise. Not strong enough to harm them unless their target had been weakened, but perhaps Heinmyets without Inharise was vulnerable.

No surprise for Katerin that they had such things for her. Leaving strands of her hair had been the price for her to leave Waykemin so she could train at Keldara's Healing House. Not wanting to be drawn further into their circles was the reason why she left once her mother had fallen into the dreamless, endless sleep. Keeping the Witches from striking at her was why she had sent regular payments for her mother's care while Terani lay senseless on the altar in the middle of the Council chambers.

Katerin had not wanted the Council to think of her as a foe then, had wanted them to forget that the unwanted, unacknowledged daughter of Terani-the-God-Killer and Alame en Miteal (even though she had not known who her father was) might possess enough power to challenge them.

Then she stumbled across the small village of Wickmasa, whose healer Makri had been corrupted by the Twin Gods, straying from Dovré, the healers' patron. Wickmasa, where she had encountered and fallen in love with Metkyi. Where they became entwined with Rekaré's fate, and challenged the Twin

Gods Karnoi and Cirdel, Terani's patrons—and the patrons of Waykemin.

Katerin's fingers tightened even harder on the rock, the faint warmth from its creation heating her hand. She had to thwart this working. Let the witches know that she and Heinmyets weren't without defenses. Something to let them know that she —not just anyone, but a daughter of Waykemin—had managed to breach their defenses and spy on them.

Put fear in their hearts, to counter what they have done to us.

Yes. A good first test of this tool that her land had given her. Would it be enough?

Only one way to find out.

A light fingertip brush on her cheek, signaling that the Goddess was with her but not revealing her presence otherwise. But that light touch was enough to bolster Katerin's confidence. She strode boldly to stand by the altar, then dropped her shielding so that the witches could see her. She knocked the poppets off of the altar. They crumbled into dust, no longer able to affect anyone.

Too late.

If only she had known in time.

The Priestess's drumming halted in mid-chant as Katerin turned to face her. Katerin stifled a laugh as the Priestess stared at her, eyes widening. Not the Priestess of her youth, but that one's daughter.

Tranarin!

The epithets from childhood came back to Katerin, all led by Tranarin. She-Who-Should-Not-Have-Been-Born. Cursed and

Fatherless. Half-breed, not full Waykemese, one to be cast out, never to set foot in this holiest of holies. And more.

But those hurtful words no longer injured her. Katerin ea Miteal, Banisher of Shadows, Leader of Medvara. Tranarin no longer held any power over Katerin. If anything, she cowered as Katerin marched toward her, until a single stride separated them, Tranarin quivering as Katerin had once quaked before her.

Do you know who I am? Do you remember me? Terani's daughter, the waif you so scorned?

Katerin leaned forward, glaring into the Priestess's face. Tranarin staggered back two steps.

No. You cannot be her. Not Katerin the Cursed, Katerin the Fatherless. She was never strong enough to breach the Circle, much less touch the altar!

I am she, indeed.

Katerin smirked at the Priestess.

And I am not fatherless. My father was Alame en Miteal. I am Katerin ea Miteal, Banisher of Shadows, Leader of Medvara. Beloved of Dovré and Staul. You dare to curse me and those I love. I warn you. While you have prevailed for now, your victory will not last. Vengeance is coming.

Tranarin shrieked and stepped back further, screaming curses.

Staul's presence washed over Katerin.

Enough. You have given them plenty to think upon. Do not overplay your hand.

Much as she wanted to see the Priestess cower further, the God was right. Petty vengeance now was less satisfactory—and a risk to their long-term goals. Katerin let the vision go.

Then the God was gone.

Awareness returned. She was on her knees, in a patch of icy snow. The sharp clean scent of pines in snow smelled much better than that dank stone cavern.

Katerin inhaled deeply, rocked back onto her heels for a moment, then bent over deeply to the land, pressing her forehead against the soil to give thanks, stretching her arms forward so that her palms touched the earth.

She rose and rolled into a squat, brushing bits of ice and damp sandy soil off of her forehead, arms, and legs. Then she opened the belt pouch on her right side, extracting a small piece of wool cloth woven from the magical fleeces of the Medvaran-raised Stardance sheep breed, the traditional source of the magical cloth that was the original source of Miteal power.

She wrapped the stone in the cloth and tucked it deep in her pouch.

"The land gives you a token?" Jeralte asked.

Katerin startled. She had been so focused on the land that she hadn't realized he stood beside her. "That, and a vision. It will keep watch over me as we battle against Waykemin."

"Good." There was no mistaking the approval in his voice. "I would not lose you to the Witches of Waykemin, Katerin Leader."

"That is hardly to be my fate," she said, rising.

She staggered halfway up and almost fell sideways, suddenly aware of the toll this vision had taken. Jeralte steadied her until Rainin sidled alongside them. Slowly, deliberately, Katerin undid the flask on her saddle horn and took two swigs from it. Then she reattached it before remounting Rainin.

"But now the Witches know that they should fear me," she continued.

I will come upon them like the ghost from their past that I am, she vowed. *The prophecy years ago claimed that one of their own would destroy the power of the Witches' Council. It is time.*

Gods, she hoped that prophecy was still obscure and forgotten. But her presence amongst the poppets on the stone altar suggested otherwise.

Perhaps their fear will give me more power. And now they know I am not toothless.

All the same, best that she not count on the Witches being intimidated. Rekaré needed to know about this. Together they could break the power of the Council.

And with it, Chatain's strongest tie to Varen.

She urged Rainin forward into the grassland, impatient to meet Rekaré.

Only fools ride eagerly to their fate.

But hadn't that been the story of her life for the past nineteen years, ever since she first cast eyes on Wickmasa?

The land's teeth released her as she crossed the invisible barrier that marked its boundary, less reluctantly than before.

But she still sensed a part of Medvara's presence with her, hidden in the pouch at her waist.

It was surprisingly comforting.

THE SUN WAS THREE-FINGERS' WIDTH FROM SETTING OVER THE western peaks when Basnen slowed from the fast jog to a halt. The road before them emerged from the mixed pine forest they had been riding through onto a snow-free but dry flat. The daranval mare raised her golden head high, silver mane spilling over her neck. She nickered loudly, coupled with the buzzing sensation of daranval-to-daranval mindspeech that Rekaré couldn't understand.

Then she snorted, sending a picture to Rekaré of

KaterinandRainin close, other side of the draw ahead of us.

Satisfied feelings as she imaged the four of them by the fire, showing her approval of where she had stopped.

Rekaré looked around Basnen's chosen meeting place. The flat dropped sharply into the draw, and from what she could see of the road, it curved to angle sideways along the canyon wall. The flat and forest edge still had enough dry grasses on it for their combined groups to graze lightly. The presence of as-yet-leafless aspens on the eastern side of the flat suggested a spring for water. They could have fire and a meal going by the time Katerin and her riders reached them.

"We wait for Katerin here," she said, dismounting. " Build small fires and heat water for tea and a light meal. It will not be long before she arrives."

"What should we prepare?" Detaluna asked. "We have the rabbits Tlliek shot."

"How much dried fruit is left?"

"Enough for a light meal. We also have enough dried fish as well. We can restock in Chellni."

"Good. Let's finish off the waybread, too. Might as well leave Chellni with fresh provisions."

Detaluna nodded. "I will see to that, then."

Sesenth took Basnen's reins. "You are all right?"

"Just tired. I shouldn't be tired."

Sesenth rested her hand on Rekaré's shoulder. "You have seen visions today and ridden hard. Why should you not be tired?"

Rekaré shook her head. "I should be stronger than this. I used to ride for longer periods without rest."

"And did you have visions as well during that time?" Sesenth snorted. "We've been in winter camp. None of us are riding with the strength we will have later."

"I know. It worries me, especially going against Waykemin." Rekaré pressed her lips tightly together. "There would be better times to battle than early spring."

"And there would be worse times."

Like when Cenarth and I rode to depose my father.

Then she only had Katerin and Metkyi to depend upon for support—that and the wrath of Dovré and Staul, both gods riding the four of them. She and Katerin were magically stronger now, and they would be leading more than a few tens, once all their forces were gathered. But these days she was not driven by the passion and boldness of youth coupled with righteous fury. Now she was more aware of the fates lying ahead of her.

I do not want to be Empress.

Rekaré shook herself free from brooding. "You're right," she said to Sesenth. "There would be worse times."

Sesenth hugged her. For a moment Rekaré let herself draw strength from her. Then she pulled back, sighing. "We'd best prepare for Katerin's arrival. Thank you for taking Basnen." She rested her hand on the golden mare's neck, scratching her under the mane near her poll, a favorite place.

Thank you for finding the perfect site,

she mindspoke to her daranval.

Basnen nuzzled her, projecting smugness. Then Sesenth clucked to the daranval to catch her attention. Basnen followed Sesenth toward where the daranvelii were gathered, waiting to be untacked and turned free to forage.

Rekaré watched her go. She stretched, then joined the riders gathering branches and dried grasses to build several fires, bigger than their midday stop, making a temporary rock fire ring around a central fire. Before long they had kindled four small fires at compass points twenty paces from the central cooking fire and placed the iron teakettles on rocks at its edge.

Detaluna supervised the cooking of the rabbit carcasses at that main fire, along with strips of backstrap from the fat young doe that Kovi had spooked up near camp. Rekaré stood with several riders at the northern small fire, waiting for Katerin. A growing sense of Medvara's presence warned her of their arrival, as if the land moved with Katerin.

How can that be?

They weren't in Medvara. She turned away from the fire to watch for their arrival. Closer, closer. She walked away from the fire toward the road, waving back a couple of riders who would join her.

"I don't need a guard—my cousin is close," she told them quietly.

She watched the grazing daranvelii in the meadow. Basnen was first to raise her head, staring toward the road. Then she nickered a welcome, joined by the other daranvelii that gathered around her. An answering whinny came from the road, still out of sight. Rekaré halted where she was, waiting.

Katerin and her riders came into view. The loose daranvelii galloped toward them, tossing their heads and prancing around the riders before falling in behind. A smile spread briefly across Katerin's face as she spotted Rekaré, then faded. She dismounted five strides away from Rekaré. Jeralte took Rainin's reins as Katerin walked toward Rekaré. Her face was drawn and pale, tight with fatigue.

The gods have been riding her hard today.

"Cousin," Katerin said in greeting, eyeing her knowingly. "So you have had visions?"

They clasped right forearms in the traditional greeting.

"Yes. I have had visions. You felt it too?"

Katerin pulled back and nodded. "Heinmyets's grief roiled Medvara." She took a deep breath. "We have much to speak about, cousin. My visions and yours. I have seen things we must discuss before we go to Chellni."

"Come to the fires. We have venison and rabbit, and tea is ready." Rekaré put her left arm around Katerin's shoulder.

Katerin sighed happily. "Ah, Gods, the hospitality of riders. I miss it. Townfolk are not the same, especially in Medvare-the-city." She gulped. "I have not yet cut hair for Inharise. You?"

"I sacrifice my hair regularly," Rekaré said as they walked together to the northern fire. "It is part of who I am now."

Once they reached the fire, Rekaré poured tea into carved wooden cups, handing one to Katerin. They solemnly touched rims, then sipped their tea.

Katerin set her cup on the ground next to the fire.

"Time to cut hair for Inharise." She took off her hat to reveal her thick black braid and pulled a knife from her belt, handing it hilt-first to Rekaré. "Years ago, I asked you to help me cut hair for Metkyi. Now I ask you to help me cut hair not only for Inharise, but for those who will die for our vengeance."

"Do you want to sacrifice this much hair?" Rekaré pulled off cowl and cap to reveal her freshly shorn head.

Katerin studied her for a moment. "Perhaps later. But not now. That is not what I am called for. Take the braid."

Rekaré set down the cap and cowl. She took Katerin's braid in one hand and cut as close to the scalp as she dared. Katerin's knife was as sharp as ever, slicing easily through her cousin's gray-streaked dark, lustrous hair. She held knife and braid out to Katerin when she had finished.

Her cousin took the knife first, wiping it on her sleeve before sheathing it. Then she took the braid with both hands, kissed it and touched the tip to her forehead before tossing it into the fire and raising her hands high, her lips moving silently.

Rekaré remained silent, letting her cousin grieve in silence. At last Katerin dropped her hands. Weariness seemed to flow over her now that she was done with cutting hair for Inharise, her face softening from its tight lines and her shoulders sagging.

"A day with visions like this is tiring," she said.

"And it is not yet over."

"No. It is not." Katerin squatted by the fire and picked her cup up again. Rekaré donned first her cap then her cowl, then joined Katerin, reaching for her cup. "What forces can you call upon?" Katerin continued. "We should not only plan for the attack on Waykemin but also to protect Medvara."

"The Hidden One will pledge Saubral's support where we need it." Rekaré studied her cup, considering the discussions she and her riders had held while riding. "I don't know how quickly Larij can respond but we can call upon Keratil for support from the south."

Katerin nodded. "Toran is still fostering with us. He will be able to summon Larij's help."

"Still? Is it Witmara that draws his interest or someone else?"

"Witmara. Though I do not think they have promised themselves to each other yet." Katerin set her cup down and opened and closed her hands, wincing. "Gods, my hands hurt. She still does not want the Leadership of Medvara."

"Then take it for yourself in truth."

Katerin grimaced. "I am not by nature a Leader."

"What does the land say?"

Katerin's grimace deepened. "It clings to me like a foal that doesn't want to be weaned." She drew a deep breath. "And more. It has given me a gift, a part of itself."

She reached into her right belt pouch and withdrew something carefully wrapped in undyed woven wool cloth. She unwrapped it to reveal a rock with green globules clinging to a gray base. She held the stone on her palm and extended her hand so that Rekaré could look at it.

"That is—it's beautiful. Katerin, you can't just walk away from Medvara. Not when it gives of itself like that."

The land never gave me a gift like this. Gods, Katerin, she wanted to say. *Do you realize what this means?*

"I know," her cousin said, gazing at the stone in her palm.

Her fingers itched to touch it but Rekaré held back, knowing better. This was not a gift for her, and Medvara was a possessive land, had been so when she had been Leader.

"How powerful is it?"

Katerin continued to study the stone in her palm. "Strong enough that it allowed me to see the Witches Council of Waykemin as they celebrated Inharise's death," she said, a bitter tone coming into her voice. "Strong enough that I saw effigies of Inharise, Heinmyets, and me on the great stone altar. Strong enough for me to break through the shielding to knock those poppets off the great altar and reveal myself as I truly am to one of my childhood tormentors, the current Chief Priestess Tranarin." She looked away from the stone, baring her teeth as she grinned at Rekaré. "Is it bad of me that I exulted in the fear Tranarin felt? That I rejoiced in showing her who I had become?"

"I would not judge you." *She broke through the Witches' Coun-*

cil's shielding? Rekaré eyed her cousin. "Not when you are powerful enough to defeat the Witches' defenses like that."

"Good, for I do not feel guilty." Katerin rewrapped the stone and replaced it in her pouch. "Though, strategically, being sneaky would have been a better choice. That is my one regret for taking that action." She sighed. "I would have done more, but Staul reminded me that petty vengeance is less important."

"The Witches had figures of you, Inharise, and Heinmyets upon the great altar?"

Katerin nodded, her mouth tightening. "The one of Inharise had fallen. Heinmyets had buckled. Mine still stood strong. They crumbled into dust after I knocked them off the altar—but I should have done it sooner. Would have if I had known."

"You still broke through the shielding."

Katerin flexed her hands again, studying them. "Remember that I am also part-Waykemese—so breaking the protections over the Council may be easier for me. At first—the last time I saw that altar in something other than a nightmare, the Witches had consecrated my mother after she conquered Nitel—and fell into the dreamless sleep." She looked back up at Rekaré. "I was not certain if what I saw was nightmare or vision." Her voice faltered. "Then I saw the poppets...and I *knew*. I...knew for certain. Rekaré. I have no doubt that the Witches are responsible for Inharise's death. My kin. My thrice-cursed kin, who had no use for me because of who my father was—but would not tell me of him." Her lips tightened again. "They will pay for this. It is long overdue. Gods. I did...not...realize...how dark they were."

Rekaré nodded. She remained silent, sensing Katerin wanted to say more and not wanting to interrupt.

Katerin shook her head. "I know that Chatain is a threat to Varen. I knew that Waykemin has committed to supporting him. But by Dovré's gold necklace, Rekaré, I did not realize it had gone this far. We should have moved on them sooner, after

Chiral. I hesitated then, wanting to focus on mending Medvara instead of punishing Waykemin for its role. That was wrong. Even though we followed the Gods' council, *it was wrong.*"

"No, Katerin. Medvara was in shreds after the deaths of my mother and daughter. It would not accept me after I killed Chiral. And you as a new Leader couldn't draw upon its strength like you do now."

"True."

"And...." Rekaré paused, picking up a twig and scratching idly in the dirt at her feet. "I had not yet gone to Gulter. Had not been acknowledged as *benghaalph* and *quixnafal.* Had not spent time building alliances between the Saubral and Larij, the Saubral and Keratil, the Saubral and—" she gestured, "—nearly every nation in Varen this side of the Barrier except for Waykemin itself."

"But Inharise would be alive today if we had attacked Waykemin," Katerin said in a low voice.

"Yes. Maybe. And perhaps there would be more dead, because the Saubral would be battling any who dared cross their lands." Rekaré broke the twig, tossing it into the flame. "What's done is done. The Gods gave us council, and we chose to trust them. What do they say now?"

"They don't disapprove."

"Then first, we strike against Waykemin to finish unifying Varen on this side of the ocean. Next—Chatain. It is time."

"So the Gods tell you?" Katerin's tone was flat, unreadable. "Are you going to accept the title of Empress?"

"I need no Gods to tell me it's time to end the corrupt rule of the house of Ralsem and free Daran to follow its own fate. And no, I will not become Empress of Daran. I will *never* take on that title, even though I am both Ralsem and Miteal."

"It will fall to one of us, then. Or our children." Katerin stared into the fire.

Silence held between them. Rekaré bit her lip, not wanting

to blurt the thought that came to her. While Linyet was her son and therefore eligible to rule the Darani Empire—his heart belonged to the Two Nations. She could not ask this of him, or of Cenarth.

But Witmara—

Years ago, when Daro was but a foal and had bonded early to Witmara, Katerin had shared her fear with Rekaré that the two were meant to be Sacrifice for the Two Nations. That had not come to pass, thankfully.

However, Sacrifice could take many forms.

And Witmara showed little interest in Medvara.

One step at a time, Rekaré reminded herself. *Consider the entire picture, but remember...one step at a time.*

"Let's eat," she said finally.

Katerin stood up slowly. "Yes. Let's."

But even as they rejoined the others, those last thoughts lingered with Rekaré.

They needed to do more than just tear down Waykemin and Daran, lest both nations create something worse than what already existed. New leadership, perhaps even new governing forms.

What would that look like?

She didn't know. Yet.

UNCOMFORTABLE MEETING

WITMARA, TORAN, AND LINYET SAT AROUND A TABLE BY THE fireplace in the chambers that Chellni's Headwoman, Mohanisha, reserved for visiting Leaders. They played the long version of a chip toss game popular in the Two Nations while they waited for her mother and Rekaré's arrival. Daro lurked in Witmara's thoughts, curious as always about this odd human behavior.

Linyet yawned. "How much longer do you think it will be until your mother arrives?"

Witmara shrugged and tossed her chips again. "Sometime tonight. Who knows where your mother is coming from, and as for my mother—she felt certain they would meet up by dusk. It could be as late as the middle of the night."

She scowled at her cast. It kept giving her repetitive results, the lines and spaces adding up to *change, drastic change, ascension to great power.*

Truth or a reflection of her hopes? Frustrated, she scattered her chips.

"I've had enough of this. The chips keep coming up the same. It's just a game, but it gets frustrating when this happens."

"Agreed." Toran shoved his chips to join hers.

"I've never seen them in so much of a pattern," Linyet agreed, tapping his fingers on his thigh. "Not for years." His lips tightened.

Daro nudged at her thoughts.

They are here.

Relief spread over Linyet's face, and she realized that Yaranei had spoken to him as well. "Shall we go meet your mother and Rekaré?" he asked.

"Might as well," Witmara said.

They pulled on their heavy jackets before going down the stairs.

Elenari met her at the bottom of the steps. "My Leader, you know?"

"Daro told me. We are going to meet my mother and Rekaré. I do not anticipate a need for a guard."

Elenari nodded. "Not with Jeralte, Sesenth and Detaluna there."

"Have you received any further word from Haran and Orlanden?"

"Nothing more than they would be here in the morning," Elenari said.

She hoped that Haran could confirm that he had indeed been able to find a good supply of glimmer dust.

Toran lit a lantern from the collection hanging by the doorway, opening its shutters for full light. He led them out of the Great House. Witmara took his free hand as they walked, stars shimmering bright above them as they headed toward the stables on the edge of the permanent structures that made up the main Chellni village. The Trading Grounds closer to the river glowed with light from campfires, torches, and lanterns.

Faint shouts came from that area, interspersed with barking dogs and occasional music.

"Night Market starts tomorrow," Linyet said. "At least that's what Yetklet told me. They're hurrying to get it set up."

"Good timing for final provisioning," Toran said.

"Not so good for secrecy if Waykemin has spies here," Witmara mumbled.

"Can't be helped. How quickly do you think Rekaré and Katerin will want to leave for Dera?"

"As fast as possible," Witmara said. "The sternwheelers can carry provisions for twenty tens. The five tens will meet Mother and Rekaré at Nixyin because of limited dock space, and supplies are more important. Provision ships arrive here tomorrow afternoon."

"The vendors will be quite happy to provide all our needs."

"That timing is favorable, at least."

They approached the stables, the bustle testifying to the arrival of her mother and Rekaré. The Light of Medvara pulsed strongly against Witmara's chest without warning. Then she spotted her mother, Rekaré next to her, talking to the captains. Witmara held back, waiting until they were done, fighting back the Light's yearning to be with her mother. Linyet slipped slightly behind her.

She noticed that short strands of hair poked out from under her mother's cap.

She has already cut hair for Inharise.

One thing less to do tonight, then.

Then her mother looked toward them and smiled. "Witmara. Toran."

"Linyet is here too," she said, waving him forward.

Rekaré turned as Linyet hesitatingly walked ahead of them, shoulders tight and stiff. Her face went blank.

"I did not expect you to be here," she said. "It is good to see you—son."

"It is good to see you, too," Linyet said. "I came with Yetklet and the delegation from Wickmasa."

They stopped an arm's length from each other but neither reached out. Certainly not like Witmara and her mother would do after a long parting.

"Ah. Your father is well?" Rekaré fumbled over the words.

"As well as can be, given the circumstances," Linyet said, voice tight and harsh.

"Well. Yes." Rekaré looked down, then back up, her lips tightening. "Your grandmother was doing poorly when you left? I *am* sorry. I had planned…."

"If I had known…" Linyet's voice caught, and he choked slightly. "If I had known this would happen, I would not have come—Mother." His voice caught again. "But Father wanted me to warn you that this time was approaching. It was…it was like seven years ago. Like what happened with Grandmother Alicira. Father did not think she would survive another winter, but she was stable for now. Yevtin gave her another summer. She was fading but not that fast. He stayed because—because…."

Katerin joined Rekaré. "You could not have known, Linyet." She glanced at Linyet. "I saw a vision of Waykemin. The Witches worked a curse on her—on me and your grandfather as well. I thwarted it."

"Thank you, Katerin," he whispered. "I would not lose both of them like this." He gulped.

Rekaré softened and stepped forward, wrapping her arms around Linyet. He leaned against her but kept his arms at his sides.

"I am sorry you were not there," Rekaré murmured. "I should have been there too, to say farewell to my Secondmother. But I am glad to see you, son."

"And I you."

To Witmara's ears his words seemed forced.

Her mother sighed and turned to them, embracing both

Witmara and Toran. "Witmara. Toran. What's the lodging situation?"

"We have the entire Guest House," Witmara said. "Elenari is making sure that rooms are warm and there's a late supper prepared if you need it."

"Things here are sufficiently organized that we are done for the night. Rekaré?"

Rekaré released Linyet quickly. "I'm ready as well." She and Katerin turned to pick up their saddlebags.

"Let us do that," Witmara said. "You two have ridden far." She, Toran, and Linyet picked up the saddlebags.

They walked back to the Guest House in silence.

"I am tired," Rekaré said when they arrived. "Which room is mine?"

"I'll show you," Linyet said quietly. He had all of his mother's gear. "Do you want me to send for some supper?"

"No," Rekaré said. "I am tired more than hungry."

Her mother watched as Linyet and Rekaré climbed the stairs toward the sleeping rooms. She shook her head and turned back to Witmara.

"I hope they talk." She started up the stairs and Witmara followed. "My usual room?"

"Yes."

Witmara and Toran carried Katerin's saddlebags into her room. Witmara would have left but her mother shook her head.

"Witmara. Stay. Please. Tell me what you have done. Toran, can you bring some of that supper?"

Witmara told her mother of the messages sent, the orders for supplies, the status of sternwheelers available to carry troops and supplies upriver. Her mother listened quietly while she pulled off her boots and changed out of her riding leathers into a soft gown, climbing into her bed.

"Thank you," she said after Witmara finished, smiling at her. "You have done well in such a short time."

"I—well, I have had good teachers. Not just you but Haran and Orlanden."

Toran knocked, then opened the door. He carried a tray with dried fruit, a steaming bowl of mush with meat and vegetables mixed in, and an ewer with three cups. He set the tray on the small table in the middle of the room and brought the bowl over to Katerin, then poured drinks for all of them.

"And I thank you too, Toran." She set the bowl in her lap. "The two of you work well together."

Toran glanced at Witmara, smiling. "Easy enough after years of fostering." Warmth spread through her at his smile.

"Our families have a strong tradition of cooperation." Katerin took a bite of her mush. "How is Linyet faring?"

Toran and Witmara exchanged glances. "Inharise's death hit him hard," Witmara said. She sipped from her cup. Golden wine from Larij. Light and fruity, but not too heavy.

"To be expected." Her mother sighed. "Well, perhaps some time with his mother will help."

"He had left her room and was going to bed when I brought the tray upstairs," Toran said.

Katerin winced. "I was afraid of that. Rekaré is—she seems more detached from the world than before."

"I've never been that close to her," Witmara said. "I wouldn't know."

"No. You wouldn't. There is one more thing I need to show both of you." She looked at Toran. "But first. What are your upcoming intentions? Are you returning to your father or staying here?"

"I will ride with Witmara as long as she will have me," Toran said. "We've not discussed it much, but...."

Her mother nodded, clearly unsurprised. "Alas, there is not time to negotiate a marriage agreement with your father before I must leave for Waykemin. Not like it should be between Larij and Medvara."

It will not be a matter of Larij and Medvara, Witmara thought rebelliously. But she was not about to bring up *that* topic right now. *Not until after Waykemin.*

"I do not require anything elaborate," Toran said. He clasped Witmara's hand. "Not under these circumstances. And, being a younger son, I doubt my father will be much concerned."

"Nonetheless, I will send him a message in the morning letting him know that I approve of a match between you two. No time for more. Not until the matter of Waykemin is settled. I will feel better about Witmara in Medvara with you supporting her." She took several bites of mush. "Witmara, could you hand me my belt? I need to show you this before we part for the evening."

Witmara rose and picked up her mother's belt. As she touched one belt pouch, it shocked her, a sharp bite that was more than static electricity. "Oh!"

"I was afraid of that." Her mother's voice was resigned as she took the belt. "Things—happened on my ride to meet Rekaré." She fumbled in the pouch that had shocked Witmara and brought out something wrapped in undyed wool cloth. "First—this."

The Light of Medvara warmed against Witmara's chest once more as her mother revealed a palm-sized gray stone covered with green globules.

"What is that?" she asked.

Daro roused, echoing her question.

"The land gave it to me before I crossed the Dry Line." Her mother studied it, lips pursed. "It is a token to keep us connected while you wear the Light of Medvara." She looked away from the stone. "It gave me the power to break through the shields guarding the Witches Council in Waykemin, and see the curse they unleashed against Inharise—as well as myself and Heinmyets."

Shock jolted through Witmara. "Are you all right?"

Katerin half-smiled. "I broke their spell. It will take more than that sort of magic to injure the Banisher of Shadows, my dear!"

"Good." But her heart still pounded as the Light of Medvara pulsed against her, communicating its distress in conjunction with hers. How much of it was her concern and how much of it was the land's? "So. What does this mean?"

"I do not know." Her mother returned her gaze to the stone. "Right now I am grateful for every small bit of help against what lies ahead of us. Fighting Waykemin face-to-face will not be as simple as it is in the spirit world." She closed her hand around the stone, then rewrapped it and placed it back in her pouch. "But I thought you should know about this." She resumed eating.

"I suppose this means we should not be too concerned about concealing your intent toward Waykemin," Toran said.

Katerin drained her cup. "No. It is not a secret at all. The Witches know I am coming."

That was enough to make Witmara drain her own cup. She reached for the ewer and refilled their cups. Her mother took hers with a quickly fleeting smile, then alternated sips with bites until her bowl was finished. Toran took the bowl and placed it on the tray. Katerin settled back in her bed.

"I am grateful for all you have done to prepare the way," she said. "So. How soon do we leave?"

"Toran and I will return to Medvara tomorrow via ship," Witmara said. "I do not feel comfortable leaving the land for long, not with a battle impending. You should be able to proceed to Nixyin by late afternoon the day after to meet the five tens from Medvara. The provision ships arrive here tomorrow afternoon to stock up while the other ships go to Nixyin."

"That is good. Thank you." Katerin drained her cup again. Witmara took that as her cue to leave.

"We will see you in the morning," she said. Toran picked up the tray as she gathered her mother's cup. After they left Katerin's room, he hesitated.

"Shall I come to your room tonight, or you to mine?" he asked softly.

"Better my room than yours, should someone need to contact me." She grimaced. "Leader's responsibilities now."

He grinned at her. "You wear it well, my dear."

"I wait for you." She went to her room and began preparations for the evening, donning a soft gown, then unbraiding her hair and brushing it out. Tears blurred her eyes as she fingered the rough edge where she had cut a lock to honor Inharise earlier, with Linyet. Then she wiped them roughly away, bidding Daro good night in her thoughts. Their connection faded.

Did the land's gift mean her mother was more open to the possibility of keeping Medvara for herself? It would certainly make things easier.

Toran tapped on the door, then slipped inside. He took her into his arms. She held him silently as he stroked her back, humming softly.

"And now our fates call us forth," she said finally. "I am glad to have you at my side. I wanted to ask, but—" An unexpected laugh broke from her. "I suppose my mother wants things settled between us before battle. Do you think your father will have issues?"

He shook his head. "I suspect he hoped this would happen as a result of my fostering in Medvara."

"If I do as the Gods bid, we may be ruling much more than Medvara," she warned.

"Wherever you go, my dear. Even if it means Daran."

"I both fear it and look forward to it."

"I know your heart and trust your choices." He stroked her cheek, then leaned forward.

Their lips met.

PREPARATION FOR BATTLES

Rekaré stirred. Sesenth coiled close, her transformed skin no longer rough and scratchy now that she was warm, the scales pliable even though firmer than flesh.

She blinked. Darkness no longer dominated the room. She made out the forms of chairs and saddlebags, but not much more. She stroked the ridges beginning to form on Senth's cheek as she nuzzled catlike into Rekaré's palm. Then Senth settled back into sleep, her eyes still closed, her nostrils fluttering in steady sleep rhythm.

Rekaré rose and went to the east-facing window. Senth grunted in protest at the loss of warmth.

Rekaré peeked around the curtain's edge to check the horizon. Lighter but no glow of yellows and reds yet. Not sunrise, but soon. Time to get up.

More grunting, and then a long sigh behind her accompanied by the rustle of covers.

"Is everything all right?" Sesenth asked. "It seems damnably early."

"It's morning. Or will be soon enough." Rekaré dropped the curtain and returned to their bed, sitting on the side.

"Something else still bothers you." Sesenth sat up and kindled the magically powered lantern next to the night table, pulling the bedding around her to keep her warm. Without her cowl and cap, the gray-green, rougher skin marking Sesenth's transition to Shadowwalker was more visible, gray-green partially up her scalp and forming ridges on her otherwise yet-unscaled face. "I noticed your mood when I came to bed. What is wrong?"

Rekaré shook her head. "It's nothing."

Deep inside, she wanted to scream. That expression on Linyet's face last night—oh Gods. Witmara didn't look at Katerin like that, even when they were arguing. She had failed him as a mother, just like she had his sister Melarae. And she couldn't break through the walls she had built around herself ever since Melarae's death to unbend and show him the love she felt. She buried her head in her hands.

If I let myself care for him, for Cenarth, then I doom them. I cannot show that I love them. I dare not risk them becoming pawns in this game with Chatain, at least not any more than they already are.

But Gods, it hurt to keep Linyet away. He had been her little boy when she last saw him—boy no longer, now a man.

I've missed so much. Gods.

But after losing Melarae, she just couldn't risk Linyet. Or Cenarth, much as she missed him.

Sesenth was safe. Senth had taken her as *quixnahi* and more, and if that marked her as a target since she was beloved of *Rekaré Kinslayer*, then what did it matter? Sesenth's doom matched hers. She knew the cost of becoming full Shadowwalker, especially the Shadowwalker who followed Rekaré Kinslayer. She had chosen this fate.

Rekaré drew ragged breaths, fighting back tears even as Senth rested a reassuring hand on her thigh. Her choices rode heavy on her this morning, now that they were on the cusp of *things coming to pass.*

This feeling will go away, she told herself. *This feeling must go away. For my good, for Cenarth's good, for Linyet's good. But oh Gods, this is hard not to feel sometimes.*

The cold prickling that went along with Staul's presence ran down her spine. Then a *heaviness* that told her that the God was manifesting, not just speaking to her. She dropped her hands and stood to face him. The God ran a bony finger down her cheek, the skeletal grin of Staul the Destroyer somehow softer than usual.

> Your fate is not an easy one, Rekaré Kinslayer. If you accept Empire, you could have your kin back.

Rekaré shook her head.

> I would not condemn them to Empire, to Daran. The hearts of both Cenarth and Linyet are centered here in Varen, and I would not take that from them.

She raised her chin, staring straight into the God's golden eyes.

> And their fate should they join me in Daran as Empress? Varen's fate? No. Better they stay here in Varen to care for the Two Nations and guard against what waits beyond the Nerean Gate. You know as well as I do what will happen if I become Empress. By the Goddess's golden tits, I will not become another Elithtra!

Staul cupped her cheek.

> You are wise, Rekaré Kinslayer. But you know what fate that dooms you to.

Rekaré shuddered.

The God leaned forward and took her head in two bony hands. His teeth brushed against her forehead.

Then he faded away.

Rekaré shuddered and drew a deep breath. She realized that Sesenth had rolled off of the bed and now prostrated herself before Rekaré.

"Get up," she said. "He's gone. There's no need for this, Senth!"

"Beloved of the God," Sesenth breathed. "I have known that about you, but to see it with my own eyes? I am truly blessed."

"It is but one appearance, nothing more." Had the gray-green moved further up Sesenth's scalp? Were those scales now forming around those cheek ridges?

"I disagree. *Quixnafal. Benghaalph.* I am blessed to see the God's blessing on you with my own eyes at long last, not just sense its presence."

Rekaré sighed. "Dear Gods, Senth. I do *not* need worship. I need *you.* I need someone to make me feel alive, not cold and isolated. Especially since I dare not reach out to my son and...." Her voice caught. "And his father," she whispered. "Please don't do this to me. Please. I need someone to keep me human. I'm sorry, but you're the safest one."

"As you wish." Sesenth rose and took Rekaré into her arms. "But you are still God-kissed, Beloved of Staul, and ever will be for me."

"There are times when I wish I was not God-kissed."

"Does it do you any good to fight your fate?"

"No. But what does that make you? Sometimes I feel as if I am only using you but Gods, Sesenth. I need someone to make me feel human."

Even if that someone is transforming into a Shadowwalker.

Sesenth held her close. "My fate is my fate, Rekaré Kinslayer, beloved, *quixnafal* and *benghaalph.* I will share your fate. I have known that since I first shaved your head." She took Rekaré's hand and twined their fingers together. "I become Shadowwalker through you, just as my mother did through her *quixnahi.* You are the fulfillment of the Shadowwalkers. You will bring much needed sorrow to Waykemin and Daran. I am honored to walk by your side and support you. I chose this path with clear mind and open heart."

"Waykemin will be Katerin's work."

"She who would strike down Waykemin will deal with that aftermath."

"I know," Rekaré whispered. "I know and I falter for a moment. Keep me strong, Senth. Please. My son—Gods. Gods. And soon I must face his father."

"I will be there for you, as ever," Sesenth breathed. "Without you my life would be much darker and dull. I know the choice I made when I decided to follow Rekaré Kinslayer and become her beloved. I know what fate it dooms me to—and I accept it with an open heart."

They held each other for a few more moments, then separated.

"Sailship coming to the docks!" Hanmit, one of the young Chellni who worked for Mohanisha as a runner, stuck his head into the rough office in the Guest House. Witmara looked up from making notes about more needs on the supply lists Haran had brought that morning, blinking to regain focus, only now aware that she had been sitting for a long time. "Gnengir said you should know."

She pushed her chair back and stretched, glad for the break. "Which one?"

"*Heart's Desire.*"

Setkin's ship. "I will come right away. Please tell Toran, then wait for us at the docks. Which berth?"

"Deepwater Two." Hanmit slammed the door.

Witmara pulled on her sheepskin jacket and wrapped a scarf around her neck, adding a hat and gloves. Even though the sun shone palely outside, it was chilly enough inside by the fire. The docks would be breezy and cooler.

Once outside, she made her way along the boardwalk rather than slosh through the mud in the streets and pathways. No need to muck up her boots after last night's cleaning. The streets were full of riders and wagons, busy not only due to the opening of Trade Fair this evening but the rapidly assembling forces intended for the battle of Waykemin.

No possible means of keeping this quiet.

Meanwhile. Setkin was here. Why? The sorcerous sailships rarely traveled past the junction with the Saktrin River that led to Medvare-the-city. They were ocean-going, beloved of the Goddess Terat, and the interior rivers were not necessarily friendly to them.

There must be a message from Betsona that couldn't wait for me to get back to Medvare.

But what could it be?

She would find out soon enough.

Toran joined Witmara at Deepwater Two and wrapped his left arm around her, pulling her close against the brisk east wind. She leaned into him as they stood at the waiting berth, a frisson of joy shivering through her as *Heart's Desire* came about. Watching an experienced Sorcerer-Captain sing their ship into mooring always gave her a thrill, and Setkin along with his protégé Vered were the best of the current fleet.

Desire's sails were furled but the masts glowed a pale green, testifying to the presence of magic that needed neither sail nor oar to guide the ship. Few noticed the amplifiers embedded in the base of the masts, a device Witmara had rediscovered in some of the old papers that Betsona had sent from Daran, and recreated with the aid of Setkin and Vered.

Setkin's deep baritone sang a chant in the secret language known only to those who had earned a Captain's ring, his voice guiding *Heart's Desire* as she settled, her sailors leaping onto the dock to secure her. His tone changed to that of praise and thanks for his ship's performance, the chant concluding with the traditional acknowledgement of the Goddess Terat's favor. The pale green glow faded at song's end. The ship quivered and fell silent.

They moved closer once the gangplank had been set into place. Setkin called to his sailors, then marched down, his weathered face softening into a smile.

"Lady Witmara. I came as quickly as possible. I bring news that may not be pleasant. Her ladyship imparted much of it to me. We sailed hard and fast—but perhaps not quickly enough." He extended a sealed letter. Witmara recognized the obscured seal that meant it came from Betsona.

She impatiently broke the seal and skimmed what Betsona had written. Toran read over her shoulder.

Cousin,

That long-anticipated revival of the play Elithtra's Dream is now being cast here in the Ourigny Islands, of all places, instead of the Grand Stage at Adalane. My brother is taking particular interest in the casting and rehearsals of this new version of that old drama. But no matter how he polishes it up, it is still the same coincidence-driven, cliché-heavy, melodrama.

Prickles ran down Witmara's spine. *Elithtra's Dream* was their established code for *Chatain is organizing an invasion of Varen.*

The ink in the next paragraph was slightly different in shade, the handwriting an urgent scribble.

The production of the play has been rushed. By the time you receive this message, the first performance will have been launched.

Gods, Witmara thought, looking up. Toran's face was tight, lips thinning. She had shared the code with him long ago.

Chatain's fleet is on its way. How many?

She looked back at the letter, biting her lip.

Rumor has it that this is a leaner, tighter production than past performances. I do not know for certain as our dear cousin Larien has been conscripted to play the role of the Betrayer. I have not seen him for many days now.

Larien was another Ralsem cousin who had been exiled with Betsona. Witmara was uncertain if he served as jailer, confidant, or an ambiguous combination of the two. He had been mentioned in past letters as a source of the historical manuscripts Betsona sometimes sent to Witmara.

More importantly, he was Betsona's usual contact with Setkin.

"Did Larien bring you this letter?" she asked Setkin.

He shook his head. "Seijina my cousin brought it this time, in disguise. I worry."

"For good reason." Seijina was Betsona's closest servant—more than servant, she suspected. Witmara continued reading.

> I wish I had more news and new documents to send to you, dear cousin. Not only have I not been well, but even if I had been, my access to the simplest transport around Lanivar has been restricted. With Larien gone, the mechanical wheelchair falls into disrepair quickly and there are none available to maintain it since he was called away.
>
> Betsona

"What does that mean?" she wondered out loud. "Setkin, is there a shortage of those able to maintain mechanical devices on Lanivar?"

"Magitechs are plentiful throughout the islands," Setkin said slowly. "Few ships put in at Lanivar, but it is not that different from the bigger islands. I usually do not—no need to draw attention to your correspondence. For Seijina to leave Betsona to deliver this message is most unusual."

She handed him the letter. "Tell me what you think." After all, he had played a part in developing the code. Perhaps he could see something in it that she did not.

Setkin skimmed through the letter, his jaw tightening as he read.

"There was no sign of a deficiency in mechanical experts on the main island of Ourigny," he said. "The fleet she refers to must be gathering on Lanivar. That makes Seijina's ability to deliver this message to me even more remarkable." He shook his head. "She had to be able to sail a small boat—and she used to claim she had no skill with them."

"So you think this is real?"

"Oh Gods yes. There's another factor. Lanivar does not have a large port. That would match what Betsona says about the size of the fleet. Lanivar is also the island closest to Varen." He stroked his curly, gray-streaked dark beard thoughtfully. "This also suggests that this fleet will be heavy with magitech."

"Then we must prepare for an attack on Medvara," Witmara said.

"Agreed," Toran said. "Nine days, do you think, Setkin?"

"If the winds are right and they departed when Betsona thought they would—then yes. There is one other thing in your favor," Setkin said. "His ships depend on technologists, not magicians, for shielding and guidance. Given the right location, your devices may disable his. With a site close to land, such as, say, a river mouth or bay, you can defeat his forces. A passage upriver would be effective as well." Setkin eyed Witmara. "That is what I would recommend."

"Oh Gods, most of my devices are untested in battle." Witmara bit her lower lip. "But—in the river rather than the open ocean?"

"That would be my advice. Use the land to amplify the power of your devices. And as for them being untested in battle? The ones I have used are effective against technology-only creations."

"Good. But I do not know if what I have will be enough."

"Coupled with magic, they should work," Toran said.

"I hope so." Witmara tapped the scroll against her palm. "We need to meet with my mother, Rekaré, and Haran immediately.

Setkin, can you carry me and Toran back to Medvare this afternoon?"

"Rekaré and your mother will want to drop the fight with Waykemin and go to meet this threat," Toran cautioned.

"They dare not do so. Waykemin will move on the Two Nations if they focus on Daran's invasion. Setkin. How many of the Sorcerer-Captains can you summon on short notice? Can someone sail to Leithra to let the Mershaunten know this is happening and bring forces from Larij?"

"We are at your service, Witmara. Vered awaits your command in Medvare-the-city. I will communicate with her immediately. Dolenin is in Cooscol, organizing our fleet. I took it upon myself to command the Sorcerer-Captains to do what is necessary to delay Chatain's fleet as much as possible. We too will lose should Chatain gain a foothold here in Varen." A tiny smile quirked the right corner of his lips. "Fortunately, his technologists are not as consistent as our magic, coupled with your devices. May I make a suggestion about strategy?"

"Absolutely. You have fought in many more battles than either of us. I agree with your recommendation that we fight in the river. But just how do we get Chatain's fleet to engage there?"

"A lure," Setkin said. "*Heart's Desire* and I can do it. Enchant one of your devices to project a false image of your presence mocking them, without shielding. They will engage because that's what they would expect Chatain to do—if he dared leave Daran."

"He would?" Toran scowled. "That's the action of a fool."

Setkin shrugged. "Or of someone convinced of his absolute power."

"He would not be the first Miteal to act so," Witmara said dryly. *Or Ralsem,* she thought, remembering Chiral. "So. Make them believe that they are chasing my ship and lead them into the Chellana's mouth. You don't think they would be discouraged by its difficulty?"

"The roughness of the Chellana bar is notorious, but there are still many captains from Daran who believe those accounts of the crossing's difficulty to be overrated," Setkin said. "None with actual experience. Vered, Dolenin, and I have heard plenty of bragging in the Ourigny bars. How much of it is actual conviction and how much is idle boasting attempting to build confidence—I do not know. *We* know that passage. Lure the survivors into the Chellana. Engage them from land and on the water. But not right away."

"Draw them upriver to Medvare," Witmara said, remembering her studies. "No direct engagement, nothing that appears to be organized. But keep the lure going, so they don't stop to offload their troops for a land march. Lead them to where *we* want to fight, while reducing their numbers."

"Exactly," Setkin said, grinning. "You remember my teachings about sea and river battles."

"Serennismis," she said. "Right? But won't their leaders remember Serennismis as well?"

Setkin snorted. "My dear, that was a loss for the Darani Empire, and Chatain like his father Dunaran and his grandfather Etikar does not hold with remembering defeats. Especially when it comes from two hundred years back. Chatain is confident of his coastal technological networks that defend Daran. His captains will only be aware that Varen lacks such established networks, and be overconfident. Once they have committed to the river, then Dolenin can bring in the shielded fleet."

"They will not detect Dolenin and the fleet?"

"I doubt it. Their devices do not depend upon magic skill. Chatain discourages the use of magic except for specific leaders he magically binds to his will. There will be magicians amongst his fleet, but they will be harnessed and limited."

"Thank you for your wisdom, Setkin." She turned to Toran. "Nine days. That will match how long it will take for Rekaré and my mother to get into position in Waykemin."

"The fleet can be at Chellananit in two days, Medvare in three. My father has been keeping it in constant readiness. Land forces—" Toran scowled. "They will take longer. Five days."

"We can bring Haran's brigade." Witmara turned to Setkin. "I hope to be ready to travel downriver by early afternoon. We can make further plans on our way."

Setkin bowed to her. "*Heart's Desire* will be ready."

"Thank you." Witmara turned to Toran. "Make certain our guard is ready to travel. Alas, they will not be able to attend the opening of Spring Fair, but—I think this news will have many of the vendors preparing for battle rather than trade. If you can let people know that we need help in Medvare—I will accept any and all support."

Toran nodded. "I will personally inform the vendors as well as gather our people."

"Thank you."

Toran kissed her forehead. "Stay safe. Stay strong. Promise me."

"I will."

He kissed her again before hurrying away.

"Hanmit. Tell my mother, Haran, and Rekaré to meet me at the Guest House. Have them bring Linyet, too."

He nodded and sped away, deftly dodging through dockworkers, riders, and wagons.

Witmara drew a deep breath before she started for her office.

Oh Gods, Staul, Gods.

It was one thing to speculate about what was happening.

Another to have it confirmed. She reached for Daro.

78

. . .

Daro returned thoughts of himself larger than life, trampling the ships.

Despite her worry, she couldn't help chuckling. If only this upcoming battle would be as easy as her daranval thought!

Katerin frowned at the letter from Betsona, her heart sinking.

War on two fronts. Gods. I have to deal with Waykemin. But I can't just leave this to Witmara—can I?

At some point she had to trust her daughter's ability, especially if she wanted to hand the Leadership over to Witmara. But this? Gods. Not at all what she had envisioned.

"Does Setkin confirm this?" she asked.

"Yes. And he has noted the presence of more soldiers and ships than usual in the Ourigny Islands."

Rekaré snorted. She sat up from where she had sprawled in her chair. "I thought Chiral was reliable. Are you certain of this Betsona? She could be yet another of Chatain's disruptive elements."

Witmara's lips tightened at the challenge. "Staul also confirms what she says. I have learned much about our family's past in Daran, and current conditions from Betsona. Our ancestress Elithtra was not as wonderful as we have been taught."

"I—see." Katerin had briefly glanced at the papers Betsona sent Witmara. "I did not realize your research extended to that era."

"I was trying to understand the technologists and how they became dominant under Etikar, Dunaran, and Chatain."

"I know of the lady Betsona," Detaluna said from her position behind Rekaré. "She is beloved by the workers of Daran.

There was some outcry at her exile—which Chatain quashed. For what it's worth, Chiral never spoke well of Betsona."

"You and Betsona have been busy indeed, Witmara," Katerin stroked her chin, fumbling for words. *I should have known, given some of the devices she and Toran have created.* Too many holes in her own knowledge. "What have you discovered, and how does it relate to us?"

"The history of Elithtra's colonial ambitions is not exactly as it is told in Medvara, Mother. The histories from Daran and the Ourigny Islands are damning to our ancestress. The devastation Elithtra wreaked in Varen when she first attempted a colony, before exiling our family here, made the spread of Plague at her death much more destructive. It is why Medvara and Keldara were so shattered before our ancestors came to Varen." Witmara paused, leaning back in her chair, pressing her fingertips together. "But there's another issue. From what Betsona says, the Islands cannot accommodate all of Chatain's dissenters. He needs to look to the East—to us—as a place to exile his opponents, even more than any dream of power he has."

Rekaré shuddered and sat straighter than before. "It is as Witmara says," she spoke, in a tone deeper and detached from her usual voice, her eyes blank and staring at the far wall. "Elithtra sowed the seeds of her own doom in Varen, and cursed this land when it would not yield to her. It drew her to the reddest paths and in turn condemned her when Etikar saw her as an obstacle to his ambitions. Alexran fell to the same delusions. It must be made right, both in Waykemin and in Medvara." She sagged back into her seat, rubbing her eyes and sinking her head into her hands. "Gods, I hate when that happens," she finally muttered. "Another *benghaalph* moment."

Linyet frowned at his mother, clearly uncomfortable. *"Benghaalph?"*

Rekaré grimaced. "One of those moments when I am the prophet of the Saubral, the One Spoken Of. And we're haring off after distractions. The prophet spoke through me to confirm the truth of what Witmara says and convey the urgency of action. She confirms Witmara's source. So what are we going to do about it?"

"Toran and I leave this afternoon to organize Medvara's defenses," Witmara said firmly. "With the aid of the Sorcerer-Captains, we will lure Chatain's fleet into the Chellana. I am sending Vered to ask the Mershaunten for his ships." She and Toran shared a quick glance and smile. "I am also letting him know that we intend to be vowed."

"I—congratulations." Much as she had hoped for this turn of events, part of Katerin ached. Her bonding with Metkyi had been overshadowed by the necessity of supporting Rekaré—and had ended with his death during her victory. *I wish Witmara didn't face the same sort of urgency.* "But we can't leave you without support."

"I will have forces in Medvara. Cooscol. The Mershaunten's forces. The Sorcerer-Captains." Witmara rose, resting her palms on the table before her. "We will draw them inland. Toward Medvare-the-city. That is a better ground for us to fight on than the open sea, and a more attractive target than small coast towns with no power and few resources. If we can lure Chatain's force inland, whisper in their ears that *Medvare is vulnerable, take Medvare and you will control Varen,* then the fleet from Cooscol can bottle them up on the river once they commit. We can weaken their technology."

"She's right," Haran interjected.

"But will they take the bait?" Rekaré asked. "Crossing the bar at the mouth of the Chellana is not easy to do for most non-sorcerous ships."

"That is part of the strategy," Witmara said. "Setkin says that the captains of Chatain's ships do not believe the stories about the difficulty of the Chellana's crossing."

Katerin sighed. She didn't like this plan, but what other

options did they have? She stroked the pouch that contained Medvara's token. Was she doing the right thing in leaving its defense to Witmara? Would she be safe?

Resigned acceptance came back to her.

I have seen. You are the one who must deal with Waykemin,

the land whispered, its tone unhappy.

It is a rot that must be treated.

The land's approval didn't make her feel better, but—there were no good options.

"If we focus on protecting Medvara, then that leaves Waykemin free to wreak whatever harm the Witches will choose—not just on the Two Nations but on Keratil and Saubral." Katerin shook her head. "I don't like a battle on two fronts. But. One thing I would ask of you. When you return to Medvare-the-city. Please commit yourselves to each other. I will not be able to be there but the land will stand witness. That way if the worst should happen, Toran will be able to command the land's strength until I return." She fixed Witmara with a stern glare. "Promise."

"I will," Witmara said. "But I do not intend to fail."

Katerin stifled a shudder at her boldness.

Don't tempt the Gods, she wanted to say.

But would her daughter listen?

Be happy that she has accepted her role as Leader, she told herself.

It was small consolation.

Heart's Desire FLED DOWNRIVER FASTER THAN ANY sternwheeler. Witmara and Toran sat on the main deck, out of the way. Setkin did not have time to talk, especially on this stretch of the Chellana which had many powerful rapids made bigger by snowmelt. The walls of the river's canyon rose high above them, waterfalls which they couldn't see from the road spilling from the cliff tops on the south side. Daro's annoyance at being on water instead of the land, below decks on the ship where he couldn't see outside was a niggling irritation at the back of her thoughts.

> Patience. We will be home soon.

He sent her an image of the two of them galloping across fields.

> Soon. Eat hay now.

> Treats?

> When we arrive.

Then she closed that part of her mind off, damping the connection.

Toran balanced a lap desk borrowed from Setkin on his knees, sketching a schematic for Witmara's lure.

"An array of amplifiers mounted on the prows of our lure ships will be better than a single device," he said. "We'll still need a primary focus for the lure. But if we can project from multiple ships, then the Darani cannot target one ship in particular. They will know you are present, but not be certain just *where* you are. It will also allow us to create an illusion of a fleet just outside the mouth of the Chellana, and hopefully provoke them to pursue it into the river without pausing. Then Dolenin and his fleet can follow."

Witmara looked up from the desk on her lap. "A stronger signal as well?"

"Yes."

"I like that." She frowned at her sheet. "May I look at your design while you look at my letter to your father?"

"Absolutely." They exchanged desks. Witmara's personal lap desk was heavy with paperwork and notes she had made for battle preparation. Toran's borrowed desk was much lighter in comparison. She pored over the details of the schematic, frowning at the amount of magical power the device would require in order to function.

*My magical strength will be an issue. I'll have to be on a ship nearby and even then it's going to drain me more than I would like with battle impending. Unless...*she tapped the end of her hand-carved pen against her lips, careful to keep her fingers away from the ink-stained tip.

The Saubral used magic-charged quartz crystals from the desert to power lights in their settlements and camps. Rekaré had given some of those crystals to Katerin two years ago, for Witmara and Toran to examine. There was one big crystal which could be inserted into the device that would be strong enough to drive a projection of that size without draining too much strength from her, especially if she paired it with a lesser but complementary crystal. It was doable, from tales she had heard—even if it was beyond what she and Toran had already done with the crystals as motivators. And a messenger bird that had arrived before they left Chellni brought the word that the Hidden One would be coming to Medvare. They could call upon her skill to set up the illusion.

Yes. That would solve the problem nicely.

"I added a few words to your letter," Toran said.

Witmara looked up from the schematic, noting that they already were passing the island of the dead, where Medvarans from the small settlement of Dankar maintained a cemetery. It was supposed to be blessed by the Goddess Terat, though Witmara never had experienced a sense of that Goddess's presence there on the few occasions when she had gone with her mother for a ceremony. Not that she understood burial. Funeral pyres sparked by Dovré's cool fire were the means of disposing of dead bodies that Witmara knew. But Dankar's people had always buried their dead on the island, long before Alexran brought his exiles to Daran.

Goddess, I hope our losses are few.

She nearly dropped Setkin's lap desk as she felt something like the touch of ocean waves wash around her feet, foam brushing against her anklebones as if she were walking in the surf.

> Loss is always something we must contend with, ᴢ_ᴢ

Terat's unfamiliar voice breathed into her mind, accompanied by a faint scent of salty ocean air and the distant cry of shorebirds coupled with the thunder of waves crashing on a sandy beach.

> Nonetheless, I, too, will aid in the battles ahead of you, Lady Witmara. Call upon me when the time is right, and I will aid your cause.

And then the sensation was gone, as the island receded behind them.

> What was that?

Daro's thoughts worriedly stirred against hers.

He settled at her response, thoughts of hay and a wistful longing for cookies coming to her.

"Witmara?"

She realized that Toran had been speaking to her.

"The Goddess spoke to me and I didn't hear you," she said.

"I didn't know that Dovré spoke to you."

Witmara pulled her jacket closer, suddenly chilled and not from any stray breeze. "No. Not her. Terat spoke to me as we passed the island. She promised her aid when the time is right."

She glanced down at Setkin's desk on her lap and wondered if there was a connection between her holding a possession of a powerful Sorcerer-Captain dedicated to Terat and the Goddess's speaking to her.

"The Gods are aligning with their favorites." Toran rested his hand on hers.

"I did not hear what you said after you mentioned adding a few words to the letter." She didn't want to talk about the Gods and their plans. Not yet.

"Oh. I informed my father that you and I would be vowing to each other—a mere formality of a ceremony—before the battle. That we would wait for a larger, formal ceremony until after Medvara stands or falls."

"You think he will be good with quiet ties and not the large formal ceremony?"

Not that she feared his father would object to the match. Gods, from the records she'd read of Alexran's last year ruling over Medvara, there had been talk of Haran and Alicira vowing —until Alexran said no to it. How long had the Mershauntens of Larij hoped for a match with the heir to Medvara? Three generations, at least.

Toran shrugged. "We'll have to watch out for Haran and

Orlanden. Both those men love ceremonies, and they're good at sneaking them in. I suspect my uncle already has Orlanden busy planning something. One thing in our favor—with your mother fighting in Waykemin, we really can't do anything large and formal. Even Haran and Orlanden can't get past that." He leaned over and kissed her. "I look forward to our formal promises. I've loved you ever since your fourteenth birthday."

She laughed. "And why is that?"

She couldn't remember anything good about her fourteenth birthday celebration. A year after she had attained her magical majority, true, and she had demonstrated the creation of a tiny flying machine upon which she placed a scrying spell, so that it could send back images of what it flew over to a linked mirror.

The demonstration had been cut short when an eagle knocked it out of the air. Besides, she had also been sad because it was her third year in Medvara and she missed riding the canyons with Heinmyets, sorrowing because her birthday was close to the deaths of Alicira and Melarae. For some reason that had struck close to her heart that summer.

"Because of that flyer," Toran said. "When it went wrong you didn't cry or fuss, just worked to get it back flying after the eagle attacked it. You didn't give up, but kept trying."

"Doesn't everyone handle failure like that?"

"No. Not by half, especially magicians." He gazed at her with a half-smile on his lips. "I knew then that you weren't just another Aireii magician but someone who understood that unlike spells, technology doesn't have to be completely correct the first time."

She laughed. "If you knew how hard I worked to get that tiny thing functioning, you'd have a different story! There was plenty of crying and fussing as I worked."

"True for anyone who invents."

"I suppose. Technology is more forgiving than magic, which

sometimes means the meld of magic and technology can be really frustrating when it's not quite right. Meanwhile." She tapped the schematic in front of her. "I've figured out what we can do about the drain on magical strength. If we incorporate some of the quartz crystals the Saubral use into this design, then that will give us additional motive power. The Hidden One can advise us about fine-tuning them when she arrives in Medvare-the-city."

"You think she'll get there in time to help us?"

"Setkin told me that Dolenin had messaged him of her arrival in Cooscol. It will only take her a day by sailship." She brushed a strand of dark curly hair out of her eyes, blown there as *Heart's Desire* picked up speed in a stretch of slack water. "I wish our people had access to the communication magics the Sorcerer-Captains use. But it's a matter of the Goddess Terat, and I don't think it is something she easily shares with non-devotees."

"Even though she's promised you a favor?"

"I don't think that's the kind of favor she meant." Witmara frowned. "And in any case, I'd want to ask for her help in a water battle. Perhaps even when we're luring the Darani fleet across the bar."

"I see. So where do you want to fit the crystal into this design?" Toran set aside her desk and pressed closer to Witmara. She eased Setkin's desk partially onto his lap so that they could pore over the schematic together.

If it wasn't for the dire necessity that drove this creation, she could be happy. Creating devices that integrated magic and technology with her beloved? If only they could do this peacefully forever without the bother of needing to rule right away, with no greater concern than creating things and taking their daranvelii for gallops through the oak savannahs of the Saktrin Valley.

After Medvara and Waykemin.

Right now she wasn't going to think about Daran and what happened once those battles were done. Not time for that yet.

One battle at a time.

Daro sent her wordless reassurance, an image of him nuzzling her shoulder gently. She was grateful for his presence.

PLANS IN MOTION

A NON-SUPPLY STERNWHEELER STOPPED TO PICK UP KATERIN, Rekaré, and their tens in Chellni late the next morning. Katerin felt torn in two as she led Rainin up the ramp and into the hold of the sternwheeler they were to ride upriver. Part of her wanted to turn around and go back to Medvare-the-city to help Witmara create its defenses. But another part reminded her of the dangers of Waykemin—dangers that required the presence of the Banisher of Shadows, the daughter of Terani-the-God-Killer, to defuse.

Waykemin. She had hoped she would never return to that place. But after that battle where Rekaré had killed Chiral on the boundaries of Waykemin seven years ago, Katerin had known *this isn't finished.* Not when the Witches were clearly allying with Chatain. And if they went by the old prophecies, only someone born of Waykemin could overthrow the Witches Council.

So why did the Witches let me leave Waykemin so many years ago? They knew I was born of Miteal. Did they think I would remain forever ignorant of who my father was?

Then again, she had been determined to become a Healer and study at Keldara's Healing House. The Goddess Dovré had claimed her—and Dovré had no place in Waykemin. Perhaps it had been more dangerous to harbor the quiet daughter of Terani-the-God-Killer in a land recently rededicated to the Twin Gods Karnoi and Cirdel. As a young Healer in perpetual debt to the Council for Terani's maintenance while she lay in the dreamless sleep, perhaps they had gambled that Katerin would have no time to investigate her origins and gain any power beyond that of a Healer. And Karnoi and Cirdel had certainly dogged her steps for years, keeping her distracted from any possible exploration of her heritage.

Until Katerin came to the village of Wickmasa. Until Karnoi and Cirdel tried to use Wickmasa's overly ambitious Healer Makri to bring her down. Makri, who had been jealous of his twin Metkyi, who had secretly been aiding Rekaré and Cenarth. Katerin and Metkyi had banished Karnoi and Cirdel from the Two Nations and she had met her father, though neither of them knew that until his death, when he had passed on his powerful magic to her.

Now she wondered. Her father Alame had studied with the Witches for a year, until he had been driven out after Terani learned of her pregnancy. He had not been allowed to know of her existence. Had the Witches hoped they would never cross paths?

She would never know for certain just how much he knew. He had not acknowledged her until his death. Alame's spirit was quiet in the Other Side, not seeking contact, not even as she changed from Katerin Healer to Katerin ea Miteal. And except for her periodic contacts with Metkyi, Katerin had no desire to summon the shades of the dead.

She leaned on the ship's railing as its whistle sounded as it left the docks, continuing to wrestle with her desire to follow her daughter downriver and protect her from the battles to come. Witmara was so young. Young to be vowed to Toran. Young to command Medvara's forces in battle. And still—

Witmara is but six months away from assuming the leadership of Medvara in her own right. She has been training for this. Leadership includes willingness to go to war. Rekaré was Witmara's age when she challenged her father Zauril and killed him. Witmara has studied not just with sorcerers but also with Vered and Setkin. She is better prepared for a battle that includes ships than either you or Rekaré were at her age. Thanks to Toran, she has the Mershaunten's support. By the Goddess's golden tits, relax!

But she was still uneasy about the prospect. And the devices that Witmara and Toran used so easily. That reeked too much of Chatain to her. The integration of magic and technology was a skill she feared as much as she appreciated it—and yet it might be their best chance for defeating Chatain.

Rekaré joined her, seeming to be more relaxed and less driven than she had been for the last seven years. They stood together in silence, watching the dry canyon walls that reared high above the Chellana as the sternwheeler steamed up the river, heading the procession of ships toward Nixyin, their evening stop.

"It is a very different world now from when we rode downriver to challenge my father," Rekaré said finally.

"I would not have thought our lives to be like this eighteen years ago."

"I thought that deposing my father would be enough to fix Medvara. That despite the whispers from the Goddess that a different fate awaited us, Cenarth and I would live in peace, raising our children to make Varen strong." Rekaré laughed bitterly. "I should have known. The Goddess Nitel named me as Sorrow. It seems as if Sorrow is all I can bring to the nations and to those I dare to love."

"Linyet will be a strong leader for the Two Nations."

"He will indeed. But how much of that is Cenarth's doing, and that of Heinmyets and Inharise?" Rekaré exhaled, shaking her head. "Certainly not mine."

Katerin snorted. "He is your son as well as Cenarth's. You helped lay the foundation of what he is now. Eighteen years ago, I was nothing more than Katerin Healer, the unwanted daughter of Terani-the-God-Killer. I never expected to become Leader of Medvara, much less knew that I was a daughter of the house of Miteal. Talk about unprepared for what I am now! Both of our children are better prepared for what lies ahead than we were."

"Yet here you are. Here we are, facing Waykemin." A distant look passed over Rekaré's face and she straightened up. "I must go."

So suddenly?

Katerin watched her cousin walk away. Uneasiness nagged at her. Perhaps it was that odd look Rekaré had, or perhaps it was the secretive way that she looked around when she thought that Katerin wasn't watching. Whatever triggered her worry, Katerin decided to skulk behind her cousin.

Rekaré ducked into an alcove. Katerin held back.

She inhaled sharply as Rekaré collapsed to her knees, the air shimmering about her. Rekaré unsheathed her sword and carefully set it point-down, leaning against its haft for a moment. Then she rocked back on her heels, reversing the sword, and touched its point to her lips, kissing it. After that she pressed her forehead against the blade, crooning words that made the hairs on the back of Katerin's neck stand up while the sword shimmered with a blue-gray light edged in magenta that enfolded Rekaré.

Katerin backed away from the sight, uneasiness roiling through her thoughts.

What was her cousin becoming? It was something unknown to Katerin.

Is this just Rekaré Kinslayer, or is it something else?

WITMARA KNELT BEFORE HER MOTHER'S GREAT TAPESTRY IN THE Great Hall. This was not the Great Hall of her childhood visits to Medvara, but the new one her mother had built after the fire that consumed the Leader's House following Rekaré's abdication. Unlike the gloomy old hall Alexran had built, Katerin's Hall was bright and airy, constructed of light-shaded pinewood, with rugs that Witmara and Katerin had woven together to augment their magics. Witmara had contributed a small bit to the weaving of the Great Tapestry, *so that passage of the Leadership to you will be simpler,* her mother had said. Daro had not been included in this weaving, as he had been too young to partner in her magic at that time.

As Witmara reached out to the land through the Light of Medvara, it responded to her willingly.

> Show me the progression of the Hidden One.
> Then show me the state of the coastal
> defenses.

If their lure failed, they needed to be ready to repel the invaders.

The Tapestry's map of Medvara showed a bright indicator near the mouth of the Chellana. Good. The Hidden One would arrive by midday tomorrow. That gave them time to integrate her spells into the devices that Toran now labored over in the forge, with the aid of artisans and technologists. Then the Hidden One could help them activate the primary crystal. Witmara could probably do it herself, but—she wanted to wait for the Hidden One's guidance. What little she had learned of these magics from Sesenth and Rekaré these past three years made her want the Hidden One's help.

Witmara stood and ran her fingertips down the coastline, pausing at each fort. In each place she sensed activity, increased fortifications while the young and feeble were sent to inland strongholds in the Saktrin Valley through the few hidden passes in the forbidding Larisdinnei. The steep mountains that rose almost directly out of the beaches were Medvara's best defense against ocean attack.

Still, there were weak spots on the coast, places where a determined force could find passage through the Larisdinnei to reach the Saktrin Valley and attack Medvare-the-city from the south. Cooscol was not one of those sites, but Flornol was—it had been where Zauril had first come ashore in Medvara and built a following. Both Rekaré and Katerin had subsequently reinforced that port, staffing it with their most loyal followers.

Finally, she bade the Tapestry to rest. It was tempting to check on her mother's progress up the Chellana, but Witmara could anticipate where she would be in any case. Sternwheeler ports were predictable. They were en route to Nixyin, with two more days on the river. One day to Dera from the port at the mouth of the Kitskan River. A day to gather forces in Dera, and then—

Gods, watch over my mother and keep her safe. If she falls, that changes everything. We dare not lose her.

KATERIN SAVED HER VISIT TO STAUL'S SHRINE IN NIXYIN UNTIL well after dark. Jeralte came with her as she walked disguised through the streets to the shrine on the waterfront, her only companion in spite of his objections. She had never required a full escort when coming to the shrine before, despite the roughness of the area, and she wasn't about to start using one. Nixyin's waterfront was much calmer than it had been when she was younger. Besides, she had this sense that bringing more than one escort would somehow offend either Metkyi or Staul. At the very least it could provoke the Chief Priest and she didn't need that, either.

This time the Priest who greeted her did so with a sad smile, his necklace of teeth and finger joints rattling on its own, as if the bone pieces of the necklace still lived.

"Leader Katerin. Banisher of Shadows." He was someone new to her, a change since her visit last spring. She noted that his red cowl was styled similar to those worn by Rekaré and her Mer Galad.

A devotee of Rekaré Kinslayer?

She had heard of such a thing amongst the followers of Staul, but to see it now…. Furthermore, this priest was not Saubral but Larijian—and Larijians usually followed Artel the Judge.

What does this mean?

The Priest's red cowl made her uneasy, coupled with her stolen observation of Rekaré on the ship.

Perhaps the God, if not Metkyi, can tell me what is going on. What is Rekaré becoming?

She half-bowed to him, hand over her heart. "Priest. You know why I am here."

"Yes." The Priest sighed. "Your daughter is not with you?"

"No. She has duties to attend to in Medvare-the-city."

Lately, Metkyi had been more inclined to speak to his daughter than to her when they came. She understood why. Metkyi had warned her repeatedly that their tie must fade as he grew deeper into the Other Side (though that did not seem to apply to Witmara, perhaps because Staul was her patron), but the process still hurt.

She dropped two silver pieces in the Priest's hand to begin the familiar ritual. "I would speak with one who was beloved of Staul the Balancer during his life."

The Priest inclined his head slightly. "I must ask—do you have need of assistance to summon the one you seek?"

Once she would have dismissed the question without thought. "The one I seek grows deep in the Other Side." She gulped and blinked hard. "This may be the last time I can speak to Metkyi without my daughter. I would ask that you remain present, to help me if necessary. You and no other."

The Priest put his hands together and bowed to her. "Then, Banisher of Shadows, I will do that."

"I thank you."

She followed the Priest down the hallway and into the inner chamber, where golden sage-infused beeswax pillar candles carved in the image of the God burned before tall back-to-back statues of Staul in his aspects as Balancer and Destroyer. The inner chamber was empty for once, no acolytes kneeling before the God's images, the scent of sage from candles and smudges filling the room. The Priest locked the doors behind them, a standard precaution should Staul's power overwhelm the supplicants and send them crazed out into the streets. He stood in front of the doors.

"I wait here, my lady Banisher, should you need me."

"Thank you." Katerin pulled the necklace that Metkyi had given her years ago out from under her tunic. She rubbed the purple and white stone in the silver ring that matched the necklace and raised her hands high, so that the stone faced the statues.

"I wish to speak to a beloved of Staul," she said.

The heat and pressure of the God's presence came upon her. Katerin endured the sudden greater weight in her arms and legs, the accompanying cloying damp heat of the air she breathed, the faint booming as the God approached her in full aspect. The candles flickered, the scent of sage growing stronger, and then Staul of the Balance stood before his statues, a tall, attractive, dark-skinned man. Though this manifestation of the God was not bald, different from his statues. His dark hair was neatly braided just like Metkyi used to do, in the same impeccable court dress, except this time it was red instead of Metkyi's favored black.

If not for the dark red shade of his clothing, he could be a duplicate of Metkyi as he had been in life. But she recognized this manifestation as the God and not her lost love.

"My Lord Staul."

"Banisher of Shadows."

Katerin reached in her pouch for Staul's gift. Her fingers brushed against the wrapping of Medvara's token, warmth radiating through the cloth. She brought out the palm-sized cedar bentwood box and handed it to the God on an upraised palm.

"Here is my gift, Lord Staul. Smoked salmon from the fall run up the Saktrin, dried Coos berries, and filberts. I would have brought fresh, but this is not the season."

"I understand." The God took the box between index finger and thumb, then popped it into his mouth, half-smiling. "And what else do you have in the pouch with my gift? I sense an artifact of great power."

"It is a gift from the land of Medvara."

"May I see it?"

Reluctance warred in Katerin with the desire to fulfill the God's request. "The land is—rather possessive of me, my Lord. I would honor its wishes."

Staul cocked his head, another Metkyi mannerism.

Does this mean he's being absorbed by the God?

"I understand, Banisher of Shadows. I merely want to look at it. I will not touch it or interfere with your link to Medvara. It is somewhat unusual for a land to gift its Leader. I am curious about what Medvara gave you."

Katerin nodded. She pulled the stone out of her pouch and partially unwrapped it, the cloth spilling over her clasped hands as she held it forth. The God put his hands behind his back and bent over to examine it closely. At last he straightened up.

"You may put it away, Leader Katerin. That is a generous gift indeed, and not at all usual. Did you find it or did the land extrude it?"

"The land *made* it somehow. The earth cracked and this flowed out."

Staul nodded. "Medvara gave you a piece of its deepest self. It is a great honor to you as a Leader for your land to do this, but it also means that it perceives you to be facing great danger. It has marked you as its own. It is a testament to the esteem it holds for you—something great for poor, broken, Medvara. Be honored—not many are capable of healing a land."

"Thank you." She rewrapped the stone and put it away. "It has power that I do not understand, and I have not had time to explore it."

The God nodded. "It is a power that will need to grow with you, both as Leader and as Banisher. Medvara has given you a tool beyond price, especially given what you face. But it also requires a toll."

"Witmara." Her breath caught, waiting for the God's pronouncement.

The God shook his head. "Yourself. Your daughter is mine as you are not. The land desires you, not her."

Katerin exhaled slowly. "She prepares Medvara's defenses even now."

"I know." The God smiled. "She is very dear to me. But Medvara does not fit my aspirations for her."

Rebellion stirred within Katerin, and she dared speak sharply to the God. "And what of my plans for my daughter? My goals?"

The God sighed, a world's weight of sorrow in it, clearly accepting her insolence. "Alas, my Banisher of Shadows. Our desires do not match. Not just mine but of Artel the Judge. Witmara is needed for more than Medvara."

"But I am no Leader."

"Medvara says otherwise. I will also tell you this—greater things lie ahead of you as well, but for that you must speak to my sister Dovré."

"Not Daran!" she protested.

"No," the God said slowly. "Not Daran." He shook his head. "I can tell you nothing more about the fates of you and your daughter."

"Then what about my cousin? What is happening to her?"

The God shook his head again. "I cannot speak to you of what Rekaré Kinslayer is becoming. This is a judgment of Artel."

Those words sent a chill through Katerin in spite of the damp heat in the shrine.

Oh my cousin, what is your fate?

But she dared not push the God any further.

"I would speak with my beloved," she said.

The God arched a brow at her, again like Metkyi. "You have very few moments left with him before you cross to the Other Side. Are you certain that now is the time?"

"I—I need it." Katerin pressed her lips together. "What lies ahead of me is challenging. I need the bolster of his presence, even if this means the last time I can meet with him like this."

"Ah, Banisher of Shadows. You are stronger than you believe yourself to be. Nonetheless, I will bring him out."

She expected the God's presence to fade away, followed by a period where Metkyi's spirit formed in a mist that rose from the votives. That had been the usual process when she previously spoke with Metkyi's shade.

Instead, the God's form shrunk, the features he shared with Metkyi becoming more prominent until her late beloved stood before her, though still attired in red rather than his usual black. Katerin brought out the second bentwood box she carried in another pouch and offered it to him. Like the God had, this time he swallowed it whole instead of scooping the offering out of the box. Then he straightened up, holding himself stiffly, formally, almost as if he were carved from the same material as the statues behind him.

"Katerin." His voice seemed very far away. "Banisher of Shadows. Leader of Medvara. Staul's Messenger acknowledges you."

Staul's Messenger.

The title struck her hard. He hadn't used it the last time she had spoken to him. He had clearly grown to great power on the Other Side.

"Oh Gods, Metkyi. I—I would see you *as you* once more before I go to Waykemin."

"You confront Waykemin at last." His posture finally softened and he took her in his arms.

He knew.

Gods. He knew. Of course he would, as Staul's Messenger. Katerin buried her face in his chest. The faintest trace of his own scent remained, overpowered by sage.

"I fear this upcoming battle more than any other I've faced," she said into his chest. "Waykemin. The Witches. And the Chief Priestess—Tranarin. She tormented me as a child. She knows my deepest hurts. She can devise a spell to harm me like no one else can."

Metkyi stroked her chin, then gently lifted it so that she gazed into his eyes. "Medvara gave you that piece of itself for a reason. Your land protects you, more than you know, and it will be useful as you battle in Waykemin. My Lord Staul spoke truly. Few Leaders are given so great a gift, and it speaks to Medvara's gratefulness for the work you have done."

"Is it strong enough to keep Tranarin from casting spells to entrap me?"

"Yes." He kissed her forehead. "You are born of Waykemin

and will still have power over elements of it as a right of birth, especially since you are the daughter of Terani-the-God-Killer. But Medvara's gift establishes its claim over you. You are also the daughter of Alame en Miteal, a strong sorcerer in your own right. More than that, you belong to Medvara, not Waykemin. Trust your land, and Tranarin will not be able to touch you."

Katerin inhaled sharply. "And Witmara. The God says—she will not replace me. I have planned this for seven years, ever since Rekaré passed the Leadership to me. And now—was this what you saw at your death?"

"I did not see it clearly then, dearest. But Witmara's fate is greater than Medvara. As yours will be, eventually."

"That's what the God said." She blinked back tears. "Hard to reconcile myself to that promise. I have never felt called to be a Leader. Not like Rekaré was." Her voice faltered as she remembered how *that* had turned out.

"But you *are* Leader of Medvara, and a very good one at that. Its gift proves that."

Katerin sniffled. "I only ever set out to be a good Healer."

"And you were. Are. There are more ways to be a Healer, and you have become a healer of the land."

"Oh Gods, Metkyi, I wish you were next to me in this battle."

"I cannot be there, dearest." He kissed her forehead again. "I cannot speak regularly to both you and Witmara, and she will have the greater need of my help, very soon. You are strong and powerful. She is still developing her strength and will need me to bolster her."

She had expected this, but it still hurt. Tears oozed out of her eyes. "Oh *Gods,* Metkyi."

"Ah, Katerin, Katerin." Metkyi took her head in his hands and kissed her eyelids. "I am sorry."

"But it is the way of the Gods," she choked out. At least Witmara could still see her father and talk to him. Maybe she could still see Metkyi when their daughter spoke to him. "You do know that she has committed to Toran, the Mershaunten's youngest son?"

"I do. And I approve. He is a good match for what she faces."

"And what of me?" she whispered.

"You have been faithful to my vision for many years. The time will come for Katerin Leader and Healer to find her living joy, her support. He will come to you in a most unexpected manner." Metkyi kissed her again, this time full on the lips. "Beloved, I wish I could keep speaking to you. But I promise you —the time will come for us to walk together on the Other Side. Go forth with the courage you always have had and know that my blessing still rests upon you. I must direct my strength to our daughter and what she faces. You have other supports. Embrace your gift of the land. And when opportunity comes to you—do not reject it."

He stepped back. Katerin blinked through teary eyes as his form grew back into that of Staul's.

"My lady Katerin," the God said, more softness and compassion in his voice than she had ever heard before. "I am sorry for this but needs demand. However. I place my highest blessings upon you as the Banisher of Shadows. I will answer when you are in the reddest of shadows. Know that both Dovré and I agree on this."

"I thank you for your blessing, Lord Staul." She did not wipe away the tears rolling down her cheeks. The God reached out and delicately brushed them away, bringing that finger to his lips.

"Your tears are a further gift and I thank you for that," he said.

And then the God was gone.

Now Katerin wiped her eyes. She shuddered, feeling the weakness in her body that always occurred after a meeting with this God. Then she straightened her shoulders and turned to face the Priest.

"I am done," she said.

The Priest bowed to her. "Staul's blessings upon you, Banisher of Shadows. Know that those who serve Staul support you. Waykemin is a grave danger that threatens all of us."

"I thank you."

She walked out of the shrine, head high. Jeralte appeared out of the shadows. He did not talk as they walked back to the Guest House and tears slowly trailed down her cheeks.

She was grateful for his silence.

CENARTH AND HEINMYETS

Four days later, Rekaré and her Mer Galad riders scouted ahead on the main road descending into the Keldaran Valley as they approached Dera at dusk. She was content to let Katerin ride behind with the forces they had accumulated on their trip up the Chellana—local forces stationed at Larijian river forts, and isolated Saubral tribes recruited by Sesenth, the more organized groups from Medvara, the motley assembly from vendors at Chellni lured by the thought of battle, and other stragglers. Linyet rode with Katerin rather than his mother. If Rekaré thought about the way he eyed her distrustfully, her heart ached.

She tried not to think about it. His behavior was a consequence of choices she had made, and that could not be changed.

Still she—she needed to ride on ahead. Not only to avoid the pangs that seeing Linyet gave her, but to give herself time to prepare for meeting Cenarth and Heinmyets. Gods, she hadn't seen either of them since she left the Leadership of Medvara. Didn't dare let them back into her heart. More than that, she wanted to have time alone with the land of her childhood. It was easier to think about Cenarth and what she would say to him if she rode ahead alone, scouting to ensure that no stray foe or spy from Waykemin would challenge their main force.

She rested her hand on the hilt of her sword.

Remember that you bring sorrow to those you hold close. Except Sesenth.

And Senth became more Shadowwalker with each passing day, a force for sorrow herself.

Memories tore at Rekaré as she rode, some from childhood, some from her teens when she and Cenarth rode hard, attempting to avoid her father's hunters and the Shadowwalkers and Houndriders they employed to pursue her. They dared not descend into the Keldaran Valley that held Dera, but skulked around the ridges to gather information and stay hidden. She practiced and honed her sorcery in secret with the help of her great-uncle Alame, Katerin's father (though neither had known of the relationship then), building her strength in order to face Zauril and avenge the sorrow he had brought to her mother.

Now Rekaré looked back at her younger, wilder, self and wondered if those choices had been wise. How much sorrow had she brought upon herself? What would have happened if they had followed the original plan and she had gone to Zauril at age thirteen, waiting for a chance to strike at him? Perhaps Medvara would not have rejected her in the end.

And perhaps things would have been worse if she had made that particular choice.

Second thoughts do you no good.

She brought a force of Shadowwalkers into Keldara. Best to ride alert. Even though there had been peace between Keldara and Saubral for some years now, thanks to her negotiations since she had left Medvara, that didn't mean that there weren't still passive traps waiting to be triggered. Or that Keldarans who had suffered from past Shadowwalker incursions didn't still carry grudges. This close to Dera there would be hunters and foragers riding off-trail. Those would include people whose past included bloody encounters with Saubral raiders. At least there wouldn't be herders yet. Not enough grass for the herders to take to the mountains.

Herders would have the worst memories of Saubral raids.

Basnen snorted as the road broke free from the trees into a broad grassy clearing. Ever since they had set foot in Keldara the golden mare had been prancing, up on her toes, more energetic, remembering her birth land. She tossed her head, sending her silver mane shimmering. Rekaré sent her a wordless question, projecting the image of Cenarth's daranval Quartel.

Nearby and behind us. Not close enough to be a danger yet. Between us and Katerin. The land hides him and his riders.

A half-smile pulled at Rekaré's lips as she recognized one of Cenarth's preferred tactics. And the land shielded him—good. That meant he had fully committed to becoming Leader of the Two Nations.

See? Things would have needed to change between us. At some point he would have needed to return here with Linyet while I stayed in Medvara with Melarae.

But oh, she wished it could have been different. That their children could have become Leaders, and they could have ridden free together again.

Sesenth emerged from the pines edging the clearing. Rekaré had sent her riders to scatter in the woods to survey for any signs that the Witches had established outposts near Dera.

"Riders behind us," she said.

"I know," Rekaré said. "Cenarth leads. The land has been shielding them. They may have already spoken to Katerin."

"I don't think they have gone that far. We're quite a bit ahead of the main force. They've been watching us. If they wanted to engage, they could have done it many times over."

"Katerin sent messages ahead to let Cenarth and Heinmyets

know that she rode with a troop of Shadowwalkers," Rekaré said. "Cenarth will be looking for me."

As if mentioning his name had summoned him, Basnen halted, sending Rekaré an image of

> Cenarth and Quartel nearby, almost within sight.

She half-reared and whirled to face the road behind them, shaking her head and prancing. Cenarth emerged from the trees. Basnen broke into a gallop, calling to Quartel. The bay stallion bellowed a welcome, galloping toward them.

Rekaré allowed her to run, just as Cenarth did with Quartel. The daranvelii dropped to a trot, then halted nose-to-nose. She kept her focus on Basnen, waiting just in case the daranvelii decided to scuffle as part of their greeting. Basnen in particular was likely to strike. Unusual behavior for a mare, but Basnen had always been prickly, which had made training her as a war mare easier.

The daranvelii nuzzled each other. Quartel nipped at Basnen's face, lips only, no teeth. Basnen pinned her ears and snapped back, teeth bared, a mare's warning against silly male bitey-face games. She stomped a forefoot but did not strike.

Quartel chuckled deep in his chest. Basnen answered first with a squeal, then a softer nicker. She relaxed under Rekaré, her ears coming forward, and gently touched Quartel's right nostril with the edge of hers, a greeting familiar to both daranvelii.

And that was that. Rekaré felt the faint rumble of daranval-to-daranval mindspeech between the two. No further worries about either daranval arguing. If only she could be certain that things would be that way between the humans.

She dared look up into Cenarth's eyes now that the daranvelii were settled, and struggled to conceal her shock at his appearance.

Gods.

He seemed to have aged more than twice the seven years they had been apart. The redbark-shaded skin of his face was deeply lined, sagging from his high cheekbones. Darker half-circles under his brown, gold-flecked eyes spoke of little sleep. Silver marked what she could see of his hair under his knitted tight-fitting gray cap, roughly cut edges showing at the nape of his neck instead of the single braid he preferred—*so he has cut hair for his mother*. When he was younger he had looked like Inharise.

Now, he resembled a paler, slimmer version of Heinmyets.

"So," he said bitterly. "I had not expected to see you wearing a Shadowwalker cowl."

"They are vowed to my service."

He sighed. "Yes. I know. We could have attacked you many times over. The land shielded us from their vision."

"I know. I warned my Mer Galad riders that you would be watching and that Keldara guarded you." She waved Senth forward. "This is Sesenth, one of my Seconds. Detaluna is still out there."

Cenarth acknowledged Sesenth with a nod, brown eyes surveying her closely. "I saw Deta."

"Yes." Gods, she felt like a young girl caught between two loves. But wasn't that exactly what this situation was?

Sesenth is not my love—but what was Senth to her, really, if not a love? For a moment she entertained the thought of a marriage between the three of them, such as Heinmyets, Inharise, and her mother had maintained. What would Cenarth think of that?

It cannot be. You dare not risk that fate. It would bring harm to him and Linyet.

But Gods, the temptation was very sweet, especially as she saw how sorrow sat on him.

"Did Linyet return with you?" Cenarth finally asked.

"He rides with Katerin. He—they have much to discuss."

"I suppose they would."

She swallowed hard. "I—I don't know what to say about your mother. My Secondmother. Heinmyets's sorrow roiled the lands. I—I should have been there."

"It was no easier being close. She died hard."

Rekaré closed her eyes for a moment, cringing. "Linyet said she was failing. That she would live to summer, but that Yevtin did not expect her to survive to winter. Is that the truth?"

"Yes."

"He said she was declining like Alicira was at the end."

Cenarth looked down at Quartel's silver-streaked mane. "It was very similar, Rekaré. A slow decline. Mother was looking forward to a summer in the mountains with the herds. She didn't say, but I think she was planning to go into the canyons in the old Clendan tradition rather than return to Dera in the fall. Then she suddenly took a turn for the worse. We couldn't identify any magic."

"Katerin's vision showed a curse from the Waykemese Witches Council."

"So the messages said. It would explain Father's decline as well."

"He is not well?"

"Not as bad as she was, but—still, he suffered harm."

"I wish Katerin could have intervened before..." Rekaré's voice trailed off.

"As do I." His face tightened. "She hoped you would return to say goodbye."

"I—I would have come sooner if I'd known," Rekaré choked. "She was my Secondmother. My lawmother."

Cenarth glared at her. "And yet you rode away from us."

"Cenarth. Please. I only do this to protect you."

"And what if I don't *want* to be protected?"

"My path leads those around me to doom. The Two Nations need you and Linyet. I can't ask you to walk away from that."

"You never asked. You only told me what you planned to do. Rekaré, that wasn't right."

"I only sought to protect Linyet and you!" She drew a ragged breath.

"And what about Sesenth? You do not care that she shares this doom you fear?"

"Sesenth carries her own doom," Rekaré said. "But you—Cenarth, you and Linyet are the hope of the Two Nations. I can't take that away from Keldara and Clenda." She gulped. "Cenarth. I am sorry for the hurt I have caused you. Caused Linyet. But I saw no other possible option that would not pull you two down into the same destruction that struck my mother and our daughter. Losing them was enough. I would much rather you two survived the storm to come."

The laden, choking sensation that meant *benghaalph* was coming upon her was an unwelcome intrusion.

Not now!

"And I would have risked everything to remain by your side, as I did for many years."

She shuddered, her vision blurring as *benghaalph* came over her.

"And that is not your fate, Cenarth son of Heinmyets and Inharise, father of Linyet the Lightbringer. Would you see the failure and destruction of all you hold dear? Varen laid waste while Chatain feeds himself on lives, a bloated spider seeking divinity? It is not Rekaré who speaks to you now but *benghaalph*, the One Spoken Of. Without her sacrifice Medvara would be a curse upon Varen. My people the Saubral would not be allies but his weapons, destroying all to feed Chatain's hunger until they too fell to his desires."

Her vision blurred even more as *benghaalph* whisked away as abruptly as it had come upon her. She slumped over Basnen's neck, forehead almost resting on her mane, and stared at the silver strands until the individual hairs became clear, breathing heavily as if she had been running full out for a long time.

Her mouth was dry. She pushed herself upright, fumbled for her waterskin, and drank. Then she dared look away from Basnen's mane to take in Cenarth's stricken face.

"I am sorry," she whispered.

"Rekaré. Oh Gods, Rekaré. What have you become?"

"I do not know. But I am no longer Rekaré ea Miteal. She died with our daughter."

He shook his head. "I have only seen you like this twice before—at Alame's death, and then again at your father's death."

"The face of Rekaré Kinslayer, carrier of the Saubral prophet *benghaalph*. You did not see me when I killed Chiral. The reason I dared not return to Medvara, to bring a further curse on that land." Rekaré swallowed hard, her throat still dry. Something still choked her throat hard. "The face of *benghaalph*, though I did not know it then. Gods. I would not impose this upon you."

Cenarth urged Quartel forward and took her hand. "I would still walk with you if you said the word."

Gods, it was tempting. As she looked into his beloved face, into those familiar gold-flecked brown eyes, felt the touch of the hand she knew so well, for a moment she let herself consider the possibility.

Linyet as Heinmyets's successor in the Two Nations. Herself and Cenarth as Empress and Consort in Daran. Witmara settled in Medvara, the land still aching for Katerin but accepting. And then her vision lengthened (although this time *benghaalph* thankfully remained quiet), and she saw the future that path led to.

A path where an unexpected foe burst through Barrier and the Nerean Gate in Keratil to the southeast, bringing devastation as yet unheard of in either Daran or Varen. Where Linyet fell to the wraith of her father just as Melarae had, only worse because Linyet was older. Where she was loved and praised during her lifetime, but after her death—after her death she was as reviled and cursed as Elithtra was now.

And Chatain had attained the Godhood he desired, wreaking his wrath upon the world and turning it toward his own twisted version.

"I wish I could," she said in a low voice. "I wish I could put aside what I see coming toward us and think about just us. But for the good of Varen and Daran—I dare not."

"It would be that bad?" he asked. "Everything I saw?"

She nodded. "You saw what I just did?"

"Yes."

"Then you know what fate drives me. I will not be a curse upon the nations. I will not be her!"

His hand closed more tightly on hers. "I don't like this fate. But Gods, Rekaré, much as I hate to admit this—you are right. You made the right choice. All the same, I wish it could be otherwise."

"So do I." Her voice caught on those words. "I miss you more than words can ever express."

"As do I, my dearest heart. Perhaps in another time." He raised her hand and kissed it. "I would be the beloved of she who the Gods have touched," he said ruefully, squeezing her hand one last time before releasing it. "But now I must be nothing more than a mere commander in the forces you lead. I do not like it—but the alternative is much worse."

"The forces Katerin leads," she said. "I merely support her in this battle. Mine is what comes after this."

"You will play a greater role than you expect." He backed Quartel five steps and whistled. "Riders! To me!"

Rekaré added her own call. As she watched for them to come in, she noticed that Cenarth and Sesenth had pulled apart and were talking quietly.

At least they are at peace together.

She hoped.

IT WAS ALMOST FULL DARK BY THE TIME THEY REACHED DERA. Katerin felt strange riding as a Leader toward the capital city she had known as a Healer. Rekaré rode on one side of her, Cenarth and Linyet on the other, Detaluna and Sesenth and Cenarth's seconds immediately behind them. Heinmyets stood at the head of an unmounted torch-lit delegation at the edge of the city. The sight pricked tears in her eyes. She had never seen Heinmyets greeting a delegation without his daranval Elantai before, much less without Inharise. But Elantai had gone to the canyons last fall, after she had met with them at Chellni. And now Inharise….

She halted Rainin fifteen strides away and dismounted, not wanting to tower over Heinmyets on horseback. Rekaré and the others followed her lead, their seconds coming forward to take the daranvelii reins. Katerin hesitated for a moment in case Rekaré wanted to go first, but Rekaré jerked her head toward Heinmyets, indicating that she should lead.

Katerin straightened her shoulders and marched toward Heinmyets. He leaned on a stick, his dark skin wrinkled and sagging. His right arm appeared to be withered and as she drew closer she realized the muscles on the right side of his face sagged lower than those on his left side. He hadn't looked like that last fall in Chellni.

Aging, illness, and grief. The healer in her wondered how long had it been since he'd had that stroke. Before or after Inharise's death? She stopped in front of him and bowed low.

"Heinmyets. Words cannot express my deepest condolences at your loss—at the loss to all Varen."

"I have none left to me." The anguish in his voice struck deep into her heart. "Those closest to me have passed on, leaving me alone save for my son and grandson." He raised his head and stared at Rekaré behind Katerin. "And my Heartsdaughter moves beyond us as well."

Katerin impulsively took his withered hand, gently checking it for strength as well as offering comfort.

"We ride for vengeance upon Waykemin," she said. "It is but the first step in the war against Chatain."

His hand clamped down hard on hers, harder than she expected given his observable condition. "Yes. We have raised many tens to ride with you—to Waykemin and beyond."

"I thank you for that."

"I thank you for doing what I am no longer able to." His hand dropped from hers. "Come into the city. Let us speak of strategy, and what those of us left behind can do to aid you, oh Banisher of Shadows."

She winced at the title but it was hers, as much as *Kinslayer* was Rekaré's. "I welcome your hospitality with many thanks."

He turned and she walked with him, the past Healer in her noticing how he favored his right leg.

Must talk to Yevtin about that.

"I am so sorry," she repeated. "It—her death was unexpected. The last I had heard was that Inharise was fading, but not in immediate danger of dying."

"It *was* so sudden," Heinmyets said. He grimaced. "One day she was well. Tired and weak, but we knew that process from Alicira's slow dying. We knew the time was coming, but we hoped for one last summer together in the mountain pastures. And then—She collapsed. We were sitting down to supper—she hadn't even taken a bite yet—when her eyes widened. She stared across the room and shouted *NO!* I saw red swirling in front of her, and then she—she just went down. I ran to her but was stricken with sharp pains in my head that made me pass out.

When I woke, we were both in her bedchamber, in our bed there. My right hand and side were weaker, and they have yet to regain their strength. We tried everything to treat her. Magic. Eldoran came out of retirement to help Yevtin. Nothing worked for her—though I regained strength after her death."

The stroke was part of Waykemin's curse, then. Gods have mercy on those Witches because I cannot.

"I saw part of it in a vision. Your grief roiled the lands." Katerin drew a deep breath. "First the vision of her dying, and then that of the Witches Council in Waykemin. They had figures of all three of us on the great altar and were working a spell. Inharise's image had collapsed, and you were faltering. As one born to Waykemin, I was able to break into the Council and destroy their spells—but alas, too late to save Inharise."

"Thank you for trying." He glanced back. "And what about Rekaré? What part is she to play in all this—and will she return to her family?"

Katerin shook her head. "Alas, no. She is fully Rekaré Kinslayer now. I swear at times she seems like she is half-Shadowwalker herself—only it's more than that. Much more. I've asked the God Staul what she is becoming. He refuses to tell me and says it is a judgment of Artel."

"I notice she is not walking with Cenarth and Linyet."

"No." Katerin stared straight ahead, words now coming hard to her. "The meeting between her and Linyet was—difficult, happening as it did after we became aware of Inharise's death."

"He was close to his grandmother after Rekaré parted from them. I know that Cenarth was very bitter when he rode out this morning."

"At least those two appear to have come to some agreement," Katerin said. "But. We've also received warning of an attack on Medvara, from the Darani Empire. Witmara has returned to Medvara to defend it in my place. I can't be there—I am needed to lead the attack on Waykemin, since it appears I am the only one who can." She grimaced. "And we dare not ignore Waykemin, for fear they will try these spells again, or lead an attack on the Two Nations, Keratil, or Saubral."

"What times we live in. I had hoped for a peaceful old age and death, like my parents." Heinmyets halted, breathing heavily. "Forgive me my weakness."

"Do not apologize. I have been walking too fast for you."

He shook his head. "No, you are not walking too fast. I am just an old man." Frustration edged his voice. "I do not appreciate aging. But I do wish that either my last days could be more peaceful or that I had my daranval and the strength to ride with you, so I could die fighting."

"We still need you." Fear clutched at Katerin's gut. How many times during her years as a circuit healer had she run into the situation where an elder surviving the death of a beloved passed on shortly afterward, unable to face life without that other? "*Linyet* needs you," she stressed. "We've had enough death already."

He groaned. "And so I sit on the sidelines, alone, a useless old man. At least if I fought my death could be of service."

"You are *not* a useless old man. You are still the Leader of the Two Nations and will serve a valuable role in keeping it safe while we ride forth."

"Forgive me my weakness in wishing this had not come to us in this time."

"You are not being weak. From what I have seen and heard, from what Rekaré reports when she is possessed by *benghaalph*, if we do not act now we will leave the world worse for those who follow us. We must do something about Chatain—and Waykemin has been a silent ally to him, until now. The Gods themselves are concerned."

"So it has been for a generation," Heinmyets sighed. "So it was when Rekaré became Leader. When Alicira died. And now —" his face twisted with grief and wetness glimmered in his eyes. "Both of my wives are dead at the hands of Chatain's allies. They were dying, true, but we would have had more time with them if not...." He choked and shook his head, gulping and blinking hard. Katerin waited, letting him mourn.

At last Heinmyets raised his head. "My daranval has gone to his forebears. My son grieves for the loss of his wife as she follows whatever purpose it is the Gods have for her, and my grandson has lost his mother. I know that things could be much, much worse should Chatain attain his goals—but for me personally, I would see the Gods *act* rather than worry!" He thumped his stick. "I may be a selfish old man but I have lost far too much that is dear to me because of their willy-nilly, back and forth, *concern* that never leads to action! I have been ready to ride for years—but the Gods kept saying no! Why now? Why when I am an old man?"

Katerin took both of his hands in hers. "I promise you, Heinmyets. The time has come for action and even old men have a role to play. The conditions are now right for us to move. It is important for you to be here. Now." She squeezed his hands tightly. "Waykemin comes first. Then Chatain. I swear it to you as the Banisher of Shadows. *We will make an end of this.*"

"I hope you are right," Heinmyets said. "Oh Gods, I hope you are right."

"We will make it so," Katerin said. "I, too, am tired of this doom hanging over our heads." Impulsively she reached out and pulled him close to her. "I have been alone for years," she said softly to him. "And now my daughter has a beloved. We depend on your strength, Heinmyets. We are not ready to see you go, too—we need you as the bulwark of the Two Nations, to guard our flank as we ride out, to keep the lands safe."

"Does it get any better?" he asked bitterly.

"Sometimes." Katerin released him. "And sometimes the loss bites harder than ever."

Heinmyets shuddered. Then he straightened. "The Gods do

as they will. Thank you, Katerin Banisher of Shadows, for bolstering me as I faltered. Come into my house of sorrow, as you prepare for battle."

"My thanks, and I will cherish your advice."

"Your knowledge of Waykemin will serve you better."

Katerin shrugged. "Who's to say? It's been many years since I crossed the Kitskan from Waykemin."

He nodded. "I have called in riders who have patrolled that border for the past few years to brief you about the conditions they have observed. It is the least I could do."

"And it will be very useful indeed."

They resumed walking toward the city and the Leader's House. Katerin took his free hand, as much to console him as to sneak in a check of his pulses.

She might be Katerin Leader, Banisher of Shadows, but she still remembered aspects of Katerin Healer.

"So this is your gadget," the Hidden One said, leaning on her cane as she hobbled into Toran's workroom beside Witmara. "A wedding of technology and magic." She squinted at the amplifier constructed of thin slabs of pine and finely woven magical wool. "Does it flap wings like a bird to fly?"

The Hidden One reminded Witmara of a spider in the way she scuttled about the table studying the amplifier, bent upon herself, arms and legs ready to close in tight if needed. No. Not quite a spider. A desert scorpion? Cowled and veiled, her form and face a mystery.

And yet there was no question of who she was. Her gray-green skin was similar to both Houndrider and Shadowwalker, at least what little of it was visible at the gaps between the gloves the Hidden One wore and her sleeves. Both Shadowwalkers and Houndriders bowed deferentially to her and the power she projected—yes, it was a match for every story Witmara had heard about the Hidden One who lurked in Gulter and never left.

Except that she *had* left Gulter to come to Medvara, to help fight Chatain's invasion force. To battle for Varen.

Extraordinary times.

"Not quite," Toran said. "Witmara has placed spells on it to project her image to our foes, to lure them over the Chellana bar when she activates them. But they are of short duration and require her to be nearby."

"Which puts her at risk in the upcoming sea battle."

"Exactly. We think that if we could combine her spells with the charges your people use to power those quartz crystals, then we can project her image further and she will not need to be as close. Perhaps she could even be ashore, or in a swift ship in the river, not out in the ocean."

"Hmm. Let me think about this." The Hidden One leaned on the table the amplifier rested on, peering even closer at it. She pointed with one red-gloved finger. "Where do you place the crystal?"

"Here." Toran tapped the small tab that led to the open space in center of the amplifier. "I have not put it in yet because I didn't know if we could activate the charge in the crystal once it was inside."

"Wise choice." The Hidden One nodded. "The magics in your cloth and the existing spells will interfere with charging and inlaying the spell in the crystals. Let me see the primary crystal you have selected."

Witmara pulled the primary quartz out of one of her pouches. She carried all the crystals with her. The longer they were close to her, the more attuned to her presence they became. Hopefully that meant they could project her image more strongly when the time came.

The Hidden One pressed her fingertip against it. "An excellent choice. You have been trained in the selection of crystal?"

Witmara shook her head. "I only chose this crystal as primary based on clarity and the number of flaws within the stone. But I did not know what else I needed to consider. I tried to choose based on what made sense to me."

The Hidden One cackled. "Exactly the criteria required, my dear. But why should I expect otherwise from one such as you? Power and knowledge sits easily on you, Witmara, daughter of the Banisher of Shadows." She pushed herself upright and tossed back her veil. Piercing gray eyes in wizened skin studied Witmara closely as she pulled off her gloves to reveal tattoos that writhed from her fingers up the back of her hands and under her sleeves. "Consider yourself honored. Few see me as I truly am. But for those such as you and your beloved—yes." She picked up the crystal in her bare hands. A faint golden glow slowly brightened within it.

The Hidden One lifted the crystal high, turning it back and forth in her fingertips. Witmara could see the flaws more clearly in the greater light. None of the cracks extended to the center of the stone. The core was solid and clear, radiating that bright golden glow that was only diffused and muddied around the flaws. The Hidden One nodded abruptly, lowering the crystal. The light snuffed out. She placed the stone on the table next to the amplifier.

"The others?" she asked. "Please hand them to me, one-by-one."

Witmara gave her the next crystal. It lit up in the Hidden One's hands, not as bright or clear as the primary. She saw how one flaw pierced closer to the stone's core. The Hidden One's examination of this crystal was shorter, but ended with the same sharp nod. She placed it to the left above the primary and held her hand back out to Witmara.

"The next one, please."

They repeated the process until all six of the secondary crystals Witmara had chosen circled the primary crystal. None showed flaws that pierced the entire stone, but all of the secondaries had cracks that edged their cores.

"Excellent choices," the Hidden One said. "Not a one is flawed all the way through." She rapped a gnarled knuckle on the table. "Mark my placement of these other crystals around the primary. If possible, you must replicate this configuration when it comes time to project your image."

"They will be mounted on ship masts," Toran said.

"Then you will need to provide the captains with a map to show the ideal staging," the Hidden One said irritably. "This alignment is crucial for the best effectiveness."

"I will ensure that this happens," Witmara said. "So how do we go about energizing the crystals when the time comes?"

"You need to link them now," the Hidden One said. "But make certain you know which crystal goes where in the alignment."

"All right. So we link the crystals. Then what?"

"You must then further align yourself with the primary. It will be the key to awakening the others."

"Will I need to be on the same ship as the primary?" Witmara swallowed hard. Water bothered her less than most of the other sorcerers she knew, but still, she hoped to avoid it.

The Hidden One shook her head. "No. Once we have prepared the crystals, I will teach you the awakening spell." She glanced at the amplifier. "Will you have one of these on your person?"

Toran and Witmara exchanged glances. She raised a brow at him questioningly.

"We had not planned for her to carry one," he said.

"So just how did you intend for her to project her spell without her being on the same ship as the primary crystal?" the Hidden One growled. "Crystal magic is powerful but not that strong. And if I understand how these—*things*—work, and the strength of the spell you want her to project, she needs a personal amplifier."

"I have smaller ones we can convert into a pendant," Toran said.

The Hidden One pursed her lips thoughtfully. "Good. Let me see one."

Toran went to his workbench. He took down a bentwood box and extracted an amplifier from it that was the size of the stone in the Light of Medvara, an orb about the diameter of the length of Witmara's thumb. He held it out to the Hidden One.

"Will this work?"

She took it from him, examining the details of the intricately carved cedar framework covered with a thin layer of magic-woven cloth, popping open the small door tab to peer inside.

"What goes here?" She pointed to the empty space inside.

"Whatever token is required," Toran answered. "Or a spell that can be contained by the fabric."

"I see. Well, this will do." The Hidden One placed the orb on the table, reached into her pouch and extracted a length of braided leather. "Watch closely, both of you. This spell for the necklace must be made from living materials, not stone, not metal, not cloth. Leather is good, and so is daranval hair." She handed the leather strand to Witmara. "Take this."

Witmara obeyed.

The Hidden One wrapped her hands around Witmara's. They were warm and rough, scratchy against her skin. Power prickled like a cluster of small needles in those hands, jangling against Witmara's.

"Look at me and repeat what I say."

Witmara met the Hidden One's gray eyes steadily. She echoed the unfamiliar guttural words, doing her best to commit them to memory. As she spoke, the Hidden One's power smoothed, pressing hard but no sharp prickling. The leather glowed sage gray, then faded, though the leather shade changed from tan to gray.

"Good," the Hidden One said. "This spell's effectiveness will always show as a gray shade on whatever material you use. If it does not turn gray, you have not said it correctly." She took the leather from Witmara's hands and placed it in a coil around the primary crystal. "You *will* remember these spells." Her eyes met Witmara's again.

Think them back to me,

she mindspoke.

Witmara mindspoke the spell back to the Hidden One.

"Excellent. Now we work with this." The Hidden One pulled a chip of obsidian out of her pouch and picked up the orb. "This part is more complex. Always use obsidian. It will expire when your spell is done—nothing to be done about that, it is just the way it is. Quartz is too strong for this binding and other stones are too weak. Solid black obsidian is best. Red and black is dangerous. It verges on the reddest of red paths. Black and white obsidian is weakest."

"I understand."

"Hold out your hands."

Witmara did. The Hidden One placed the chip in one palm, the orb in the other. She flicked the door open in the orb, then wrapped her fingers around Witmara's.

"Again. Look at me and repeat what I say."

This time Witmara had the sensation of sinking deep into the Hidden One's gray eyes as she echoed the spell. A smile twisted the Hidden One's thin lips as they finished. Once again she commanded that Witmara retell her the spell via mind-speech to ensure she had it correct. This time Witmara had to repeat it three times until the Hidden One was satisfied.

"Place the chip inside the orb."

After Witmara did that, the Hidden One reached for the length of braided leather. She threaded it through the clasp on the orb and tied it.

"You will only wear this when you need to command crystals," she said. "You now have a power normally given only to those of us of the Saubral—the ability to waken and control spells through crystal and stone."

"Is this the spell I would need to waken the primary crystal before transmitting my image?" Witmara asked.

The Hidden One shook her head. "These are lesser spells. That greater spell? It is one we learn next." She glanced at Toran. "For your safety, you must leave."

Toran hesitated, looking at Witmara, brows raised questioningly.

She nodded.

He sighed, but came over and kissed her before leaving. "If you need me, just call," he murmured.

The Hidden One remained silent until the door closed behind Toran. Then she pulled off cap and cowl, followed by her robes. Tattoos and scars covered her wizened and twisted body, her skin gray-green and scaled. She stepped out of her slippers to reveal fleshy cloven feet, like those of a Shadowwalker.

"Few of my people have ever seen me as I truly am without my robes and cowl," the Hidden One said. "Of your kind, only you and Rekaré Kinslayer have had this privilege, Witmara the hope of Varen." She gestured to Witmara. "Remove your clothing. We must do this next spell sky-clad."

At least today she was dressed for riding and work, not Court function. Otherwise, undressing would be more complicated without help. Witmara shed trousers and tunic.

The Hidden One surveyed her. "Good. No one has marked you. I did not think any had—you have been carefully protected

—but best to be certain before we work this level of magic. Do you have issues with bearing a tattoo?"

"Not if it is necessary to work magic."

"It is for you to have easy access to this spell. I will embed it into a small mark on your wrist."

"Then go ahead."

"Good." The Hidden One stretched her arms over her head, then placed her hands on the small of her back, groaning softly.

"Do you need help?"

"No. I need to straighten myself out, and my back dislikes that." She chuckled. "It is easier to convince others that I stand taller and straighter when I am covered. Ah. There." The Hidden One sighed with relief, then held her arms out. "Entwine your forearms with mine."

Witmara did as she was bid, clasping the Hidden One's sharp elbows. This close she realized suddenly that even standing up straight, the Hidden One was a head shorter than she was. Her surprise must have shown because the Hidden One cackled again, looking up at her.

"I told you it is easier to convince others that I am taller when I am fully dressed. A necessary façade. Now. Witmara daughter of the Banisher of Shadows, granddaughter of Alame the Exile. Place your forehead on mine."

Bending over to do that felt clumsy. The Hidden One spoke again in that unfamiliar language. Small hot sparks tingled around Witmara's feet, until it felt like flames licked them. Then, suddenly, the flames went cold, shooting up her legs and body until a cold flame consumed her—no, both of them.

How could something be both cold and searing? She wanted to scream with agony but bit her lip instead. Any noise would summon Toran and that could not happen.

This is a test.

Her grip tightened on the Hidden One's elbows, just as the Hidden One's fingernails clawed into her own.

Hold on,

the Hidden One mindspoke.

You do well for one of your kind who has not
been trained to this. Hold on.

Witmara clung to that assurance as the cold conflagration
blazed through them. She gripped the Hidden One as if her life
depended on it, gasping and panting. Burning. Burning. Burning, a fire that consumed both of them.

Then she felt the ponderous weight of the God's approach.

My Lord Staul,

the Hidden One said.

I offer this one as worthy of my deepest
secrets. Empower her with that knowledge and
skill. Mark her as an adept of the Red Flame.
Burn this into her, body, mind, and soul, so that
she will never forget.

Familiar bony caress from Staul's fingers on her cheek. And
then the skeletal touch on her wrist, tracing a sigil that burned
more painfully than ever.

She wanted to cry out at this. Wanted to scream for Toran.

But if I do then I fail—everyone. I cannot fail. I must not fail.

Gods, it felt like a sharp hot needle drilling into her wrist
bones. She bit down hard on her lower lip to keep from screaming, until the sharp coppery tang of blood ran into her mouth.

Then it ended. Witmara gulped at the sudden cessation of
heat and pain, weakness pouring wave-like over her. She started
to sink to her knees but the Hidden One shook her head and
forced her back up.

"Now is not the time for that!" she snapped. "If you are to

wield the Red Flame, you must stand strong in the face of exhaustion!" She dropped her arms and stepped back. "Stand tall and proud!"

Witmara gasped for breath. She forced herself to stand upright, blinking hard until her vision cleared and she could focus upon the Hidden One in front of her.

"Now. Activate the primary." The Hidden One's eyes drilled hard into her.

What do I do?

For a moment, she was confused. Then it all fell together. The Hidden One had spoken of a spell contained within a tattoo. Witmara pressed on her wrist where Staul's touch had burned hottest. A glow radiated through the fingers of both hands. She picked up the primary crystal and held it high in her fingertips, like the Hidden One had earlier. Now she could visualize the sequence unique to that crystal encoded within it. Use her mind to press here, and here….

The crystal blazed bright, just as it had for the Hidden One. Witmara stared at it, entranced by the light within the suddenly fluid stone. There was a doorway….

"Tsk, tsk, tsk," the Hidden One clucked, breaking into Witmara's concentration. "That is not for you yet! You are now aligned. Encode your projection spell."

Witmara closed her eyes, visualizing the matrix within the crystal. She placed the image of herself laughing at Chatain.

> I dare you to find me!

that part of herself snarled.

> I dare you to capture me! You cannot catch me! Chatain and those who follow him are but offal below my feet!

She let herself pour the smallest bit of anger, frustration, and rage into the projection that she had carefully held apart from herself ever since her grandmother's death. Since Melarae's death. Since Inharise's death.

Too many dear to me have died!

That is enough,

her father's shade suddenly whispered to her.

Too much rage and you will frighten and drive them away. Focus your anger. Control it. Make yourself appear vulnerable.

She slowly damped down that projection, twisting it into the shape of a young woman's petulant temper tantrum rather than pure anger. A memory of Chiral's peevish behavior came to her, and she reshaped her projection so that instead of an angry, powerful woman, she was nothing more than a defiant, sullen young adult miffed at an intrusion.

Enough?

Witmara asked him.

Yes.

He smiled at her, then faded.

Gods, she was tired. She carefully damped the glow in the crystal and replaced it on the table, staggering slightly.

"Is there more?" she demanded of the Hidden One, a tinge of Chiral's petulance bleeding over into her voice.

"You have done well," the Hidden One said. "Now we can dress, then recall your beloved."

It seemed to take forever to pull her clothing back on. Witmara needed to pause and catch her breath, and sat down to pull her tunic on. But she noted that it took the Hidden One even longer to dress.

As she pushed back her sleeve, she spotted the sigil tattooed on the inside of her right wrist. A tiny red flame, with her initial in silver outlined in black over the top of it. The tattoo containing the spell. But what did it mean?

"What does this tattoo mean?" she asked the Hidden One. "I know it contains the spell, but what does it *mean?*"

"It is the mark of the Red Flame," she said. "It identifies you to other adepts of the Flame as well as containing the spells you need to activate the crystals. Press it and memory will tell you what you need to do when you need to activate the spells. When someone else identifies themselves as being of the Flame, ask them for their mark, and show yours."

"I—see." Witmara raised her wrist high, studying it.

Daro's awareness broke through the shield she had raised against him and pressed hard against her thoughts, uneasiness roiling from him. She sent him an image of the tattoo.

Uncertainty came back from Daro at first, then approval. Now she realized that the red of the flame matched the blood bay daranval's coat, and the silver and black were the same shade as his mane. He reared high, seeming to loom larger, almost as if he were a living manifestation of that tattoo.

Then Daro's projection shrank into his usual shape, satisfaction coming back from him.

Somehow this tattoo enhanced *his* magic as well.

Witmara slowly pushed herself up from the chair, her body aching. "May we call Toran back in?"

The Hidden One picked up her cane and hobbled to the door. "I will send him in." She hesitated. "I will tell you this. You are truly the hope of Varen, Witmara ea Miteal. Our future depends on you."

And then she slipped through the door. Witmara leaned against the table.

No more magic today.

She wanted nothing more than to spend some time with Daro and Toran for days. Even if it wasn't really possible, it was what she wanted. But since it wouldn't be—at the least she would steal some time with her husband-to-be. With her daran-val. Perhaps they could ride out to the Western Parade Grounds, just to have a good gallop. A break would improve their focus.

And then it will be back to preparations.

Gods, she wanted Chatain to feel *her* wrath.

Soon. Soon.

REUNION AND A MARRIAGE

Rekaré rode toward the waiting army behind Katerin and Heinmyets in the clear dawn, Cenarth at her side. A few clouds scudded overhead as the sunrise touched the snow-covered western range that curved south to join the eastern mountains that divided Keldara from Clenda, a pinkish salmon-shaded glow illuminating the peaks.

Had it only been two days since more troops started assembling in the meadow south of Dera? It seemed like ages.

And Cenarth had been at her side most of that time, as she and Katerin worked to integrate the different units into their existing organization. He glanced at her, a faint smile touching his lips. Not mindspeech, but that awareness of each other they possessed for years.

Until now, she hadn't realized how much she had missed that connection. He meshed well with Sesenth and Detaluna—especially Senth. It was a relief, and allowed her to focus on melding the assorted Saubral bands which had become part of the Mer Galad. The amount of anger at Waykemin from the

Saubral surprised her. It spoke of a vulnerability she hadn't been aware of until she had taken on *benghaalph*. Most of her life she had been trained to consider the Saubral as a uniform, shadowy, malign power.

Now she knew better. She would wonder if the same held true for Waykemin, except—in closed sessions with their army's leaders, Katerin had tersely recounted her experiences growing up Waykemese, in the heart of the Witches Council as Terani's daughter. A land where magic was used not as a tool for bettering the lives of all, but to further empower the strong. Where thousands labored with no will of their own, save during those times when rest was allowed them. Many were not allowed to function with their own minds even then, their spirits eaten by the Witches.

"There will be impacts when we break the controlling spells," Katerin had said. *"I cannot tell you how the freed Waykemese will act. Some of those with minds left to them will be angry toward their masters and align with us. Others—both with their own minds and those without—will see the stripping of those controls as a betrayal, and attack us. Others—mostly those whose minds who have been eaten— will be adrift. We will not know which is which until the spells are broken. When I was younger I could predict what would happen with more accuracy. But now—leadership has changed. Dynamics have changed. It's been over a generation since I have been there. We must gather intelligence from those freed ones as we move into Waykemin."*

And the Mer Galad was the group designated to take in those willing Waykemese, as the unit with the greatest experience in integrating differing groups.

By the Goddess's golden tits, it's going to be complicated.

Rekaré sighed. And yet she couldn't argue with Katerin's logic. Not only could the Mer Galad take these renegades in more effectively—sending them to one unit would isolate potential infiltrators and saboteurs from the rest of the army. Her Saubral Shadowwalkers would help identify them.

But Gods, that means I need to watch my back.

The Witches were well aware of what Rekaré Kinslayer meant to the Mer Galad and to the Shadowwalkers. She would be a target.

Cenarth cleared his throat. "I've one question for you about the Mer Galad organization, if I may."

"Ask away." She missed this aspect of him. Clearly he had spotted a flaw.

"Sesenth and Detaluna do an excellent job as your Seconds. But they're going to have their hands full keeping their sections under control as we add Waykemese to your unit. Who is acting as your personal protection?"

"That's been both Sesenth and Detaluna. Most of the time I've been my own protection."

"Works with a smaller unit. But with doubled size and the potential of Waykemese joining your command, you need a direct bodyguard."

"Katerin is more significant for our success," she pointed out. "Without her knowledge of Waykemin and her blood tie to the land there, we won't be able to get close to the Witches Council, even with a large force. We might conquer Waykemin physically, but unless we can defang the Council and break those controlling spells, Chatain still has them to work with and attack us."

"I *know* that," Cenarth said impatiently. "But Katerin depends upon your magical strength for the battles in Waykemin. You do still carry the Maker, the Strength, and the Vision, right?"

Rekaré shivered at the mention of the magical artifacts in one of her pouches.

Only Cenarth would dare to bring them up.

Her discovery of those artifacts, meant to be used by one

who aspired to Godhood, twisted by her father, had been a factor in her leaving Medvara. While they traveled well-wrapped in a belt pouch, she hadn't touched them for years. Hadn't needed them since *benghaalph* had come upon her.

But she would need to use them in Waykemin. She just—they twisted her thoughts. She dreaded needing to take them up again.

"Yes," she said quietly. "Though I have not brought them out for some years."

"You are vulnerable when you wear them. I *remember*," he said roughly.

"I've hoped it wouldn't come to that. Hoped *benghaalph* would be sufficient." Rekaré shook her head. "*Kinslayer* is bad enough. To bring out the Maker, the Strength, and the Vision...." Her voice trailed off.

"Katerin can't battle the Witches alone. You need someone to watch your back—not just physically but magically, for protection from what those *things* do to you. I've brought this up to her and she keeps shoving me off to you. I'm bringing it up now. What are you doing about your personal security, especially once we start taking outsiders into your unit? Who is keeping you centered so those artifacts don't take you over?"

"Spells," Rekaré said. "My powers as *benghaalph*. And Sesenth's presence."

"Sesenth will be busy integrating outsiders and you want her focused on that. And as for spells—" Cenarth shook his head. "Don't you remember Alame's training when we first rode on our own? Always have physical protection as your backup, even when working magic?"

"There's no one available to coordinate that now," Rekaré said. *You used to do that.* "You're right. I don't want either Sesenth or Detaluna distracted from their necessary work to protect me. And Sesenth has never been exposed to the Maker, the Strength, and the Vision, so she will not know what to do to recenter me. But who can do it?"

"Me."

"But your responsibility to the Two Nations—you will be Leader soon." She fumbled for words, suddenly feeling awkward and yet relieved.

"No. I have already spoken to the Council. I have made it known that I will not accept election to my father's position. Linyet is young but well-loved. He will be the Leader the Two Nations needs after my father, not me."

"But why?" Oh Gods, how was she going to explain this to Sesenth?

"I spent enough time as your consort in Medvara to know that I am not cut out to be Leader when my father passes. I have said I will serve as an advisor to Linyet. But should the Council elect me instead, I will decline."

"Does Linyet know?"

"Yes. He was in Council when I told them yesterday, was one of the voices asking me not to do this." Cenarth paused. "Rekaré. You are not the only one who feels the need to walk away from Leadership. Perhaps I don't have your reasons—after all, no one calls me *kinslayer*." His voice turned bitter. "But Medvara marked me as well. I have no desire to act as the servant to a land's magic again, even though the Two Nations would sit much more lightly on me than Medvara did you. I've seen how the people and the land respond to Linyet as compared to me. How Katerin carries Medvara and the way that land cherishes her as it never did us."

"But why ride with me? Why not Linyet? You do intend to advise him, after all."

It would be a relief to have Cenarth at her back along with Sesenth and Detaluna. They knew each other's ways so much better. All the same, he could protect their son, the future

Leader of the Two Nations. Wasn't that more important than protecting her?

"Oh, I'll do some of that. But. I see a greater need here. Rekaré, you've reverted to what you were doing at the end of our time in Medvara. Sacrificing yourself for everyone else. Those artifacts will eat you alive if you don't take care. I would see you survive Waykemin to challenge Chatain, and I am the best person available to make certain that happens."

"Things are—different from what they were before. We cannot be the same to each other that we once were. You know that."

"I have eyes to see what Sesenth is to you. I do not expect what we had before. On the other hand, remember how our mothers worked with my father. Your Heartfather. Perhaps not the same level of intimacy that we had in the past, but—I would ride with you again, Rekaré Kinslayer, Rekaré who once carried my heart. I do not have a place riding with our son in this battle. He has his own connections, his own ties—I have spent the past seven years encouraging that. But now we face the battles that you and I have known could come to us. I would much rather fight them at your side."

Rekaré shook her head, laughing softly. "Oh Cenarth, Cenarth. Do you know how my heart leaps to hear this?" She reached out to take his hand. "I can no longer promise you much of my heart—Sesenth will tell you that she has little of it herself. But to have both of you to sustain me—gods. I did not expect such a favor."

He smiled at her, that slow smile with that had always brought warmth into her life, until the very darkest days at the end of her rule of Medvara.

Gods, how she had missed it.

Dovré. Artel. Staul. Whichever of you Gods are responsible for influencing Cenarth to offer this—I thank and bless you.

TWO DAYS TO GO. WITMARA SAT BY THE FIRE PIT IN THE GARDEN house after a long soak in the heated tubs there, along with her dinner guests. She kept an eye on the informal service presided over by Cantiste, who had served as majordomo for both her mother and Rekaré. Much as she wanted private time with Toran, the Mershaunten and his fleet had steamed into Medvare that morning. That afternoon a large force from Chellni had arrived. They needed to meet, they needed to eat, and everyone complained of the cold. She couldn't think of a more pleasant option than the garden house to deal with all three.

The soak had banished the pervasive damp chill that penetrated to her bones. The garden house's minimal walls of the same light pine as the Great Hall, and transparent spells that channeled out the smoke while keeping the warmth in, was just the right setting. As she sat next to Toran, holding his hand, nibbling on the first course of nuts, smoked salmon, and dried berries, she noticed that the others were equally relaxed. A nice break from the hectic day just past and the days ahead. Good.

She signaled Cantiste that it was time to serve the main course and bring wine.

"Come, my friends," she said to the others. "Comfortable as this is, it's time to move to the table."

One of the Chellni delegation—Nemit, she thought, the trade representative, groaned, along with Aldan, Toran's older brother. Mohanisha, Chellni's headwoman, elbowed him. Haran and Orlanden didn't groan but she saw how Haran winced.

Getting older and stiffer. A good thing he came to Medvare instead of following Mother and Rekaré.

"There will be wine," she added.

Nemit's expression brightened along with Aldan's.

"What kind of wine?" Aldan asked.

Witmara raised a brow at Cantiste.

"A white from the lower Saktrin Valley," he answered.

They settled themselves as Cantiste and his staff brought out the platters of venison, assorted roasted root vegetables, squash, and bread, setting them not only at the table for the notables but on another table for the staff.

Witmara rose and raised her glass high. "To success in the battle ahead."

"Success!" the others echoed.

"We've done the best that we can to prepare. I am grateful that Medvara does not stand alone against the incursions from Daran. Together, we show Chatain and his lackeys that Varen is not a land to be colonized and controlled. That we are our own peoples and that we have no need of his twisted and oppressive ways. Thank you once again for coming together." She fumbled a little, trying to think of a good way to end her speech, wryly thinking that Betsona would have come up with something longer and more lyrical. "Let's eat," she said finally.

The meat platter was closest to her so etiquette stated that she would need to serve herself first. But as she reached for the serving fork, the Mershaunten rose.

Witmara stifled an inner groan, hoping he wasn't about to begin a long speech. She was hungry and she was certain that the others were as well. She politely set the fork down, waiting as he studied her and Toran.

"I am given to understand that we will have cause to celebrate, though I have not been told when the happy occasion will occur. Witmara, Toran, when do we observe your vows?"

"We had planned a quiet ceremony tomorrow morning, before we leave," Toran said. "We've not had much time to put one together. All of us have been busy, including the shamans of Artel and the priests of Staul. And since Katerin will be fighting in Waykemin, we did not want a big event. We had agreed to that."

"Understandable. But why wait until the morning?" his father asked.

"Well, it would be a matter of bringing a shaman and a priest here," Toran said slowly. "And then there's the matter of witnesses, our vowing gifts, the recorder...am I forgetting anything?" he asked Witmara.

"Nothing that I can think of," she said. "We wanted to keep it small, so as not to detract from battle preparation. The morning appeared to be the best timing for that."

The Mershaunten winked at Haran. "Brother, what do you think? What better witnesses do we have than those of us gathered here? Have you worked your usual magic?"

Haran grinned back at his brother. "Cantiste," he called. "I believe you have some packages in the kitchen, correct?"

"Absolutely." It was hard to say who was grinning the hardest, Cantiste or Haran. "And there is a special dessert prepared," Cantiste continued. "My staff and I will stand witness for the people of Medvara."

"My lady, if you so desire, I can stand as your second," Tlikset, her personal servant, chimed in.

"Thank you." She didn't know whether to laugh or cry. Planning the vowing had taken second place to everything else and pushing it off to a hurried ceremony the morning of their departure had seemed to be the easiest solution, especially since she hadn't seen obvious signs that Haran and Orlanden were planning something.

I should have known better. Should have known they were waiting for the Mershaunten and Aldan's arrival. Mother cannot be here, but we will have at least some family present.

"I stand ready to serve as second for you, brother," Aldan said to Toran.

"I—yes." Toran looked as flustered as she felt. They had both intended to ask their proposed seconds tonight, but she hadn't gotten around to it—obviously neither had Toran.

"Orlanden. If I recall correctly, you are certified to record for the Mershaunten," Aldan said.

"Have been for years." Orlanden smirked. "I am certified for both Larij and Medvara, so both nations are covered."

"And I have been dedicated to Lord Artel for many years," the Mershaunten continued. He bowed toward the Hidden One. "As you have been to Lord Staul, correct?"

"Indeed," she said. "This will not be the first vowing I've performed."

"The same is true of me. I would say we have all those present and qualified to witness your vowing tonight." The Mershaunten turned serious. "Katerin Leader cannot be here. As the only other living parent of the happy couple, and since we are on the eve of battle, and cannot have the sort of celebration that the union of Medvara and Larij would deserve, I say that tonight is a better time for your vowing than in the dark of morning, before hustling aboard ship. More auspicious to do it amongst friends and fellow leaders."

"I—well...." Witmara looked at Toran. He shrugged and she smiled. "As long as we get some dinner first," she said finally. "It is a simple vowing, and I will be taking him as consort."

"Understood." The Mershaunten smiled at them. "Let's eat a hearty dinner, have your vowing and then dessert. Does that sound good to all?"

The cheers spoke for themselves. Witmara fancied that the most enthusiastic ones came from the staff table.

"Then let's eat."

She picked up the fork and dished up the meat.

IT TOOK MORE THAN CLEARING THE DISHES TO PREPARE THE MAIN room of the garden house for the ceremony. Witmara would have pitched in to help move tables and chairs, but Mohanisha and Orlanden whisked her off to a smaller room where Tlikset, once nanny and now personal servant, waited with a change of dress and—to Witmara's surprise—Davni, from Wickmasa, a former healing apprentice of her mother's. Orlanden left Witmara to Mohanisha, Davni, and Tlikset.

"How did you come here, Davni? How did you know?" Witmara asked, slipping out of her day dress. Tlikset helped Mohanisha slide the hooped underskirt over Witmara's head and lace it while Davni waited to slide on the next layer of ruffled underskirt. "And just how am I going to get out of all this when we are done?"

"We will help," Mohanisha said, waving Davni over. Together they deftly arrayed the ruffles of the underskirt over the hoops.

"I came to Chellni with Linyet and Yetklet as part of the trade caravan," Davni said as she worked. "It appeared to be more important to stay and finish our trade than go back upriver to battle with Waykemin. Then when we decided to come to Medvara to fight those Darani colonizers—well, I could hardly stay behind, could I?"

Witmara hugged her. "Thank you." Words couldn't express how it felt to see a familiar face from her childhood. "Did Colerei come?" she asked, naming her mother's other Wickmasan apprentice.

Davni shook her head. "Hidebound baker that she is, she stayed in Wickmasa. But if she could, she would have been here, baking an elaborate cake and fussing. But you have Tlikset and Cantiste to fill her place."

"Thank you, Tlikset."

"It is my pleasure." Tlikset and Mohanisha carefully pulled the soft blue dress over Witmara's head and laced it. Davni adjusted the necklace that Witmara always wore under her clothing, the first magical jewelry she had been gifted. It was short, and did not interfere with the longer chain of the Light of Medvara, which she had slipped off before getting dressed.

Witmara now put it on. The center citrine glowed golden. Tlikset produced a fine silver ring with a small blue and green stone set into it, a match for the stone in her necklace. "Haran thought this would be best for you to give Toran."

Witmara took it in her fingertips. The power that stirred in the stone reminded her of that in the necklace and bracelet she wore, also a present from Haran on her eleventh birthday.

"It's a match for my necklace and bracelet," she said. "I know where he got it."

Mohanisha studied the ring. "That is from Jeral of Wixtnal. Not surprising, considering he's in Haran's holding."

"That is where Haran got my necklace and bracelet." Witmara smiled to herself, wondering how long he had been holding this ring in anticipation of her bonding. She gave the ring to Tlikset to carry for her.

Then it was time to go out to the main room. As she entered it, she saw Toran first, standing beside his father and the Hidden One, his brother Aldan on his left. He too had been taken aside and garbed in more formal clothing, for him a black swallow-tailed coat over tan breeches, and a puffy shirt with an elaborate blue and silver cravat. His eyes remained fixed on Witmara as she entered.

Blue for Medvara.

Tlikset, now also changed to a more formal but less elaborate dress than Witmara's but in the same shade of blue, walked on her left. As they joined those waiting, Witmara took Toran's hands. They faced each other.

"Toran int Mershaunten, I propose a lifebond to you," Witmara said. "As Leader-to-be, I offer you a life at my side. Not above me or below me, but equal with me, a consort to a Leader, our bond second only to those I must make with the land that I rule. Our children will be eligible for election to Leadership, if they indeed prove worthy. I give you my heart and my soul, in the name of my patron Staul the Balancer. I, Witmara ea Miteal, do swear. Do you accept?"

"I accept your offer in the name of Staul the Balancer," Toran said.

"The ring," the Hidden One said, holding out a red-gloved hand. Tlikset placed it in the center of her palm. The Hidden One took the ring and held it high. It glowed as she murmured soft words, silver and blue and green light coming from it. Then the light faded as the Hidden One lowered her hands. She offered it to Witmara. She took it with fingers that trembled. Toran held his left hand out to her, ring finger extended. Witmara slipped it onto his finger, worried that it wouldn't fit.

She needn't have been concerned.

Toran clasped her hands. "Witmara ea Miteal. I propose a lifebond to you. As the youngest son of the Mershaunten of Larij, I bring you no position in Larij other than my personal holdings. I accept your offer of a life at your side, as your consort, and acknowledge our bond will be second to yours with your land. Our children will be eligible for election to Leadership, if they indeed prove worthy. I give you my heart and my soul, in the name of my patron Artel the Judge. I, Toran int Mershaunten, do swear. Do you accept?"

"I accept your offer in the name of Artel the Judge," she said.

Aldan produced a ring—a match to the one she had placed on Toran's finger—and the Mershaunten took it. After the God had blessed it, Toran's fingers quivered as much as hers had while he guided it onto her finger.

Then the Hidden One and the Mershaunten both placed their hands on top of hers and Toran's and consecrated the lifebond as final. Toran's hands closed even tighter on hers once they were done. She wasn't certain which of them initiated the kiss, but as their lips met, she felt power rumble through them. Suddenly she was deeper into his thoughts than she had ever been, as he was in hers, and not only her patron Staul but Artel the Judge were present, the Judge closer to her than he ever had been, both approving.

"A true bond," she heard both the Hidden One and the Mershaunten pronounce as if from a distance. As it were, she marveled at the depths of Toran that she had suspected were there but now confirmed.

Together, we will be great indeed.

She wasn't certain if it was her, him, or both of them who thought that.

EXPEDIENT AND EMPTY

As they rode to the fords of the Kitskan, long-forgotten memories stirred in Katerin's mind, roiling her gut. The curses of the then-Chief Priestess as Terani collapsed. The bullying led by Tranarin that increased as Terani faded into the dreamless sleep, deep in the core of the Council's tower in Forsim, Waykemin's capital. The curses that the mindless ones threw her way as she skulked through the streets of Chiyan, where she had been born and had fled to once Terani fell.

The final decision in Chiyan to leave Waykemin after encountering a solitary wandering healer from Keldara, to ride with him to the Healing House there for study.

The memories of rejection, hurt, and the anguish of *I don't belong here*, so much a part of her childhood and youth, kept pouring over her to the degree that she knew she would need to retreat and meditate that evening. The last time she had come this close to Waykemin, she had been focused on capturing and killing Chiral in recompense for the evil she had done. Had been more concerned about Rekaré would do, driven as she was by grief, rage, and the influence of the Maker, the Strength, and the Vision. She hadn't had time for memory.

Now she had a surprising amount of time available for those memories to grab at her.

I will need to reconcile them in camp tonight. Alone.

It would serve as part of her preparation, since tomorrow she would need to lift the spells on the Kitskan that would keep their army from crossing.

Detaluna trotted down the column toward Katerin, her face tight. She spun her daranval to ride next to Katerin.

"We've run into our first Waykemese," she said sharply. "Rekaré would like you to speak to them. There are—problems."

"I will be right there." Katerin waved to Jeralte and Abeyets, her assigned guards, and urged Rainin to follow Detaluna. As they passed the head of the column and picked up a gallop, a curious relief coupled at dread of what she was riding to see eased her mind.

Action. Riding.

No more anticipation of what was to come. Rainin picked up speed, and she had to tighten the reins to keep her from outrunning Detaluna's daranval.

All too soon they rounded a corner and came upon a small cluster of riders surrounding ten people on foot, spears drawn. Rekaré glanced toward Katerin and jerked her head toward Cenarth. He galloped Quartel toward her, his face equally as hard and tight as Detaluna's.

"We thought you had best hear this," he said sharply.

But she already knew, suspicions confirmed, from a glimpse of how those on foot were dressed. Dirty, ragged trousers and tunics, headwraps, no footwear.

I didn't think we would encounter these folk until after I had the chance to break the spells!

Dismay tightened her gut even more than the memories had. She knew how to manage this but—she should have anticipated that the Witches would condemn certain ones to march out from the land.

Goddess's gold necklace, how best to counter them? They'll be worst of the lot, the ones they won't trust to protect the homeland, those they can't really control, the most broken.

"These are but a few who recovered who they were," she said. "At least that is what the Witches would claim. They can't trust them. We may not be able to either, even if we convert them. I—I should have spoken of this phenomenon, but I didn't think the Witches would be so desperate as to send them out before we reached Waykemin itself. They must want to slow us down."

"You know what they are?" Cenarth flinched.

"Yes." She urged Rainin forward, noticing that those in the forefront of the circle around those on foot were Shadowwalkers, their faces also tight and grim, ready to use their spears at the slightest provocation.

Shadowwalkers would know and recognize these wretched ones. These would be the ones sent to prey on Saubral.

At least none of this batch had revealed themselves to be magicians under the Witches' control. She didn't think that even Rekaré's Mer Galad Shadowwalkers could hold themselves back.

"Stand back for your own safety, but strike if I tell you," she commanded them. "Let me through." Then she rode Rainin into the midst of those on foot, easing between two Shadowwalkers who gave her unhappy looks. "Speak!" she ordered in Waykemese, the words coming back surprisingly fast as the mindless ones now recovered backed away from Rainin. "Are you the empty ones or the expedient ones?"

"What do you mean?" A tall man with matted dark hair glared up at her, speaking in halting Varenese rather than Waykemese.

Rainin bared her teeth at him, pinning her ears, recognizing him as a threat. Katerin drew her sword.

The Spear of War and Unmaking, the tool of the Banisher of Shadows, took form in her hand and she pointed it at him.

"Do not try to deceive *me*," she snarled, still in Waykemese. "Are you the empty ones or the expedient ones? I am Katerin ea Miteal, Katerin daughter of Terani-the-God-Killer. I am the Leader of Medvara, the Banisher of Shadows. You may fool others but not *me*." She glared down the Spear at him. "Empty or expedient?"

His face contorted. "So *you* are the one responsible—" He howled and lunged toward her.

Before Rainin could set teeth on him she impaled the tall man with the Spear. His shape writhed and twisted on its shaft, his form turning to smoke and mist that faded away.

"So he was one of the empty ones." She glowered at the remaining nine. "So are you all empty or is there a one of you who is expedient?" She raised the Spear. "Who cares to meet their fate?"

"Move in closer," Rekaré commanded.

Katerin dropped Rainin's reins and raised her free hand. "Hold. Let them answer." She repeated it in Waykemese, studying the others who shrunk further away from her. "I am Katerin ea Miteal, daughter of Terani-the-God-Killer," she repeated in Waykemese. "*What kind are you?* Answer me or die!"

"As if you'd let the empty ones live!" one woman spat bitterly. "We know what you are, God-Killer's daughter. Just another one who would use us for a different cause."

Katerin pointed the Spear at this one as the others shrank away from her. "Empty or expedient?" she demanded. "Answer!"

"What is it to you?" the woman sneered. "You're just another tool of the oppressors. You'll kill us all."

"If you are empty we have the means to repair that. If you are expedient but willing to change your alliance, then I have a place for you in my army."

"Why should we care?"

"Would you see the Council overthrown? Would you desire to live a free life, rather than be subject to the whims of the Witches? Be able to travel the lands of Varen, buy and sell your own goods rather than labor solely for the glory of the Witches?"

"That's not possible."

"I left. I became my own person."

"And you are half-bred!" The woman shook her head, but Katerin saw the tears welling up in her eyes, testifying to the battle within her. She knew that struggle. Sympathy warred with anger.

I'll wager this one's expedient.

Still, she hardened herself and placed the Spear's tip on the woman's chest. If she were expedient then there would be a greater challenge ahead to turn her, especially since she hadn't prepared for this contingency.

Fool. Blind fool. Luckily none of yours have paid the price—yet. Getting out of this situation...you should have realized it would happen!

"Empty or expedient?" she pressed. The Spear strained against her hand, eager for more blood now that it had tasted the first one.

"We cannot break free like you did. You are half-bred. The rules are different for you." The woman gulped, lowering her eyes as tears ran down her cheeks. "We have no hope."

Katerin carefully moved the Spear's tip to raise the woman's chin. "I offer you hope if you are willing to change your alliance. I tell you, it is possible."

"And what becomes of those we love? Of those who remain?"

Katerin let a feral smile touch her lips and bare her teeth, mimicking one she had seen on Terani's lips in the past. Or was it Tranarin? Did it really matter?

"You have a choice. Cling to the Witches and fall, or hearken to me and mine, and build a new Waykemin free of their grasp. Now. *What kind are you?*"

The woman glared at Katerin down the Spear. And then she transformed into the visage of the Goddess Cirdel, that Goddess's presence filling out the emaciated woman's body.

The kind that will see you die, half-breed Aireii trash!

Cirdel shrieked through the woman.

We will see you all die, freak!

"Strike!" Katerin screamed and shoved the Spear through the woman's throat.

Do not let them injure you!

she warned Rainin.

They bring a possession worse than wild Shadowwalkers would!

The Shadowwalkers descended on the remaining eight. Katerin backed Rainin to stand by a shaken-looking Cenarth and grim-faced Rekaré and Sesenth as the Shadowwalkers tore through their opponents. At least it was over quickly.

"I would have killed them all without thought," Sesenth growled. "That's what we should have done in the first place."

"If there was half a chance of turning them I would have done that instead," Katerin said.

Sword,

she thought to the Spear, noting that it had absorbed the

blood and gore already. The Spear reluctantly transformed back to its sword shape.

"We need to turn some of them," she continued. "We cannot kill them all! That is what the Witches hope we will try to do."

Sesenth glared at her. "You saw how Cirdel rode that one! They need to be eliminated."

"But some will turn," Katerin countered. "Those are the ones we need to find."

Sesenth started to speak but to Katerin's surprise Cenarth put a hand over hers, just as he used to do with Rekaré.

"Hold," he said quietly. "Katerin knows her own people. She's right. We cannot murder all of Waykemin."

"He's right." Rekaré shook her head. "But how do we weed them out, Katerin? You can't be here to interrogate every band we capture."

"Make them tell you whether they are empty or expedient. *Ushar belost*—empty," she translated. "*Kendar minost*—expedient. You must use the Waykemese words as they will not respond truthfully to Varenese. They can lie in Varenese but not at all in Waykemese—part of the compulsions the Witches put on the mindless ones they control." She gulped, surprised at the sudden anger pulsing through her. "They will have no choice. Believe me, the Witches know what fate these met for they still have a hold on them this close to Waykemin. Until I break their spells over the land, they still control these, even though they are the least trustworthy of those they control."

"Artel's curse on the Witches. These are their *least* trustworthy?" Cenarth groaned. "Then what of their more trustworthy?"

"The Witches' spells will be broken over them once the land's spells are destroyed. At that point they will be as I told you earlier."

"This is a risk we must manage until we reach the fords and you can break the spells, then," Rekaré said.

"Yes. Meanwhile. When you encounter these bands—and

they will be in bands, not solo, and probably close to the road—should they refuse to answer you, keep pressing until they react. You saw the difference between *ushar belost* and *kendar minost*. *Ushar* will react mindlessly if challenged. *Kendar* will argue until the God takes them. If they are ready to turn, they will yield after a short argument. I don't know if we will see any of those. Even if we only can turn a handful of what comes against us, though—that will give us strength when we invade tomorrow."

"But that will take time," Sesenth persisted.

"And if we can turn them, they'll be the first to attack their masters and the Gods who betrayed them," Katerin countered. "They will be a more effective voice to turn their compatriots than we will ever be." She looked at the remaining bodies. Three had vaporized like the man who had attacked her when challenged. The other five lay with the body of the woman Cirdel had ridden. She rode Rainin over to the pile of bodies. "Meanwhile, Rekaré, Cenarth, we must call down the cool fire on these. We dare not leave corpses behind. The Witches will reanimate them. Can you still call the fire, Rekaré?"

"I—can. Even as the Kinslayer." Rekaré stepped aside and began the ritual.

"Good. Begin, and I will finish. Move away from the bodies," she ordered the Shadowwalkers. Once they were clear, she closed her eyes, pulled the Eye of Dovré out from under her tunic, dropped her reins to spread her arms wide, turned her face to the sky, and called upon the Goddess. More than the simple cool fire was needed.

> Dovré, Dovré the Blessed. Find a place for their lost spirits amongst your own. And help me to find a way for others to break the spells on the ushar belost and kendar minost without needing to kill them all, until I reach Waykemin and can lift the spells myself. I pray for this in the name of my lost homeland. Help me to free them.

The glow from the golden needles in the clear stone of the Eye was so bright that she could see it even with eyes closed. Then the Goddess touched her whole body, first drawing her tight, then easing into a warmth that burned deep inside of Katerin.

> Take the ashes,

the Goddess commanded.

> Mix them with glimmer dust and the soil of this land on the edge of three nations. Have the Shadowwalkers draw lines on the foreheads of any captured after this before interrogation. It will not work for all, but until you can break the spells over Waykemin, this will have to do.

Then the burning sensation faded. Katerin opened her eyes. The Goddess's cool fire had reduced the bodies to ash. The Shadowwalkers stared at Katerin, murmuring nervously.

"The Goddess's cool fire has consumed their bodies," she said. "I must mix the ashes with glimmer dust and soil. Stand back."

The Goddess had not said who was to gather the ashes and mix the mud and dust. She might as well do it. She dismounted and retrieved the big bag of glimmer dust from her saddlebags.

"Bring me small bags," she commanded. "One for each Shadowwalker."

Katerin gathered the ashes, mixing them with the glimmer dust and the mud of the road while she waited for the bags. It felt good to be working the earth, and as she worked the ashes and glimmer dust into handfuls of earth, the mixture turned powdery.

Persuade, persuade, she thought as she stirred the mix together. *Persuade and convince.*

She had no charm for this, but perhaps the magic of the glimmer dust plus the Goddess's touch in the cool fire would be enough.

It is what the Goddess promised. Trust the Goddess.

One of the Shadowwalkers brought Katerin a collection of woven wool bags—magic wool, she noted approvingly—and she filled them. Then she went amongst the Shadowwalkers and handed each of them a bag, instructing on the use of the mixture as she gave them the bag.

That done, she rejoined Rainin, handing the remaining three bags to Rekaré, Sesenth, and Cenarth, leaning on the bay mare as fatigue took over briefly before she straightened up.

"The Shadowwalkers must lead as they are the only ones who can safely be the first ones to interact with the *ushar belost* and *kendar minost* without risking themselves. But these bags are for you just in case—use the mixture of ash and dirt to draw a line on their foreheads. Should you need to call the cool fire down on others, collect the ashes. I can use them to attack the spells on Waykemin."

If there were enough ashes. Would they encounter more groups like this one? Most likely. At least there weren't waves of the *ushar* and *kendar* descending upon them—and yet this was worse in a way, because that meant there were more strong and reliable ones within Waykemin's boundaries that the Witches did not consider sufficiently expendable to risk outside the border.

"This will work?" Rekaré asked. "It will break the spells?"

"So the Goddess said. It may not work on all. The empty may still fade. The expedient's eyes may be opened." She drew a deep breath. "They may still choose death. But they will not be a threat to us. The empty must be given names and a purpose to keep from fading. Pick whatever name comes to you. The expedient must be given a purpose and made to remember who they were—it will be child-names for most but that will be sufficient for now. They will be angry. Focus that anger toward the Witches. Speak to them of self-rule."

"And we need to do this to all as we fight?" Sesenth asked skeptically.

Katerin shook her head. "Only today, to the bands you encounter outside of Waykemin. Once the spells are lifted and we enter Waykemin—it will be different."

"Gods, Katerin, is this what the entire population of Waykemin will be like?" Rekaré sounded sick.

"Many but not all. I was never placed under spells. The wealthy, the privileged, the traders—all will be more like I was because I was privileged, the daughter of a priestess and witch. But those who labor in the fields, in the towns, who serve the Witches—yes. Many will be under these spells. Children under the age of thirteen will not be."

"Empty. Expedient. I'm guessing the empty are those whose wills have been completely devoured?" Cenarth asked.

"Yes. And the expedient are those who commanded them. There will be many more empties than expedients." Katerin sighed. "I had hoped we would not face this...but clearly the Witches are sending out advance forces to slow us down. I should have warned you."

"You can't think of everything," Rekaré said.

"But this is something I should have considered." Katerin remounted Rainin. "I will pass the word along. We need to slow so that the Mer Galad has a sufficient lead to intercept more of these parties without risking them coming in contact with our main forces."

For there will be more, she thought, sick at heart.

Gods. Why?

Because you are the one who will repair this ill,

came to her. But she couldn't tell which God sent that response—or even if it was herself and not the Gods speaking.

IT WAS NEARLY DARK BY THE TIME THE ARMY REACHED THE FORDS of the Ollonit River where it joined the Kitskan River. Full dark had fallen once camp had been established and a meal prepared. Katerin set out to check with her leaders. Fires on the other side of the Kitskan testified to the presence of a sizable army just within Waykemin's boundaries. Katerin studied them grimly between her stops, Rainin a silent shadow at her back, Abeyets and Jeralte a discreet distance behind. At last she reached Rekaré and the Mer Galad, separated from the rest of the army. Jeralte and Abeyets took up a position near the camp, looking uncomfortable at being that close to so many Shadowwalkers.

"Watch the fords," she directed them. "Check with the Mer Galad watch, and keep guard with them. I'll call for you when I'm ready to leave."

How many of the mindless did Rekaré encounter and how many survived?

She scanned the group of scraggly *ushar belost* and *kendar minost* that clustered together around a separate fire. Ten *ushar* and twenty *kendar.* Better than she had expected. She could use the *kendar*, and to a lesser extent, the *ushar.*

Rekaré joined her. "That's what remains of nearly eighty we encountered."

"Thirty out of eighty is a decent ratio when dealing with such as these. How fare your people?"

"I had to draw on Cenarth and Sesenth to protect my non-Shadowwalkers at the end. We were swarmed by a mob as we approached the fords. I scattered what was left of your ash mixture around us while the Shadowwalkers took them. They are more aggressive the closer we get to Waykemin." She took a deep breath. "I suspect we have more lurking around the edges, waiting to strike if we let down our guard. Katerin, by the Goddess's golden tits, how do you expect to keep the army safe?"

Katerin studied the remnant. "By removing the spells. I will need you and Cenarth to support me."

"Me, Cenarth, and Sesenth," Rekaré corrected. "That's the safest way for us to draw power. Sesenth can integrate my Shadowwalkers into the mix to give you more strength."

"And I need some of the *kendar*."

"You'd trust them?"

"I won't know until I speak to them. But yes, if some of the *kendar* will join us—the more we can recruit, the more effective my spells will be."

Rekaré took her arm. "Katerin. Are you certain of this?"

"They will follow the Banisher of Shadows." Her mouth tightened. Gods. There had been a time when she shied away from that role.

What have I become?

Rekaré surveyed Katerin carefully. Then she nodded and released Katerin's arm. "We will stand with you."

"Let me speak to them alone first. Were you able to gather the ashes of those you burned?"

Rekaré went to her tent. She returned with a bag that she handed to Katerin.

"This is good," Katerin said.

"Will you need to mix it with glimmer dust? I have more if you need it."

"Yes, but I have a higher quality batch that I held back for this working." Katerin turned to Rainin and extracted another bag from her saddlebags, smaller than the one she had used earlier in the day. "Can someone bring a bowl to your tent?"

"I believe so."

"Good. Send Cenarth and Sesenth to the tent as well." She turned to Rainin.

Wait outside,

she told the daranval mare.

I may need to call on you, but otherwise this is a human matter. Stay here with the others, even when I leave to do the greater working.

Rainin sent wordless agreement as they walked. She joined Basnen, Quartel, and Sesenth's daranval outside of Rekaré's tent, clustered around a hay pile. The three daranvelii made room for Rainin.

The faint mental buzz that meant the daranvelii were mindspeaking rose in her thoughts and Katerin sent a wordless thanks once again that daranvelii got along better together than their ordinary horse counterparts. Rainin lifted her head and snorted, flicking one ear and working her lips. The other three imitated her face and Katerin got the sense that the daranvelii were laughing at her.

Of course we do not fight each other! We are kindred,

came to her, a sense of combined daranval thought. Then it faded, replaced by the buzz.

"I guess I've been told," Katerin said as she entered the tent. Cenarth and Sesenth sat around the small fire inside, on reed mats. She set the two bags on an empty mat and dropped onto it.

Cenarth raised a brow at her. "Couldn't miss it. All four daranvelii are projecting what passes for daranval humor."

Sesenth smiled faintly. Inside the tent, she was capless and cowlless. Her scalp revealed the mix of leathery and scaly gray skin gradually overtaking her natural brown shade. Her ungloved hands were completely gray but she still wore slippers so Katerin could not tell if her feet had changed yet.

"Rekaré is getting a bowl," Katerin said. "I mean to mix up more ashes with glimmer dust, then speak to the *ushar* and *kendar* you have turned. We need to break those spells over Waykemin tonight—the four of us."

"Do you need more earth?" Sesenth asked. "I can have someone bring drier soil."

Katerin shook her head. "What was gathered along with the ashes is plenty for this working."

Rekaré entered the tent and closed the flap behind her. She placed a large wooden serving bowl in front of Katerin.

"I hope this is big enough."

"It will do. I need enough to mark those of the *kendar*—and perhaps even *ushar*—who will join us in this spell raising, and put down markings."

"You would trust them." Skepticism colored Rekaré's voice. "I would not."

"All have either been given names or remembered names, and been marked?"

"Yes," Rekaré said slowly. "But you would consider that enough?"

"With the mixture I am about to make, yes."

The one enchantment of Waykemin she had learned before Terani confronted Nitel was the making of the *ushar belost* and the *kendar minost*. She had hated it then, had cringed throughout making as she held the bowl for her mother. But if one knew the spell of making, one could unmake it—and this unmaking provided a foundation for destroying Waykemin's defenses.

Katerin poured ashes into the bowl—a deep banquet dish meant to hold enough cooked grains to feed twenty to thirty people—until it was a quarter full. Then she shook in some of the dark blue glimmer dust, a higher quality than the dust she had used earlier in the day, until she judged the amounts were equal, leaving about a third of the glimmer dust in its bag.

She frowned. Something more was needed, but not until the two were mixed. She looked up at Rekaré, Cenarth, and Sesenth, noticing how fixed their gazes were on the bowl and how they had arranged themselves to sit on one mat, shoulders touching, Rekaré in the center, Cenarth on her left, Sesenth on her right.

"The working begins," she said. "I may draw upon your strength. Do not think in words. Think of images—preferably of the land."

"Land magic is best, then," Cenarth said.

"Yes."

He glanced at Rekaré and Sesenth, as if the three of them communed without speaking. Sesenth frowned, then nodded. Rekaré raised her brows at Cenarth. He interlaced his fingers and stretched, cracking his finger joints, and shifted to his knees, as did Rekaré and Sesenth. Then, carefully, precisely, he bent over until his belly rested on his thighs, pressed his forehead on the ground, and extended his arms above his head to place his palms flat. Rekaré threw an arm around his shoulders, leaning across him and burying her head in his back. Sesenth squeezed into the small space between Cenarth and Rekaré so that her back pressed against him while her arms wrapped around Rekaré. She rested her cheek on Rekaré's back and stared unblinking at Katerin.

On guard, Katerin thought as she felt the stir of their combined sorcery.

No bonds involved, save the long-quiet one between Rekaré and Cenarth, the newer one between Sesenth and Rekaré. Nothing at all like what had been between Alicira, Heinmyets, and Inharise—and yet in other ways, rather reminiscent of how the three of them had woven their magics together.

Battlefield necessity.

She mentally reached out, lightly touching Cenarth's mind since he was the earth magic's channel. His sorcery stirred against her connection, ready, waiting should she need it.

She did not use words for this working. This close to Waykemin, the Witches could capture a word-based spell and twist it unless she raised a shield as complex as any incantation. She would save her spoken spell for breaking Waykemin's protections. But images were how any rebellious *kendar* and *ushar* would communicate. The Witches couldn't track images effectively—unless they had grown significantly stronger in the many years since Katerin had left.

Remember your childhood. Remember Katerin the unhappy, Katerin the scorned. That last awful working where you held the bowl for your mother as she made more ushar and kendar.

She stared into the bowl, remembering her anger at being forced to assist Terani under threat of being made *kendar* herself.

Sesenth's eyes flashed gray-green, mirroring Katerin's rage.

The glimmer dust began to glow, a soft blue light hovering over it. Katerin eased her hands into the mixture. She visualized a dome vibrating with red and magenta energy over the land of Waykemin, remembering the curve of the Kitskan just before the Ollonit ran into it. The huts of Chiyan, deep in a mountain canyon. The gloomy stone city of Forsim, shadowy even on a hot summer day with the sun directly overhead. The Council chamber in Forsim, where light penetrated only through narrow slits in the stone. The broken image of the goddess Nitel in the Chamber, flanked by fresh stone statues of Karnoi and Cirdel. Katerin paused, imagining those statues darkened by age. The stone altar as she had seen it in that vision of Inharise's death, now empty.

She sifted the mixture in the bowl through her fingers, holding that last vision of the Council chamber paramount in her thoughts, mixed with her rage at being forced to be part of Terani's spellcasting, until gray ash and blue dust were thoroughly combined. The blue glow faded in intensity as it mixed with the ash. Time to test the mix. Katerin imagined the top of the stone altar cracking, shattering.

The vision did not hold. The altar remained whole.

Not enough.

She studied the bowl, then looked up to meet Sesenth's steady gaze. Pictures of green stone on gray came to her. She dusted off her hands, careful to keep the grains of dust and ash within the bowl so as not to scatter the incomplete spell and reached into her pouch for Medvara's gift, unwrapping it, then sitting it in the middle of the bowl. Contemplated further, then reached for Cenarth's sorcery for more strength.

The stone glowed green and the blue shimmer of the glimmer dust shone brighter. Katerin tried the visualization of breaking the altar again. Cracks, but still not enough. She inserted an image of the green stone in her hand, smacking down hard on the altar's surface, channeling her anger at this last foul thing of Waykemin. At all the sour, corrupt things she remembered of her homeland.

Crack!

The surface shattered as the stone sank deep into the mix of dust and ashes.

Fix!

Katerin commanded, confident enough now to use the single word in her thoughts. The image held.

She dug out the buried stone and traced her glyph into the mixture, blue light edged with green illuminating the design.

Katerin smiled.

Yes. This would work. She used the stone's wrapping to dust it off, then replaced it in her pouch. Then she obscured the glyph with her right index finger. The green-edged blue light shimmered along the top of the mixture, spreading until it completely covered the dust and ashes. Once the glow settled, she put half of the mixture in the bag that had held the ashes.

"There," she said. "We are ready."

She watched as Sesenth uncoiled herself from wrapping snake-like around Rekaré, then Rekaré from Cenarth. He straightened up, shaking his hands and stretching his back.

"What is next?" Rekaré asked. Her expression was troubled as she studied Katerin.

"First, I recruit those I can amongst the *ushar* and *kendar*. I need you to clear a space by your fire closest to the Kitskan." Katerin thought about who else she wanted there. "Have the full Mer Galad there, not just Shadowwalkers. Keep them thirty paces away from the fire. No daranvelii. We need human magic for this working." She set the mixture bag next to her glimmer dust bag. "These bags need to be guarded. I will not need them for what I do next, but I can't take them with me until I am done. The Witches may still give direction to one of the *ushar* or *kendar* we have yet to convert to steal these bags. I'll send Abeyets and Jeralte to guard the outside, but I want someone trusted to sit with the bags inside, until I can return for them."

"Will Detaluna be sufficient?" Rekaré asked.

"Yes. Anyone who is trusted."

"She is still one of my Seconds."

Katerin noted the *still* and wondered what that meant. "Good." She rose and carefully picked up the bowl. "I will meet you by the closest fire—hopefully with some of the *kendar* and *ushar* who want nothing more than to see the end of their oppressors."

"Good luck, and may the Goddess go with you," Sesenth said, fixing Katerin with a steady, unblinking gaze.

Somehow it surprised Katerin that Sesenth and not Rekaré was the one to say that blessing.

THE ROAR OF OCEAN WAVES BREAKING ACROSS THE MOUTH OF THE Chellana echoed through the great bay that had formed behind the narrow opening, seeming louder than any other time Witmara had been at Chellanasit. It echoed her mood as she and Toran sat alone by a small fire just outside their lodgings, a guesthouse near the docks that was located above the Great River's flood level. *Morning Star* and *Heart's Desire* bobbed at the nearest berth. The rest of Chellanasit's berths were filled with the bulk of the Medvaran fleet and a few Larijian ships. The main Larijian fleet was moored across the bay at Chellananit, Toran's father and brother with them.

Tomorrow, she thought. *Tomorrow it begins.*

She stared at the twinkling lights on the combined fleets. The ocean's roar drowned out the sounds of sailors preparing for battle. How many would survive until tomorrow evening? What *would* tomorrow evening look like? Would she be able to make her lure work as they had planned? They had tested it in the bay before dark fell. It had performed as expected—then. But at a further range?

"You are quiet," Toran said.

"Worry about tomorrow."

He rubbed her shoulders. "Normal to do so the night before a battle, from all I have heard."

She leaned against him. "At least we can spend this last night on land." While being on water didn't disturb her magic as much as it did her mother—it was still problematic.

"And you'll be safe in the bay with Setkin."

"Now to hope that the Darani fleet takes the bait." She didn't have access to the Tapestry here—not that it would show the Darani fleet until it was actually in the river and within the bounds of Medvara proper—so she couldn't track the movement of the Medvaran fleet following the Darani. But messenger birds had kept them updated. So far the Darani fleet was aimed directly at the mouth of the Chellana and not at Cooscol or the other Medvaran ports along the coast.

That means Medvare-the-city has been the target all along.

So perhaps her lure didn't need to be quite so important. And yet they needed to have the Darani fleet move upriver quickly, not linger in the bay here and create fortifications.

Something didn't feel right, though. If Chatain meant to attempt a conquest of Medvara, wouldn't he have sent a larger fleet and be targeting all of the major Medvaran ports, not just Chellanasit? Or was his intent to blockade the Chellana and restrict Medvaran trade? The coastal mountains restricted much of Medvara's ocean access. Blockading the Chellana would have an impact on Larij, true, but not as great as it would on Medvara, Chellni, and the Two Nations.

And perhaps his goal is not conquest but capture.

If that were the case, who would be their target, especially since Waykemin was also stirring?

Me.

And there it was, the source of her uneasiness. Drawing her mother and Rekaré off to Waykemin left Witmara apparently unprotected, a young Leader who might be easily captured. Rekaré had refused to take the bait of attacking Chatain and battling for the Empire. What if Chatain thought that he could eliminate the prospect of a younger challenger by this invasion?

But that possibility was one reason why the Mershaunten and the Hidden One had come to her aid.

"They may seek to capture me and not conquer," she said finally, giving voice to that nagging worry.

Toran's arms tightened around her. "I will do my best to keep that from happening."

"I know. But I wish Mother and Rekaré had given more consideration to this option."

"I mentioned it to my father." Toran sighed. "As did Haran. You will have me, and Haran's forces around you. If we can lure them upriver to the Melanut Plains then we can do battle. The key is to keep them coming quickly."

"I know. We've planned this."

"Then trust the plan. Keep faith with Staul. And don't forget the goal."

Yes. She knew the goal.

Now if only the invading fleet knew it as well.

Witmara closed her eyes.

Empire.

Her dreams the last two nights had been of running from pursuit in an unfamiliar city. A land that resented its ruler, rife with technology that stank with the fumes it ejected. A city who sought to rid itself of the Emperor who ignored the needs of the land, not fully in tune with the land's magic as he sought to destroy all sorcery and magic save that subordinate to him alone.

Was she creating a construct of her own wishful thinking? For all she knew, Chatain was well-loved by his people, ruled wisely, and that their information about the awfulness of Daran came from those with strong interests in attaining power for themselves.

But did that include information from the Gods? She sighed, frustrated. She knew that ruling the Empire had been dangled in front of both her mother and Rekaré, her cousin more than her mother. Was it her turn to be tempted? Should she settle for Medvara?

"Thoughts?" Toran kissed the top of her head.

She shifted in his arms so that she could see him. "Thinking about the Empire, as always."

"If it calls to you, then perhaps you should follow that invitation."

"Tch. And perhaps I'm just being an imaginative fool who was raised on dream stories, puffing up the importance of the exiled Miteals to the Empire."

"My father thinks it's a very real possibility that we can overthrow Chatain," Toran said. "So do your mother and Rekaré."

"My mother still entertains the notion that I will become Leader of Medvara in truth and not as her regent."

"She can't keep that up and still be in touch with the land. Even I can tell that the land only tolerates you as a substitute, not its real choice."

"Then what do I do to change that perception? Medvara isn't mine. But Empire? Really?"

"I know," he said. "Oh Gods, I know. I've had the same dream. But. Tomorrow is not Daran. Tomorrow we lure the fleet up the Chellana, fast enough to keep you from capture."

"We hope."

"We will."

The fire popped. She closed her eyes and rested her head on his chest.

Waiting was the worse of all.

"Do you think she'll be able to break the spells?" Sesenth quietly asked Rekaré as they waited beside the fire. This close to the Kitskan they could hear the rhythmic, grunting, drum-driven chants of the forces on the other side. Occasionally the upriver breeze brought wisps of foul smells—rot and offal. And that was just from the edge of their camps. Rekaré dreaded what they would face once they entered Waykemin.

"We are talking about the Banisher of Shadows, born in Waykemin," Rekaré said. "I have faith in Katerin."

"Did you see her memories as she created that mix?"

Rekaré nodded. "Those experiences are what made her the Banisher of Shadows. I had always wondered why a circuit Healer like Katerin became what she was. Even though she is the daughter of my great-uncle—that was never quite enough to explain her choices and her power. I did not know about her past before she came to Keldara."

"I...." Sesenth fell silent as the drums roared louder, then faded.

The Mer Galad around them parted. Katerin carried the wooden bowl and led ten of their prisoners to the fire. Her cheeks and forehead bore three blue parallel lines from the glimmer dust and ash mix. Those who followed her also wore those marks, in addition to those the Shadowwalkers had placed on their foreheads. Rekaré noticed that the prisoners carried themselves with more awareness and a certain pride that had not been present before, their eyes fixed adoringly on Katerin.

Has she bound them to her instead of the Witches?

A worrisome development. What could the Banisher of Shadows become?

Katerin halted by the fire. "I bring you ten who have chosen to lend us their strength for the spellcasting ahead." She nodded to the group that silently lined up behind her, six to her left, four to her right. "Four *ushar belost*. Six *kendar minost*. All remember enough of their old selves to lend us aid."

"We are grateful, Banisher of Shadows," the first woman on Katerin's left said, in halting Varenese.

"My *kinforost*—my coterie. Ten plus you three is an auspicious number." She gestured to Rekaré, Cenarth, and Sesenth.

"*Kinforost.* Rekaré. Cenarth. Sesenth." She continued in a language that Rekaré didn't understand—Waykemese—except for their names. Perhaps it was an introduction. The ten bowed to them. Then, one by one, they said their names. Durast. Serani. Keenst. Ylittim. Wisknani. Garanst. Nenanim. Huttim. Karatani. Teranst. As each spoke, they stepped forward and bowed to Rekaré, left hand clasped over their hearts.

Cenarth stepped forward and returned their bows. After a moment's hesitation, she and Sesenth joined him.

"Now I must mark you, and then we begin the casting," Katerin said. She went to Sesenth first. To Rekaré's surprise Sesenth did not flinch from Katerin's touch, like she did with anyone except herself, Cenarth, and Detaluna. Next, she marked Cenarth, then came to Rekaré. Her fingers were cool but still tingled with something akin to Dovré's cool flame as she traced the lines on Rekaré's forehead, right cheek, then left cheek. Katerin set down the bowl.

"Now we align ourselves. I will stand here, where the bowl is." She guided Rekaré to a position directly opposite her, on the other side of the fire, then Cenarth and Sesenth in opposing positions so that they would form a square. Behind them, she aligned the ten, four directly behind their positions, four in between, and then the remaining two next to the ones behind herself and Katerin.

Katerin returned to pick up the bowl. She dropped a pinch of the dust mixture where the bowl had been, then scattered the remainder of the mix in a path that wove around each of them so that they were completely encircled. At last she traced a circle around herself, then upended the bowl over her head so that what remained of the dust fell upon her. She set it down at her feet and spread her hands wide, turning her face upward to stare into the moonless sky bright with stars overhead.

"With me," she began. "All. Repeat what I say.
Waykemin the cursed must fall.

Waykemin the cursed must fall.
Waykemin the cursed must fall.
Waykemin the cursed must fall.
Shred the spells over the ushar belost.
Shred the spells over the kendar minost.
Dissolve the protections over the Witches.
Bring the fear to them that they have created.
Let them know the dread of their making.
Open them to their true fate.
Waykemin the cursed must fall.
Waykemin the cursed must fall.
Waykemin the cursed must fall.
Waykemin the cursed must fall."

Rekaré's neck prickled as the lines around them glowed blue and green during their chant. The Waykemese mouthed the Varenese awkwardly, but still close enough that she could recognize the words. They became more fluent as Katerin finished.

Katerin repeated the phrases in Waykemese and it was Rekaré's turn to stumble over words and phrases that suddenly became easier as they finished.

"Ha!" Katerin raised her hands high. "As the Banisher of Shadows, I call upon all of you for support! Help me smite the protections of the Witches! Show them the wrath of a true-born Waykemese returning to free her people! In the names of Dovré, Staul, Artel, and Terat, I call down vengeance upon the Witches Council. Break its power and give us the victory!"

Power shuddered through Rekaré as the land under her feet quivered. Besides the familiar touch of the sorcery of those she knew, a second, bitter-tasting strength rose around her. The Waykemese marched in to fill the square, clasping hands. The ones identified as Serani and Nenanim took Rekaré's hands, cold and clammy to the touch as they formed a living link around Katerin and the fire.

"*Break!*" Katerin screeched. "Break, break, *break!* I command this as Katerin ea Miteal, Katerin daughter of Alame ea Miteal and Terani-the-God-Killer, Katerin the half-breed, Katerin the Banisher of Shadows!" The Spear of Unmaking and War appeared in her hands, and she thumped its butt on the earth.

Rekaré's muscles tightened. Her head jerked back involuntarily to bellow inarticulately at the sky. Still roaring, she fell to her knees along with the others save for Katerin who still stood tall, raising the Spear high with both hands. A sensation of rending and breaking, tearing and shattering whipped through Rekaré.

And then it was finished. Rekaré fell forward, breaking free of the clammy hands she held. The earth quivered under her touch. Dismayed shrieks echoed from the now-darkened fires on the other side of the river. Only Katerin stood tall, gazing now into the fire with a tiny smile quirking one corner of her lips.

"Let us see what the Witches think of *that*," she said. "Oh. Rekaré. Double the watch. I don't know if the Witches' forces will be ambitious enough to cross the river for a sneak attack after *that* spell, but best not to take risks. I'll spread the word on the way back to my camp."

Katerin turned away from the fire and motioned to Jeralte and Abeyets, then strode off. Her *kinforost* followed twenty strides behind.

Rekaré noticed that Katerin still carried the Spear ready for quick use, and that she scanned the shadows as she walked away.

"I think we'd better double the watch immediately," she said to Cenarth and Sesenth.

"What about the—*others?*" Sesenth asked. "How capable do you think they are?"

Rekaré sighed. She didn't have enough people to set a double watch *and* guard twenty unpredictable refugees—if that was what they were.

Detaluna joined them. "Katerin is sending escorts back to move our—guests, she calls them. She warns that they are unstable and not capable of much thought. They'll go to the back of our column, with the Healers."

"Good."

Rekaré left Cenarth, Detaluna, and Sesenth to divide up the watches and returned to the tent. Detaluna had kept the small fire burning. Rekaré added a limb and sat next to it, head on her knees, her thoughts whirling as she contemplated what they would face tomorrow. What kind of horrors lay ahead as they marched on Forsim? Who would be lost in this battle? Would *benghaalph* stir as she led her Shadowwalkers against an old foe?

Her hand crept to the hilt of her sword. Slowly, she drew it, gazing at the blade while it glowed with a blue-gray light edged with magenta. The glow soothed her restless mind, drawing her closer to calmness and acceptance. What would be, would be. She was *Rekaré Kinslayer* and that path could not change. She kissed the blade, then pressed her forehead against it, as peace flowed over her.

It was not until Cenarth sat beside Rekaré and laid a hand on her wrist that she realized he was there. On her other side, Sesenth copied him. They did not attempt to pull Rekaré away from the sword but just sat there, hands on her wrists, quietly meditating with her.

BATTLES BEGIN

THE *HEART'S DESIRE* ENDED UP CROSSING THE BAR ANYWAY AS dark clouds hung on the horizon, a brisk, chill wind whipping up the waves in advance of the incoming storm. Reports from the Larijian small scout ships had the Darani fleet turning toward Cooscol instead of braving the mouth of the Chellana, perhaps because *their* scouts had sighted the Medvaran fleet, perhaps trying to avoid the Chellana's mouth in the face of this storm coupled with an outgoing tide.

"You sure you want to do this?" Setkin tied Witmara and Toran to a mast so they wouldn't be washed overboard during the rough passage. "You could probably project just as well from my cabin, in more comfort."

Witmara blinked strands of hair out of her eyes. "But then I couldn't see how effective my projection is. And wouldn't an outgoing tide be favorable for a smoother trip?"

"True," Setkin conceded. "But still. You're going to get wet. And cold, in this wind."

"With this gear?" They wore spare oilcloth rain slickers and pants borrowed from Setkin's crew. "Something you not telling us about it?" she tried to joke.

"It will keep you as dry as anything short of spell casting."

"Then that will work just fine. It will be worth it." She took a deep breath. "Can't be that different from getting caught out riding in a mountain storm."

"If you say so." Setkin checked the knots. "Good luck."

"You want the thrill, don't you?" Toran asked quietly after Setkin had moved to the wheel and started to sing spells to move the *Desire*. "Isn't that part of being dedicated to Staul?"

"The weather helps my magic."

Which was the truth. But something deep inside her thrilled at the thought of facing the rain. Her magic coiled at her fingertips, steady, calm, waiting.

The *Heart's Desire* plunged into the channel, followed by the other ships. Between the current and the outgoing tide, they rolled up and over waves as tall as the *Desire's* masts. Witmara yelled for joy, grabbing Toran's hand. Then they were free and angling out of the current, sailing south toward where the Larijian scouts had spotted the Darani fleet. *Desire* steadied into a smooth, rolling flow with the waves as the clouds loomed closer, faint lines of rain trailing down from them. Setkin turned the wheel over to one of his sailors and came to Witmara.

"Now that we've crossed the bar, the other ships are moving into formation. The *Star* will tell *Desire* when they are ready." A rare smile that bared his teeth faded. "Will you be prepared?"

"Yes."

"Do you wish to be unbound for this working?"

"No. I would sooner be safe than risk being washed overboard."

"Good idea, in these seas." Setkin returned to the wheel.

Witmara rested her head against the mast, eyes closed, fighting back nausea as she waited.

Damnable water.

Toran's presence was helpful, steadying. If she thought about his hand in hers, she didn't get quite as nauseous.

Footsteps. She opened her eyes. Setkin stood in front of her.

"The ships are in place."

"Good." She slipped her hand from Toran's, concentrating on the amplifier hanging around her neck while she rubbed the tattoo on her right hand. Daro stirred below decks.

WitmaraandDaro,

he insisted, sending the image of the two of them bonded together. She remembered how he had become part of the tattoo.

DaroandWitmara,

she responded. Her magic eagerly absorbed his. Then she drew upon Toran. He lacked magic but their bond was enough that she could use his strength, along with Daro's, to push her spell more strongly.

And then the primary crystal wakened. Its power startled her at first, but she kept pushing, pushing. Suddenly her awareness expanded and she was part of the sending, screaming across the waves at the unfamiliar ships heading south. Her heart sank at the sight. Could she turn them?

She would have faltered save for Daro and Toran's support.

Push. Push. Push. Repeat the projection. Push. Was it actually working?

Then she saw motion on the nearest ship, sailors scrambling up the masts to adjust the sails. The first ship to come about had no sails but puffed steam out of huge smokestacks on the ship, slipping through the fleet from where it had been concealed in the middle. Made of metal, not wood. Another like it followed, and then more. The pale smoke from their stacks abruptly darkened as the metal ships outpaced the sailing ships, picking up speed.

How can that be?

The metal ships were coming quickly enough that they might catch the decoy fleet before they reached the safety of the Chellana.

They are shaped wrong! No masts, square in form, low in the water—Gods, how do they move? What causes the smoke? Is this all technology or is it technology plus magic?

We must flee.

She forced her awareness back into her body. While part of her pushed the projection, she called out.

"Setkin! The Darani fleet has turned, and they have mostly metal ships without sail! Turn about and sail as quickly as the *Desire* will go! We will be swiftly overtaken otherwise!"

"I hear you and see for myself!" Setkin bellowed back.

She fought to keep control of her magic as Setkin's sorcery flooded through *Desire*, his deep voice carrying an urgent note as he sang them along, aided by the cold wind.

CROSSING THE FORDS OF THE KITSKAN WAS DECEPTIVELY SIMPLE, as the forces that had been camped on the far side were gone. As Rainin set foot on Waykemin proper, Katerin felt the land stir.

It wasn't a welcome, but it wasn't the bitter repulsion she had experienced as a young woman when leaving her homeland, either. She and her *kinforost* stood watch while the army crossed the river, the *kinforost* holding hands as they circled Rainin.

Meanwhile, she worried.

There was no resistance at all—no one living left to give it.

The camps they had seen the night before were gone, leaving only scattered bodies, dead fires, and a foul stench. The bodies did not bear signs of recent death but were half-rotted, *ushar belost* that had been completely drained. Katerin kept an eye on the *ushar* that were in her *kinforost,* concerned about the impact of seeing those like them in such condition.

Their calmness at seeing the corpses disturbed her. *Ushar* had not behaved like this before. Even those whose pasts had been completely wiped should still react when they saw the final deaths of others like them.

What have the Witches done to the people?

At least no spells lay within her awareness so far. Nothing snatched at the riders as they assembled in the ruins of the camps. No traps lay around the fires. Yet.

But they couldn't leave things like this. It would be possible for the *ushar* to be reanimated. They deserved a final rest. Katerin ordered that while the rest of their people crossed over into Waykemin, their first crossers dealt with the carnage.

At first the entire force worked on it, but the *ushar* bodies left the non-Shadowwalkers sicking up and ill. Katerin had non-Shadowwalkers do other cleanup while Rekaré directed her Shadowwalkers in stacking the *ushar* corpses into great piles, then calling down Dovré's cool fire on them. The stench eased with each burning.

It was a delay, but a necessary one. She would be as bad as the Witches if she let her people ride away without proper respect for those who had died. Even if they were only *ushar*.

Still, something else wasn't right.

She felt it in the way the land brooded. With each fire that Rekaré lit, each touch of Dovré, the land seethed, offended by contact with the Goddess when it should be soothed by the respect shown to its abused own.

She needed to warn Rekaré. Katerin couldn't feel any spells, but it was entirely possible that the land cloaked them. Traps would be subtler than the protective spells. Last night's working dealt with the great sorceries, but the minor castings?

That possibility was another thing that she had overlooked about her homeland, but remembered now that she was actually here. Waykemin's enchantments weren't as potent as the remembrance spells used to block knowledge of places with secret meanings and uses in the Two Nations. Within a limited range, however, Waykemin's enchantments could be just as potent. Remembrance spells in the Two Nations kept people from speaking about those hidden places. They hid the past of those places. Only skilled sorcerers could create the remembrance spells.

Waykemin protected itself, hid facts about itself, even without remembrance spells. Or was it the weight over the years of the Witches' sorcery? Whatever it was, Katerin had the sense that further magic protected this land, clouding memories and things important to know until it was almost too late.

Remember that Karnoi and Cirdel now protect Waykemin.

That might explain the difference in Waykemin's feel from her childhood, when Nitel still reigned as patroness. The Twin Gods thrived on chaos, and while Nitel's bloody domain had become too much for their tolerance—that didn't mean they wouldn't exploit the chaos after Nitel's expulsion and twist it for their own ends. Her questioning of the *kinforost* last night about the changes since the Twin Gods had become Waykemin's patrons had been unproductive. None remembered what the land had been like before Terani banished Nitel, though some were clearly of an age that they *should* remember.

Frustrating. But she was unwilling to spend time digging any deeper when they needed to move quickly and reach Forsim before the Witches built up much of a resistance.

Who should she send to warn Rekaré about the spell traps? Which *kendar* spoke the best Varenese?

Nenanim. He had been a scholar once, before conscripted into the kendar.

Another task from last night—learning about her *kendar.* The *ushar* had no memory of life before they had been compelled into the ranks of the *ushar belost.* The *kendar minost* were in little better condition, remembering their names but not much about their past lives. There was something familiar about him, something she was missing—but then again, unlike Rekaré (*and Metkyi,* she recalled with a moment's brief anguish), she had never been a great scholar beyond what she needed to know as a Healer.

She should have remembered Nenanim. He knew too much to be a low-level scholar. She had heard of him during her years riding as a circuit healer. She was sure of it. But memory refused to stir.

Oh well. Rekaré might be able to help him remember who he had been before he had been made *kendar minost.* Something else tugged at her thoughts, then escaped.

Feels like one of those damned remembrance spells!

She remembered that sensation from her first visit to Wickmasa, the clouded mind and the sense that *you needed to remember that* which faded, leaving her uneasy.

"Nenanim," she called. "Go to Rekaré. Tell her to shield herself as she works the cool fire. The land is angry with us. Give her this."

She reached into a saddlebag and pulled out one of the small bags of the mix of glimmer dust and ashes she had made last night before going to bed, a quieter sorcery than the casting she had used to break Waykemin's protective spells.

The *kendar* bowed to her and took the bag, carefully holding it by the strings so that his fingers did not come in contact with the dust, even with the shielding of the leather. He broke into a steady run, heading for the latest flash of blue light from the Goddess.

Gods, she hoped this would be enough.

And then she remembered, briefly, what she had forgotten.

Where were the *kendar* amongst the dead? So far she had only seen *ushar.*

Just as quickly, that thought fled.

Katerin shook her head, annoyed. She had just forgotten something important. But what?

No time to figure it out right now.

"ONE OF KATERIN'S *KINFOROST* IS HERE WITH A MESSAGE," Sesenth said to Rekaré, her nose wrinkling in distaste.

Rekaré sighed, turning away from the newest pile of corpses that weren't yet high enough to call down the cool fire. By the Goddess's golden necklace, this work seemed to be never-ending. She had sent her non-Shadowwalkers including Cenarth to help Linyet move the supply caravans across the oddly quiet river, sparing them from the sights and smells. The Shadowwalkers, as devotees of Staul, didn't find the handling of corpses to be as repulsive a task as the others did.

But it was still grim work. She wasn't Kinslayer enough to find this an easy task.

I suppose that's a good thing.

She gestured to the *kendar* waiting politely behind Sesenth. He looked at the ground in front of him instead of at either of them.

"Come on, you," Sesenth growled when he did not respond to her gesture. "Rekaré waits."

"Thank you," he said in reasonably passible Varenese, albeit with a strong accent. He minced forward carefully, eyes still fixed on the ground, stopping five paces from her.

At least this *kendar* looked better in the light of mid-morning than any of them had last night. His skin no longer appeared blotched and gray, and while he was still too pale under red-brown, he no longer seemed desperately thin, as if he were a walking skeleton. Magical influence? Katerin had renewed the markings on his cheek and forehead. Perhaps that was the factor.

He kept his eyes downcast as he bowed. "I bear a token and words from the Lady Katerin, Lady Rekaré."

"You don't have to do that," she snapped, annoyed by the way he avoided looking at her. "No need to speak so formally or to look away from me. Katerin has taken you as one of her own."

He shook his head. "It is not the way things are done in Waykemin. You are of a higher caste than I am. I am not worthy to meet your eyes."

Annoyed, she strode forward and lifted his chin with her right hand so that he looked into her face. "You are dealing with the Varenese forces now. We do not operate like that. Look at me when you speak!"

He swallowed hard, fear tightening his face, doing his best to look at anything but her, obviously wanting to pull away from her but trying to obey as well.

"It is not done, Lady Rekaré. Not for one such as me."

"*This*—what was done to you—is not done amongst *my* people. You are one of us now, for better or worse. Nor do we require titles, or looking down, or kneeling, or any of this abject crap! I am no Lady. I am Rekaré Kinslayer, leader of the Mer Galad. Katerin does not use the title of Lady. None of us do. Now. Speak Katerin's message."

His golden-brown eyes settled on her, focusing on her right shoulder instead of her face.

"La—*Katerin*—sends a warning that the land is angry and that you should shield yourself when working the cool fire. She gives you this to use as part of your protection." He held out a leather bag to her by its strings.

She took it from him and eased the strings to peer inside. More of the glimmer dust and ash mixture.

"Did she recommend how to use it?"

He shook his head. "However, I would advise that you mark yourself and those working with you like the La—*Katerin*—has done us." A tinge of frustration colored his voice. "Too much of my knowledge has passed, and Katerin's spell will not restore everything. At least not right away. But before I became *kendar*, I was a scholar."

Her eyebrows raised and she studied him more closely. "A scholar of what?"

"Magic and the history of Waykemin." He startled. "I—I did not remember that until just now." His eyes darted to meet hers for a moment before they flicked away to stare over her shoulder, shy as a frightened deer.

"The Witches made you—a scholar—into *kendar*?" She couldn't hide the outrage in her voice. "A scholar? Goddess's golden tits—*why*? You are a scholar! You should be honored!"

He flinched from her tone as if she had smacked him. "I obviously must have overstepped my bounds and stumbled into something secret," he said in a monotone, his gaze focusing on the ground yet again. "That would be a reason for making me *kendar*."

"Reaching out for unfettered information is what scholars are *supposed* to do." She forced herself to soften her tone, reading his skittish reaction to her sharpness. "They share knowledge. They learn. Those who would restrict knowledge are—are—are..." she fumbled for words that would express her indignation without sounding too harsh. "Rulers cannot act this way," she said finally.

"It must have been for the good of Waykemin," he mumbled.

She reached out and lifted his chin so that he would meet her eyes again. This time he trembled at her touch, shoulders pulling away from her, eyes wide with whites showing all the way around his pupils. He clearly wanted to run from her—but discipline and fear at what might happen kept him there. His quaking intensified, jerking his whole body. But he stayed.

"What is your name, scholar?" she asked as gently as was possible for her.

"Ne-Nenanim," he whimpered.

"Nenanim," she said softly. The name was familiar—from what? Nenanim. A scholar. Not a common name, but not someone recent, not—

And then remembrance came to her and she stared at the terrified man in front of her, horrified at her discovery.

"You wrote *The Lay of Terani-the-God-Killer*," she murmured. "I read your *History of the Great Plague* when I was young. You are *famous*."

"I do not remember those, La—Rekaré. Perhaps that was why I was made *kendar*—because I became known outside of Waykemin. Because I was more popular than the Chief Priestess, and I wrote about Terani."

She released his chin, shaking her head, clenching and unclenching her fists. He staggered back a step, panting.

"Gods. To do that to one such as you—Nenanim. Your writing is—was—exquisite. Your analysis of the spread of the Great Plague in Varen is classic."

He shrank into himself. "I'm sorry. I don't remember."

She studied him. He had to be older than Katerin, almost the age of Heinmyets.

"Do you know how long you have been *kendar*?"

This wasn't right. Even if he had written the most scurrilous of passages, he hadn't deserved this treatment. The name Nenanim was synonymous for even-handedness in historical writing. No wonder there hadn't been any writing from him for years—gods, since before she had become Leader of Medvara. So it had been at least eighteen years that he had been *kendar*.

Eighteen years!

Oh Gods. It spoke to the strength of his spirit that he now remembered who he was.

He shook his head. "Again, I am sorry. I do not remember."

"Never mind." She drew a ragged breath.

She should not distract Katerin with this information right now. But Gods—if Nenanim the Great was amongst the *kendar*, then who else was in that group around Katerin? Her cousin deserved to know that at least one Waykemese person of note rode with them.

How many others were as famous as Nenanim? How many of the carcasses now burned by Dovré's cool fire had been amongst Waykemin's notables—or would have been, under different rulers? Just who had the *ushar* and *kendar* been? Dissidents? Lower caste? All of those?

Gods. I will do all I can to help Katerin destroy those Witches.

"Return to Katerin with my thanks, and tell her I am honored to have spoken with Nenanim the Great," she said softly.

Without hesitation he fled from her presence, not daring to run until he passed the pile of corpses. Rekaré watched him go, then turned back to the dead. She stared at the bodies, wondering.

Just who had they been?

Gods, these Waykemese Witches were as exploitative as her late father had been. No, they were worse. Zauril did not steal his subjects' minds for years. He wanted them aware and suffering, which was dreadful enough, but he didn't steal their minds and turn them into the living dead as the Witches did. She clenched her hands hard as anger surged through her.

They will pay for this.

But she needed to make sure that those she was responsible for were not vulnerable to the same treatment. Anger was a luxury. She opened the bag of ashes, marking her cheeks and forehead before she moved amongst her Shadowwalkers to mark them as well.

❧

HEART'S DESIRE MANAGED TO CROSS THE BAR IN FRONT OF THE strangely shaped pursuing metal ships, racing hard across the ocean through periodic squalls while the storm blew onto shore. Several times the setting sun peered through the dark clouds long enough to reveal the malign squat outlines of the ten metal ships on the horizon behind their lure ships, their foes no longer maintaining the pretense of being a primary sailing force.

How many of the sailing ships in that fleet are disguised metal ships?

A shower of cold rain pounded the deck while they thrashed through the worst of the roiling cross-waves, the tide still outgoing. Finally, the storm-driven ocean overcame the Chellana's vast current, and they made progress. Witmara continued to maintain her awareness of the Darani fleet, turning her head to monitor their progress as best as she could, grateful for the skill of the Sorcerer-Captains as they pushed their ships to beat the Darani to the river. But still, the Darani gained on them.

Faster than we expected. Oh Gods.

They broke through the churning surf. The ship leapt ahead as they reached the calmer bay waters, a ray of sun briefly warming them. No time to stop at Chellanasit to catch their breath, no choice but to forge on to the Melanut Plains and hope their forces would be prepared to fight, even if it was full dark by the time they arrived. Toran untied himself.

"Untie you, too?" he asked.

Witmara shook her head. "Be careful. Both flags and birds?"

He kissed her. "I will be careful. Signaling my father's fleet, sending birds to Melanut."

"Don't forget to warn them about the nature of the ships. Your father's fleet might not expect that."

"Sending a bird to Chespir," he said. She hadn't met the admiral of the Larijian fleet since he had remained in Chellananit, preparing his sailors. "He will know what to do."

I hope you're right.

"Be careful," she repeated.

"I will." He kissed her.

Witmara closed her eyes as he left, focusing hard on projecting her image to the fleet behind them. Daro sent her reassurance but all the same, she didn't dare reopen her eyes until she finally heard Toran's light step on the deck.

Setkin drove *Desire* hard upriver, edging as close as he dared to treacherous sandbars that might entrap their pursuers unfamiliar with the river and unable to read its currents after dark.

As they rounded a bend and passed in the lee of one of the big islands in the river, Setkin came to her.

"Their fleet is committed to the crossing, and you should be safe from being washed overboard now."

"How many survived?" she asked as Toran untied her. Witmara released the projection and dropped to her hands and knees, shaking, fighting off the exhaustion from so long a working. Toran knelt beside her, holding her close.

"Not sure yet. Are you all right?" Setkin asked.

"Nothing that food and rest won't fix. It was a long working." She pushed herself to her knees, resting her hands on her thighs.

He nodded, reached in his pocket, and shoved a cloth-wrapped bar toward her. "Take this. It's a staple of Sorcerer-Captains—one way we sustain ourselves."

Witmara unwrapped the bar and took a bite, handing the wrapper back to Setkin. "Thank you."

It consisted of pressed fat, nuts, grains, dried fruit, and meat chunks, similar to a travel bar that the Clendans made. Saltier than the Clendan version, and the fruit was less tangy as well, though creamier and richer. She wolfed the bar down in three more bites, the shakes fading as she ate. She brushed off her hands and wiggled out of Toran's grip before she pushed herself to her feet, able to stand steady as a single bright ray from the sunset shot up in stark contrast to the dark storm, then faded.

I hope they lose at least one ship in the crossing.

Perhaps those strange ships would struggle more than sailing ships to get across the roiling currents. But she couldn't count on that. Best to assume they all survived the passage and engagement with the Larijian fleet to continue upriver.

"Continue or stop?" Setkin asked. "Night travel on the Chellana is risky."

"Can we continue? We're so close—I'd like to reach Melanut if we can, have the support of our ground forces. Is it possible for us to do without running aground?"

Night travel was an issue for the sternwheelers above the Saktrin—one reason why they stopped overnight at various ports. The Sorcerer-Captains and their ships should have a greater ability than the sternwheeler captains to avoid sandbars, logs, and other hazards in the river—shouldn't they?

"I need to get back to the helm," Setkin said. "Yes, we can do it. Carefully—but doable."

"Then perhaps we'll run our followers aground."

"One can only hope." He frowned. "Though who knows what kind of technology those metal ships possess? I have heard reports that they have lights that allow them to run at night and systems—magic? technology we don't understand?—to detect obstacles. I did not think the Darani had so many working metal ships. I had heard of only one or two, not ten. And the ships I knew about weren't shaped anything like these are."

"We haven't had much of a spy network in Daran since Rekaré resigned the Leadership of Medvara. My mother hasn't found anyone to replace Detaluna—and Betsona is hardly the same as Detaluna for effectiveness."

"True. At least the darkness will slow them. In our favor, *Desire* remembers the channel. Our other sailships will do the same. But our non-sorcerous ships will be at risk—and the metal ships will have to slow."

"Do what you can."

He nodded and left. She clutched at the amplifier around her neck with her right hand. Perhaps she could use a little more energy to determine the status of the rest of her ships before going below.

Then cannon rumbled downriver, making the choice between staying on deck or going below easier. Witmara hurried to *Desire's* stern, straining to see something—anything— behind them as the light faded and they cleared the island. An explosion. Bright flare of red and yellow light that faded. Another boom from the opposite direction. Toran joined her.

"The Larijian fleet has engaged the Darani ships," he said, pointing to the right as light blossomed again, followed by a roar. "That's one of ours shooting now."

Witmara's hands tightened on the railing. "Do you think I should reawaken the sending to keep them coming?"

And then another light flashed bright and steady on the river, closer than the booms and roars. One of the metal ships rounded the end of the island and Witmara saw that it followed a single white glow that hovered low over the river.

Toran's hands tightened on her shoulders.

"I don't think reawakening the sending will be necessary," he said. "It looks like we have at least one follower. And where one comes, others will follow."

After scrambling over a low pass that separated the valley of the Kitskan from the rest of Waykemin, Katerin's forces camped shortly before dusk on a ridge in the mountains above Chiyan, still without encountering any resistance.

"This doesn't feel right," Rekaré fretted during Katerin's camp rounds. As always, the Mer Galad watch camp was on the eastern perimeter, at the head of the column. "I would think we would have run into something besides piles of *ushar* bodies. There's a trap somewhere and we're marching right into it."

"I don't know. Over the years there hasn't been much between the border and Chiyan, just a small guard station at the fords." Katerin eyed the rock outcropping past Rekaré's camp. She knew that outcropping. It was part of a cliff overlooking Chiyan, and she was oh-so-tempted to shinny out on the point to gaze down into the valley where she had been born and spent her first years. She had done it when following the herds as a child, and it was free from snow and ice. Treacherous though it looked, she knew the pathway to the edge.

"All the better for a fighting area without risking civilians—Katerin! Are you even paying attention?"

Katerin jerked her head toward the outcropping. "Just thinking about going out there to take a look at Chiyan, see if there are any fortifications there."

"You *wouldn't.*"

"Why not? I used to do it on that exact chunk of rock. There's a path—or used to be one."

"That was years ago."

Katerin shrugged. "If I can't see a path, I won't go out there. But if I do, then it's a good viewpoint to scope out Chiyan. Want to come with me?" She glanced at Nenanim. "You will join me, right?"

For the first time since she met him, Nenanim chuckled. "My la—Katerin," he amended, as Rekaré glared at him. "The reputation of Chiyani-raised climbers is something I recall even with *kendar*-muddled memories. If you find a way, I will follow."

"I..." Rekaré spluttered, throwing her hands high. "Katerin. It's crazy."

"You could come with me. It's no worse than scrambling around the outcrops in Clenda. Didn't you do that as a child?"

Few could keep up with Katerin during her scrambles around cliff faces and outcrops. Granted, it had been a few years since her last climbs, but still—she had taught Witmara climbing during their summers in Clenda, before the Leadership. But she hadn't done much since Medvara claimed her.

It will be a good way to reconnect with the land.

"No!"

"Well, I think it's an excellent idea. Perhaps you should send some of your riders out to check conditions ahead."

"Now that is something I can support." Rekaré turned away, gesturing to several of the Mer Galad.

"Shall we?" Katerin asked Nenanim.

He bowed and gestured toward the outcrop. "Lead the way. You are Chiyani. I trust your skill."

"It has been a few years."

"I trust you."

She wanted to laugh at that, but didn't. Trust her? She had already demonstrated problems with that sort of faith. Not remembering things. Susceptibly to remembrance spells. What else was she getting wrong?

All the same, she marched toward where the trail had been. It was still there. Overgrown over the winter, but the track looked much the same as it had in her childhood. The footholds and handholds were in the right place, and remained sturdy. The stone didn't stir under her hands as she edged out on the narrow ridge, no indication that it would crumble and send her catapulting into the valley.

Katerin reached the tip, where there was a narrow ledge

wide enough for several people to sit. She chose a natural seat on that ledge, the spot that had been her favorite in childhood. Nenanim crossed behind her and sat an arm's reach away.

Perhaps this excursion would help him remember more of his past—and do the same for her.

How could she have forgotten Nenanim the Great? She had saved up her early Healer earnings to purchase a copy of his *Lay of Terani-the-God-Killer*. They had read parts of his *History* during winter trainings at the Healing House—she had taught some of it.

Even if being *kendar* had erased much of himself, she hoped that if she dragged him along with her, asked him questions, his memory would return. Gods only knew they could use his knowledge. It was encouraging that flashes of the old scholar returned through the day, and while his memory was impaired, his reasoning and analytic abilities did not appear to be.

Remembering the Chiyani climbing reputation was a good sign. Now if only they could see something here. Chiyan was the next logical fortification where the Witches might make a stand. She pulled her spyglass from its holster, and peered through it to pick out faintly remembered landmarks.

Her birthplace looked much the same, exactly like she would have expected this time of year. It was too early in the season yet for planting, and herds were drawn close in for lambing and calving, as protection against predators with a taste for young flesh.

Or invaders seeking to feed an army.

Not that they would need to provision just yet.

She didn't trust what she saw. There should be differences.

"It hasn't changed," she muttered. "At least not from this distance. I wouldn't expect it to look the same as it always has."

"Chiyan the enduring," Nenanim said. "Chiyan the foundation of Waykemin—or so it appears."

Another flash of memory.

It certainly sounded like something Nenanim the Great had written. She examined the buildings more carefully. Even Dera and Wickmasa had changed more than this over the years—Medvare-the-city could not be a comparison, not after all she and Rekaré had done to it. She didn't see much to suggest further fortification here, certainly nothing more than she remembered from childhood.

Unlike the Clendan and Keldaran villages on the other side of the Kitskan, the Chiyani had built a wall around the town and its fields, ostensibly to keep the herds safe and invaders out. She had been old enough to participate in the annual reinforcement of that wall before leaving for Forsim. With an anticipated invasion, she would expect to see more activity below. After all, this was on the direct route to the capital city, and it was a logical place to harry and repulse invaders. She would have staged a defensive force here, were she planning the defense of Waykemin.

But she didn't spot much activity below. Nothing unexpected. Just flocks and herders. Certainly no sign of defenders preparing for battle.

Katerin lowered the spyglass, frowning. "That shouldn't be right. Don't tell me the Witches expected their magic to guard everything! Nenanim, does this seem right to you?"

She offered him the spyglass. He took it awkwardly, obviously uncomfortable at being treated as a regular person instead of *kendar*. But as he raised it to his eye his grip eased into a practiced handling. He peered through the glass, then handed it back to her.

"I admit, it does not seem right to me." He frowned in puzzlement. "Logic suggests that we should see more activity."

"And it looks *exactly* like it did when I was a child. That doesn't seem right after all these years. Do you suppose there is a glamor on the land?"

Frustration crossed his face. "Once I could have told you.

Now I do not know. Neither my forgotten past nor my link to the *kendar* tells me anything. The sense of the *kendar* is fading, especially when you renew the marks on my face. But I am caught in between the two, neither who I used to be nor *kendar*! What use am I?"

"More than you realize." She bit her lip as she raised the glass to her eye again. "Perhaps I should probe with my sorcery to see if there's a glamor on the land."

"I do not recommend it. That may be a trap."

Katerin nodded. "Tranarin would set such a trap."

Nenanim shifted on the rock next to her. "It would be more than her who knows of your ties to Chiyan." His voice seemed distant. "A memory stirs, of the Council arguing over what to do with you after Terani went into the dreamless sleep." His hands moved. "A writing."

She lowered the glass and focused on him. "Tell me more."

His hands kept moving—apparently helping his recall.

"I had been called into the Council to record the proceedings that day. I felt much honored as a younger scribe to receive the recognition. *Daughter of Alame the Cursed*, they called you. *Betrayer of Terani. Dangerous half-breed. She should be killed.*" His voice changed to a higher note. "*Limit her to Chiyan. Make her kendar. No. She is beloved of that cursed Goddess and of the Destroyer. We dare not touch her. But she will destroy us. No, not if we do not give her cause. She desires to be a healer. Let her go to that fate. But bind her. Demand that she owe us tribute for her mother's support. She will be so busy paying that price that she will have no time to seek out her father and her fate. Warn the Healing House in Keldara of the danger should she ever learn what she really is. Threaten them.*" He stopped. "Gods. I remember how I felt that day, in agreement with the Witches that you should be bound to the Healing House of Keldara with unbreakable links, saddled with an onerous payment. How could I have been so blind to what the Council really was? Can you forgive me?"

The Healer in Katerin wakened. "You were young and ambitious." She hesitated. "If it is painful for you, you need not continue. But I would hear more about what was said, if you can still remember."

His jaw tightened. "I will try. Some of these memories are slippery, but they are older. I'm—finding it easier to bring back these earlier memories." He stared toward Forsim and the east, where the violet glow of approaching night rose behind the peaks on the other side of the valley.

Then his face softened. "*The Goddess and God appear*," he chanted in a sing-song tone, as if he recited a poem. "*Karnoi the Great, bloody and strong, sly and conniving. Cirdel the Glorious, mistress of enchantment and misdirection, twin with her brother and lover, both entwined with love of chaos. Let her go, they say. We will watch over Katerin to-be Healer, keep her distracted. Keep her from Alame the Cursed, deny memory to both of them. Bind her to Terani-the-God-Killer, weight her steps with the heritage of her dam. Terani will be hostage for her daughter. To keep Katerin here, to turn her kendar, brings swift destruction to Waykemin. We dare not risk the curse of the Miteal. Let her go, to avoid certain ruin.*" His voice broke off. "That is all I can remember. I am sorry for it being so little."

"Do not be sorry. I—that explains much."

Katerin sighed, looking back down at the village of her birth. She reached down to press her fingers against the lava rock she sat on, to see if the land responded at all to her touch.

A faint recognition was all. She eased herself back from the edge of the outcrop so that if anyone were looking up from below they would not spot her silhouette. Nenanim followed her back down the trail.

"Well," she said once they were safely off the outcrop. "We should assume that we will face opposition once we ride into Chiyan. After what you have told me, I expect that Karnoi and Cirdel hope to obscure my sight." Her fists clenched. "But between Rekaré Kinslayer and the Banisher of Shadows, with the patronage of Bright Dovré, Staul the Balancer, Artel the Judge, and Terat of the Waters, the Twins' manipulations will be overcome forever. I swear it, on the soil of my birth. I swear it to you, Nenanim the Great, and to all who would stand in my way. We will enact our vengeance and end the corruption of the Witches. I swear it to the Seven Crowned Gods!"

Now she felt the land stir under her feet. Though whether it was in support or rejection of her vow, Katerin could not be certain.

BETRAYALS

Witmara and Toran waited tensely on *Desire's* deck while Setkin flashed the signal lanterns at the Melanut Plains moorage. Witmara wrapped her fingers in Daro's mane, prepared to leap on his back and swim for it if their pursuers came too close. Toran stood next to his daranval, also ready.

She was *not* going to look back at the lights that marked the seven ships following them. Setkin had already signaled the Medvaran ships and the shore cannon brigades about their pursuers. Now they just needed to reach land.

Light flashed back, three longs, a pause, one short, pause, two shorts, then three more longs. Then lanterns flared and they could see the dock clearly, and more lights among their waiting forces.

"At least something's going our way," Setkin grumbled. He unshuttered the signal lanterns and stepped back from them, his deep voice rising as he sang the spell to guide *Desire* into port swiftly, without need for oars or wind.

Witmara swung into Daro's saddle. Toran and their guards mounted up. Setkin planned to dock just long enough to set them off before taking *Desire* to a safer harbor in an island cove upriver, along with the other magic sailships. She waited tensely while the ship glided next to the dock. As soon as the sailors ran the plank out and pronounced it steady she urged Daro forward. He trotted down the plank and exploded into a gallop once all four hooves touched the dock. They thundered past the startled group waiting for them.

The sailors hustled the plank back as Witmara reined Daro in and whirled him about. He snorted and reared as the sailors finished unmooring and Setkin sang the *Desire* away.

"Leader Witmara! What is happening?" Korien, general of the forces she had staged here, ran off the dock after her. Daro reared again and screamed a challenge as the light of the first metal ship became visible from the shore.

"Did you not get our message?" Toran yelled. "The Darani have technology-powered metal ships hard on our heels! Seven survived the bar and the Larijian fleet! They come now! Prepare for battle."

"We had received the message but hadn't expected you to be here this soon...." Korien answered. "Ready for battle!" he bellowed at one of his aides. He turned back to Toran and Witmara. "Will they follow the sailships or come ashore?"

Witmara swallowed hard. She took the amplifier around her neck in her hand.

"I will do my best to call them in," she said. "They follow me."

REKARÉ COULDN'T SLEEP. WHILE SHE HAD ASSIGNED HERSELF THE first watch, Cenarth a protective shadow beside her, she had remained on guard when Sesenth came to relieve her. Their restlessness infected the rest of the Mer Galad as clouds obscured the sliver of moon overhead, prowling around the edges of the camps. Waiting. Waiting for the next morning, when *surely* they would encounter something besides abandoned corpses. If not before then.

Something was going to happen soon. Her magical perception warned that there was *something* out there, even if they couldn't see it. The way her skin crawled brought back bad memories of that last summer in Medvara, when the vengeful ghost of her father stalked her and, through Chatain's agent Chiral, her daughter. If only she could pinpoint *what* it was that was going to attack and *when* it was going to happen. There was an anomaly that she just couldn't finger, something she was missing—but what?

Gods. This *was* just like being back in Medvara during those last days, complete with second-guessing her senses. Rekaré fought the urge to pull out the sorcerous tools she had taken from Medvara, the gems known as the Maker, the Strength, and the Vision. Magic in the camp was under Katerin's command, not hers, and until Katerin told her to don them or she had a clear reason to use those tools, she wasn't going to do that.

But Gods, she didn't like being this blind.

Two people approached the watch post—not signing their identification like her Mer Galad would do when they drew near, their hands spread wide as if they planned to surrender. The back of Rekaré's neck prickled and she drew her sword. Cenarth was quicker, and advanced to meet them, Sesenth a shadow by his side, spear at the ready, both placing themselves between the intruders and Rekaré.

"Identify yourselves!" he snapped.

"We are part of Katerin's *kinforost*," the taller one answered slowly, in accented Varenese. "I am Ylittim and this is Wisknani, both formerly of the *kendar*." He gestured at the person next to him. "We were warriors before we were *kendar*. Katerin thinks we would be best here on watch, not back with her. She sent a message for Rekaré."

"Give it to me." Cenarth held out his hand.

Wisknani handed him a folded paper. He opened it, glanced, and nodded at her. "Watch them," he said to Sesenth, then strode to Rekaré. "This is a curious message from Katerin. I understand part of it, but the rest? Is it a code?"

Rekaré took the paper from Cenarth. One look told her why he called it curious. "Yes. Sending written coded messages is something we've done since I left Medvara. Katerin and I stopped using the speaking squares because we couldn't coordinate times and locations," she said. *And with my mother dead, we didn't have any real need for that level of urgent communication.* "It is authentic." She reread it.

Cousin of fire, my heart and blood, sharer of hidden regard, from she who was Healer.

They only used this salutation phrase to validate urgent written communications. She and Katerin never spoke of each other in this manner in public, only in private.

These things are important to remember.

Remember. A laden word. Did Katerin also suspect a remembrance spell? She would know, after past experience in Wickmasa.

One. Memories of Wickmasa and that which Eldoran did for me.

That phrase referred to the head Healer Eldoran's removing the influence of the Wickmasa's remembrance spell over Katerin, so that she became aware of Wickmasa's secrets.

*Two. The same is true here. I write this down as a
result.*

Rekaré raised her brows. That was interesting, especially given what she was sensing. What was Katerin forgetting and why did she think it was spell-linked? Did this mean that the Witches still maintained protective sorceries? Not surprising—and a good reason to bring out the Vision, at least.

*Three. Your burials are missing those who are like
the ones that bear this message.*

Rekaré inhaled sharply through her teeth. Of course. They had only burned *ushar* bodies and the message bearers were *kendar*. So there should be *kendar* lying in wait for them—why hadn't it happened during the day? Perhaps the spells that hid the *kendar* were more effective after dark. And two warriors that had been *kendar* could tell her how to discover them.

Four. You have the tools. Use them as you see fit.

"I hear you and obey," she breathed, a fierce joy leaping in her heart. She could use the Vision, at least.

*Five. Be careful. Those I send you know of appro-
priate strategies to match your tools.*

Your cousin in fire and blood. K.

Fire and blood. That plus the initial instead of her full name meant that Katerin expected an impending attack.

She crumpled the paper in her fist, then strode past Cenarth and Sesenth. "How will the *kendar* attack us?" she demanded of Ylittim and Wisknani.

"Shadow spells," Ylittim said. "Something conceals them. They will come upon us by surprise. They...." His voice trailed off as he frowned.

"And you couldn't tell Katerin this?"

He and Wisknani exchanged glances.

"We tried to tell her," Wisknani said. "But she is bound by this spell very tightly. She could not hold the memory from moment to moment, even when Nenanim wrote it down for her. It was hard for him to get the words down when we spoke...." Her voice trailed away and confusion crossed her face. "It's happening again!"

What were they talking about? Something about the paper. Rekaré uncrumpled it, scanned it again. Oh. Remembrance spells.

"Do you forget?"

"When she does." Wisknani shook her head. "*Shadow spells. Shadow spells, shadow spells, shadow spells!*"

Rekaré held a hand up, recognizing the strategy to try and counter remembrance spells.

"I have another means to deal with this. Sesenth. In my saddlebags. There is a box wrapped in purple Medvaran wool cloth. Bring it to me." She turned, waving to the two *kendar*. "Come to the fire. I have something that may help."

Sesenth joined them at the fire, holding the small purple-wrapped box at arms length, her fingertips barely touching it.

"I do not like the feel of this magic," she said.

Cenarth scowled. "If that's what I think it is, then you are correct to feel that way, Sesenth."

"Tch!" Rekaré snorted. "Sometimes one must be willing to walk the red paths. Katerin has told me to use these tools. We need to see things more clearly, and this is how we are going to do it."

She took the box from Sesenth and knelt beside the fire, setting the box on the ground, using the lid to weight the unfolded paper so that she could glance at it to remember why she did this when her memory failed. Once she activated the gems, she would not forget.

The first item she removed was a necklace with a pendant of citrine, amethyst, peridot, garnet, and pearl on a gold chain. "Maker-of-Gods," she said, laying it on the purple cloth. She didn't want to don this one, not until they marched on Forsim. Of all the gems, this one was the most likely to betray her.

"Gods, Rekaré, I did not know you still held those!" Cenarth shook his head.

"They belong to me, not to Medvara. Katerin agreed."

A foul inheritance from my father.

While she had been able to purge some of his influence from the Maker and expelled its links to the Goddess Nitel with the help of Staul, she did not like to wield it.

Rekaré extracted the second item, a silver bracelet with a plain amethyst. "Strength-of-Gods." The Strength was a different matter. The Goddess Dovré's presence pulsed through it. It had taken little work to purify it from her father's use.

She laid it down and pulled out the last item, a gold ring with a garnet set into it. "Vision-of-Gods." Like the Strength, the Vision was easy to cleanse, being dedicated to Artel the Judge. She set the ring below the necklace and bracelet.

"I thought of these earlier tonight. I have not used them since Chiral's death, but I put them away fully charged. I knew that I might need to call upon them at some point—and they are the only tools I possess that will counter this damn spell."

Especially the Vision.

Gods, they could all use some vision in the face of this

remembrance spell and the *kendar* that should be there but weren't.

"I don't like this, Rekaré," Cenarth said. "Those gems are dangerous. They caused your break from Medvara."

"I agree with him," Sesenth said. "They don't feel right."

Rekaré picked up the Vision, holding it high as the red stone glittered in the light of the fire. "They are dangerous tools and not to be taken up lightly. But after what I have seen today, I see no other option to stop the Witches." Her fingers closed around the Vision and she held it to her chest.

> Staul. Dovré. Artel. You know I wield these tools to prevent a greater evil. Do I wield all of these, or is Vision enough to banish these damned remembrance spells?

She devoutly hoped that was the case.

Artel remained silent but Staul's ponderous presence came near, Dovré lurking behind him.

> The Vision and perhaps the Strength will be sufficient.

Well, that was a relief. She really didn't want to use the Maker until it was utterly necessary.

Rekaré held the Vision high as Staul waited.

"My lord Staul. I put on the Vision-of-Gods to see what would not be seen." *Benghaalph* stirred within her, approving, as Staul reached out to touch the garnet. It flared bright red. "Thank you for your blessing."

She slipped it onto her finger. Power stirred and she looked beyond the fire. Transparent figures crept in the furthest shadows. Rekaré blinked and shook her head, but the shadows remained mere outlines.

Do I need the Strength to see more?

Her hand trembled slightly as she picked up the silver

bracelet and raised it high. A lighter presence approached. Dovré.

"My lady Dovré. I put on the Strength-of-Gods to call forth power to help battle what would not be seen."

The Goddess smiled wistfully at Rekaré. She caressed the amethyst, stroking it gently so that the glow became first lavender, then deepened into a rich, clear violet while the silver shone with a bluish tinge. Rekaré clasped the Strength on her wrist. Dovré touched her forehead.

I fear you are growing beyond me, Rekaré. Use these tools wisely and well.

Then both Gods disappeared. Rekaré carefully wrapped the Maker in the purple cloth and tucked it into a belt pouch for safekeeping. She looked up. The transparent figures were more solid, clustering at the edges of camp. Thin, emaciated, dark skin gone gray-blue, teeth elongated. They clutched bone knifes but seemed to stop moving as Rekaré gazed upon them.

"Ylittim. Wisknani." She kept her eyes on the figures, her voice low and steady, heart pounding in her ears.

Gods. I knew something was wrong.

"I see figures at the edges of camp. They looked much as you and the others did when you came to us last night. Only more skeletal."

Gods, had it only been that short a time?

"I cannot see anything," Ylittim said.

"I see shadows," Sesenth said.

"*Kendar.* Come to me." Rustling in the dry grass behind her, then Ylittim and Wisknani stood next to her, Cenarth and Sesenth bracketing them. "Kneel for better contact with the land. Put a hand on my shoulders."

A moment, then first Wisknani, then Ylittim knelt and rested their hands on her.

"I see them," Wisknani said quietly. "They are our *kendar*

siblings, under a shadow spell, as we thought. Worse than we thought." Her hand tightened on Rekaré's shoulder. "The Witches didn't just spell them. They ate their souls. I am surprised that you have influence over them."

"I have powers that surprise even me," Rekaré said. "Tell me more."

"They carry bone knives," Ylittim said. "These are not ordinary *kendar*. They cannot be brought back to themselves. They are owned by the Witches body and soul. The enchantment on them can only be broken by their death. They are *shalkendar*."

"*Shalkendar?*" Rekaré asked.

"*Kendar* of the shadows. There are several ways to counter them, but the best means is to use fire," Ylittim said. "Arrows, torches, whatever it takes. Strike them with fire, and they cannot survive. But those who are wounded by their knives must be treated quickly before they are lost."

"How do we get enough of our people to see them so we can effectively fight?" Cenarth's hand joined the others on Rekaré's shoulder. "Ugh. They are far from pleasant to view."

Benghaalph stirred within Rekaré, husking her voice deeper. "This is a spell known to me. Bring me a torch, one of you."

"Ah." Sesenth said, nodding. "Take fire to them? Now I remember it as well. I will fetch the best torch I can find."

"How does that spell work?" Cenarth asked. "You're not going to need to fight all of them yourself, are you?"

"No, no, no. I will strike the first blow with a glimmer dust-enhanced torch. That will make the rest visible since they are controlled by a linked spell." She paused. "Cenarth, arm the Mer Galad and bring me some glimmer dust. Wisknani and Ylittim, warn the rest of the camps. Once the *shalkendar* are revealed we will need to strike hard and fast. You will not have much time to raise the call."

"The bow is my weapon, and I can make fire arrows," Wisknani said. "Ylittim. Our kind will know what to do. Let's use them as messengers to each camp." She hurried away with him.

She had a few moments alone by the fire, waiting while Cenarth got the glimmer dust and the *kendar* scattered around the camps. Rekaré kept her gaze steady on the one *shalkendar*. As long as she stared at that one directly in front of her, the others didn't move. The slightest glance away, and they skittered a few steps.

What was it about her that seemed to control them? The Strength and the Vision? The presence of *benghaalph* lurking just under her skin, ready to explode with rage? Herself as Rekaré Kinslayer? All of those elements in combination?

She wasn't sure. But it was a relief when Sesenth handed her a thick pine branch with a pitchy knot at the very top, knowing that soon she could strike and not worry about having to freeze the *shalkendar*, especially since she didn't know *why* they stood still when she gazed at them.

"I picked the biggest knot I could find in the woodpile," Sesenth said. "Our Mer Galad stands ready once you strike the first blow. The *kendar* have spread the warnings around the camps."

"Good."

Rekaré touched first the Strength, then the Vision to the knot, keeping her eyes fixed on that one *shalkendar*.

"Glimmer dust."

Cenarth thrust the bag toward her, the top already untied so that all she had to do was plunge her hand into the bag and seize a handful of dust. Rekaré sprinkled the knot with the dust, then lit the torch. She rose quickly, careful not to look away from the closest *shalkendar* as she ran toward it. It remained frozen to the ground, immobile, eyes widening.

"May the unseen become seen!" Rekaré shrieked. She smacked the *shalkendar* with her torch. *"Begone, all of you, by the powers*

granted me by the Lord Staul and the Lady Dovré! Forces of Varen, strike now!"

Outcries arose as the *shalkendar* became visible. Fire arrows launched from the nearest camps. Rekaré swung her torch as the Vision blazed red and the Strength glowed violet, shrieking unfamiliar words as *benghaalph* overcame her, battering the *shalkendar* with a force she rarely felt before, all the frustration and rage at what she had seen of Waykemin this day exploding out of her. The flame of her torch flared with a cool blue light.

Feel the wrath of Rekaré Kinslayer! was the only coherent thought in her mind as she fought, instinct and reflexes keyed toward keeping those bone knives away. It was satisfying to see those horrors fade away.

GODS, I WISH I COULD DO SOMETHING.

But Korien and Toran both insisted that Witmara didn't belong in the fray, so she was banished to a vantage point on the bank next to the beach, only able to follow what was happening by the torches and occasional flashes of moonlight when the clouds parted. Four of the metal ships rumbled toward the beach as cannon blasted at them. The cannonballs hit an invisible barrier and pinged into the river.

Sorcerers on each ship.

But that blue-white light guiding the ships was another sign of sorcerous support.

Maybe if one of the cannoneers were to aim at those lights....

As if one of the cannon crews could read her mind, *something* crashed into the guiding light of the furthest upriver ship. It winked out. The ship faltered. The current grabbed the bow and it swung toward its neighbor. A roar came from the threatened ship and it lurched back, water churning around it.

Oh Terat of the Waters, if only you could take all four of those ships out!

Should she call for that Goddess's favor? She hadn't done so on the open ocean, her concentration on keeping her projection going filling her thoughts.

No. Not yet, something cautioned her. *That time has not arrived.*

Cannon rumbled, the fire of their explosions briefly illuminating the water. Cannonballs peppered the careening ship and it exploded like a huge pitch knot, just as it crashed into the bow of its neighbor. More cannon fire, and that ship exploded as well.

Yes! Two ships down. *Thank you, Goddess.*

The remaining two surged ahead faster, charging the beach as if they planned to ram themselves into the sand. They beached themselves before the next round of cannon fire. Doorways creaked open above the waterlines and soldiers poured out of the narrow portals, more fighters than Witmara thought those ships could carry. The blue-white lights retreated to their ships' decks.

She vacillated between fascination at this new technology and dread of what it meant for this battle. The fighters charging through the water and up onto the beach were taller and broader than her own people. And even though the invaders were on foot compared to her soldiers on horseback, it seemed to take a long time for her riders to take them down—and both horses and riders fell to the invaders' attacks.

The ships' cannons fired, some at her soldiers, some at her cannon. Not all their projectiles were cannonballs. Some burned en route and crashed amongst her cannoneers, flames rising high on impact. Loud screams and shrieks came from the cannon forces and she closed her eyes.

Goddess Dovré, ease their pain. Please.

So two ships down. Two landed. A third without a light circled aimlessly in the current. Where were the other two ships? Had they run aground?

Daro snorted and pawed, pulling at the reins and chewing his bit, shaking his head. Had she and Toran not been circled by a double row of guards, he might have galloped into the fray. Witmara patted him on the neck.

"Easy, boy," she said out loud, sending reassurances she didn't really feel as she watched the battle. Their torch spluttered as a soft breeze whispered upriver, bearing a cool damp that warned of the approach of more heavy squalls.

Just what we need, more weather, she thought, straining to watch the battle below them.

It was a grim play of light and shadow. Some of the Darani wore lights on their helmets similar to those that had hovered before the ships, only not as bright, enough to show clusters of warriors. Witmara yearned to call forth a spell so she could see more of how the battle progressed. But light would aid their foes as much as it would help her fighters.

Gods, she felt silly sitting up here, out of the way of battle, watching her people battle and die. She should be down there with them. But Toran and Korien had vetoed that notion when she brought it up. They wanted her safe, away from the fray.

She didn't feel safe separate from her warriors.

Where were those last two ships?

Daro wordlessly shared her worry, snorting and pawing. Witmara tried extending her awareness, but she couldn't sense the ships in front of her, much less any others. Even when she linked to him she couldn't. Was it because they were technology and not magic?

If it hadn't been for the Shadowwalkers and Houndriders from Saubral, they'd be in trouble. Only the Saubral seemed able to hold ground against the sorcerers intermingled with Darani warriors.

I thought Chatain was supposed to prefer technology to magic! Wasn't that what Chiral had told Mother and Rekaré?

Witmara closed her hand around the Light of Medvara.

> Respond to me, please. Gods. Staul. Dovré. Artel. Terat. Waken the land.

If her mother was here, she could rouse Medvara to fight for them. Why couldn't she do that herself?

> Mother. Hear me. Answer me. What am I doing wrong? Help us!

A rider galloped toward them. "Korien advises you move back," he gasped as he halted. "A spell on their fighters…." He jerked hard, arms thrown wide, eyes nearly popping out of his head, gasping for breath before he fell from his horse. Witmara saw the red arrow in his back, a fiery glow spreading from it as he convulsed. The horse spooked away, galloping off in panic, screaming in terror.

What caused that glow?

She had to do *something.* Witmara dismounted and pushed through her guard to reach the fallen rider before Toran or anyone else could stop her, instinct and her mother's training driving her to help if she could. Daro bellowed in distress and shoved through their protective cordon, pressing his nose against her back as she knelt beside the rider. She reached for his neck to determine his pulse, as her mother had taught her.

A sharp hard sting knocked her away from the rider as her fingers contacted flesh, sending her sprawling on her behind. Her fingertips tingled and her heart pounded.

What was that?

Daro rumbled deep in his chest, nostrils flared, blowing hard, sharing her bewilderment.

Witmara pushed herself back up and crawled to the rider's

side. He was dead. She wrapped her hand around the arrow to try to discern what that glow was.

A curse on their weapons. But what kind of curse is it?

Daro snorted a warning as the bright red light covering the rider suddenly coalesced as a pulsing globule in front of her.

Laughter. Then a man appeared inside the mist, red hair and beard streaked with gray. She recognized him from projections she had seen seven years ago, during that horrible time when first Alicira and then Melarae died—though he had appeared younger then. Now he was much older, more so than the progression of seven years should have shown.

Witmara rose cautiously to her feet. She greeted him without ceremony or deference.

Chatain. So this is your invasion force.

I bid you greetings and curses, oh ambitious cousin. How do you like my new toys? Were you surprised?

How much dare she admit?

They are different from what I expected. But my forces will win. The land of Medvara will not tolerate your incursions. Varen holds firm against you.

He laughed.

I admire your delusion in the face of adversity.

His form changed slightly, becoming more menacing.

But despite what platitudes you spout, you're still overmatched. My Eyes ride with my fighters. I can see how the battle progresses.

He was right. They had grossly underestimated the number of fighters on those ships. If they could hold until daylight, until the Larijian fleet could bring more warriors…if they could hold until daylight.

One of my fighters is worth three of yours.

She thrust her chin up defiantly, meeting his gaze from within the red mist.

Ha! I like your pride and courage, little cousin. But let us face reality. You're doomed to lose this battle. Submit or fall. Your forces cannot prevail.

No!

A sinister smile spread across his face.

A pity. You are young and strong. You could rule beside me as my Empress. I offer you power with my blessing. Submit or fall.

I will never submit to you!

Then you will die.

He reached for her. Daro bellowed and struck at the apparition, his presence larger than life. Chatain shrank back from the daranval.

Damned beast!

The light within the red globule faded in intensity and a victorious cheer rose from her people.

I must counter his magic directly. Perhaps if I try drawing from the land—there has to be a way.

Then she remembered the tattoo left by the Hidden One. Worth a try—and Chatain had yet to see her display *her* sorcery.

Watch, cousin,

she told him.

Watch and see how we win.

She rubbed the tattoo on her hand as she knelt.

My Lord Staul,

she called. Would he answer?

Heed me.

In response, power surged through her at long last, and the Light of Medvara flared bright on her chest. The ground vibrated under her. Witmara placed one hand on it. The land responded.

Finally.

She pulled strength from it.

Deny the intruders their power! I command you as Regent, as daughter of the true Leader! Deny the intruders!

She shrieked defiance as Chatain's projection faded. She rose and stood tall, light flowing from her hands. Her fighters seemed to pick up more strength, pushing back against the intruders. Would this be enough to win the battle?

The line broke as the Darani started to backtrack toward their ships. Daro stood beside Witmara, nuzzling her. She drew strength freely from her daranval, not daring to lower her hands as the Darani were in full retreat. One of the ships pulled off the beach—*how did they do that?*

Screams from behind her. She dared not look to see what that was, focusing instead on the fighters before her, trusting to Toran and Daro to keep her safe.

And then something hit her head hard. She fell to her knees as Daro bellowed, daranval blood splattering over her.

Chatain appeared to her again before she lost consciousness.

Little cousin, you have much yet to learn about fighting with sorcery,

he sneered.

KATERIN DIDN'T KNOW WHAT REKARÉ HAD DONE, BUT THE remembrance spell was gone and she remembered *we didn't see any kendar bodies.*

Skeletal gray figures with bone knives appeared around them, suddenly unmasked.

"*Shalkendar!*" Nenanim bellowed. "Do not let them cut you with their knives! Fire is the only weapon against them!"

Shalkendar. Kendar sucked so dry of their souls that they were beyond recovery. Source of nightmare bedtime stories for Waykemese children.

"*Be good or I'll make you shalkendar,*" Terani had threatened Katerin on days when nothing seemed to go right between mother and daughter. And she was hardly the only mother in Waykemin who made that threat.

Shalkendar.

Only now they were real and not the stuff of nightmare—except oh Gods, oh Gods, *oh Gods they're scarier in real life than in those childhood stories.*

No time to let childhood fears take her over. She was Leader. She had to fight this and not give way to the stuff of nightmares. Even if doing so made her skin crawl. Even if she had to make every move deliberate, careful, and slow, so that she didn't break and run off gibbering in terror.

Dovré. Goddess. Protect me. Don't let me falter. Please.

Katerin summoned the cool fire as she implored the Goddess, but it didn't stop the *shalkendar* charging at her. Nenanim threw a burning chunk of firewood at it and the *shalkendar* burned.

Gods. Shalkendar. Tranarin dared that working!

Katerin retreated to the fire and seized a limb, swinging the burning brand about her.

Luckily the word seemed to have spread amongst her people for she saw many with firebrands striking at the *shalkendar*. Sesenth ran toward Katerin, swinging a torch at any *shalkendar* that dared to cross her path.

"Rekaré saw these with her gems," she gasped.

"*Shalkendar.* She broke the remembrance spell," Katerin said, swinging a brand at one of the *shalkendar* who dared venture close.

"You remember them."

"Now. How does my cousin fare?"

"She fights like one enraged. *Benghaalph* has her."

Katerin paused, not seeing any more of the *shalkendar*. Had they actually defeated them? It appeared to be so.

And then a low laugh came from the fire behind her, along with heat from the pouch where she had tucked Medvara's gift.

Her land screamed within her.

Dread tightened Katerin's gut and she ripped the green and gray stone out of her pouch with one hand. Then she dropped her torch to the ground, tearing off the wrappings off the stone.

Medvara continued to wail in her head, counterpoint to the cackling coming from the fire.

Oh Gods, what's happened to Witmara?

Katerin raised the stone with shaking hands, trying to make sense of disjointed images of metal ships that didn't look like ships, bright white lights, fighters swarming the gathered forces by the river—where was that? The Melanut Plains? Yes.

> You could ask me what is happening.

More chuckling.

She whirled to see Chatain's figure standing in the flames of the nearest campfire.

> Greetings, oh foolish and distracted cousin.
> Your daughter is mine.

"NO!" Katerin screamed as the meaning of Medvara's sudden desolation came to her. "Goddess, *no!*" She dropped to her knees and pressed her head to the ground, shaking with sobs.

It wasn't supposed to happen like this!

Chatain's projection kept laughing until it was suddenly cut off. Katerin raised her head.

Rekaré, her eyes wild, pointed at Chatain.

"By *all* the Seven Crowned Gods, I will make an end of you, *cousin.* Empire will not protect you from my wrath," Rekaré snarled.

> I have already taken your mother and daughter,
> Kinslayer. I look forward to seeing you humbled
> and destroyed in person.

Rekaré bared her teeth. "And you would do best to consider how I earned the name *Kinslayer, cousin!* If you were wise, you would not play with things that will bring us together in the flesh. Remember that I claim both Katerin and Witmara as cousins. If any harm comes to Witmara, *you will pay*. Enough!"

Cold fire pulsed around the Strength and the Vision as it leapt from Rekaré to the projection of Chatain. He writhed and twisted, then disappeared.

She turned to Katerin. "Cousin. Witmara still lives and may yet escape before we can reach her. Let us make an end to this distraction in Waykemin. We must eventually go to Daran, but we dare not leave this festering mess behind us."

Katerin drew a shuddering breath and pushed herself up, rage and sorrow filling her in equal measures.

"Is this Rekaré Kinslayer or *benghaalph* speaking?"

"Both." Rekaré bared her teeth again. "I promise you, Katerin. Chatain owes me much, and taking Witmara is just one more strike against him in my ledger of grievances. *He will pay.* Also remember that Witmara is beloved of Staul. She is no small sorceress herself. He will discover that she has strengths of her own."

"Thank you." She exhaled. "What is our status? Have the *shalkendar* been dealt with?"

"Yes. No *shalkendar* remain. Our people are secure and safe. The *kendar* are tending to our wounded."

Katerin nodded, not trusting herself to speak. Rage flooded through her.

He stole my daughter! He dared to take her!

Oh Gods, what had happened to Toran? To Daro? She closed her fist around the stone, but the land did not tell her anything more.

CAPTIVITY AND CHIYAN

HER HEAD HURT. THE WORLD ROCKED AROUND HER. WITMARA blinked awake, curled on her side in damp straw. She strained to make out something, anything, that could tell her where she was in the warm, clammy darkness around her.

A distant chugging roar vibrated through the surface she lay on. The smallest bit of light spilled from a narrow slit up high. A foul, unnatural scent of something oily burning choked her and made her cough. The weight of heavy chains pulled at her wrists as she tried to cover her mouth when nausea stirred in her gut. She swallowed back the sour stuff that tried to come up.

What happened? Why am I here?

She tried to reach out with her magic to gain *some* knowledge about where she was.

Pain shot through her wrists and ankles, sharp, hot, knifing pain that caught her by surprise and forced a scream out of her. Witmara doubled up hard, jamming her knuckles in her mouth to choke back any further noise. Her body jerked as her stomach tightened and she once again fought the urge to vomit.

Fetters on her wrists and ankles. That meant she was a prisoner.

But who had done it, and most important, where was she?

Swaying, with the additional vibration that matched that chugging roar akin to that of the Chellana sternwheelers—only the sternwheelers were quieter with less vibration. She was on a ship, below decks.

How had that happened?

She had been using her magic to fight back against Chatain's soldiers, when something had smacked hard against her head. But how on earth could an attacker have gotten through her guards, Toran, and Daro?

Daro.

She tried to reach for her connection with her daranval. The burning pain knifed through her wrists and ankles, worse this time. But she choked back screams and sour bile, shaking with the agony. She remembered daranval blood flying as Daro screamed—oh Gods, had he been killed? And what had happened to Toran? Were they both dead?

No. No.

She lay shivering in the straw as the last traces of pain faded, the sour taste remaining in her mouth. She couldn't use her sorcery. Her captors had placed shackles on her to control her magic—but this was more intense than any previous shackling she had been witness to—which had been only Chiral, and Chiral had been bound by slender bracelets, not heavy fetters with chains attached to them.

Well. Since she couldn't use magic, she needed to use other means to figure out where she was.

Witmara carefully pushed herself up until she sat with her legs extended in front of her. She felt about her. No drop, so she must be on a floor and not a cot. Her fingers traced the length of the chains attached to the cuffs on her wrists—from the weight and what felt like chunks of rust on them, they must be iron. The chain ran to a palm-sized staple in the wall —an iron wall, not stone. More evidence that she was on a ship, probably one of the metal ships that had followed her upriver.

Her ankle chains were attached to the same staple. Witmara fingered around the base of the staple. Pulling on it didn't budge it one whit, and she couldn't feel any softness where it was attached to the wall. So how far away could she move? She carefully rolled to hands and knees, and crawled to the end of her restraints. Not very far, maybe about half her body's length. But long enough that she could at least lie down comfortably.

She must be alone down here. With all the groaning and rattling of her chains, if someone else were in this cell with her they would have spoken up by now.

Worth a check.

"Anyone here?" she asked, keeping her voice low.

Nothing. She sat quietly, straining to hear anything besides the deep rumble of whatever it was that made this thing run.

All right. She was alone. Could she stand up? Crawling back over to the wall and using it for a support was one possibility, but something deep inside her rebelled against that idea. She would lean against the chains to stand. Perhaps that could reveal some weakness in them.

Her head pounded as she slowly moved from hands and knees to a crouch. Then she leaned back, pulling hard on the chains, and straightened her legs to stand, using the chains to keep her from falling when her legs wobbled. She made it to her feet, only to stagger sideways and collapse into the straw.

Very well, then. Standing wasn't a good idea. Did she have anything to eat or drink within reach? Back on hands and knees, she explored every bit of the area allowed her by her constraints.

Nothing.

Witmara groaned. She crawled over to the wall and sagged against it, leaning her back against the metal. No magic available. No food. No water. How badly was she injured? She started at her feet, pushing and prodding at her body, working her way up to her head. She still wore the tunic and trousers that were under her protective rain gear. But the rain gear was gone, along with her boots, hat, and heavy jacket. The back of her head was sticky and matted. She hoped that was just her blood and not anything else.

If it were brains you wouldn't be moving around like this, she told herself grimly.

The dubious asset of being a Healer's daughter, even a retired Healer, was that she knew far too much about what could go wrong with a body. She had received a heavy blow to her head, and that was why nausea kept roiling in her gut. Had probably vomited already, though she couldn't smell it over the oily stink. But other than the head injury she appeared to be all right. And no one had apparently raped her when she was unconscious, probably for fear of what potential protective magic *that* would trigger.

Witmara smiled bitterly. There were advantages to being known as a sorceress.

Now. As for what she could figure out about what magic she had available to her without actually *using* it—what tokens had been left to her?

She started with her hands. Toran's ring was still on her finger. The bracelet that had been Haran's eleventh birthday gift still clasped her wrist, surprisingly not removed when she had been shackled. Not much magic in either item, but they were something. The Regent's Ring was gone. She felt at her waist. Pouches had been taken off of her belt, so no glimmer dust, no small tokens, no bandages or healing supplies. The knife Inharise had given her on her seventh birthday was gone—Witmara's lips tightened at that. She would need to find it.

Her head throbbed and she didn't have the strength to continue chronicling what was gone. She closed her eyes and rested her head against the wall. But her thoughts continued to spin.

Where were they taking her? Directly to Chatain or somewhere else?

Gods, this would trigger a major war. She couldn't see either her mother or Rekaré accepting this abduction as anything other than a reason to attack Daran. But after this battle, oh Gods. It was going to be a slaughter. Even with the combined magics of her mother and cousin, even if Staul and Dovré plus Artel and Terat themselves came to fight…magic plus technology and the support of the other three of the Seven Crowned Gods made it an unequal fight.

Unless she could find a means to make it equal.

Witmara exhaled hard. She needed to figure out how to attack Chatain and Daran from within. He would want to see her himself, gloat over her—what was it he had said to her—he desired to make her Empress?

That makes him vulnerable.

Perhaps if she could communicate somehow to Betsona, link to that resistance she had alluded to, she would have a chance to weaken him. These ships would have to stop by the Ourigny Islands to restock. Betsona was there. If she could only find a means to escape….

Meanwhile, she should finish inventorying what tools she had left. Her hands went to her neck. One of her necklaces was still there. But only one—the necklace that matched Haran's bracelet. The amplifier was gone and—the Light of Medvara was gone from her neck.

Despair washed over her. Were both the Light and the Regent's Ring stolen by her captors or lost? Gods, she hoped that the Light and the Ring had managed to escape her capture. If they were lost, someone could pick them up and return it to her mother, that would give Katerin more strength. But if they had been captured—oh Gods. Gods.

Her head throbbed and her stomach spasmed, sending the sick bitter bile up her throat again. Witmara rested her head on her knees, wrapping her arms around her legs to hold herself tight.

My lord Staul,

she thought, holding herself tense, preparing for another jolt in case her restraints interpreted prayers as magic.

Nothing, not even the slightest bit of heat from the manacles.

At least prayers weren't restrained. Perhaps a call to the God would bring help.

Come to my aid, Lord Staul. Please. Let me know what has happened to those I love. Help me escape.

No answer from the God. Did that mean she had failed? That he had washed his hands of her?

Witmara shook her head. No. There had to be another explanation. Perhaps the sorcery that drove this ship was strong enough to keep Staul from hearing her.

But what kind of magic was this that shut out the Gods entirely? And oh, Gods, what had happened to Toran and Daro?

She moaned. Sobs broke free in spite of how hard she fought against their escaping. They wracked her body along with stomach spasms that brought up the bitter bile, until she crawled away from the wall and let herself vomit far away from where she intended to lie down. Then she wiped her mouth, tried to clean off her hands as best as she could with the straw, crept back to the wall, and collapsed, curled up with her back against the cold iron, shaking with tears for an untold period until everything faded around her again.

THEY SWOOPED ONTO CHIYAN AT FIRST LIGHT. KATERIN WAS IN A fell mood that frightened Rekaré. Her cousin had been the solid one in their past battles, the one who didn't fall apart even when the world went to pieces around them.

Now she led the charge on the village of her birth, the Spear of War and Unmaking clenched in her fist as she let Rainin thunder down the last length of the road winding down the ridge toward the gates of the walled town. She lowered the Spear as if it were a ram instead of a spear as she approached the gate, shrieking in Waykemese that was echoed by the *kinforost* immediately behind her, now mounted on good warhorses that could keep up with a daranval for a short period. Katerin had armed the *kinforost* with pairs of curved swords sheathed behind their backs.

"They will know how to use them on horseback," she had told Rekaré.

As they approached the gate, the *kinforost* dropped their horses' reins and drew their swords, holding them vertical while they screeched in concert with Katerin.

Katerin struck the gate with the Spear. It exploded apart as if it had been made of kindling shreds. Rainin leapt over the remnants of the gate and charged in, the *kinforost* on her heels, slashing with both weapons as they engaged fighters.

Rekaré had no time to think about what others were doing as they battled, Cenarth on her right, Sesenth on her left, Basnen biting and kicking at ground foes. They hacked and slashed until no resistance remained, surrounded by bodies and fighters on their knees, holding hands high to show they carried no weapons.

She eased Basnen to a halt and looked around. They had

reached Chiyan's main square, the force of their charge carrying them through the main street into a village that was about half the size of Dera. Stone and earthen buildings two and three stories high surrounded them, frightened faces peering around the edges of the windowsills.

"Who here has the power to surrender to me?" Katerin bellowed. Her voice echoed around the square, above the moans and groans of the surviving fallen. To Rekaré's relief most of those were not from their fighters.

No response.

"Who here has the power to surrender to me?" Katerin repeated. "I am Katerin ea Miteal, Banisher of Shadows, Leader of Medvara, daughter of Terani-the-God-Killer and Alame en Miteal, Alame the Cursed! You know who I am, Chiyan! Surrender or I put you to the flame!"

Gods. Katerin wouldn't, would she?

Cenarth and Sesenth rode up next to her.

"She isn't going to do that, is she?" Cenarth hissed.

"I do not know," Rekaré said.

"Battle rage has her hard," Detaluna said from the other side of Sesenth.

"She is possessed of the rage," Sesenth added.

"You're the one who can stop her," Cenarth said.

A bitter laugh broke free from Rekaré. "Who, me? *Rekaré Kinslayer?* Some will think I grow weak if I do that."

Nonetheless she understood the truth of what they said. She was the only one who could stop Katerin from doing something foolish and evil, intervene in the mixture of the rage and grief that drove her, remind her that she was not the only one who had lost a daughter to Chatain.

Oh Gods, I hope we can retrieve Witmara.

With a sigh she urged Basnen forward, Cenarth next to her. The *kinforost* moved to intercept her until she bared her teeth at them.

Before she could reach Katerin, a scar-faced young man leaning on a cane hobbled out from what appeared to be the town hall, a whitewashed earth two-story building with a bell tower. He stopped ten paces from Katerin and the *kinforost.*

"Katerin, daughter of Terani. Welcome to Chiyan." His voice carried like hers.

"Do you have the power to surrender to me?" Katerin raised the Spear. "I warn you, I am not in any mood to play word games."

"Oh, I am not here to play games, either. I thank you for ridding us of this plague upon Chiyan." He gestured at the fallen. "As always for our home of Chiyan, we have been viewed as rebels and suspected by the Witches Council. The Witches stationed these soldiers to prey upon us in the guise of keeping Chiyan compliant." He spat, then drew a ragged breath. "I am very happy to surrender to anyone who has rid us of this filth. I am Yitlisk, son of Marneri, daughter of Arendri."

Katerin startled. "Is that Arendri mother of Terani?"

He nodded.

Katerin shuddered. To Rekaré's relief the battle rage seemed to slip from her face. "Then we are kin," she said in a quieter voice.

"Yes. And since Marneri was called to the Witches Council as your mother was, that leaves me as mayor of Chiyan," Yitlisk said. He clutched his cane with both hands as he stiffly went to his knees. "I gladly surrender Chiyan to you, kinswoman, with my thanks for your elimination of these cursed soldiers. I surrender and implore you to rescue my mother from the Council. She went reluctantly—five days ago. Under extreme compulsion."

For a moment the battle rage tightened Katerin again.

"*They dared,*" she growled.

"Yes," Yitlisk said. "She was quite unwilling. I hope—I hope she has not been made *kendar* because of her resistance."

"We battled *shalkendar* last night," Katerin said in an odd, tight, voice. "She would not have been amongst them?"

"She would have died the final death first." Yitlisk's voice was flat.

"A woman of honor." Katerin sighed and seemed to sink into herself. Then she straightened up. "I add her to my list of grievances against the Witches Council."

"I thank you for that."

And I thank you, Yitlisk.

He had snapped Katerin out of her battle rage much more effectively than Rekaré ever could have—and Gods, she had learned so much more about the way Waykemin operated from that short exchange between Katerin and Yitlisk than she had over the years with Katerin. How much of her past before the Healing House had Katerin kept to herself?

We need to talk.

The *kinforost* also seemed to read Katerin's change of mood, wiping their swords clean and sheathing them. The Spear shifted to its Sword form so that Katerin could sheath it.

"I accept your surrender of Chiyan, Yitlisk. I ride hard to Forsim on a mission for vengeance. The Council caused the death of Inharise of Clenda, one very dear to me and mine. The Witches are tools of the Emperor-over-Sea, Chatain, who has captured my daughter. I mean to put an end to their misbegotten abuse of Waykemin before I deal with Chatain."

Yitlisk clung to his cane. "Chatain." He spat again. "Thank the Gods that deliverance has come at last. The Council is more than mere tools of that abomination. His visage strides openly in Waykemin. He aids the Council in their oppression, and Chiyan has been one of his primary targets. Chiyan willingly lends you aid, kinswoman."

Rekaré and Cenarth exchanged troubled looks. Cenarth raised his brows and she nodded. If Chiyan had been a primary target of Chatain, then its connection to Katerin—and Witmara

—must have been one factor. But she had never heard that Chiyan had been a hotbed of rebellion.

There is much we do not know about this place, she mouthed to Cenarth.

Yes, he answered.

Katerin sighed. She dismounted. "Call me cousin, Yitlisk." She glanced around and spotted Rekaré. "Another of my cousins rides with me, my father's great-niece Rekaré."

"Rekaré Kinslayer." Yitlisk flinched.

"My *cousin*." Katerin's voice was firm. "And I am hardly better. How many of Chiyan's own have fallen to my swords? How much blood price do I owe?"

Yitlisk ducked his head deferentially, leaning his head against his cane. "You owe no blood price for those who died. Those of Chiyan who died did so willingly." He groaned and his next words came out as a whisper. "My brother led the troop stationed here. He would not listen to me or our mother, but only sought glory. I saw him fall."

"My regrets for your loss. Have one of your people identify his body and we will give him appropriate respect."

"No need." Yitlisk grimaced. "We have been alienated for several years."

"As you wish." Katerin offered her hand to him. "Stand and tell me more. I have time for a cup of tea while you tell me about these." She gestured toward the fallen and surrendered. "Will I be able to gain their support? Or are all of them from elsewhere? How many were conscripted?"

Yitlisk seized her hand. Katerin braced and pulled him to his feet.

"Cousin, many of those conscripted soldiers from Chiyan took refuge in the alleys once you broke the gate. Those of Chiyan you battled were dedicated to the Council." He raised his voice. "Chiyani. How many of you will ride with Katerin daughter of Terani to overthrow the Witches Council?"

"Who do you intend to replace the Council with? More Witches?" a voice called from amongst a cluster of kneeling soldiers.

"Do you *want* more Witches?" Katerin challenged.

"Gods *no.*" The speaker rose slowly to her feet. "Once upon a time Waykemin was a haven for scholars and artists."

"That was before the Great Plague." Nenanim rode forward. "Waykemin used to have an elected Council before the Witches came through the Nerean Gate."

"What?" Katerin turned from Yitlisk, raising her brows. "The Witches are not from Waykemin?"

Nenanim shook his head. "They fled the Divine Confederation. Keratil would not have them, so they came to Waykemin."

"I had not heard of this before," Katerin said.

Rekaré shivered.

More hidden knowledge. Gods. This land is rife with twists and hidden history. What else don't we know?

"It is known only to scholars and the Council." Nenanim swallowed hard. He pointed to the standing woman. "Kirest, there, was once of the Scholars. I am pleased to see you were not made *kendar*, Kirest."

"I volunteered for the Swords of Chiyan before they could touch me," Kirest said. "So. Katerin, daughter of Terani. What will it be?"

"An elected Council as Nenanim describes, I suppose. Certainly no more Witches." Katerin pursed her lips. "But we have a battle to win before we can do that. Who chooses to ride against the Witches with me?"

"I will." Kirest pushed through those around her. One by one they rose to follow her. As she walked by other kneeling fighters, they slowly joined the line following Kirest, until two-thirds of those surrendered stood behind her. When she reached Katerin she knelt, bowing her head. "I offer you my sword for the liberation of Waykemin, Katerin daughter of Terani, Katerin ea Miteal." The others behind her did the same.

"And all of you are with her?" Katerin scanned the line. "You will work together after we win to rebuild Waykemin in a new image, one without the Witches?"

"Yes!" they cried.

"You offer me your swords and your hearts for the good of Waykemin?"

"Yes!"

"You swear this on the gold necklace of my patroness, Dovré the Golden?"

"*DOVRÉ!*" The crowd bellowed back. "*KATERIN! KATERIN! KATERIN EA MITEAL!*"

Was it Rekaré's imagination or did the land quiver under them at the mention of the Goddess?

Katerin ignored it if that was so. "Then I accept your vows. Your first task. Imprison those of you who have not sworn. Do not harm them but do not allow them to escape." She turned to Rekaré. "Cousin. I would have you meet with me and Yitlisk to gather information." She turned her attention to her *kinforost*. "Nenanim. Ylittim. Wisknani. Work with the Mer Galad and my commanders to ensure that our new recruits are integrated with our units, and that they are supplied and ready to ride by midmorning. We must ride fast now because at least one of those out there—" she waved toward those who had not vowed to support her. "—will have informed the Witches of what has happened here."

Rekaré dismounted as Katerin took Yitlisk's arm.

"And now," her cousin said as they walked. "Speak to me of what I can expect between here and Forsim."

METAL RATTLING ON METAL WOKE WITMARA. A FEEBLE LIGHT revealed three men in light armor on the other side of a set of bars, one inserting a key into a heavy lock on a narrow gate. She glanced around to take advantage of the light, quickly getting a measure of her cell before the men entered, looking for possible escapes. Her chains restrained her to half of it. Other chain sets hung from the wall—so this cell could hold four people. She returned her attention to the men entering the cell. None were bound, so what was their purpose here?

She used the wall as support to push herself to her feet without trembling. Her head still ached but not as bad as it had before.

"Do you bring me food and water?" she demanded, making her tone as imperious as she could in spite of a stuffy nose and scratchy throat from the damp and the straw chaff.

The tallest man strode across the cell and smacked her hard. She swayed but refused to let herself cry out or fall.

"Arrogant little half-breed Miteal witch scum. *Maybe* we will give you food and water, if you change your tone to something that better befits your station in life."

She managed to work up enough saliva to spit at him. "In your dreams, chattel of Chatain! I am Witmara, Regent-Leader of Medvara, daughter of Katerin ea Miteal and Metkyi beloved of Staul. I speak as I will!"

He flushed red—Gods these men were pale-skinned, as pale as Alicira had been—it didn't look right—and would have slapped her again except that a smaller man, the palest of all, stepped forward, seizing his hand.

"That's enough, Rearnex." He looked Witmara up and down appraisingly. "Quite the little sorceress you were there at the end. Too bad your spells were lacking." He sneered. "To be expected of a half-breed with aspirations above her station."

"Your people retreated because of my spells," she countered.

"So we did. But that doesn't matter. We obtained our prize."

He looked up and down her body again, then stepped forward to grab her chin.

As soon as he touched her she knew him as the magician who drove the ship.

But she hadn't felt him until he touched her.

Was that an effect of her bindings? Or some other magic she couldn't sense or counter because of her restraints?

She wrenched her chin free from his grasp and snapped at him, almost catching one finger in her teeth. He jumped back.

"A mistake, foolish little sorceress. I look forward to teaching you the consequences of such mistakes." He slammed her body hard against the wall, then punched her hard in the gut. As she doubled over, moaning in pain, he jerked her upright and planted his lips on hers.

Outrage pulsed through her.

My lord Staul, this is not right! Answer me now!

Warmth radiated from her bracelet and necklace. Power exploded from her, sending him reeling back even as she doubled over with sharp pain that quickly faded. His companions rushed forward as a shape shimmered into being, that of a neatly dressed man in black swallowtail coat and breeches with tall black boots, a bone and tooth necklace laced around his neck, his black hair plaited into a heavy braid, skin the redbark shade of the Keldarans, akin to her own. He looked familiar, like a portrait her mother had—her father? But she had never seen him attired like a Medvaran court dandy. Was this her father or was this another form of Staul?

Stop,

he commanded.

Rearnex and the other man halted.

"Who are you?" the man who had assaulted her demanded.

I am Metkyi, Messenger of Staul, and you touch this woman at your peril.

It *was* her father. But Gods, she didn't know that he was so exalted in Staul's ranks! He had never appeared as such in his infrequent visits.

"What does the Messenger want from us?" the man who had assaulted her sneered. "Why does Staul care about a Miteal?"

Larien en Ralsem.

Her father pointed at him.

You will pay for hurting my daughter.

He snapped his fingers. A bruise rose on Larien's cheek. Another snap, and Larien doubled over, clutching his gut. A third snap, and Larien screeched, his eyes widening as his hands moved from gut to crotch, collapsing to his knees.

And that for what you intended. My daughter is not for your foul uses.

Larien.

Was this Betsona's mysterious cousin? Then why was he so rude to her? Surely he knew that Betsona had written of him to her.

Larien gasped for breath as her father scowled at him.

"What. Do. You. Want." His voice might have been submissive but his expression was wrathful.

You will treat my daughter with honor and respect. You will send someone to tend to her hurts. You will feed and water her, and provide her with means to care for her bodily functions.

"I suppose you want me to tuck her into bed every night and read her bedtime stories, too? Perhaps even turn her loose?"

Oh that was a mistake.

Gods, didn't the Darani understand what happened if you angered even a Messenger of Staul? Or was this an example of the things Betsona had alluded to in her messages—that Chatain and his followers already imagined themselves to be as powerful as the Gods?

But I thought Larien was one of her allies.

Her father strode forward and punched Larien.

> The God allowed her capture for a purpose. But she is not your toy.

He towered over Larien.

"You have no power over me, you and your God! I am a follower of Nitel!"

> If I have no power over you, then how could I do this?

Her father ripped a necklace off of Larien's neck, holding it high.

Witmara's eyes widened as she spotted Nitel's glyph on the silver disk hanging from the broken chain.

"No," Larien gasped, grabbing at the disk as her father dangled it just out of his reach. "*No.* You can't do this! The ship will sink and all will perish, especially your daughter! I need that to motive the ship!"

> Perhaps she should become a ghost to haunt your family,

her father snarled.

He pinched the disk. Tarnish spread over it. Nitel's sigil glowed, briefly, then faded. He threw it on the floor in front of Larien.

There you are. You can continue to motive the
ship. You can even keep my daughter under
magical restraint. But you will not harm her, nor
will any of your people cause her harm. She is
under Staul's protection—and mine. Now. Get
her water, and food. And bring a Healer to deal
with her head injury.

Larien snatched up the necklace. He stared at the disk. "Gods. You've marked it for Staul." He turned the disk toward Metkyi, his voice rising hysterically. "You don't understand! Chatain will—will hurt me for this. This makes my warship nothing more than a cargo hauler!"

Witmara saw that the disk was not just tarnished, but that a small glyph of Staul's was stamped at the bottom of it, directly below Nitel's mark.

Then a cargo hauler it will be, and you will
suffer whatever consequences Chatain has in
store for you. Now. Get care for my daughter.

Larien stuffed the disk and broken chain into a pouch. He crawled away from her father before he stood.

"This isn't over, for either of you," he hissed. "Nitel will have her way."

No. It is not over. But bring care for my
daughter, or by Staul, I will be a terror on this
ship of yours. NOW!

The three men fled, leaving the cell door slightly ajar. Witmara listlessly rattled her chains. They were no looser than they had been before. She sank back to the floor.

"Thank you, Father," she gasped, shivering as she realized what had happened. "But why can't I go free?" She winced at how petulant that sounded, but *Gods.* She hurt. She was hungry and thirsty. And what had happened to Toran and Daro?

He dropped to his knees in front of her.

We are constrained in what we can do for you,
my daughter. Not just by the magic present in
this ship but by the judgment of Artel. Staul
pushes his limits by allowing me to protect you.
I had to plead to Artel to be granted this much
power, and it only came about because of other
elements in the mix.

Spectral hands stroked her cheeks and took hold of her face. The contact warmed and became more solid the longer it lasted —something she remembered her mother mentioning about her sporadic visits with him.

If I don't touch him first, he becomes more material, more solid.

"Oh, Father." She blinked hard, fighting back tears. Why was she so teary?

Witmara. Daughter. Witmara of the promise, as
I told your mother when I died.

His hands slipped from her face. He wrapped his arms around her and held her close. She buried her head in his chest. He smelled faintly of musk, and horses, but it was an old scent, as if she had opened a long-closed storage chest. Or was this just a memory of the few things of his that her mother kept stored, and brought out to brood over on the anniversary of his death every winter?

He was a shadow. A ghost. He shouldn't have a scent.

But he shouldn't have been able to attack Larien and imprint that disk, either.

Messenger of Staul.

That was no small position serving the Gods, but a rank just below them, with its own power.

And she was his daughter?

Witmara shivered, and his arms tightened on her.

Footsteps. Metkyi pulled back and rose as Rearnex returned

with two women bearing a waterskin, a tray with something liquid in a bowl, and healing supplies in a shallow bowl. They both wore bonding bracelets and were darker-skinned than any of the men, though their skin was more yellow-brown than Witmara's redbark tan.

The woman with the tray and waterskin set the tray down in front of Witmara, bowing nervously first to Metkyi and then to Witmara. She reminded Witmara slightly of Setkin.

"It's not much, my lady, my lord, but it is what my lord Larien commanded," she whimpered.

"It's food."

Much as she wanted to gobble it down, she needed water first. Witmara picked up the waterskin and took a cautious swallow. She grimaced at the brackish taste of the water but drank anyway. It eased the scratchiness in her throat.

Not too much,

her father advised.

She scowled at him. Gods, he sounded just like her mother in Healer mode. Still, she set the waterskin aside.

"Thank you—what is your name?" she asked the woman.

The woman glanced worriedly at Rearnex. He stood there impassively, arms crossed.

"Nereast, my lady," she said finally.

Witmara coughed, a hacking cough that brought up crud and muck from her lungs. She scuttled sideways and spat, wanting to aim it at Rearnex but deciding against that petty rebellion, then returned to take another sip of water.

"You do not need to use 'my lady' when speaking to me, Nereast," she said. "It is not a title used in Varen except when speaking to the Gods."

Rearnex snorted.

Witmara reached for the bowl. A thin film of grease floated on the top of brown broth-like liquid.

"I'm sorry my lady but that's all we have for those such as us," Nereast gabbled.

"That is all right." She took a tentative sip.

Gods, the soup was every bit as greasy and sour as she feared. But it was still nourishing. She carefully sipped some more, then drank a couple of mouthfuls of water.

"My lady," the other woman said. "May I tend to your wounds?"

Witmara eyed her. The woman was filthy. Her mother would have had a fit.

Healers must be clean.

A fundamental precept of the Keldaran Healing House. But something had to be done about her head.

"Yes," she said. "But wash your hands first. What is your name?"

The woman scowled and shook her head, less deferential than Nereast.

Remember this one.

Witmara vowed not to take any food from this woman. Healer she might be, but she certainly was not in the same class of Healer as her mother.

The healer picked up the waterskin and sloshed some water into the shallow bowl, then dipped the soap in and washed her hands. Then she picked up a rag, dipped it in the bowl, and moved toward Witmara. The water stung as the woman dabbed at her wound, muttering softly to herself.

"Is it infected?"

"How should I know?" The woman dipped the rag in the bowl again, rinsing out mud and blood. "Not enough light to see here, and there's so much *stuff* caked in your hair that I can't see it."

"You could shave around it."

"I have nothing useful for shaving." The woman resumed dabbing at Witmara's hair. "At least nothing I would choose to use on any person that mattered."

Those comments appeased Witmara somewhat. Perhaps this healer just had the coarse manner because she spent so much time in the company she did. How many of the tortured and tormented did she have to deal with on a daily basis?

The healer finished, applied an ointment to the cuts on Witmara's head, then wrapped a bandage awkwardly around it. Witmara sat back up and reluctantly reached for the greasy goop. She forced herself to consume the mess sip by sip, then fish out the meat chunks from the bottom that were mostly gristle and fat. Then she drank more water.

"All right. That's enough," Rearnex said. "Let's go."

The women scuttled out, leaving her in darkness except for a faint glow where her father stood. Witmara settled back against the wall.

"Well, that was something," she said. Her father stirred, now looking more wraith-like and transparent, at least from what she could see in this damn darkness.

Alas, it is the minimum that these barbarians give a prisoner.

"You can't do anything about that?"

He shook his head.

"Can you tell me...." She paused, and swallowed hard. "Did Toran and Daro survive?"

I cannot tell you that. I am bound only to protect you and keep you alive.

Regret colored his voice.

> If it were up to me, I would tell you. But Artel
> keeps us on a tight rein, and if I cross his
> bounds, you lose my presence here.

"I understand. Thank you." She sighed, wondering if petitioning Dovré would be of any help.

Probably not.

The Goddess faced the same restrictions. Besides, she had protection and had been given food and drink. What else could be done if the God couldn't get her free? Staul was more fearsome than Dovré, and if these lackeys disregarded him, then they were even less likely to respect the Goddess.

She yawned, sleepy again, and eased herself back down into the little nest she had created in the straw. At least she had the straw to insulate her from the floor.

Her father settled next to her head.

> You may not see me here, but I will stand
> watch. We may have other visitors who will not
> be as amenable.

"That's fine. Thank you."

As she slid back into sleep, she fancied that she felt his hand gently stroke her head.

Fantasy or not, it was comforting to have her father's protection. Even if he was only a shadow—he *was* the Messenger of Staul. She doubted that anyone with foul intentions would bother her for a while.

Not even Larien en Ralsem.

DAUGHTER OF THE PROMISE

Late afternoon brought Katerin and her army to Forsim, approaching from the east of the city instead of the west as would be expected from an invader, tracing a route that cut over a high mountain pass. Yitlisk's advice and his identification of a shorter route from Chiyan to Forsim proved valuable, saving them half a day's ride as well as routing them around several loyalist towns. They descended from the mountains rather than riding across open plains bracketing the Waykemin River. Kirest knew many of the hidden routes used by Chiyani rebels to harass the Witches' forces.

Katerin brooded as they looked down on Forsim from one of the foothills while their forces organized for attack. Like Chiyan, things looked normal, with people passing in and out through the various gates of the walled city, moving along the banks of the Waykemin.

Nenanim rode next to her. "Looks quiet."

"We thought that about Chiyan. And they knew we were there."

"They know we're here too. Probably know that you broke

the gates at Chiyan. I don't know if you'll be able to do that again. They'll have them magicked up beyond belief."

Katerin shivered. "*I* don't want to do that again."

But after the *shalkendar* attack, after Chatain's bragging about capturing Witmara—she was crazed and just wanting to *be done with it.* And it had almost gone bad.

Almost.

It had been so bad that Rekaré had been moved to intervene —Rekaré, of all people, *Rekaré Kinslayer.*

Katerin Butcher of Chiyan they would have called her. She would have been in the wrong—and after listening to Yitlisk, she was ever-so-grateful that he had snapped her out of that course. His account of what had happened in Waykemin since she left at thirteen gave Katerin a much different picture of her homeland than she had been imagining, confirmed by those of her *kinforost* that she had spoken with after talking to Yitlisk.

Waykemin had always been a land of inequality—she had known that from dealing with the *ushar* and *kendar* as servants (*slaves,* she corrected herself) when young, had shivered at the rare appearances of the *shalkendar,* but this?

Things had become much, much worse here since the fall of Zauril. Perhaps she should have returned to see things for herself before now—but then again, given Chatain's apparent close ties to the Witches, would *Katerin ea Miteal* have even been allowed to leave had she ever returned to Waykemin?

Waykemin was not your responsibility, she told herself, as she had been telling herself regularly since they left Chiyan. Even as Yitlisk's presence reminded her that there was more to Waykemin than just her needs.

You were glad to leave and they were glad to see you go. You are now Leader of Medvara—and that brought a twinge, with worry about Witmara. But she dared not let herself succumb to the same battle rage that had possessed her in Chiyan. She had been oh-so-close to doing something awful.

"Yes," Nenanim said, bringing her back to the present. "Repeating a previous strategy isn't going to work. We have to do something different."

"We're not set up for a siege."

Nor do I have the time. Not if we have to pursue Witmara to Daran.

"You have your cousin. You have the *kinforost*. You never were going to defeat the Witches by sheer force of numbers at Forsim—or by breaking down the gates."

"I'm surprised that Karnoi and Cirdel haven't moved against me themselves since we entered Waykemin."

One reason why I don't have much of a plan for Forsim. I thought we would have seen the Hunt by now. Some manifestation. Something that the Witches would work through to bring about the battle.

But she wasn't going to share that with Nenanim. She had thought they would have more time to prepare for this confrontation. Now, with Witmara captured….Gods, how had her daughter managed to get seized? Between all the support she had, and fighting on home ground, she should have been able to evade Chatain's forces—at least for longer.

What had gone wrong in Medvara?

Not that it mattered, except that she had to defeat the Witches quickly. It was a blessing to find Yitlisk, who had plenty of ideas of his own about what Waykemin would look like without the Witches. She just needed to set things up so that he could go about fulfilling those visions. The Chiyani seemed dedicated enough to him. Hopefully that would extend to all of Waykemin.

"And you think what you've gone through hasn't been due to their influence?" Nenanim said, once again drawing her back from her brooding. "The Gods can't intervene that directly but as a former *kendar,* I can tell you that Karnoi and Cirdel worked directly through us as their tools."

"You didn't see what happened in Medvara when Alicira

died," Katerin said. "Or Wickmasa, where the Twin Gods tried to kill me and Metkyi. The manifestations of their Hunt in both places."

"And what happened after that?"

"We banished Karnoi and Cirdel from Keldara and Clenda. And Medvara…." She swallowed hard. "Eventually even from Medvara. At the cost of Rekaré's daughter."

Nenanim nodded. "The Balance at work. I saw what happened when Karnoi and Cirdel rode your mother to banish Nitel from Waykemin. There are reasons why the Seven Crowned Gods do not normally directly interfere with a human country's political affairs. The Balance doesn't allow it. Things —happen."

"And yet Nitel was allowed to do just that, not just here but in Medvara. To hear some tell it, Daran as well."

"I don't know what to say about that, save that Nitel went rogue."

"Many times. When are the Gods going to stop her?"

"Perhaps they are doing so, in their own good time, for their own purposes." Nenanim shrugged. "Who is to say what their ultimate goals are?"

"Sometimes I wonder." Katerin sighed. "Well, this speculation gains us nothing. How are we going to take Forsim?"

"There are magical vulnerabilities. I've been talking with Kirest, and that's brought back memories."

"Really." Katerin focused on him. "Tell me more."

"A charge like you did on Chiyan won't work for all the reasons we just discussed. But a slow, measured approach will. There are traps set all around Forsim meant to stop a fast charge, but not riders approaching at a slow pace."

"And then?"

"Summon magic when you reach Forsim's walls. Attack with magic. I need to sketch the layout out for you and your commanders, so you know the best way to array yourselves."

"Let's discuss this as part of the commanders' meeting."

Nenanim almost seemed to bounce on horseback at that prospect. "Yes. Oh yes. It has been ages since a scholar like myself has been taken seriously in a commanders' meeting." His face tightened. "I also remembered being made *kendar* and why. I discovered some old records that discussed the coming of the Witches to Waykemin. It countered the legends, and—well, they don't come off that well."

"I am sorry for that."

"But it helped me remember vulnerabilities. After I faced that memory and accepted it during our ride here, I remembered what I had learned about the vulnerabilities of Waykemin —and Forsim. All that is why I was made *kendar.* I went too far and knew too much."

"I look forward to hearing all about this." She turned Rainin back toward the main body of their force.

"Oh, there's quite a bit of lore about the founding of Forsim," Nenanim said. He continued, clearly eager to share what he had learned.

Katerin let him speak, half-listening as she thought about how best to attack Forsim.

MORE RATTLING OF METAL ON METAL. WITMARA SAT UP FROM her drowsing. Her father's presence suddenly became more *there,* as if he had been leaving a shadow of himself to monitor her while doing other things. She supposed he had other tasks as the Messenger of Staul besides defending his daughter.

She relaxed as she recognized Nereast and the anonymous healer. A different guard accompanied them and stood stiffly by the door. Nereast carried a tray with a bowl and small water-skin on it, while the healer carried the same shallow bowl she used to clean Witmara's wound previously.

"This food is better than what I brought this morning, my lady," Nereast said. "It's mush but at least it's still warm."

"Mush?" She had to wonder if that was the best available—or was she sharing servants' food?

"Dinner leftovers for us lesser folk," the healer said dryly.

Nereast cringed at the criticism, glancing back at the guard. He didn't seem to have noticed.

"I thank you for this," Witmara said. She took a bite. Not greasy. There was even a little sweetness to it that suddenly tasted very good, enough to make her gobble it down.

As soon as she finished eating, set the bowl down, and sipped from the waterskin, the healer moved in.

"Nereast, can you keep the guard busy?" she said in a low tone.

Nereast's eyes widened but she nodded and gathered up the bowl. "Petronin, what did you think of Kalinera's mush tonight? The prisoner seemed to like it and you know how picky those Miteal and Ralsem are."

"Bend over so I can check your wound," the healer said loudly. She started to unwrap the bandage and bent close to Witmara's ear. "You are a friend of Betsona?"

"Yes," Witmara whispered, suspicion creeping on her. How would this healer know of Betsona? "The shadows are our friend."

"Shadows protect us from the reddest of red paths." The healer repeated the correct response.

"Shadows slip through the darkness that covers those red paths."

"Shadows hide us as we walk in parallel." The healer straightened up. She dabbed her cloth into the bowl and began to clean Witmara's injury again. She winced at the touch of water on the injury.

"Until the day that shadows reveal themselves." There, that was the last phrase. Would the healer identify herself now?

The healer bent close to Witmara. "This light is difficult," she complained loudly. In a quieter voice, she continued. "Ankari ea Ralsem at your service, Witmara. Betsona is the daughter of my mother's sister."

"I understand." She wished she could look up, assess Ankari's body language, but that would interfere with Ankari's work and raise suspicion. "Ouch!"

A dab of Ankari's cloth was too hard. Something wasn't quite right here, even though Ankari had given her the proper answers.

Best to play along.

"I'm sorry, but I need to clean this more. I brought some ointment that should work better on your scalp this time."

"Understood. What ointments are you using? My mother was once a Healer."

"Willow bark powder mixed with a clear gel solution."

"Do you not have arnica? My mother used to use it on many of the cuts and scrapes I gathered as a girl out playing."

"Arnica is not available to me," Ankari said, her voice suddenly going dead. "Not to healers who work with the lesser folk."

Strange. It grows freely in Varen.

Perhaps it was different in Daran...but the lore around arnica had come from Daran originally, hadn't it?

"What do you know of Betsona's work?" Witmara whispered as Ankari secured a less awkward bandage on her head.

"I monitor the movements of Chatain's navy," Ankari answered softly. "Or at least I have been. We will see what happens to Larien once we reach port. While he will be favored for bringing you in, losing the value of this ship as a warship is not good."

"Are you about done yet?" the guard—*Petronin,* Witmara reminded herself, she needed to remember these names— snapped. "I've more to deal with than tend to Miteal scum."

"Done." Ankari guided Witmara back up. "You should find that more comfortable, my lady."

"It is. Thank you."

Ankari bowed to her. Petronin herded both Nereast and Ankari away.

So that is an interesting development,

her father commented softly once they were alone.

"Do you think she was telling the truth?"

In part, but there are pieces that don't fit. Do you know what relation Betsona's family is to Chiral?

"Chiral was Zauril's niece, if I remember correctly, the daughter of his brother Zauberin. Betsona is Chatain's surviving sibling, the daughter of a slave concubine. Not a close relationship."

He nodded.

This Ankari doesn't fit. Plus, why would she be a slave on this ship if she is kin to Betsona? Betsona is not a slave. Why does she not call Betsona cousin? That is a common usage amongst Aireii kin.

"Agreed. And—she doesn't know arnica. What healer would be ignorant of arnica? As you said, the pieces don't fit."

Her father smiled.

Ah, daughter of mine. I am glad to see that a head blow has not completely muddled your thinking. Something else. Neither Larien en Ralsem nor Ankari ea Ralsem feel right. Both are glamored by the same source.

"Chatain?"

So it appears. They are protected, and the wards reek of Nitel, Karnoi, and Cirdel. Do not trust either of them until we gain more information.

"She did know the code phrases for Betsona's networks."

Are you sure Betsona is not another of Chatain's tools?

"She hates her brother. I don't know the whole story, but he is the reason she is crippled."

It was magitech gone bad. Did she ever give you a reason for contacting you and your mother?

"To keep us aware of events in Daran. To provide me with the true history of our origins in Daran."

And conveniently inspire you to lead a rebellion.

"Not Mother. Empire has never been her interest. And Rekaré denies any desire toward Empire, even though she has vowed vengeance on Chatain."

I wonder what notion Rekaré has now.

Metkyi's form grew more solid, glowing faintly as he tapped his fingers on his knees thoughtfully.

I do not know her as I once did—when she became Kinslayer her purposes became hidden from me. Ah well. We have more urgent concerns. What is your goal now, daughter?

"Escape, if I can once we reach the islands."

An island escape has limits. How do you plan
to get back to Varen?

"I don't know. But should I manage to get ashore, lose myself for several hours to several days—that will delay my meeting with Chatain, and perhaps give time for a rescue party from Medvara to reach me."

That depended on how badly the battle had gone after she had been knocked out. On whether Toran and his father survived. Or whether any who followed her had to wait for her mother and Rekaré in Waykemin. Pacing. Pacing was everything.

Rescue?

Her father's tone went sarcastic.

Seriously? You contemplate delay in hopes of a
rescue?

"Father, I fully intend to meet Chatain face-to-face and defeat him. Eventually. But without the opportunity to find support within Daran, any rebellion I might lead is wasted time. Escape gives me time to muster a force to meet any rescue party and build the foundation for a rebellion."

I see.

A subtle red glow rose from his hands, a welcome break from the unrelenting darkness.

You want time to create a resistance force, not
a rescue.

"*I* will be Empress of Daran," she said, the words startling her as she said them. "It is time that the Miteal reclaim the throne. Rekaré does not want it. Betsona faces health challenges and is of the Ralsem, and Medvara is enough for my mother. It needs her healing touch and responds much better to her than it ever has to me. If I had the same ties to the land as she did, I wouldn't be here now. Medvara would have warned me that danger approached. Instead, it remained quiet. Even in the midst of working my spell I would have known."

Chatain would have been aware of your mother's connection to Medvara?

"I think that any with eyes to see would notice how Medvara has thrived in the past seven years since my mother became Leader. The land did all right under Rekaré and Cenarth—but Mother makes it blossom."

What of Rekaré and Cenarth's son?

"Linyet is committed to the Two Nations. He always has been, and we knew that as children. No. I will be Empress."
Her father chuckled.

Witmara, daughter of the promise. Gods, if I'd truly known what that meant in my death vision. It is a gamble. You know that. You face a very powerful foe. Rekaré quailed at facing her father for several years before dueling with him, and Zauril was no Chatain when it came to strength of magic. That was one reason why Rekaré ambushed him instead of swooping down with an army. She felt that stealth would be more effective. You are bolder than she was.

"I am not Rekaré. I grew up around the court of the Two Nations, both summer and winter, as well as learning the traders' craft in Wickmasa. I spent the last seven years in

Medvara. I do not fear facing the Darani Emperor. And I am descended from Alame en Miteal, not the Miteals cursed by Etikar, Dunaran and Chatain. I am also a daughter of Wickmasa in Keldara. My father is the Messenger of Staul, and I am dedicated to Staul." She set her jaw firmly. "I will admit I am nervous. But. If any of us have been trained and prepared for this—besides Alicira—it has been me." Something inside of her released. At last. She had toyed with the idea, but now—it rang true.

She would become Empress or die.

A slow smile spread over her father's shadowy face.

> Gods. I doubt that either your mother or I had any understanding of what we made in you. But I am grateful to Staul for you. And to your mother's Dovré. Well. We have time. You have more lessons to learn.

He gestured and a board with alternating red and black squares appeared between them. Three rows of black figures appeared on the black squares in front of him, then three rows of red figures on the black squares in front of her. The innermost figures were the smallest and all the same.

Witmara picked up one of hers. It was a foot soldier carrying a spear. She set it back and picked up a figure from the middle row—archer. Only half the figures in this row were archers. The others were horse soldiers. The back row was a mixture of two of Dovré's healers, two priests of Staul, two of Terat's Sorcerer-Captains on tiny ships, two shamans of Artel, and the center-most figure—a sorceress. Witmara picked up the sorceress.

It had her face.

"What game is this?" she asked her father, her voice tight. "I have never seen this before."

The Great Game of Nations, as played by the
Gods. It is time you learned how to play it,
given your aspirations and what it will take to
reach them. Few living beings are so privileged.

"I—see." Witmara swallowed hard. "I do not aspire to Godhood."

But you face one who does. One who has been
prepared by Nitel.

He cocked his head as if he were listening to a speaker she couldn't hear.

Ah. We are fortunate. The Speaker for the Lady
Dovré comes to aid in your coaching.

A blue shimmer. Witmara gulped as she saw who it was.

Alicira ea Miteal as Speaker for Dovré was gloriously radiant, her silver hair unbound and glowing bright enough to illuminate the cell. Though she retained the lined and mature aspect that Witmara remembered, she was whole and strong, her hands straight and not gnarled and twisted, her body no longer frail and sickly, but reasonably plump, truly the Star of Medvara that she had once been called. She bent to kiss Witmara on the forehead.

Greetings and blessings, kinswoman, beloved
of Staul. It is time that one of us finally stepped
up to righting this wrong.

"Alicira," Witmara breathed. "I—does Rekaré know how honored you are?"

Alicira shook her head.

My daughter has her own path. I will not interfere with it. I cannot interfere with her, not even to share my exalted status. As for you— there are things you must learn, and not much time left to study them.

"And Melarae?"

Sorrow crossed that bright face.

My granddaughter is safe with the Goddess, and heals, though it is a slow process.

She tapped the board.

Now. Metkyi, are you ready?

As always, Alicira.

Then let us begin.

She settled next to Witmara.

First, know your opponent's pieces.

Alicira pointed toward the pieces in front of Metkyi. The innermost two rows were the same as hers. But the back row… Witmara recognized the Voices for Nitel, and four wolves were clearly from Karnoi and Cirdel's Hunt. She didn't recognize the two figures who wore grotesque masks, and the central piece….

The Sorcerer, with Chatain's face.

Witmara drew a ragged breath. "I see this matches my foes in real life. But who are the masked ones?"

> The Witches of Waykemin. There is much more involved in this war than you realize. Than any of you have realized. Time for that to change for all of you, including your mother, as she is now learning while she proceeds to battle in Waykemin.

Alicira snapped her fingers.

> The Board as it currently appears in Artel's chambers.

The pieces rearranged themselves.

It was not much consolation to see that both sides had lost equal numbers of players.

FORSIM, AND THE GREAT GAME

BASNEN WAS TIGHT AS A COILED SPRING UNDER REKARÉ AS THEY approached Forsim at a steady walk, following Katerin, her *kinforost*, and the Chiyani former troops who knew this land, no matter what illusions the Witches raised. The Maker snarled restlessly on her chest as the latest shadow bore down on them.

She was back on that hillside with her great-uncle Alame down, dying, and the Shadowwalker Gegarth charging toward her.

Her fingers itched to draw her sword and hack his head off with one God-enhanced blow, like she had done in real life.

End it now!

the Maker demanded.

No. Hold.

Gegarth jabbed at her with his sword.

Rekaré stared straight ahead, not reacting. He faded away with a scream.

"Forsim guards itself with illusions," Nenanim had said in the commanders' meeting. *"Shadows. You must not engage with them. If those in the lead ride through them without reacting, the shadows will fade. Those who follow you will not see them. It is a flaw in the Witches' plans because it depends on the assumption that there are few who have the discipline to pass through those shadows without engaging with them. If an army is led by those with such discipline, however, that defense fails."*

When pressed as to the nature of those shadows, Nenanim could only say that it was individual to each person.

Time for the next shadow. Rekaré tensed, not knowing who would be next.

Her father galloped toward her, sneering. He swung a sword at her, the first stroke of the battle they had engaged in before she had beheaded him.

Rekaré closed her eyes, but that didn't banish the vision as his sword aimed for her neck.

Another ghost she did not regret. Murderer of her grandparents and great-grandfather, he who had caused the death of so many others. Killer who had left only Alame and Alicira alive, and had he not sought to breed a master sorcerer—herself—Alicira would have died in that bloodbath as well.

Why do you refrain from battling, Lady of Sorrow?

the Maker queried querulously.

Hold. Hold,

she responded. She *had* to remain in control.

Zauril's sword passed through her neck without harm, and he faded. Basnen quivered and Rekaré patted the golden mare's neck.

Katerin continued to scatter the mixture of glimmer dust and ash as she rode in the lead. It shimmered blue and gold above them but did not dissipate the Shadows.

"This will shield us from archers, at least, once they attack," Katerin had said. *"And it will make passage easier for those who follow us."*

Next came Chiral, sniggering and sneering as she seductively minced toward Rekaré.

Rekaré focused on Katerin's back and kept Basnen walking straight through the shadow, ignoring Chiral as she swiped at Rekaré with elongated claw-like fingernails. Basnen would have reacted to this one except that Rekaré's fingers closed tightly on the reins.

She killed your daughter!

the Maker screeched.

Why do you not act?

Hold!

Rekaré commanded. She didn't need to justify herself to the Maker. It had guided her hand when she killed Chiral, after all, and earned herself the epithet *Rekaré Kinslayer.*
Basnen continued to fuss.

It is not real, dear one,

she repeated to her daranval.

Not real at all. Do not let the Maker bother you, nor the images. Listen only to me.

Basnen snorted.

Chatain sneered at her and raised his hands high to attack.

Rekaré tamped down the surge of anger she felt at his sight —the Maker would take that as permission to act, as touchy as it was now. He and his father had brought so much harm to her family. She needed to exact her revenge on him—but not now, not now. He was an illusion, nothing more. *Just an illusion,* she reminded herself as he raised a spell and threw it at her.

> Just an illusion!

she snapped at the Maker.

> They are all illusions! Hold and do not react!

Then she was flooded by images. *Melarae. Linyet. Katerin. Witmara. Alame.*

> Worthless mother!

> You left us!

> Kinslayer!

> Why did you let me be captured?

> Failure! I had so many hopes for you!

Her mother, Inharise, and Heinmyets were not amongst the chorus. Those were the shadows she didn't think she could ignore without stopping to try to explain her choices. At least the Maker didn't respond to these voices.

At least.

Rekaré glanced to one side to check on her Mer Galad. All

rode with their faces set hard, staring ahead, Detaluna on this side looking grim and fell. But they all held.

The other side. Cenarth next to her held firm, but she knew his expression all too well. He was sickened by whatever it was he saw. Sesenth and the other riders held solid, unreactive, but Senth also showed signs of struggling.

"It is all illusion," she said out loud. "I see old foes and our friends turned against us. It is not real. Not real at all."

Her voice seemed to break the shrieking around her. The shadows faded somewhat.

Maybe they should talk more?

"Mer Galad!" she shouted. "The shadows fade if you speak."

"Perhaps a song," Cenarth said.

He began one of their old favorites, *The Dance of Staul and Dovré*, the story of the courtship of those two Gods. His baritone quavered at first, but grew stronger as others joined in. Even the Shadowwalkers knew this one. The voices grew stronger as the song became more ribald, the flirting between the two Gods becoming more and more seductive before the final peak.

The world around them grew brighter and the Maker calmed on her chest, still restless, still wanting to strike, but patient and ready for her command.

Katerin sang next, a song Rekaré didn't know but the Waykemese must have, both Chiyani and *kinforost*, given their enthusiastic chorus. The oppressive reek of blood and guts faded, until it was clear that they rode along a wide road, toward the closed gates of Forsim. The shadows faded away as Katerin halted Rainin forty paces from the gates.

"Riders, take your places." Her voice carried clear and loud.

Rekaré brought the Mer Galad behind the *kinforost*. Yitlisk and the Chiyani formed ranks on either side of them. She caught a glimpse of Linyet leading the riders from the Two Nations to their appointed place.

It seemed like forever but was really only a few moments before they were all where they were supposed to be, just as Nenanim had sketched. Katerin drew her sword. It transformed into a long version of the Spear. She thumped its butt hard on the ground.

Was it Rekaré's imagination, or did the earth shiver as the Spear struck the ground?

"Tranarin. Whatever you call yourself these days. I call you out as Chief Priestess of the Council of Witches. I, Katerin ea Miteal, Katerin daughter of Alame en Miteal and Terani-the-God-Killer, pronounce you and your Council as corrupt—" *thump!* went the Spear's butt on the ground again, "venial," *thump!* "and utterly without the strength, power, or integrity to rule Waykemin. Thus do I speak as the Banisher of Shadows."

Thump, thump, thump!

Laughter from above the gates. "What makes you think you have any power here, half-breed brat?" a masked figure called down from the ramparts.

"Are you afraid of me? Come on down and call me names to my face. I have authority given to me by Dovré and Staul."

"Dovré and Staul have no power here!"

"Do they?" Katerin threw a handful of glimmer dust into the air. It shimmered into a shield above their fighters. "Then what is this? I am dedicated to Dovré. I should not be able to work this magic. But here I am."

"Illusions!"

"No more than the ones your failed defenses hurled at us. The world is changing, Tranarin. Does the Chief Priestess of the Witches fear the Banisher of Shadows?"

"You are nothing more than a bastard half-breed misbegotten twerp who should have been made *kendar*! Then we would not have to deal with the likes of you!"

Katerin laughed. "And you are still as much of a cowardly bully as you were when we were children, Tranarin!" Her voice sharpened. "Are you afraid to face me? I am the Leader of Medvara. The Banisher of Shadows. Daughter of the Miteal. *I* am not afraid of *you*. Meet me now, face-to-face, and save our followers from this battle. That is what a true leader would do, not a base-born bully." She threw another handful of glimmer dust. Their shields thickened. "I call you afraid. A coward. Are you so distrustful of your magic that you dare not face a *misbegotten half-breed bastard* directly?" She spat out the last words.

Arrows rained down on them, but the glimmering shield held overhead, deflecting them harmlessly away.

The masked figure shrieked. The main gate of the city opened. Warriors poured out.

"I guess that's their answer," Cenarth growled, drawing his sword.

Rekaré cast several handfuls of glimmer dust over her riders. *"Protect,"* she whispered. That spell would not last for long, but even a short period would give them advantage.

The *kinforost* drew their swords along with Yitlisk and the Chiyani rebels. Katerin showered glimmer dust on them, just as the other commanders were doing with their forces. Then the *kinforost*, Yitlisk, and the Chiyani charged toward the defenders. Katerin held back and Rekaré brought the Mer Galad up to support her.

She let instinct take over, not activating the Maker, the Strength, and the Vision. She did not need to expend sorcerous energy just yet—that was to be saved for when they finally confronted the Witches. Cenarth kept close to her as they engaged both foot soldiers and riders. The melee led them both close to Linyet and the Two Nations. Pride rose in Rekaré as she saw how well her son battled—albeit in brief snatches between her own encounters.

For once a battle plan worked like it should. She and Basnen fought as one being, like they had learned so many years ago from first Heinmyets and Inharise, then Alame. She dropped the reins and guided Basnen by weight and leg when needed, though Basnen picked targets as well. But she was so attuned to her daranval's body that the slight tensing of a back muscle prepared Rekaré for a shift in direction or a swift double-barrel kick to dispatch a fighter approaching them from behind.

Time seemed suspended as they tore through the Forsim defenders. Some tried to use magic against her. Rekaré ripped it from them with an ease fueled by battle rage and the amount of glimmer dust floating around due to their spells. None of them matched her skill and experience.

The Witches Council is holding back.

That much was obvious.

Why?

And then it stopped. A red glow replaced the blue and gold shimmer of the glimmer dust. Rekaré and Basnen charged a Waykemese spear rider aiming for Linyet's back, sending horse and rider staggering before she dispatched them.

Laughter. All-too-familiar laughter.

"*NO!*" Katerin screamed. "MY MOTHER BANISHED YOU YEARS AGO!"

Rekaré spun Basnen and gasped.

The Goddess Nitel loomed in Forsim's gateway.

It was all she could do to keep from riding that Goddess down.

You will pay for what you have done to my family, oh false Goddess.

And still, she checked Basnen. This was Katerin's battle to wage. Unless Katerin wanted her to take on Nitel—she would wait to take her own vengeance.

"*WHAT?*"

Witmara gasped as the Voices for Nitel suddenly lay siege to the Dovré pieces. She clapped her hands over her mouth to constrain her dismay.

Your move, Lady Witmara.

The personage across from her abruptly changed to someone not her father. She sneered at Witmara with teeth bared, malign intent glittering from her red eyes. Witmara gulped, suddenly aware that she was not in her cell any more, but in a great chamber with multiple entities around her. Staul and her father stood to the side, clearly dismayed. Despair radiated from Terat of the Waters. The Twin Gods chuckled at everyone's discomfort as Nitel leaned across the board.

What is your move now, Lady Witmara?

Her head spun. What could she do now? This wasn't supposed to be happening!
Then Alicira rested a hand on her shoulder.

You do not need to rush. Metkyi. Witmara needs our guidance.

Her father was at her side, placing a hand on her other shoulder.
She became aware of another presence. Artel the Judge scowled down at the board.

You presume much to intervene in this matter, Lady Nitel.

The Goddess straightened up from glowering at Witmara.

You gave me this right when Terani banished me from Waykemin.

So I did, but your option is limited

Artel sighed.

She has unfair assistance! No Gods are allowed
to directly help mortals invited into the Game!

Nitel gestured toward Witmara.

True, true,

Artel grumbled. Then a sly smile that would have made
Witmara shiver if it had been aimed at her crossed his face, not
touching his eyes.

But. That restraint does not extend to our
Messengers, Speakers, and Voices. Especially
when a God has chosen to enter the Game
while a mortal is still learning it.

He snapped his fingers.

Alame. It is time.

A figure detached himself from the crowd and bowed to
Artel.

My lord. I am honored to serve you as Speaker.

Good. Assist your granddaughter in my name.

A smile that matched his patron's crossed Alame's face.

Gladly, my lord.

Wait! This is unfair! She has three representatives of the Gods advising her moves! And they are all part of her family!

Nitel protested.

Artel shrugged.

Leveling the playing field, my dear. She is but a novice still learning the Game. You are a skilled player who broke the rules by intervening when you should not have done so, even though you had a limited right should the daughter of Terani-the-God-Killer ride against Forsim.

His voice sharpened.

I have warned you and your allies about the dangers of arrogance for ages, Nitel. Now it is time for me to do something about this. I have withheld my hand for far too long.

Then if we are to level the field I need supporters of my own, Artel,

Nitel snarled. Her voice sent a chill through Witmara's gut.

Now who is being unfair, Nitel? Goddess versus a mortal? A novice mortal?

I am owed supporters of my own, Artel!

For far too long I have listened to your protests of unfairness,

Artel sighed. He looked up, and Witmara felt the same buzzing that she did when the daranvelii spoke amongst each other.

Artel nodded abruptly.

> Nitel, my allies and I will grant you this one
> favor. But you get only one supporter, and it
> cannot be one known to your opponent, nor
> one tied to Medvara.

Nitel bared her teeth at him.

> As it happens, oh impotent one, I have a
> specific supporter in mind. Etikar! Etikar
> destroyer of Miteal! I call you forth, as one who
> knows the Great Game so well. Come forward.
> I have another Miteal for you to consume in my
> name.

Witmara had seen a hidden portrait of the approaching shade in one of her mother's restricted libraries.

Etikar the late Emperor of Daran, Chatain's grandfather. Etikar, who had sent Zauril to Medvara. A small colorless man, smaller than he appeared in the portrait, with a receding hairline, skin paler than most with bulging, fish-like eyes. He bowed to Nitel. The portrait had not been flattering, but it had been much more so than this spectral apparition.

> I am ready to serve, my Goddess.

Nitel raised an index finger, pointing directly at Witmara.

> This one fantasizes that she can depose your
> grandson and reestablish the Miteal chokehold
> on the Darani Empire. Perhaps it is time that we
> take her down a notch or two.

She rose and Etikar took his place, seated across the board from Witmara.

Etikar studied her. Witmara straightened up, not flinching away from him, copying his intense stare.

She had heard so many stories about him. The Emperor who created a death curse on his mother's funeral pyre, unleashing the Great Plagues on the world. The Emperor who created the Darani colonies in Varen, until his brother Alexran's defiance freed them. The Emperor who exiled Alexran to Varen because he was protected by Dovré. The Emperor who sent Zauril to Medvara to depose Alexran.

Somehow she had thought Etikar would be bigger and more imposing. Instead, she thought he might be shorter than her. Her first impression of a narrow-faced, big-eyed, fish-belly pale man didn't change. He didn't *look* like he was an emperor, but rather a soft-fleshed, lower-level small town Medvaran bureaucrat of the sort who pestered her mother for unearned favors.

He flushed as her lip curled in scorn. "So this is the so-called great Emperor Etikar," she said, pouring every ounce of derision she could into her voice. Even though her heart pounded in fear, she would not show it to this fish-faced destroyer. "And *this* is what launched the Great Plagues?"

I look forward to consuming you. A half-breed descendant of the Miteal can be no match for my pure blood.

"If I'm so impure then why do you seek to sully yourself with me?" Witmara parried, her heart pounding hard. Gods. Another one obsessed about purity of blood!

Ah, you are but a tidbit before I consume your mother. Your cousin.

Alicira's hand tightened on her shoulder.

"That will never happen," Witmara said, forcing a confidence that waned as the visage of bureaucrat sharpened into that which must have been the Emperor. Oh Gods. This Game. Did this mean she was going to affect the battle in Waykemin?

Such a bold one. Shall we gamble on this?

Gods. A bet. It might fall her way—or not.

He snickered, the severe countenance of Emperor falling back into that of a bureaucrat pressing on a point he thought he'd scored, as she took her time to answer, considering her options. And *that* firmed her resolve. She would do anything to wipe that smug expression off of his face.

After all, she *did* have four of the Seven Crowned Gods on her side.

"I am—*considering*—your offer," she said finally. "Let me think for a moment on the means."

Was that dismay she saw flitting across Etikar's face at her words, making him look even more like a sanctimonious bureaucrat? His fingers twisted against each other nervously and he chewed on his lower lip.

Yes. He fears the risk.

Get him to define what he wants to wager,

Metkyi whispered.

The more he talks, daughter, the more he angers the Gods who are your allies, as well as Artel. Push him.

Remember that I gamed with Zauril in Staul's name to keep Rekaré,

Alicira added.

But do not risk moves in the Great Game, granddaughter,

Alame said.

Make it a different game.

"What is the wager?" she said.
Etikar spread his hands wide.

The lives of your mother. Your cousin.

He leaned forward.

Your life as well.

"Those stakes are far too high."
Artel intruded.

She is right. Pick one, Etikar. Then you, lady Witmara, will choose the game.

Etikar laughed.

Well, then. Your mother and cousin are currently engaged in battle against My Lady's supporters. Shall we bet on the outcome of that battle?

Witmara's throat was suddenly very dry.
Metkyi leaned close to her.

Take it.

Choose the Clendan chip throw for your game.

Alicira added.

He will need to frame a question precisely for that game—and will overplay his hand. Remember, he wants to consume all three of you. Etikar is not wise. He is greedy, and will further anger the Four on our side.

Require that the chips be of daranval bone,

Alame said.

That carries additional weight toward Dovré, though none of the Gods will admit to that. The chips themselves will demand sincerity and a concern about more than power. One question each. No need to draw it out.

Witmara nodded, acknowledging their advice. "I accept the wager," she said slowly, her throat tight.

Etikar waved a hand over the board.

So shall this be the game?

"No," she said, suddenly confident. "We will play the Clendan chip throw. With chips of daranval bone, and one question from each of us."

A small strand of satisfaction threaded through her as she saw him flinch.

I do not know that game!

"It is a very simple game," she said. "Children play it in Clenda and Keldara. We each ask a question, and then toss four chips. One side of the chip is blank, the other is a line. The number of lines determines who wins—and the pattern of the tosses adds to the interpretation as set down in *The Book of Artel.*"

Nitel scowled and whispered to him. Etikar scowled.

That is the game that Alicira used to steal Rekaré from Zauril!

"Yes. It is. Are you afraid to play that game with me? It is a game of chance, after all, like any other. Or is it too simple for you?"

> No! I will defeat you at this game, young lady, and then you shall feel my wrath!

> That is ENOUGH,

Artel growled.

> If you threaten her further you will lose.

Etikar leaned back in his chair, the smirk returning.

> I have no need to threaten her. I will win. And then....

His voice trailed off as he glowered at Witmara.

HOW CAN NITEL BE HERE? TERANI BANISHED HER!
Confusion whirled through Katerin's thoughts as she raised the Spear while Nitel laughed.

> Banishment does not last forever, Katerin Half-Breed, Katerin the jumped-up scion of Alame the Cursed. And now it is time for you to make amends for all the trouble you and your mother have caused me.

Katerin took a deep breath, drawing on Rainin for strength.
"She does not ride alone." Rekaré halted Basnen next to Katerin. "And you and I have unfinished business, goddess who allows torture of children and the sick."

> This is between her and me,

Nitel said.

"You rode my father. You led him to destroy Medvara." Rekaré raised her sword. "I may no longer be Leader of Medvara but I saw the devastation you enabled my father to wreak. And I say to you, *Rekaré Kinslayer supports her kinfolk, especially the Banisher of Shadows!*"

Golden light flashed around Rekaré's neck, matched by dark purple on her wrist and deep red from her ring.

She has activated the Maker, the Strength, and the Vision.

Now was the time to take on Tranarin and the Council, even if Nitel herself barred the way.

"Begone, Nitel!" she yelled. "Your time has ended here. Katerin Terani's daughter will banish you from this land once again if you do not leave!"

Big words,

Nitel sneered.

"With action." She didn't need to look over to know that Rekaré and Basnen would match them stride for stride. "Ride and fight well, cousin."

"The same to you," Rekaré said.

Katerin lowered the Spear for the charge. Basnen snorted and Rainin responded. Rekaré's eyes flicked toward her and Katerin nodded. Their daranvelii leapt as one toward Nitel.

You must flip to be the Questioner,

ARTEL INTONED. A SPOTTED BLACK AND WHITE HORSEHIDE replaced the Great Game's board, eight chips scattered loosely on it. *The Book of Artel* lay on the horsehide, a tattered copy that looked like the one she had used as a child.

The winner is the one with the most lines.

He picked up the book, then flicked four chips to Witmara, and four to Etikar.

Throw one chip at a time, both of you together.

First toss. A line for her, a blank for Etikar. An auspicious start, but only a start. She had seen the game twist from such a beginning.

Stupid game,

Etikar grumbled.

Witmara kept quiet. She had played this game far too many times as a child to assume the remaining tosses would go in her favor.

And yet her supporters had encouraged her to do it. With daranval bone chips. That must mean something—shouldn't it?

Second toss. A blank for her, a line for Etikar. Equal.

Third toss. Both blank.

Fourth toss. A blank for her, a line for Etikar.

Aha! I have won!

Etikar crowed.

Only the right to form the Question first,

Alame growled at him.

Oh, that is simple. How soon after her mother and cousin fall will I be able to devour her?

Invalid question, Etikar,

Artel said.

The chips do not forecast time and we have not
established that her mother and cousin will fall.

Etikar scowled.

We both have the same question. Why should
we both ask it? Let me ask openly with no
contrivances and this farce will be over.

Even though the words of your question may
be the same, your intentions may not serve the
same purpose,

Artel intoned.

The meaning and outcome you seek will put a
different emphasis on the question than you
expect.

Witmara frowned.
What does the God mean by this?
There could only be one outcome—couldn't there?

Not fair! She knows the nuances of this game
and I do not.

Etikar sounded peevish.

You are older than she is, and served as
Emperor for many years,

Staul interjected.

You should have the greater knowledge and
understanding of diplomacy.

Diplomacy is for fools! All right, then. Who wins this battle in Forsim, Rekaré and Katerin or the Witches?

Witmara bit her lip, forcing herself to keep her face blank. Was this truly Etikar? How could someone with his experience be so—so foolish?

Diplomacy is for fools?

How had he managed to maintain control over the Daran Empire for all those years without being deposed? Bullying and autocratic power? Overreliance on Nitel's favor?

Now you see what a thirst for power alone brings,

her father whispered.

The hunger continues to devour you after death. You become more of what you were in life. Do not underestimate him. Etikar was a canny and deceitful ruler in life.

Are you ready, Lady Witmara?

Artel asked.

"Yes." Witmara raised her chin defiantly, running her finger over the chips in her left hand, just as she had when younger and playing the game. One warmed to the touch. That would be her first toss. She picked it up between her right thumb and index finger.

They threw the first chips. Both blank.

Second chips. Still blanks.

Third chips. Blanks.

Fourth. Both lines.

Even without the book she knew the response to this one, even as Artel flipped it open to deliver the official response.

The chips would not answer his question because they could not.

> A tie. The answer to your question does not fall within our control,

Artel said.

> Then we will throw again until it is conclusive!

Etikar snapped petulantly.

> That is not the way the game is played,

Artel said.

> You have received your answer.

> And it is no answer at all! I demand another question.

> It does not work that way.

Artel turned his attention to Witmara.

> Lady Witmara, your turn. Remember to ask wisely and well.

Etikar glared across the horsehide at her.

> I will still consume you, upstart half-breed Miteal corrupted by dirt lineage.

"Not if I can help it," she growled back at him. "And I *will* supplant Chatain, you hateful piece of inbred dung-ridden filth, attempted destroyer of Medvara."

He recoiled at the vehemence in her voice. Good.

Now. What was she going to ask? She doubted that she

would receive any better answer if she asked the same question that Etikar had. Those last two lines were emphatic on that subject. Both her mother and her cousin possessed sufficient power that any toss involving them would come out skewed—that was her reading of the chips' judgment. No. There had to be a better question about the outcome of this battle.

What was it that Alame had said when advising her to choose this game?

The chips themselves will demand sincerity and a concern about more than power.

She needed to think beyond herself. Who else would be affected by the battle in Forsim?

Ah. She had it now. She smiled across the horsehide at Etikar. "I know my question now."

It is an illusion and not the Goddess, Katerin realized as Rainin thundered toward Nitel and her image shimmered away. That meant that Tranarin and the Witches were in the Council chamber.

Time to take the fight directly to them.

"Let the others battle!" she called to Rekaré. "Follow me!"

"Where are we going?" Rekaré yelled.

"To the Council chamber!"

"Gods, Katerin! Can we even get there without being killed?"

"We bring Sorcerer's Challenge! They *must* let us through!"

They passed through the gate and into a cluster of guards that barricaded their way. Katerin halted Rainin and raised the Spear high.

"I bring Sorcerer's Challenge to the Council!" she cried. "I am of Chiyan, the daughter of Terani-the-God-Killer! Do not stand in my way."

The Head of the Guards sneered at her. "We know you, Katerin Half-Breed. Why should we grant you this privilege?"

"Because I am also the Banisher of Shadows," Katerin growled. "I am beloved of both Dovré and Staul. I am the rightful Leader of Medvara, and I ride with Rekaré Kinslayer as my second. Do you deny me Sorcerer's Challenge?" She lowered the Spear so that it pointed directly at the Head's chest. "Do you recognize this weapon, the tool of the Banisher of Shadows?"

His face grayed, pale under mud brown, as he stared at the Spear's point just two hands-width away from his chest. It twisted in Katerin's hand, eager to drink of his blood and soul. A faint moan came from it. He leaned away from the spearhead.

"Proceed, Banisher of Shadows and Rekaré Kinslayer. But I give you no blessing."

"I did not expect one."

The Spear did not want to move away from his chest. She had to struggle against the temptation to let it feed, just a little, to prove her point.

But she did not give in to that enticement. It was a dangerous distraction, and she did not want to face Tranarin with such a petty vengeance on her conscience.

Katerin grinned at Rekaré. "Shall we go, cousin?"

"I follow your lead," Rekaré said.

"My question," Witmara said slowly. "In this battle for the soul of Waykemin now happening in Forsim. Will the outcome benefit the people of Waykemin?"

She couldn't ask directly about her mother and Rekaré. But if the battle was righteous, if the battle would benefit Waykemin —that would mean they would prevail, given everything she knew about her mother's birth land.

Was she right?

Artel gave her a slow smile of approval as Etikar scowled.

Well said, she who would become Empress of
Daran. Well said. Let us toss for this answer.

First toss. Both blanks. Her heart sank. And yet—it was only
the first toss.

Second toss. A line for her, a blank for him. Better.

Third toss. Both blanks. Inconclusive.

The final toss. Two lines. But she was up by one, which
meant she had won—at a cost. What would that price be?

She looked up from the horsehide at Artel the Judge, poring
over the interpretation in the book, though she suspected he
knew the answer without looking.

The battle outcome will be favorable for the
people of Waykemin,

the God said softly.

But there will be a price.

*A small cost. Mother and Rekaré will win—but will they survive?
Who else could be lost? Linyet? Cenarth?*

Or was the cost Artel spoke of to her and not to her mother
and Rekaré? She still didn't know the fate of Toran and Daro.

Etikar whimpered.

You were biased toward her question!

Artel bristled.

> And rightly so! She correctly perceived that the underlying issue was about what was right for the people of Waykemin, not about individuals and power. That is the question a true leader of the people should ask, in alignment with all my precepts.

> Our principles,

Staul corrected. Artel glared at Staul. Staul maintained a faint smile, but lowered his eyes, submitting to the Judge and Leader of the Gods.

Artel sighed

> Correct. It is the standard of the Seven Crowned Gods, though some do not take such to heart. Begone, Etikar. You have served your mistress's purpose. All of us have. Let us return the Lady Witmara to the original game, where she may learn and grow wise.

He waved his hand, and she was back in her dim, dank cell with Metkyi, Alicira—and Alame. Witmara collapsed against the wall, closing her eyes for a moment.

Artel had said the people of Waykemin would win, but at a cost.

What is that cost to be? Mother? Rekaré? Toran? Daro?

Not her mother and Rekaré. Artel would consider that to be a major cost. So they would come through the battle for Waykemin safely.

But who would not?

Toran. Daro. Linyet. Cenarth.

Which would it be? Loved ones connected to her—or to her mother? Or Rekaré?

THE WITCHES OF WAYKEMIN

Rekaré urged Basnen to stick close to Rainin's tail. She suddenly
realized that Cenarth rode next to her.

"This is not a place for you to fight! Your magic isn't strong
enough for this! Go back to Deta and Senth!"

"I am here to guard your backs," he yelled back. "That takes
little magic!"

Before they could argue further, Katerin halted Rainin in
front of a huge single-story stone building. Three flights of
stone steps led to a doorway covered by a red and purple
tapestry. Power radiated from that tapestry, not quite the same
power that emanated from the Great Tapestries woven by the
leaders of the Two Nations and Medvara as part of the proof of
their fitness to rule the land's magic, but akin.

It clearly had a meaning for her cousin. Katerin stared at it,
her lips tightening. Then she raised the Spear high, and urged
Rainin up the stairs without dismounting.

"Reckless," Cenarth grumbled, but he did not keep Quartel
from joining Basnen as they climbed the stairs.

Katerin dismounted when they reached the ledge at the top.

She marched toward the tapestry. The Spear changed to its Sword form, this time like the curved swords that the *kinforost* carried. She turned to face Rekaré and Cenarth.

"I need every bit of strength you can feed me," she said in a low voice. "This is our first test of power. There will be three more before we reach the Council chamber." Rainin shifted into place behind Katerin, her head close to Katerin's back.

"I understand." Rekaré dismounted, looping Basnen's reins around the saddle horn to keep the golden mare from stepping on them. Their daranvelii would follow without needing to be led.

If this tapestry represented a barrier, then it wasn't a real tapestry, but an impediment using that illusion.

Support Katerin,

she willed the Maker, the Strength, and the Vision.

Let her draw freely on what power I can give to her.

Purple, red, and yellow lights twisted together from her chest, wrist, and hand, then flowed toward Katerin as she raised the Sword high. Katerin slashed the tapestry from top left to bottom right. It screamed, power raging from it like a creek that had just burst a dam. Katerin flinched back against Rainin.

She needs aid in shielding.

Rekaré cast a protective spell over Katerin, willing herself to take the brunt of that magical deluge, wincing as sharp little points pricked her. Basnen's forehead against Rekaré's back strengthened her, but she gained more relief when Cenarth moved next to her so that their shoulders touched. She leaned into him, grateful for his support as the sharpness faded.

Katerin raised the Sword again and slashed it in the opposite direction, top right to bottom left. This time Rekaré guarded them. The barrier imploded in knife-like red and purple shards that twisted toward each of them, but fell back harmlessly when the pieces contacted their shield.

Katerin lowered the Sword and walked inside, Rainin close on her heels. Rekaré followed, Cenarth at her side, their daranvelii right behind them.

Darkness broken only by the occasional torch burning in copper sconces met them. Blue and silver light glimmered around Katerin—Dovré's mark upon her cousin. The Spear had shifted to its original form, and a golden light shone from the spearhead, bright enough that Rekaré saw ichor oozing from the stones around them.

What sort of foul magic is this?

She exchanged a worried glance with Cenarth.

A reddish-purple light shimmered in front of them. Another barrier. Katerin did not hesitate but lowered the Spear and marched directly toward it. The Spear contacted the barrier and Katerin's movement suddenly slowed. Rekaré and Cenarth had to stop hard to keep from running into Rainin and getting kicked. Ahead of them, Katerin moved in slow motion, foot rising slowly, slowly, before it descended at the same pace, then the next foot coming forward—

The narrow passageway grew hotter. Sweat broke out on Rekaré's face as she felt like she was trudging through chest-deep water with the current shoving hard against her. Rainin put her head down and struggled just like they were. Rekaré kept wide of her hinds, cautious about that mare's tendency to kick if someone followed too closely. Cenarth fared no better.

And then the pressure released. They staggered ahead. Katerin stopped, breathing hard.

"The Second Barrier," she said. "There are two more." Once again she walked on.

WITMARA TENTATIVELY MOVED THE VOICE OF DOVRÉ. ONCE THEY had been returned to her cell, the board had returned to its previous layout.

> Are you certain that is the move you want to make?

Metkyi raised his brows at her, which she was rapidly learning meant that her father did not approve of her choice.

"I—I am not sure," Witmara hesitated, studying the board. She hadn't opened her Sorceress to attack as near as she could tell. She had lost one shaman and a priest, but her father had lost two of the Hunt's wolves. She had been holding back on the healers and the sorcerer-captains.

> It is time to risk your sorcerer-captains instead of your healers,

Alicira said. Her finger traced a move.

> Never risk a healer when you have other pieces to hand. It is time for you to counter the Masked Ones.

"But won't that mean I lose a player?" Witmara pointed to the rider left vulnerable by the move Alicira recommended.

> Sometimes it is best to risk those players and win the game,

Alicira said.

"All right." Witmara moved the sorcerer-captain. Metkyi captured the rider at risk with one of his Masked Ones...and, she realized, left the Witch wide open to her priest of Staul. She captured the Witch—and realized that left an opening for her remaining shaman to capture the other one in the next move. Her father could not move it, pinned in as it were by the other players.

Suddenly she could see how the remainder of the game would play out. She could capture the Sorcerer in five moves. Even if her father countered, losing the Witches would cripple him immensely.

"How close is this to real life?" she asked.

Metkyi and Alicira smiled.

But it was her grandfather Alame who answered.

Close enough to the real thing to be effective.
Why do you think we call this the Great Game?
Excellent work, granddaughter.

Distant rustling and voices. The screech of a door being unlocked and the distant rattle of keys.

Best that we leave now,

her father said, banishing the board with a wave of his hand.

I will be watching and reappear if needed. No need to keep reminding them of my presence. We may discover more if they aren't fretting about me.

"Thank you," Witmara said as her spectral companions disappeared, though Metkyi kissed the top of her head before leaving. Now what was she going to face? On the one hand, she wished he would stay. On the other—

If it was nothing more than just Nereast and Ankari bringing food and more treatment for her head, then they didn't need that reminder.

She wondered how much longer it would be until they reached the Ourigny Islands.

If possible, she was going to escape there. What would happen after that—well, it depended on how much of what

Betsona had been telling her about conditions in Daran was truth, and how much was exaggeration.

❀

THE THIRD BARRIER WAS ICE AND COLD. KATERIN COUNTERED that easily, using the Spear as an ice axe to break through it, barely aware of Rekaré and Cenarth behind her. She wanted to stop and catch her breath after hacking her way through the ice wall, but there was danger in doing that.

The Witches' calculations had anticipated that someone bringing Sorcerer's Challenge would want to stop at this point. She faintly remembered discussions between her mother and the Council at the time as they had set up these protections. Stopping would trigger another defense that would remain quiet if they pushed on.

The Fourth Barrier will be that of endurance.

By this time any sorcerer who had gotten through the previous barriers would be tired and ready to collapse, not able to counter an all-out attack.

She thought about that one. She had used Sword and Spear, then bulled through the ice for the Third Barrier using the Spear as an ice axe. What should she use next?

Shield.

The Fourth Barrier would involve an active attack. Could she raise a large enough physical shield to protect not just herself but Rekaré, Cenarth, and their daranvelii? Not an invisible shield like the ones Rekaré had raised to protect her but an actual, physical shield that was a manifestation of the Spear.

I can try.

She visualized the sort of shield she wanted, an image from a long-ago illustration in a book she had read shortly after she and her mother had come to Forsim. She hadn't seen anything like that shield before or since. It was as tall as she was, and

288

wide, so that it would cover her entire body. Perhaps the Spear could extend its protections to those who followed after.

She held the image in her thoughts before commanding.

Shield.

The Spear shaped itself into a massive but lightweight shield, as wide as it was tall, almost filling the passageway. Katerin laced both arms into the grips of the great shield. Any moment now....

Arrows pelted the Shield, followed by chunks of something more solid. And then a single, hard thump, like that of a battering ram, vibrated throughout her body. Had it not been for Rainin leaning her forehead against her back and Rekaré feeding her strength, she would have faltered at this point. She pressed hard on the Shield, shoving, shoving, shoving.

And then they broke through.

Spear.

The Shield reshaped itself. Rekaré and Cenarth stepped up beside her as she marched into the Council chamber. Tranarin stood at the head of the great stone altar, arms raised high as her voice ululated in a high-pitched chant. Twelve other masked women circled the altar, echoing Tranarin, focused on three figures hanging from tripods erected on the altar. Some were ululating almost as loudly as Tranarin while others barely made a sound.

Their chanting broke off as Katerin approached. Those with their backs to the intruders turned to face them. All wore grotesque masks, bleached pale with features twisted into disproportionate, gnarled faces of different sizes. Six of the thirteen had Nitel's red sigils painted on the masks' foreheads and cheeks. They wore the larger masks, some covering half their upper bodies. But the other seven—those had not been personalized, and their masks barely covered their faces. Those were the quiet ones.

Does that mean that they were conscripted, like Yitlisk's mother Marneri?

Katerin saw that her shape had been raised again on one of the tripods, along with Heinmyets and—was that the Mershaunten? She didn't know if she was relieved not to see Witmara as a poppet. Or Rekaré.

No. That third was Cenarth. Dread clutched at her gut. Rekaré had been much more like her old self since he had been riding with the Mer Galad. No. He couldn't be one of their targets. No. She couldn't let this happen to her cousin. Not more losses. No.

I must stop this before it goes further.

At least Witmara and Linyet were not represented. That might mean that the Two Nations were targeted and not Medvara. Curious that they did not also include Rekaré.

Katerin drew a deep breath. "Tranarin. I am here, to wreak the vengeance I have promised upon you. I bring Sorcerer's Challenge to the Council. For too long you have twisted the people of Waykemin to your corrupt ways. It ends now!"

Tranarin laughed at Katerin. Her mask had the most sigils of Nitel on it, and extended down to her waist. It was *not* the sort of mask Terani would have worn, nor her successor. None of the big masks were.

Further sign of their corruption?

"You fool, Katerin Half-Breed! You dreamer! Katerin daughter of Terani, she who has denied her name, how is it that you are so powerful that you would *dare* challenge the Council, much less presume that you could ever do so?"

"I have wielded such power ever since I became the Banisher of Shadows and learned that I was the daughter of Alame en Miteal," Katerin answered. "I am the Leader of

Medvara and cherished by my land. And I say that this *ends!* NOW!"

She thumped the Spear hard on the rock floor. The floor and walls shuddered, hard enough to send the Witches staggering. Shards of stone fell from the ceiling and the figures on the stone altar quivered.

But the floor under Katerin's feet was steady, and the shards did not fall on all the Witches—only the six with Nitel's tokens.

Katerin strode forward four steps. "Look at you! My mother *banished* Nitel from this land! The Twins were not perfect but they would never have sold Waykemin to Chatain as you have done. And here you are, working Nitel's fell spells and enslaving Waykemese to her twisted purposes!"

"The Twins were weak and distracted!" Tranarin shrieked at Katerin. "Nitel offered us power once again! She turned the Twins into a power to be feared, as Waykemin should be! Not dependent on a Hunt! Not subject to their playful whims, but focused on power! Real power, to be feared!"

"Feared at what cost? More *ushar* and *kendar* than unbound people? More *shalkendar?* Tranarin, you have abused your power as Chief Priestess!" Katerin thumped the Spear again. "And I say you must GO!" Another thump.

Rocks showered down from the ceiling. The stone altar shivered, fissures jagging through it.

"And I say you have *no idea* about the danger we face!" Tranarin hissed back at her. "About what lies beyond the Barrier. Have you looked through the Nerean Gate? The Divine Confederation will consume all of us, no matter which of the Gods we follow or what magic we support! Talk to your friends in Keratil. They will tell you!"

"And did Keratil ask for this sort of help from you?" Katerin shook the Spear toward the shapes on the altar. "Did you go to the Two Nations with this information? The Hidden One in Saubral? The Mershaunten in Larij? The Quiet Ones of Keratil?

Even me in Medvara? No. You did not. Not a one of us! You offer mere excuses to seize at power."

"You are all mewly-mouthed, scruple-bound idiots who would be swallowed up by what awaits," Tranarin growled.

"So you reached to Chatain for help instead."

"Chatain is smarter than to let a few scruples stand in his way. And his cost is—" Tranarin shrugged. "—payable and of no importance to us. An easy price."

"My loved ones are not an easy price for Chatain's support!"

Rage swept over Katerin. She was close enough to Tranarin to stab her with the Spear, plunge it deep into her chest and let the weapon consume her soul, drink her blood. The Spear emitted an eerie, high-pitched keen as it strained toward Tranarin, ready to do it. Katerin let it almost touch her chest. Tranarin did not flinch away but tore her robe open.

"Go ahead," she taunted. "Go ahead and strike the coward's blow, half-breed. Let your weapon do the fighting for you. Let it control you instead of you controlling it."

No.

Katerin tamped down her anger and constrained the Spear. It was a violation of the Challenge. Breaking these rules would make her no better than the ones she sought to defeat.

Instead, she straightened and brought the Spear back, standing it upright and clenching it in her fist.

"Tranarin, Chief Priestess of the Witches Council of Waykemin," she said in formal Waykemese, not Varenese. "I issue Sorcerer's Challenge to condemn the actions taken by the Witches Council to oppress the people of Waykemin and sell out their birthrights to Chatain, Emperor of Daran. I condemn the deals struck with Chatain by the Council. I condemn the Council's role in the death of Inharise, Leader of the Two Nations. As one born of Chiyan, I offer Challenge in the name of the people of Waykemin. Do you accept?"

"Idealist!" Tranarin cackled. "We will swat you down like the half-breed, impotent upstart that you are. You think you know how to wield magic? We will show you what magic really can do!"

Katerin's grip tightened on the Spear as it strained against her restraint.

"And perhaps you will learn what real magic truly is," she answered Tranarin. "Are we finished with the taunts? Shall we begin the battle?"

"It starts now!" Tranarin howled. She hurled a fireball at Katerin.

Really? Katerin thought as she intercepted it with the Spear, deflecting it toward the roof. *Is that the best you can do?*

"Rekaré. If you could feed me power from your tokens?"

She reached out her free hand, waiting. Suddenly her hand sagged with the weight of the unbridled strength of the Maker, the Strength, and the Vision as channeled through her cousin, a ball of yellow, purple, and red energies swirling together. Katerin brought that hand over to the Spear. The ball expanded to join with the Spear. Katerin raised it high with both hands. She aimed it at Tranarin, who flinched back. No. That should not be the target. Tranarin was personal, where the real danger rested in—yes. The altar. She changed her focus to the altar and hurled the Spear at it.

The Spear struck one of the fissures. Energy boiled out from its head, lighting up the cracks in shades of red, purple, and yellow. They snapped and popped, widening.

"NO!" Tranarin screamed. She threw another ball of flaming energy, but at Cenarth, not Katerin or Rekaré.

Katerin and Rekaré both dove to deflect it. Before they could touch the fireball with their magic, it struck Cenarth's chest. His poppet on the altar burst into flame. Katerin pulled back as Rekaré knelt beside Cenarth, white-hot flame consuming him. She turned to the altar as she noticed the other figures trembling. Katerin leapt onto the altar. It cracked and fissured under her feet, pieces spalling off of the edges as it shook, making her footing unsteady.

Goddess. Please.

The Eye of Dovré warmed in its hidden place under her tunic. Katerin pulled it out, letting its light shine bright in the gloomy chamber. She threw the smoldering figures of Heinmyets and herself off of the altar before the flames swallowed them, damping the fire with a whispered spell. Cenarth's figure was already consumed, nothing but clumps of ash.

Katerin seized the Spear and wrenched it out of the altar.

"No more foul workings!" She thrust the Spear down hard again. "In the name of Dovré, I put an end to this obscenity!"

The altar's cracking and shattering grew worse and she struggled to keep her footing. Tranarin grabbed at her ankle. Katerin kicked it away. She pulled the Spear free from the deep hole it had made.

"In the name of Dovré, I end all the workings made on this foul surface!" She struck the altar a third time, raising the Spear immediately.

"In the name of Dovré, I call for the elimination of the Witches Council!" A fourth strike. Tranarin wrapped herself around Katerin's leg, then fell back, screaming in pain as her mask burned away.

"In the name of Dovré, I thus free Waykemin!"

Her final thrust shattered the altar. Katerin leapt free as shards spalled into dust. She crouched, facing Tranarin as the masks of the rest of the Council shattered into chunks, then pieces, then dust. The seven women whose masks had been unmarked ran to the far side of the chamber, where they huddled together. But the remaining five clustered around Tranarin.

"You dare. *You dare,*" Tranarin screeched. "You will pay for this!" She extended shaking hands toward Katerin as the five placed their hands on her, power spilling in irregular pulses of red and purple from her fingers. "That is not how a true Sorcerer's Challenge is run!"

"You lost that privilege when you struck at one of my own." Katerin resisted the impulse to check on Cenarth and Rekaré. She dreaded the worst—after all, his figure had been consumed by the flames. "And destroying the altar is a legitimate part of Sorcerer's Challenge. My mother built this altar, and I can destroy it!"

"He came with you!" Tranarin's face twisted with frustration as Katerin deflected her spell. "That makes him an acceptable target."

"And as always you are a coward, striking at the least powerful." She moved toward Tranarin. Once again heavy weight drug at her body, making each motion of hand and foot laborious as she trudged toward her opponent.

Goddess. Please.

Tranarin smirked as Katerin struggled to move herself forward. She stretched one hand toward the remnants of the altar.

"Your puny Goddess can't keep us from rebuilding." Dust resolved itself into small chunks as Tranarin's shaking hand sent streamers of red and purple power toward the altar.

"I. Claim. Waykemin. For. Dovré." Katerin managed to grab the last fistful of glimmer dust from the open pouch. She threw it in Tranarin's eyes.

"Ahh! What have you done? It burns, it burns! You have betrayed us to the Bright One!" Tranarin fell back into the arms of her acolytes, tearing at her eyes.

"I am the bearer of Dovré's vengeance." Her body no longer

felt weighted down. Katerin could move freely. She raised the Spear high, aiming once more at Tranarin.

Do not feed,

she commanded the Spear. She drew a deep breath.

Goddess. Guide me. Help me. Cleanse this foul place, starting with this.

Dovré's presence filled Katerin, the Eye glowing brighter than ever. Blue-white light shimmered around her hands.

Then Katerin thrust the Spear hard into Tranarin's chest. It burned bright with the combination of its magics and those of the Maker, the Strength, and the Vision. But it was Dovré's cool fire that dominated. Tranarin shrieked and writhed while blue-white flames consumed her living flesh. The other five women sought to pull away from her as Dovré's cool fire leapt from Tranarin to them, but could not.

Katerin held the Spear in place as the cool fire consumed Tranarin, then the other women, until all five were nothing more than small piles of ash. She pulled the Spear away. The other seven women stared at her in horror, whimpering as they held each other tight.

But there were louder sobs from behind her.

"Rekaré?"

Dare she look, to confirm what she already knew?

The continued sobs and a mournful nicker from Basnen were her only answer. Katerin slumped, leaning hard on the Spear. She didn't want to do it but she turned, to see both Cenarth and Quartel prostrate behind her. Basnen nudged Quartel's unresponsive form while Rekaré knelt next to Cenarth, sobbing over his unmoving body.

Oh Gods. That first strike of Tranarin's. She had suspected as much when the flames consumed his poppet, but to take *both* him and Quartel? It mirrored her own loss of Metkyi and Mira when Rekaré had killed Zauril. And Katerin could do nothing about it now, save provide her cousin mourning and support.

At least her cousin had not lost Basnen.

"Rekaré?" she repeated.

Her cousin looked up, gulping.

"I—do what you must, Katerin." Her voice hardened. "Finish it. Don't let his death be in vain. We will still be here when you are done."

"I am sorry." Katerin straightened up. She stepped around the ashes of Tranarin and her closest supporters—she would need to gather that ash and dispose of it properly later, another task piling up on her—to confront those who were left. She marched up to the women, who shrank back even further from her.

"Well?" she demanded. "How many of you are loyal to Nitel? How many of you wish to share their fate?" She gestured toward the piles of ash. "This land will not belong to either Nitel or the Twins. We may tolerate the Twins if they submit to Dovré's justice and follow her edicts, but Nitel—never."

"What do you intend to do with us if we yield?" One woman pushed forward, standing tall and pulling her shoulders back. "What is your intention for Waykemin? Do you intend to return to the land of your birth and rule us? Force us into submission?"

Katerin eyed this woman, noticing the strong resemblance to Yitlisk in brow and mouth shape. "Are you Marneri of Chiyan?"

The woman tightened but nodded curtly. "Yes."

"Your son Yitlisk has spoken to me of the conditions here, and he has brought Kirest and the remaining rebels of Chiyan to this battle. And no, I have no intention of ruling Waykemin. I already hold Medvara as Leader." A pall shivered through Katerin as she acknowledged to herself that whatever the outcome was of Witmara's captivity, it probably meant that she would not rule Medvara. "I do not need more. What I do not want is a Waykemin dedicated to Chatain, a Waykemin terrorized and diminished because a handful of its leaders thirst for unlimited power. A Waykemin that seeks to become a tool of another."

"That's what you *don't* want," Marneri snapped. "What *do* you want?"

Katerin paused, finding the words she wanted. "I want Waykemin to become part of the nations of Varen, not separate and shunned as it has been since I was a child," she said finally. "I want Waykemin to become like Saubral, honored and treated equally, not spurned and scorned because of poor alliances. I want Waykemin to be free of the taint of Daran. A free nation, its people not hiding in fear of the judgment of the Witches Council, of becoming *ushar* or *kendar* or even *shalkendar*."

"But such spells have their uses," Marneri countered.

Katerin pursed her lips. "They do," she said finally. "But not used by the leadership against the population, to enslave them in fear. I left Waykemin, Marneri, but I remember what it was when I was growing up in Chiyan and my few years here in Forsim. From all signs, it has only gotten worse."

"Getting rid of the Council is only a beginning." Anger still tightened Marneri's face. "If you are serious about ridding us of Daran's taint, we will need help in cleansing everything."

"I am aware of that," Katerin said. "My *kinforost* knows. Your son and Kirest know. I am sure that others will rise to leadership within Waykemin as they realize that the Council's oppression of the land has been lifted." She sighed. "I am quite familiar with what it takes to rebuild a land. But those who died have taken one of those who is familiar with that process and could have helped you." She gestured toward Rekaré and Cenarth. "Cenarth of the Two Nations aided Rekaré Kinslayer in the early days of rebuilding Medvara. His knowledge is lost—and the Kinslayer and I cannot remain. We are needed elsewhere."

"I am sorry for his death," Marneri shuddered. The tension in her body began to recede. "I wish we could have prevented it."

"There were more of you than of them."

"We were little more than *kendar* ourselves," Marneri said bitterly. "I joined—we all joined the Council under compulsion, under threat to those we led and those we loved. I wanted to protect Chiyan and my son." She waved at her companions. "We all have villages and families we wanted to protect. The best we could do during Tranarin's working was to hold back as best we could, feed them as little of our magic as possible."

Katerin studied Marneri. "Are you all rebels?"

"Not all of us. Chiyan led, and I vowed to protect those like my son who wanted the best for Waykemin, who wanted to overthrow the Witches but lacked the support to do so. When you broke the altar and the masks, I saw an opportunity to separate those of us who did not agree with Tranarin, and deny her our strength."

"A wise choice." And yet they had not chosen to throw their power to Katerin.

Could that have prevented Cenarth's death?

But if she had failed—that would have been worse than death for them if they had thrown their support to her.

Shalkendar.

"What do we do now?"

Katerin thought through what lay ahead. She—and it had to be her alone—needed to gather the ashes of the fallen so that they could be properly disposed of, so as not to contaminate this new Waykemin from the beginning. While Rekaré had not honored her father, neither had she allowed him to be dishonored. The same needed to be true for these Witches.

The Chamber should be destroyed. The chunks of stone that had reformed under Tranarin's magic had crumbled back to dust, but the rest of it? Yes. That should be done by the magicians and sorcerers who remained to Waykemin. She could lead but not be the main driver of that destruction. It was the first step to creating a new path for Waykemin's people.

And Cenarth and Quartel needed to be honored. She could call the cool fire down on Quartel in here, though she cringed at the thought of burning a daranval like him inside, not out in the open air. But moving his body would not be easy.

Forgive me, Quartel; forgive me, Cenarth.

She would take the time to ride in the ridges above Dera to return what she could of Quartel to his home, just as she had done for Mira's ashes.

Rainin nudged her and Katerin rested her hand on her daranval's neck, grateful for her quiet support throughout this battle. She wanted to bury her head in Rainin's neck, collapse and do nothing.

But she had things to do. A nation to start on the path to rebuilding. Cenarth and Quartel to mourn, as well as the others who had fallen in the battle.

Only then could she turn her thoughts to her kidnapped daughter, and whatever had happened in Medvara.

Given her preference, she would throw over everything else and ride as hard as she could for Medvara. Katerin Healer would have done that—but Katerin Healer had faded away long ago.

Witmara was nearly of age, and she had her own magic and powers. Katerin would have to trust that her daughter could keep herself safe until these matters were resolved.

"Katerin?" She realized that Marneri had been speaking, trying to get her attention.

Katerin sighed again. "I will gather the ashes of those who had ruled, for safer disposal. But first I call the cool fire down on the daranval who has died, and gather his ashes, so as not to mix any of them. Then we need to aid Rekaré in removing the body of her late bondmate, the son of the remaining leader of the Two Nations."

It gave her a grim pleasure to see Marneri's eyes widen as a soundless *Oh* rounded her lips, while she stared at Rekaré crouched beside Cenarth's body.

"What payment will be exacted from Waykemin for his fall?" Marneri whispered.

Rekaré looked up. "That will need to be decided by the Leader of the Two Nations," she said hoarsely. "Whether that be Heinmyets or—or—Linyet," she stumbled over the name, "remains to be seen."

"Not a matter of immediate concern," Katerin said harshly. "Once we are clear, then this Chamber must be destroyed. Utterly. So that it can never be rebuilt." She gazed around the room. Once her mother's senseless body had rested here in state, for years, on that very stone altar now broken into dust.

Was this abomination of a Witches Council what Terani would have wanted? After all, her mother had struck out against Nitel's oppression and an equally problematic Council in her time—though the Twins had not been a better choice of patrons for Waykemin, in the long run. Chatain had found friendship here under the Twins, and Nitel had managed to find a means of return.

She remembered the vengeful apparition of her mother during the tumultuous final days of Rekaré's leadership in Medvara. Did the bitter hatred of Katerin exhibited by that version of Terani truly represent how her mother had felt? Or had Terani's own uneasiness about her daughter as the unacknowledged child of Alame en Miteal been twisted as Nitel insinuated her way back into Waykemin's power structures? Or had that appearance of Terani even been a true manifestation of her mother?

Did it really matter if anger and hatred had really been how

Terani had felt toward her? Did it really change anything about Katerin's life?

Questions, questions, all questions.

The only one Katerin knew the answer to was the last one—and how Terani had felt about her unanticipated daughter hadn't changed anything in her life. She couldn't imagine her mother being more attentive or affectionate, given her responsibilities and roles in both Chiyan and Forsim. If anything, her mother's standoffish attitude had made it easier for Katerin to leave Waykemin once Terani collapsed into the dreamless sleep, never to wake again.

It didn't matter. What did matter was to settle Waykemin into a new, better, path. Ensure that Nitel, Karnoi, and Cirdel could not slip back in.

"So," she said to Marneri. "Those are the immediate things that need to be done. And after that? I suggest you speak to your son and to Nenanim. To those of the people who may have other ideas about what an ideal Waykemin will look like. The will to change Waykemin still exists. Whether it is the failed, incomplete vision of my mother or—something new—remains to be seen."

She was not going to bring up that Divine Confederation, whatever it was. Not yet.

Not when they still had the threat of Chatain to deal with.

THE OURIGNY ISLANDS

"So," Larien en Ralsem sneered after Petronin unlocked Witmara's cell door and let him in. Petronin stood outside with the torch. "I see your *father* can't be bothered to keep regular watch on you."

Ankari and Nereast trailed into the cell behind Larien, eyes downcast. Witmara didn't look at them but kept her attention on Larien. Why had he come now? Wouldn't he be needed to guide this ship into port—or was his motiving the ship like what one of the Sorcerer-Captains would do? Even at that, a Sorcerer-Captain would be on deck guiding the ship into its moorage.

"My father will return soon enough should it be necessary," she said. "So why are you here?"

"I wasn't aware that I had to justify myself to you! You are the prisoner and I am the jailer."

Witmara shrugged, feigning a casualness she didn't feel. "And I am not to be concerned that you have decided to visit me again? After all, last time you tried to assault me. I'd just as soon avoid that experience. Even with my father's intervention it was an unpleasant experience."

Larien inhaled sharply through his teeth, hissing as his eyes narrowed and his fists clenched.

"If I—if I—augh! You are a most vexing woman!"

"My bondmate doesn't think so," Witmara said.

For some reason a memory of Alicira came to mind, one of the times when she was dealing with a visiting dignitary who had annoyed all three of the Leaders of the Two Nations with his pompous and pretentious behavior. Alicira had affected a sarcastic concern mixed with a light air that put all but the oblivious dignitary on edge, worried that they too might fall prey to her glittering, pointed commentary.

"But then again, Toran is a man of wisdom and skill," she added in that same note of barbed ennui. "Unlike what I have seen of you."

Larien flushed. "I devoutly hope he is one of those I struck down during your capture!"

"For your sake I hope that is not the case," Witmara said dryly, choking back any other emotion she might feel.

Remember the Great Game.

It almost seemed like Alicira was there, whispering advice. If Toran and Daro had fallen—no. No. She dared not think about that.

"So. Again. Why have you come to bother me? I'm sure you have more important things do instead of annoying me. Aren't you supposed to be motiving this ship? We should be getting close to the Ourigny Islands by now."

He turned redder. "You are not the most important person on this ship!"

She arched a brow. "I have never considered myself to be that personage."

"We need to transfer you when we get to the Islands!" he shouted, face redder than ever. "Thanks to *your father's* work, I've been demoted. I have to take you off of this ship and face sentencing myself!"

"Perhaps you shouldn't have tried to assault me." Gods, it was a struggle to keep her voice calm and not shriek at this man. "And why did you need to inform me of this? Sooner or later, I need to leave this ship. Or is this happening very soon and that's why you are here?"

"We will be at the docks shortly! I have been removed from captaining the ship, thanks to you. I'm no more than your jailer!" Larien huffed and stomped toward the door.

Ankari and Nereast shared worried glances. He stopped short of the opening, breathing hard, fists clenching and unclenching. At last he stepped out and took the torch from Petronin, then clomped back toward her.

Witmara eyed the torch as he brought it close. Did he think to torture her with the flame? She had no doubt that her father would step in at that point.

Instead, Larien held it high, studying her face closely.

"There are—options. If only your skin were not so brown," he said finally. "You have the Miteal chin. The brows. But your cheekbones, and your skin. Those aren't Miteal. Your eyes. And yet," he mused. "It could work. By Artel, it could work. Especially in the Islands, where there are many of a similar shade."

Ankari frowned. An uneasy expression crossed her face before it fell back into neutral lines.

"What do you mean?"

He swore by Artel. Does that mean he's not dedicated to Nitel like Chatain is?

She had assumed that all of the Ralsem in Daran followed Chatain's lead, except for the small minority that Betsona represented. This change. What did it mean?

"What I mean, *girl,* is that you are mixed blood."

"I don't see why my blood matters."

"It matters because it's important to the Court of Daran," he said. "Not so much to the peoples of Daran, but the Court...ah. My cousin's downfall."

She didn't miss the startled expression that flitted across Ankari's face, gone as quickly as it appeared.

"It is not an issue in Varen." Witmara kept her voice steady.

"I know that!" he snapped. "It's obvious from looking at you and the position you hold. Who your parents were."

By Staul, I wish he'd get to whatever point he's trying to reach!

She remained silent as Larien paced back and forth in front of her, clutching his head, muttering. Something had changed in him. Was it the removal of his position as captain? And Ankari —there was a difference about her as well. She felt as malign as she had the first time Witmara had seen her.

If only I had full access to my magic right now, I would know.

Larien halted abruptly, staring at her and shaking his head, looking confused and somehow younger than he had before.

"I can't," he said. "I just can't. And yet. I have failed Chatain. I will pay, not only for my actions but my kinship to rebels. I have to act." He clutched his head again. "Ay. It hurts. The compulsion. And yet. I can't. But I have failed. I will pay the price, unless...." He squatted by the cell's bars and leaned his head against them, trembling. "*Oh Gods, Betsona, the betrayal, the betrayal!*"

A scowl twisted Ankari's face, fading quickly.

"I wish you would tell me what is going on," Witmara said finally.

Larien sprang up with a roar. "You'd like that, wouldn't you? Aahhh!" He doubled over, gasping. "I. Can't. I. Want. I. Can't."

Was he going insane?

Her father suddenly appeared, followed by Alicira. They strode over to Larien. Alicira rested her hands on his head and Metkyi on his shoulders.

You have a short period to speak freely,

Alicira said.

Larien straightened up, staring at Alicira in wonder. "Who are you?"

Alicira ea Miteal, Speaker for Dovré. Our magics will not give you peace for long. Do not waste this time!

"Oh Artel, at last, at long last," he said prayerfully, wiping the sweat off of his forehead. "It is simple. I am kin to Betsona ea Ralsem, and I operate this ship under compulsion forced on me by Chatain. Someone on the ship is my controller and *I don't know who it is.* Betsona says you can free me and others of our kindred, which was one reason why I volunteered for this mission. Can you do that?"

He speaks truthfully,

her father said.

His controller is with us,

he added in a low voice for her alone.

"Free me, and yes, I will do my best to rid you of Chatain," Witmara said, her heart pounding. Gods, she had not anticipated this possibility. She glanced sideways at Ankari to see her reaction.

Ankari. Nereast. Petronin. Which one of those three controls Larien? None of them were here when he attacked me, so it's someone with enough magic to manage control without being close.

Displeasure tightened Ankari's face. She shook a dagger out of her sleeve.

"You fool! For that you die."

But before she took two steps Nereast moved, dropping the tray she held, then tripping Ankari and disarming her. Without hesitation she slashed Ankari's throat.

Meanwhile, Petronin stood quietly, almost looking bored. He turned his head as distant whistles sounded, frowning.

"We don't have much time left. I hear the docking whistles." The drone of the engines changed, and the ship jerked backward.

"Faster than I thought," Larien said. He quivered and sweat still beaded his face. He rubbed his eyes and sighed. "Still, just to have a few moments free…thank you."

Nereast knelt beside Ankari's body and started pulling off her skirt. "Gods, I tried not to get too much blood on her robe." She glanced at Witmara. "They are of a size. What do we do next, Larien? We have to get her off the ship before they come for the two of you."

"Do we know which of Chatain's lackeys this one was?" He gestured toward Ankari.

"She claimed to be Ankari ea Ralsem," Witmara said, throat dry. "She said she would get me safely to Betsona."

Larien spat. "Ankari! Oh, she'd have gotten you to Betsona all right. Then she would have betrayed both of you. Did you know?" he asked Nereast.

"Yes." Nereast finished easing the robe off of Ankari's top, leaving her in undergarments. She began gathering up the dropped food on the tray, putting it into a pouch. "It's a good thing we're coming into port right now, Larien. Are you coming with us or should I hit you over the head to cover our escape?"

"Wait, what?" Witmara looked back and forth. "Are you saying that you—you came here to free me?"

Nereast finished picking up the food and rose. "Yes. We'll need to move quickly." She went to Larien. "The key."

"Petronin has it," Larien said. "Thank you, Lady Witmara, and those who guard you. It has made things easier." He sank to his knees. "Make it worthwhile, Lady. Become Empress. Depose Chatain—for the good of Daran."

Witmara swallowed hard. Here it was. It was one thing to

proclaim herself to the shadow of her father. But now here was someone, in the flesh, who had sacrificed himself, had volunteered in the hope that she would step forward to challenge Chatain....

She could not let him down.

"I will," she promised Larien. "I will become Empress of Daran."

Nereast put her hands on her hips. "This is all well and good, but we need to get moving or we'll get caught. Larien, you're staying behind?" She went over to Petronin. He handed her a key.

He nodded, breathing harshly. "I need you to pass my love on to Betsona. I—I don't expect to survive this."

Gods.

"We could take you with us," Witmara said. "My magic can hide you."

Both Nereast and Larien shook their heads. "We need to do this with as little magic as possible," Nereast said. "The next lackey bearing Chatain's countenance will have more power now that we're here in the Islands—if it's not Chatain himself." She fumbled with the shackles on Witmara's wrists. "And for the Gods' sake, *don't reach for your magic until we're clear of the ship!* That will betray all of us."

"I understand." As the first shackle fell free magic surged back to Witmara. She damped it down hard as the second shackle opened.

"I will do my best to give you as much time to get clear of the ship as possible," Larien said.

"Larien," Witmara said as Nereast freed her. "You're not one of Chatain's followers? You could have fooled me."

Larien grimaced as he struggled back to his feet. "He rides most of the family save Betsona, and keeps us under compulsion. For my part I am sorry for what I have done, but it was necessary to get you here to the Islands. To defeat our cousin."

He drew a deep breath. "The drug I took to block the compulsion will be wearing off soon. Chatain will realize that I escaped his control for a short period. That will be my doom."

"Strip down and change clothes with Ankari," Nereast said to Witmara. "Move quickly. Don't forget her head covering to cover your bandages!"

Witmara pulled off her outer clothing. While she was pulling on Ankari's skirt and robe, Larien sagged against the bars of the cell.

"Help me get Witmara's clothes on Ankari, Larien," Nereast growled. "We'll shackle Ankari and I'll hit you on the head. Maybe that will cover the drug."

He shook his head. "They will know once they wake me that I am no longer under control. Once they identify Ankari they'll know and it won't matter whether I'm conscious or not. If I'm lucky they'll just kill me before I wake." He came over and helped Nereast ease the skirt over Ankari's legs as Witmara awkwardly wrapped the turban around her head.

"Chatain will want to know what happened," Nereast said.

We can blank your memories,

Alicira said.

"That would be a mixed blessing, Lady of Dovré." He sighed, then bent to help Nereast with draping Witmara's tunic over Ankari. "That would delay my ultimate betrayal, however. But what I will go through beforehand...." He shuddered. "Worth it for a better Daran, however." He frowned at Nereast. "She's much paler than Witmara. They'll know right away."

"They don't know what Witmara looks like for certain, unless they bring Rearnex down. And he's not been to see her since the beginning, so it could be argued that she's pale after the time spent here in the hold during the voyage. We don't need much time. Just enough to get off the slave barge. Let's drag Ankari over here, get her hands and we'll put the shackles on her. Petronin, do you hear anything?" Nereast fussed at Witmara's turban, clucking fretfully. "That braid of yours is heavy."

The ship jolted under them, almost sending Witmara to her knees. Larien winced.

Petronin tilted his head, frowning. "Just hearing a commotion, not coming our way."

The ship lurched again. "Rearnex is having problems with docking," Larien snorted as he and Nereast pulled Ankari over by the wall. He held one of her hands as Nereast locked a shackle on it. "Overconfident, as usual. That buys us more time. Gods only know how much damage he'll do to the docks this time."

"Was Ankari truly a Healer?" Witmara bit her lip.

"She knew healing but I would not call her a healer. By reputation, Ankari ea Ralsem has been one of Chatain's spies for years," Larien said wearily as he held on to Ankari's other hand. "But none of us have known what she looked like. She was given to him as a young girl, along with her sister Chiral, by their father Zauberin."

So Chiral did have a real sister. Just not the one she claimed.

"Did Chiral ever have a sister named Ranar?"

"That was a code name Chiral used when she spied," Nereast said. She adjusted Ankari's body so that she was curled up with her knees against the wall. She paused for a moment, then put the dagger into Ankari's hand, curling her fingers around the handle. "This will confuse them slightly, at least. Perhaps they will think she cut her own throat for fear of failure's consequences."

"One can hope." Larien straightened up. "Lady Alicira. If you please—wipe my memory. Do it as deep as possible. I will not leave this cell alive, and I'd prefer not to betray Witmara." He turned to Nereast. "Do me a kindness. Hit me as hard as you can once the Lady is finished. Otherwise I may turn on you."

Nereast's lips tightened. "Petronin. Your cudgel."

Petronin handed it to her. "Hurry."

Larien closed his eyes as Alicira pressed a hand on his brow. "Long life and health to you, Empress Witmara."

Alicira stepped away and faded. Larien's eyes snapped open, devoid of all awareness, and he growled. Before he could move Nereast clobbered him hard. She tossed the cudgel back to Petronin.

"Let's go! Here." Nereast shoved the tray Ankari had carried into Witmara's hands.

She hurried down the hallway behind Nereast and Petronin. Nereast pointed to a stack of trays at the first doorway and Witmara happily set the tray down. They followed Petronin as he led them up several unoccupied stairways, pausing at doorways to check. She heard the footsteps of others but they didn't join them until they reached a main passageway and joined a surging throng. Petronin took one hand and Nereast the other.

"We must appear as a triad," he whispered in her ear. "Slaves are grouped into duos, triads, and quads. You are the highest in status but you are still one of us." He tapped the tattoo on her hand. "That needs to be visible. Show it to the guard when we get on the barge. It is close enough to the slaving mark that they won't look for more details—unless we are discovered."

"Understood." Witmara copied their demeanor, looking down at her feet as much as possible so that she would not be recognized as different. She was one of the lighter-skinned of those in the mass but not the palest, at least.

Light ahead revealed an opening. They shuffled toward it as part of the crowd, moving and then halting, moving and halting. Magic roiled around Witmara and it was hard not to reach for it, so hard—

Chatain was nearby.

She squeezed Nereast's hand hard, suddenly aware that she also carried sorcery, tightly shielded.

"I know," Nereast breathed. "I feel it too."

"Do you think he will see us?"

"We're slaves and you're appearing in the guise of one of his servants. We are not a priority."

"Good."

Only a few more groups were between them and the guards. They were crossing a narrow bridge onto a large barge, packed in tightly.

Witmara bit back a gasp as she caught her first glimpse of the Ourigny Islands. Gods! Not only was it much warmer than it had been in Medvara, but the sunset was brilliantly bright, in shades of red and pink and orange that made the mountain sunsets of Keldara dull in comparison. Tall trees rose high against the gold and red and orange sky by the docks, their only branches feathery clusters at the very top. A strong odor of fish and the stink of manure rose from the waters around them. Two and three-story buildings rose behind the trees, made of some sort of stone-like substance painted in shades of pink, yellow, and green.

They would be next to board the barge. She carefully watched what the previous group of four did. The man in the center half-raised his right hand to show to the bored-looking guard. He nodded and waved them on. The group dropped hands and proceeded single file down the narrow plank.

Their turn. Witmara lifted her hand slightly. The guard waved them on. Petronin and Nereast held back so she led them across the plank, remembering to keep her eyes downcast and her arms tight against her body. They jammed in tightly against the others, amongst the last to get on this barge.

The guards pulled back the plank. Something rumbled ahead of them, and then a loud whistle like she was used to hearing from the sternwheelers sounded. The barge jerked and they all jostled against each other. Witmara echoed the polite murmurs she heard from the other passengers, wanting to look at what made this barge move but not daring to.

They were near the front of the barge, it appeared. She turned to face the bow with the others around her. Gods, she wanted to stare at everything. Not even Cooscol was this warm this time of year, and it didn't have those fantastic trees and brightly-colored buildings. And while the warmth brought a heightened stink, still it felt good after the deep chill of the ship's hold.

The barge banged into a decrepit wooden dock. The passengers swayed against each other, then began to get off in the same groupings as before. A short plank made up the difference between the barge and the dock. Witmara saw that two guards stood watch on the dock by the plank.

"They count the numbers coming on and off the ship," Nereast whispered. "Don't look at them. Just keep moving. Show them your tattoo."

Witmara obeyed, taking Nereast and Petronin's hands in hers. The groups of slaves spread out, mixing amongst the chaos of the docks. This port was much, much bigger than the one at Medvare or even Chellanasit or Cooscol. At least the groups of slaves appeared to have different destinations. And the crowds were big enough that they could disappear amongst them.

"Is someone tracking where we go? I thought slaves were under more control," she said quietly to Nereast.

"That's what the tattoo is for," Nereast said. "It is a good thing you have one as neither Petronin nor I do. And it's another reason to hurry into hiding...once Ankari's body is found the hunt will be on."

They stepped off the dock and onto a cobbled street. Witmara swayed as power exploded through her, exulting. The cobbles quivered under her feet.

The land!

Is it her? Is it her?

she felt the land questioning.

Is it her at last?

Nereast and Petronin guided Witmara away from the general mass of people and buildings. After a while they turned into a narrow alleyway of dried grass shacks. More people than she was accustomed to seeing pushed past them in both directions. Witmara clung to Nereast, suddenly dizzy as the land pulled at her, its excitement rising.

It is her! It is her!

"Keep the land quiet for a little bit longer!" Nereast muttered to Witmara. "Chatain will know that you are here and that the land claims you soon enough!"

Witmara nodded, unable to speak as the land's delight pulsed through her. She wanted nothing more than to press her hands —no, her whole *body*—against the soil to suck in every bit of its rejoicing at the arrival of the leader it wanted. To drink of its power and reassure it that she would care for it until her death.

Was this what Medvara felt like to her mother? If so, now she understood so very much about Leadership than she hadn't until now.

But Nereast was right about keeping the land calm.

Wait. Soon,

she thought to it.

She desperately wanted to know what had happened to Daro and Toran. Once she was able to join with the land—perhaps she would find out.

A NEW WAYKEMIN

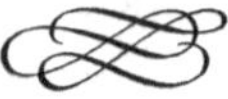

Rekaré didn't have any more tears left. Katerin had pressed the bag with Quartel's ashes on her as part of the process of clearing and destroying the Chamber. Sesenth held her other hand as they followed the Keldaran and Clendan Mer Galad members who carried Cenarth's body out of the Chamber through those narrow, foul hallways. She would have done it herself, carried Cenarth's bulk in her arms with Sesenth's aid, or had Basnen carry his body, but Katerin had held them back.

"You must be the mourner now," she had said. *"And you have Linyet to console. Let your Mer Galad do this. They want to do what is right by him."*

Linyet. Gods. And Heinmyets, if he still lived. She would have to answer to both of them for Cenarth's death. Rekaré blinked as they finally emerged from the Chamber, her vision still blurred from weeping.

I should not have let him come with me for this last fight. No. I shouldn't have yielded to him back at Dera. I should have made him stay with Linyet and the Two Nations' force, not let him come with me and the Mer Galad. Though Gods, having him ride and fight next to me was so much like it once had been....

Rekaré shook her head.

Gods, another family death to be attributed to *Rekaré Kinslayer*. Even though she hadn't killed Cenarth with her own hand, her sentimental desire to regain a lost piece of herself had put him in harm's way. It was her doing as surely as if it had been her own hand that cast the spell that killed him.

That thought brought dampness to her eyes—even though she had assumed she was cried out. No. She fought them back. The time was done for crying. Tears wouldn't fix things, not at all. She stared straight ahead, ignoring the Waykemese and the warriors from the Two Nations who now lined the street. They knelt in respect to Cenarth but Gods, it shouldn't have been him!

No more. No more yielding to sentiment. No deviation from my path of vengeance. I must completely become Rekaré Kinslayer, she who brings sorrow, and remember that I bring death to those I love.

She half-expected *benghaalph* to stir but it remained quiet within her.

Sesenth's hand tightened on hers, the faint cool scaliness of it somehow reassuring as they processed outside of the gates of Forsim toward Linyet, his personal command from the Two Nations, and the remainder of the Mer Galad forces.

"Stay strong," Sesenth said softly.

Rekaré's hand closed down hard on Sesenth's. This was one person she could not harm, one person who expected nothing more than the sorrow that trailed Rekaré Kinslayer. For better or worse, Sesenth's path joined with hers.

Yet as they drew close to Linyet, her resolve not to yield to sentiment flew away. The anguish on her son's face as he stared at his father's body made her want to take him in her arms. He,

Heinmyets and Katerin were the only close family remaining to her.

You do not want to be the cause of harm to him.

Katerin followed her own fate, intertwined with Witmara's, and Heinmyets was old and alone. But Linyet…no, Gods, she dared not lose him. Not for her, not for the Two Nations.

"Halt," Rekaré croaked as he dismounted and strode toward Cenarth's body.

Linyet stopped short, staring at his father's body, shaking with unshed sobs. Rekaré let go of Sesenth's hand and walked to meet her son, steeling herself for the angry reaction she expected.

"I am sorry," she said from two paces away, making herself halt instead of taking him into her arms—would he even allow it? "I tried to tell him not to follow us. He should not have been in the Chamber." Her voice caught and she choked on the next words. "But he insisted. He…he said he would watch our backs. I should have sent him to you if he wouldn't stay with the Mer Galad."

"He was the happiest I've seen him in years, once you let him ride with you," Linyet gulped, still staring at his father's body.

"I—should have sent him back. He would still be with us. With you."

"The time for thinking about that happened seven years ago!"

Rekaré flinched at the anger in his voice as he kept staring at Cenarth, not looking at her.

Linyet continued. "I didn't understand why you didn't come back after Chiral's death. Why we couldn't see you. He always kept faith with you. He always said you had your reasons, and that after what happened at—at Grandmother's memorial, and with Melarae—he said you couldn't be captured. Pinioned. You needed to be free, despite what it cost to us. That our future was with Grandfather and Grandmother, in the Two Nations, and no longer Medvara." Anguish replaced anger as he finally looked at her. "Why, Mother? *Why?*"

"I—I couldn't," she murmured. "I couldn't return, and he knew it," she repeated, louder. "Chiral was a closer relative than I realized, and I didn't know that until her death. I brought down Kinslayer's curse on my head when I killed her. I dared not bring that back to you and your father. Oh Gods, Linyet." Her voice caught again and her vision blurred. *No more tears.* "I wanted to come back. But that path would have led to much, much worse. Do you think I really wanted to be away from you and your father?"

"I wondered sometimes." He moved next to her. "Especially when Sesenth clearly has become important to you."

She gulped, and buried her head in her free hand. The weight of Quartel's ashes made her slump, pulled her off-center. "I was alone. Senth was there, and helped me understand what was happening when *benghaalph* took me."

"It is a strange thing to learn that your mother is now the Saubral prophet." But that wasn't anger in his voice now, perhaps just a touch of wry understatement. "Do you know he was proud when we heard that the Saubral had embraced you as *benghaalph*? That as relations with the Saubral improved, he kept asking them how you were?"

"Gods. I...." She couldn't find any words to say. She raised her head, staring at Cenarth, not daring to look at her son. "Katerin told me how things were faring with you and your father. She relayed messages between us. Occasionally I would hear from the Two Nations—mostly the traders from Wickmasa, when we'd come across them in summertime. They gave me the news, told me how you were."

Linyet's arms closed around her unexpectedly and she buried her face into his shoulder.

"Father told me that he didn't care if he died following you. He knew it was risky, but he felt that if he were there, it would give you the strength you needed to ensure that Katerin did the right thing."

"He did."

"He seemed to like Sesenth, too. He came to our fire last night. I think he had a premonition. He told me to guard you—and Grandfather, that we all still had roles to play."

Rekaré sniffled and straightened up. "Can you forgive me?"

"He died the way he wanted to—protecting you."

She became aware of another presence as Sesenth joined them.

"I am honored to have ridden with your father, Linyet of the Two Nations," she said to Linyet, clutching her right fist to her chest and bowing low. "He spoke very highly of his son—as does your mother. His death is a great loss for all of us."

"Sesenth." Linyet's voice was noncommittal. "Close to my mother—and to my father as well?"

"Yes. We are diminished because of his loss." Sesenth hesitated. "I learned much from him, including the depth of his love for your mother. And he—I had not thought I would be close to one of the Two Nations, much less a Miteal like your mother. But he held both of us dear at the end. We knew we shared your mother's love—and he did not begrudge me the piece I have, which is much smaller than the piece of her heart that he owned."

Linyet sighed. "What became of Quartel?"

Rekaré shook the bag she carried. "His ashes are here, to be scattered in the mountains above Dera. We will take your father to the Two Nations for his pyre. Your grandfather should not be denied his right to send him off. I—I will work the preservation spell, tonight, in the camp of the Two Nations. That is where he belongs."

"The Mer Galad is welcome to join us," Linyet said.

"I thank you. Meanwhile, let's move on." She signaled the Mer Galad to continue on.

Linyet did not rejoin his riders. He took her free hand, and they walked behind the stretcher that bore Cenarth's body. Sesenth took his other hand.

"It would be so much easier if you would just accept the Leadership of Waykemin!" Marneri glared at Katerin.

"Medvara already claims me," *at least until Witmara can take it—if we can free her from Chatain—no, don't think about that.* "I cannot and will not take on another Leadership. I may be of the Miteal and Alame en Miteal's daughter, but I am not an Empress and have no desire to create an empire in Varen!"

"Then what is to become of Waykemin? Are we to be absorbed into Saubral and the Two Nations?"

"No. Not that."

But then what was to become of Waykemin, indeed.

Once the remaining Council had destroyed the Chamber that evening, the arguments began. Katerin presided over a gathering of the Council in Forsim's main square, by a bonfire fueled by wooden pieces of the Chamber that hadn't collapsed after its destruction. Occasionally, a scrounger brought more chunks to throw on the fire.

Nenanim had found a campstool for Katerin so that she sat while military leaders, guild leaders, her *kinforost*, and assorted former *ushar* and *kendar* gathered around her and the Council that remained, to argue over what was to become of Waykemin. The crowd of mostly quiet observers from Forsim expanded as the discussion grew into debate. At first each speaker glanced around worriedly, as if expecting one of the Witches to descend upon them. But as time passed without retribution, more participants spoke longer and louder, especially the former *ushar* and *kendar*.

It always came back to this. She was Terani's daughter, born of Chiyan. She had brought about the fall of Tranarin's abusive rule. Why would she not take on the Leadership?

Because I already have one land to repair.

She felt no kinship with Waykemin any more—if anything, she wanted to flee this place. But before she left—a sharp twinge pierced her as she thought of Witmara—she wanted to see her birthland set on a reasonable path toward healing. To drop the barriers that had kept it isolated and apart from the rest of Varen.

What little she had heard about the Divine Confederation on the other side of the Nerean Gate in Keratil during these arguments worried her. What would it mean for Varen? Waykemin needed to be whole and strong if the Divine Confederation was the threat that some here thought it to be.

If the Witches allied with Chatain to face it.

That spoke to the level of threat from the Confederation. The Witches she had known were fiercely independent.

Finally she could bear no more. "Enough," she yelled, thumping the Spear on the ground. "The question really is simple. The Council is gone. You need new leaders, ones not bound to Nitel, Karnoi, or Cirdel. How are you going to choose them?"

Nenanim stepped forward, his voice projecting loudly over the crowd. "Perhaps we should elect someone from the village leaders who *are* here."

"But not everyone is here," Yitlisk said. "Is this fair?"

"Couldn't you elect someone temporarily?" Katerin asked. "Or instead of a Council of Witches, a council made up of village leaders who then elect someone to speak for them?"

"Then who controls the land's magic?" Marneri raised a brow at Katerin. She had apparently become the voice of the remainder of the Witches' Council.

"Do you feel the land seeking one person to control it?" She certainly didn't get that sense from Waykemin. If anything, the land seemed to be satisfied *not* to have someone poking at it, drawing upon its power.

"There's also the question of who is going to be Waykemin's patron," one of the military commanders whose name Katerin had missed said. "Staul? Dovré? Artel? Certainly not Terat, not as far inland as we are."

A good question, and one that would point to whomever is going to take over the Leadership. Figure out which God will honor Waykemin, and find someone dedicated to that God.

Perhaps this could lead to a solution.

"Terat is the patron of Clenda and it's just as inland as Waykemin," Katerin sighed. "Perhaps we should ask the land which God it wants as a patron to replace the Twins."

"But who is going to do that?" Marneri scowled. "If we Witches do the asking it will be perceived as skewed and biased, an attempt for us to retain power. Maybe you should ask the land for us, Katerin. You have made it clear you will not accept Leadership. You don't have a ruling agenda. Your verdict will be clear."

"Perhaps a group of us should ask instead. Now. In front of everyone as witness, so that no one doubts the choice the land makes." Gods, she wanted to get this settled as quickly as possible—but also done right. Katerin pointed toward Kirest. "You. You represent the military. Come here. Marneri. You represent the Witches." She scanned the crowd. One of the outspoken merchants caught her eye. "Drestil. You represent the merchants and tradespeople." She studied the crowd, choosing Nenanim for both former *kendar* and Scholars, then picked six more people that came from various groups within Waykemin.

Katerin rose from the stool and eyed the ten people she had chosen. "Join hands around the fire and repeat what I say."

She strode into the center, next to the fire—*Gods that heat felt good with the evening chill coming on*—and drew the token Medvara had given her out of its pouch. She knelt, facing the fire so that any apparitions could manifest in the flames, and raised the stone high in one hand while resting her other palm flat on the ground.

"Waykemin! Your people seek you."

The circle echoed her words.

"Waykemin! Wake and give guidance to your people." She paused as Waykemin stirred sluggishly under her contact, resentment at being awakened again seething in the mix. "No further need to repeat what I say," she told the circle. "The land awakens. It will speak to us shortly. Watch the flames."

She trusted that anything she raised in the flame would be true—this was not gods-haunted Wickmasa, where an unwanted spirit could manifest and attempt possession of someone who watched the fire too closely. Waykemin would not allow it. *She* would not allow it.

> I do not seek to control you,

she told the land.

> I belong to Medvara. I simply am trying to guide your people toward the right path.

> No more Witches,

the land growled.

> Understood. We seek your true patron. Bear with me.

"The land has awakened," she said out loud. "It does not want any more Witches—they have depleted its strength," she added. Even though Waykemin had not told her that, she could feel its weariness under the resentment. "It needs someone who will cultivate and cherish it." Her fingers tightened on her token. "I am of Medvara. Tell us, Waykemin. No Nitel. No Cirdel and

Karnoi. Which of the remaining Gods do you choose as patron?"

The one I want most is not yet a God,

the land grumbled.

But I will choose one of those four anyway.

An image shimmered in the flames in front of Katerin. At first it was indistinct. She thought she caught glimpses of Dovré, Artel, then Staul, then Artel again. Terat. Artel. The features grew more distinct and she heaved a sigh of relief as the image shaped itself into Artel's form. First the circle around them, then the others beyond the circle, knelt.

"Lord Artel! Lord Artel of Waykemin! Lord Artel!" Was that relief she heard in their cries? Either Staul or Dovré might have been too demanding, and Terat too lax. But Artel the Judge— yes, that was the patron this land needed right now.

Waykemin. People of Waykemin. I accept your choice of me as your new Patron.

The God studied the circle of people around them.

Waykemin the land and Waykemin the people have been damaged. You need leadership that seeks to heal and rebuild both people and the land without twisting its magic. It will be a hard job.

"It is one that is worthwhile, oh Lord Artel," said Marneri. "And yet who will wield the land's magic? A Council? A Leader? Katerin ea Miteal refuses the position."

And rightly so. Katerin ea Miteal has her own destiny beyond Waykemin, and she has not lived here since she was young. No. Your leadership needs to have suffered through all that has been done to Waykemin in recent years.

The God studied the ten in the circle.

You ten are an excellent beginning for a governing Council. But you need one voice.

He pointed to Marneri.

Your son. Yitlisk. He comes from the line of Terani-the-God-Killer and has battled and suffered for Waykemin against the threat from the east. You have trained him to become the mayor of Chiyan. He has greater ability than just Chiyan. Where is he?

Yitlisk rose from where he had knelt in the crowd, his figure partially obscured by Artel and the flames in front of Katerin. "I am here, Lord Artel."

Come forward, Yitlisk, Leader of Waykemin.

"My thanks to you, Lord Artel."

Yitlisk made a fist of his right hand and struck his chest. He bowed to the God, then made his way forward through the kneeling crowd. Those around him scrabbled out of his way. Katerin noticed that he received respectful bows as he hobbled toward the circle, which he acknowledged with quiet thanks.

At last he entered the circle, pausing to kiss his mother's forehead and say a few soft words. Then he shambled toward Artel, dropping to his knees close to the flames, before the God.

"I am not worthy of this high position," he said in a firm and calm voice that nonetheless carried. "But since you have chosen me to do it, I will strive to perform my best for the good of the land."

"Speak to your land," Artel said.

Yitlisk bowed until his forehead touched the ground, extending his hands until his fingertips lay flat at the edge of the bonfire. He trembled as green and brown lights shimmered over him.

Katerin took Medvara's token in both hands, to provide its witness. Just before she raised her hand she perceived satisfaction radiating from Waykemin. She rose slowly, aware of a slight disturbance as someone else approached. No. Three people. Linyet, Rekaré, and Sesenth carefully picked their way through the kneeling people to stand outside of the circle.

The lights over Yitlisk faded. He shivered, then slowly sat up. A brown and green pendant on a silver chain glowed in Artel's fingers—amber and emerald. It looked vaguely familiar, like something she had seen as a young child. Then memory returned. It was another item she had seen in an old painting that had burned when she was young. Yes. Its bearer had been a young man who looked a little bit like Yitlisk. And after an argument-filled visit by the then-Chief Priestess, her mother had pulled down the portrait and thrown it on a bonfire, along with several books of Waykemin history.

The Heart of Waykemin,

Artel intoned as he held the pendant high.

It is the new token for leadership here, rather than the masks the Witches Council wore. Bear it with pride, Yitlisk, Leader of Waykemin.

Yitlisk ducked his head as Artel reached out from the flames and hung the pendant around his neck.

"Heard and witnessed by Medvara!" Katerin cried, raising

her stone high. Even at this distance she felt her land's satisfaction with the God's choice.

"Heard and witnessed by the Two Nations' Leader-Designate," Linyet called, his voice strong and clear until the last two words, spoken with a slight quaver. He coughed, and his voice was strong again. "Our congratulations and support to Yitlisk."

Rekaré eased between the kneeling new Council members to march toward Artel and Yitlisk. A subtle change came over her features as she bowed to Artel.

"*Benghaalph* gives honor and thanks to the Lord Artel for his wisdom," she said, her voice deeper and more raspy than usual. She faced Yitlisk. "Heard and witnessed by *benghaalph* for the Saubral. The Saubral riding with the Mer Galad join Medvara and the Two Nations in honoring the changes in Waykemin, and look forward to facing together the challenges that lie ahead of us."

She seemed to grow larger, stepping away from Artel and Yitlisk, spreading her arms wide as she faced the fire. "For more foes than just Chatain lie ahead of us, with even graver consequences should Waykemin falter."

Images of riders pouring through a narrow river canyon flickered in the flames. Katerin shuddered.

The Divine Confederation.

"Varen and Daran must join together to battle an even greater enemy," *benghaalph* continued through Rekaré. "The Witches realized that danger but chose the wrong path when they decided to ally with Chatain. He gave them power to hold these intruders back, but the cost has been dear to Waykemin. I will not say their name for fear of summoning them, but it is known to the Council."

"She speaks truly!" Marneri said. "This has not been spoken of outside of the Council. They ride with sorcerers and shamans who do not acknowledge the Seven Crowned Gods but seek to twist the world to worship of their One—the Outcast God."

The Outcast God.

Katerin hadn't heard him mentioned for years, not since she had left Waykemin. She had thought him banished, defeated. If he had a foothold in the Divine Confederation, then it was a danger greater than the one Chatain presented.

But Chatain's path is not the correct one, either. Not that level of red shadows! Not that level of oppression! I would not see Varen and Daran go the path of Waykemin. I will fight that with every breath I take.

"At this time the Nerean Gate still holds," *benghaalph* continued. "But that will not last. I call upon those here. Medvara. Keldara and Clenda, the Two Nations. Saubral. Prepare. Be ready. Do not become complacent. Prepare for the danger from the east. Be wise, young Yitlisk and his Council. Rebuild Waykemin and do not become overconfident. The land of Varen will depend upon your vigilance. I speak to you as *benghaalph*, the One Spoken Of by the Saubral. Watch. Be ready. I am done here."

Rekaré seemed to shrink as *benghaalph* faded from her. She swayed, jerking slightly, face turning to the sky, then fell toward the fire. Yitlisk pulled her back. Katerin ran to her side, kneeling to check her pulses even as Sesenth and Linyet joined them. To her relief Rekaré's pulses beat strongly under her fingers, her breath coming smoothly and regularly.

Benghaalph has overwhelmed her, that is all.
She will be well soon,

Artel said.

I take my leave of you now but add my endorsement of every word that benghaalph has said. Heed her prophecy, all of you. And once again, my blessings upon you, Yitlisk, Leader of Waykemin.

The God faded away as Rekaré's eyes blinked open. "What happened—oh. That was a strong visitation."

"I thank you for your wise words," Yitlisk said. "We will take them to heart. Right, my Council?" He rose and faced his new Council as Rekaré struggled to sit back up. Katerin supported her as they watched.

Marneri was the first to rise, march to Yitlisk, and kneel before her son, her arms crossed across her chest. "I give you my honor and heart, Yitlisk, Leader of Waykemin. I am yours to guide and command." She rose and stepped aside.

The others followed her, one-by-one, until the entire Council had vowed to support Yitlisk.

"My first request," Yitlisk said. "I want an assessment of Waykemin's condition, especially in light of what *benghaalph* has shown us. Magic has ripped our land apart, as those of us who have secretly sought to overthrow the Witches well know. I want to know who remains to farm and raise stock, who is available to fight, who can build and restore our roads, our buildings, our villages. We need to know what has been lost after all these years and plan how to restore it."

"The Two Nations will provide you with Stardance line sheep should you choose to cultivate magic fleeces so you may weave a Great Tapestry," Linyet said. "The Tapestry provides a useful means to monitor problems within a nation. It may give us aid and warning in light of *benghaalph's* words."

"I—the knowledge of how to wield the Tapestries is lost to us," Yitlisk said.

Katerin cleared her throat. "When the time comes, Medvara can provide guidance for weaving the Great Tapestry."

Yitlisk nodded in acknowledgment. "I thank you, Leader Katerin and Leader-Designate Linyet. Waykemin thanks you. I am sure we will have need of your help."

"One place we can start. There are hidden caches where old books and scrolls were stored once the Council began to destroy all old histories," Kirest said. She gestured toward Nenanim. "When Nenanim was taken as *kendar*, many of us who were Scholars realized we needed to preserve Waykemin's past knowledge safely, in secret. I was one of those granted that task. There will be more of our past available than you know, Yitlisk."

"That is good to know." Yitlisk heaved a heavy sigh. "My Council. Among other things we need to find a new place to gather. I have no desire to build a new Chamber right away. We have more important tasks."

"The Mayor's Hall is available," one of the onlookers said. He stepped forward. "Rykenst, Mayor of Forsim. We would be honored to have the new Leader and his Council meet in our chambers."

"Thank you, Rykenst. That is a beginning. Also, we of the Council should meet in other villages to hear our people's needs. Please lead us there," Yitlisk said. "Council, let us go for a short meeting." He turned to Rekaré and Katerin. "Rekaré Kinslayer. Katerin Leader of Medvara. I thank you in Waykemin's name for what you have done to free us. Our debt to you is insurmountable, but we will do what we can to repay it." Then he faced Linyet. "Linyet, Leader-Designate of the Two Nations. Waykemin expresses its deepest grief at our role in your father's death. We are in no shape to pay a blood price to the Two Nations, but we will do our best somehow."

Linyet bowed. "Yitlisk, Leader of Waykemin. We hear you and understand. This is a matter we can deal with as we go forward, after I consult with my grandfather. For now, focus on rebuilding your nation."

"We owe the Two Nations a debt of honor, and will not forget it." Yitlisk sighed. "Now. Council. Let us go."

He followed Rykenst, the Council around him.

"Wise words," Katerin said to Linyet as they helped Rekaré to her feet. "This new Waykemin will need all the aid it can get."

Linyet nodded. "It is what my grandparents would have done—all three of them." He reached to help steady Rekaré as she staggered. "Sesenth. Let us take her back to camp. Between the battle, this prophecy, and weaving that stabilization spell over my father's body, she's worn out. And I would have time with my mother."

Katerin stepped back as Sesenth replaced her by Rekaré's side. She stood by the bonfire, watching as they left.

Alone again. Witmara is Gods-knows-where. Metkyi no longer speaks to me. Oh Gods.

The stone in her hand warmed, Medvara seeking to offer her consolation even though she was far away. Katerin clutched the stone to her chest.

I am with you too,

the Goddess said, stroking Katerin's brow before fading away.

Rainin moved next to her, nuzzling Katerin's arm. She sighed and threw her arm over the daranval's neck, then buried her head on Rainin's withers, breathing in deeply of her daranval's scent.

Once upon a time, when she was still just Katerin Healer, the presence of a good daranval would have been enough. She supposed that this would still be the case. Katerin remained standing there, leaning on Rainin. Gods, she was tired.

But at least the matter of Waykemin was settled. Now they could focus on Chatain. Thinking about that now was almost a relief.

Almost. Because once Chatain was dealt with, then there would be whatever challenge the Divine Confederation brought, led by the Outcast God.

Katerin suspected that those battles would be even redder than what they had already faced.

CONSEQUENCES

Gods, her head hurt. Witmara sagged against Petronin as Nereast haggled with a pale-faced, portly woman who stank of fish. They stood in a marketplace full of pushing people. What little she understood of Nereast's words suggested that Nereast was telling the woman that their controller had taken ill and they could not drag her across the city to their usual quarters. Nereast moved boldly as she and the pale woman argued, gesturing broadly and no longer cowering, at times leaning close to the pale woman's face.

The loud voices made her nervous. If it wasn't that others around them were yelling and shoving, black and brown and white alike all pushing close as they haggled, she'd be afraid they were drawing attention

Everything around her was unfamiliar, intruding and invasive. Bright reds, yellows, and greens. Loud voices speaking words she didn't know. Spicy fragrances not just from food, but from the bodies pressing close around them. The loud *squawwwk* from a big, yellow and green bird riding on someone's shoulder, brushing her face with a wing feather as its person momentarily staggered against them, his breath heavily fragranced with alcohol.

Another time she would be thrilled to watch everything around her. Right now the chaos added to the pounding in her head.

The pale woman bellowed at Nereast and she shouted back. Gods, she wished she knew what they were saying.

I need to learn common Darani, and soon.

What she knew of the language of Daran was strictly formal, from documents she had studied in Medvara. That had to change if she were to become Empress. She needed to know not just the formal language, but enough of the common dialects that she could speak easily to the peoples of Daran. Her mother had done so in Medvara, learning coastal and mountain variants as well as the common Medvaran. Heinmyets, Inharise, and Alicira had been able to switch easily between Keldaran and Clendan tongues as well as Varenese—and her mother was fluent in all three thanks to her years spent as a traveling Healer.

A final volley of yelling, and then Nereast and the woman shook hands, four hard, distinct shakes. Nereast untwisted her turban to pull out a copper disk as payment. The woman's eyes widened when she saw the felted locks of hair hidden under Nereast's turban. She raised her hands and shoved the disk back at Nereast.

Nereast protested, shoving the disk back at the pale woman, and that led to a further round of haggling. Witmara closed her eyes and leaned harder against Petronin. It wasn't just her head. The land pulled at her, demanding her attention, and fighting it off took more effort as her head throbbed harder and harder.

What did Ankari do to me?

She buried her head in Petronin's arm, trying to shut every-thing out—the sounds, the heat, the smells, the sweaty bodies jostling against her, the incessant pleas of the land for her to acknowledge it. She wanted to answer, but not if it gave Chatain a clue to their location. She was in no shape to face him right now. She needed rest. Quiet. Food. A chance to have a *real* Healer look at her head wound, not someone posing as one.

Petronin nudged her. Witmara raised her head and straightened up.

"Well, *that* was a challenge, but I got more than shelter out of it." Nereast smirked as she juggled several leaf-wrapped packages.

She jerked her head toward an alleyway. They pushed through the crowd toward it, both Petronin and Nereast protectively sheltering her from the crowd.

"Revealing yourself could be dangerous," Petronin chided once they reached the comparatively less crowded alleyway and could walk without bumping into others.

"It got us food as well as shelter, and she claims to be a sympathizer. We're beggars right now. Until we reach the lady B, we're not safe," Nereast said. "And this places us right where we need to be in the morning, without having to go back within the walls."

Petronin snorted but didn't respond.

Nereast led them along several twisted alleyways and through a narrow gate in the city walls. Witmara drew a deep breath as people and buildings no longer felt like they pressed hard against her. They followed Nereast along a row of three-sided shacks; some open and empty, some with occupants staring out at them as they passed by, others with sheltering curtains or reed mats covering the open side. Nereast stopped in front of one of the empty ones. A thin curtain hung over the open side. The lane ended abruptly a few shacks down, changing from a wide dirt trail to a narrow pathway through a massive stand of brush and trees different from the tall, narrow ones with branches at the very top.

There wasn't much to the hovel, a grass mat-walled shack that had dried versions of the branches Witmara had seen on the tall trees for a roof. Woven reed mats covered the ground and there was a rough stand made of branches of some sort of wood that looked almost grass-like to Witmara's eyes. A metal pitcher sat next to a bowl on the stand, its exterior beaded with dampness, along with a simple clay oil lamp, a knotted wick threaded through a bead at the top. A single cot sat against the back wall of the hovel, and a plank resting on two stumps made up the rest of the furnishings.

"On the cot with you," Nereast ordered. She set the packages of food down on the plank, lit the lamp, then untied the ragged cloth that mostly screened the front. "As for revealing ourselves, our hostess for the night knows nothing other than the locks represent my rank. She didn't recognize the strands twisted into them, or my other markers. We're all right, Petronin."

Witmara gratefully sank onto the cot, swinging her feet up to lie down. The incessant din of the land's demands for her attention faded, until it was just a nagging sensation in the back of her mind.

"Chatain is here," Petronin said in a low voice. "How long can you expect Larien to hold out before betraying us? You know Chatain won't kill him outright, but torture him to death."

"His memory was altered," Nereast said.

"And how long do you think that will stand? More than that, how are we going to get *her* to Betsona? She's in no shape to walk, even with a night's rest."

"Hush. I will go out later to arrange that and pick up medication to treat her wound. Meanwhile, here's food."

Nereast brought Witmara one of the leaf-wrapped packages.

"Can you eat?" she asked. "You don't look very well." She pressed the back of her hand to Witmara's forehead. "You're feverish."

"I know. It's gotten worse. I can try to eat."

"Food will help." Nereast set the food on the edge of the cot and unwrapped Witmara's turban. "There's more here than your wound—it's warm but there's something else going on. Tell me."

"My head is pounding and the land keeps pulling at me. Hard. I need to rest, and I can't touch the ground right now—as strong as the land tugs at me. I don't have the strength to shield or control at the moment."

"Food will help. I will go find medication after you have eaten and I've looked at your injury," Nereast said. "Can you sit up and eat? I'll help you."

"Thank you. I'll try." Witmara pushed herself up with Nereast's aid, crossing her legs on the cot so she didn't touch the ground. Nereast handed her the leaf-wrapped package, and Witmara opened it to find a bar covered with something white and gummy. The paleness and texture didn't look appealing. But an intriguing smell rose from it.

It is food, no matter what it is, she told herself, and took a bite.

The inside of the bar—no, roll, she decided, was filled with a mixture of meat and some sort of bean paste. Hungry as she was, anything would taste good, but the flavor was sweet and slightly savory. After the first bite she was ravenous. The outer covering was some sort of white grain she wasn't familiar with, but it held together, only crumbling slightly.

Nereast sat at the foot of the cot. "It is good?"

"It is delicious." The leaf wrapping held the chunks that crumbled. Witmara picked out the pieces. Then she eyed the pitcher. She desperately wanted a drink, but she would have to walk to reach it. She didn't think she could resist the land's pleas, even with the boost from eating decent food. She gestured to the pitcher.

"Not for drinking," Nereast said. She handed Witmara a waterskin that she hadn't noticed before. "Open pitchers are for washing up—who knows what's fallen into that or who has contaminated it in order to harm you. First lesson of Daran. Do not drink from open pitchers. Only trust waterskins. Slavers will drug you to capture you for sale, even if you're already owned."

"Thank you," Witmara said.

What kind of society is this, that slavers prey on the already slaved?

She drank carefully, not wanting to consume all of their water.

Nereast snorted. "It's nothing. Let me check your injury with a better light, now that you've eaten. Lie back down." She pressed her hand against Witmara's forehead again. "Better." She rose and washed her hands, then removed the bandage. Her fingers probed the wound on Witmara's head, more deftly than Ankari's had.

"No infection," Nereast said finally. "But it's also not healing as quickly as it should, especially in this climate." She sighed. "Now I know what to get." She patted Witmara's shoulder. "Rest, my lady. I will return with medication."

She was too tired to object to the title *my lady.* Witmara sighed and closed her eyes, barely hearing the hushed argument between Nereast and Petronin before falling asleep. When Nereast returned, she roused just enough to be aware of a gentle hand cleansing her wound, followed by a salve that burned at first, then soothed.

"I need you to sit up again," Nereast said.

Witmara complied, blinking rapidly in the brighter light. A second oil lamp burned on the plank, while Petronin held the original lamp close. Nereast wrapped her head neater than Ankari had, muttering to herself.

"Good thing we got to this when we did. Maggots would be growing soon."

"Maggots?" That snapped her awake.

"We are in a jungle. Rot happens more quickly here than on the mainland. The wound was not fully cleansed. Ankari should have known better."

"Or perhaps she meant to sap my strength before meeting Chatain."

"That's a more likely possibility." Nereast produced a small vial of a brown liquid. "This is bitter, but it will help you with both healing and rest. I have used it myself in the past."

Witmara took the vial and sniffed it, trying to remember what her mother had used in situations like this. She recognized the scent of several herbs—willow bark, mint, cirelen—*cirelen grows here? This isn't the place for it! It's too hot and damp*—healflower, and chamomile, as well as some spicy scents unknown to her.

"Does this mixture have a name?"

Nereast shrugged. "We've always called it HealRest."

HealRest. That sounded similar to one of her mother's mixes that used the ingredients she recognized. "I think my mother has used a similar remedy."

"Oh?" Nereast's brows rose sharply. "We can only get this mixture from a Healer. How would your mother know of it?"

"My mother was Katerin Healer before she was Katerin ea Miteal and Leader of Medvara. I may not be a Healer but I possess some knowledge of the healing arts. When Ankari did not know of arnica…that should have alerted me."

Gods, she was tired. If this HealRest was close to what her mother had used, it would provide relief.

"Only drink half of it," Nereast cautioned as Witmara raised the vial to her lips.

"I have taken this remedy before, or one like it." Witmara drank the whole thing. "Half is not enough. Not for the way I feel. Not to silence the land's voice in my mind. I dare not risk our exposure."

She handed the glass vial back to Nereast as she spluttered objections. Sleep washed over her, a welcome and hopefully restful oblivion.

With any luck, she would be in better shape tomorrow.

Katerin left half of their tens in Forsim to help Yitlisk and the Waykemese first, and as a defense should the Divine Confederation attack. Now that Waykemin was settled, she had other issues to face—primarily what had happened to Witmara, and who was ruling Medvara in Witmara's absence. A smaller group would travel faster.

It felt odd to be greeted as saviors as they rode out of Waykemin. She ended up leaving even more of her force behind in the name of further assistance. All the things she had missed by taking the back route to Forsim from Chiyan struck her as they rode through Waykemin. With the Witches' glamor broken over the land, the failure of crops and the poor condition of much of the livestock was glaringly obvious.

"Gods," Rekaré said at one point, having left Sesenth and Linyet with Cenarth's body. "What a damnable mess. I thought Medvara was in sad shape after my father's death. This—this is worse."

Katerin nodded, remembering what she had seen of Medvara then. "Waykemin was better when I was younger. But I left before the Witches' Council became more twisted."

Rekaré did not say anything in response. She gazed across the land, a distant look in her eyes. Katerin wondered if *benghaalph* stirred within her. Then she turned Basnen, and rode back to join the escort around Cenarth.

They traveled well into the night, Katerin pushing hard so that they would only need to ride a half-day to reach Dera.

Circuit Healer's experience, she thought at one point.

Gods, she never thought she would use that background to calculate how far she needed to travel with an army.

How things change.

Camp that night was basic. But by midmorning they had crossed the last pass and ridden into the Keldaran Valley. She sent messengers ahead to warn Heinmyets and advise him of their victory—and what it had cost them. The contrast between the greening-up land that was healthy and prosperous as compared to Waykemin struck Katerin hard, and once again she wondered if they should not have intervened sooner.

And yet—they did not have a reason until Inharise's death. None that the Gods would approve, anyway.

Those who bore Cenarth's body moved to the front of their column once they reached the valley, followed by Katerin, Rekaré, and Linyet. At first a scattering of people stood vigil by the road, raising their voices in mournful keening as they rode by. Then more and more came to stand by the road. Rekaré stared straight ahead as they rode, lips tightening more as the lamentations grew louder, along with muttering about *Rekaré Kinslayer*.

Heinmyets awaited them just outside of the city, face grim and even more tired-looking than it had been when they left. Linyet rode ahead to greet his grandfather. Rekaré tensed next to Katerin as Heinmyets and Linyet spoke, from the gestures clearly heated, then Heinmyets rode on ahead to meet them, Linyet at his side.

"I am sorry," Rekaré said before Heinmyets could speak. "I tried to discourage him from following us into that last battle. He insisted he needed to be there to protect our backs."

"Did he do so?" Heinmyets glowered at Rekaré.

"He did so with all honor," Katerin interjected. "I witnessed it. He would not be denied. She tried to protect him, Leader Heinmyets. But he would not have it."

"I hear you, Leader Katerin." The formality seemed to ease Heinmyets' foul mood. He urged his horse further to look at Cenarth's still form. "My son. You too. Alicira, Inharise, and now you. Was it a fell mood that made you discard the election to Leadership and follow Rekaré Kinslayer, after she had rejected you?" He sighed. "I am old. I only have a grandson, and a Heartsdaughter gone rogue. What is to become of the Two Nations?"

Rekaré's face paled. She opened her mouth but no words came out.

"He was the happiest I have seen him in years, Grandfather," Linyet said, riding forward so that he was between Rekaré and Heinmyets. "He knew there was danger in following my mother, especially since she has become the Kinslayer. But he found peace in fighting for her at the end. He didn't want the Leadership. Like my mother, after Medvara he had enough of that."

"And will you tire of it as well?" Heinmyets challenged.

Linyet shook his head. "The land speaks to me, Grandfather. I want to honor and cherish it. I want to learn more from you about making it even stronger—I have learned so much from you and Grandmother Inharise, but now—I will be its Leader. After seeing what has become of Waykemin—I do not want to see our own land spiral down into that level of failure. I never want to see that again, in any land."

Their eyes met. Grandfather and grandson stared each other down, Linyet unflinching.

At last Heinmyets sighed and looked away. "We will have the bonfire for Cenarth tonight. Leader Katerin, I have messages for you from Medvara."

"And is my mother welcome?" Linyet challenged.

Heinmyets stiffened. "The Kinslayer is welcome as long as she is in the company of Leader Katerin. When Katerin goes, she must leave also."

"I thank you for that," Rekaré said in a low voice. "I would bid farewell to Cenarth." Her voice caught. "I wish he had not followed us into the Chamber. I devoutly wish that were so."

Heinmyets turned his horse away and did not answer her.

"I'm sorry," Katerin said.

Rekaré shook her head. "I expected worse. I will ride with

Cenarth. You should probably get those messages. Don't worry about me." Her brittle tone turned harsher. "I am *Rekaré Kinslayer*, after all. I knew he would be angry after Cenarth died. Now nothing holds me back from my ultimate purpose—and Cenarth is but another addition to the claims I hold against Chatain."

Katerin held out a hand. "I wish things had been different."

"So do I." She made a shooing motion. "Don't worry about me. You have Leader's business! Find out about your daughter!"

Oh Gods, do I really want to know the details?

She groaned. So much. Witmara and now Cenarth. She hadn't dared let herself think about Witmara's fate. Not if she were to keep on going. Not until she could leave for Medvare-the-city.

Katerin reluctantly urged Rainin to join Heinmyets. "What is the news from Medvara?"

Heinmyets gestured to one of his riders. "Give Leader Katerin her messages." As the rider handed Katerin several sealed papers, he continued. "I will tell you news I received from Haran so you do not worry untowardly—your messages will have more detail. Witmara was captured by a sorcerer piloting a metal ship."

"A metal ship? By the Goddess's gold necklace, however would that work?"

"I do not know—my messages did not provide details. She had married Toran just before the battle—the Mershaunten and the Hidden One stood witness. Witmara was ambushed as she worked magic to overcome the invaders. The Medvaran forces prevailed, but Witmara was taken and Finniarn killed on the battlefield."

"And Daro? Toran?"

"Both were injured but survived. Toran recovered the Light of Medvara and the Regent's ring—her captors discarded both on the battlefield. They are now in the custody of the oldest son of the Mershaunten, Aldan, and the Hidden One."

"Why didn't Toran hold onto them himself? As her consort he would have the authority to do so. Who is ruling Medvara right now, then? Aldan? The Hidden One?" She couldn't see Medvara tolerating the rule of others.

"Toran went after Witmara—her captors left a taunting message for him and he would not be discouraged." Heinmyets frowned. "As soon as he and Daro were treated, he took Daro and joined a fleet of sorcerer sailships in pursuit of Witmara's captors. The metal ships move very quickly, Katerin, from what Haran said, and he probably feared losing track of her once she left the Ourigny Islands. It is likely that Witmara is now in Daran, in Chatain's possession." He hesitated. "Haran also said that a brother and sister, Tilyet and Tilvi, administer Medvara in your name. Twins. They were guarding the Great Hall when the Tapestry spoke to them—at the same time that Witmara was captured."

Tilyet and Tilvi? Katerin frowned, trying to remember who they were—oh. Yes. Senior Agricultural Recordkeepers. Thanks to them, the Coos berry bushes in Cooscol had been restored. Finniarn had added the twins to the Council two years ago. They spoke rarely, but between the two of them they knew Medvara's agricultural production down to the smallest skein of ordinary wool and tiniest produce market, as well as trade with other nations.

If the Tapestry spoke to them, then Medvara is in good temporary hands. But Gods, Witmara.

"So we won Waykemin and saved Medvara, only to lose Witmara and Cenarth." Katerin's lips tightened. "A dire price."

Do not fret about Witmara right now. Do not. Toran is in pursuit. He is her spouse. It is his role.

"Dire indeed."

Katerin sighed. "Rekaré will be in even more of a rage about

Chatain when she hears this news about Witmara. We suspected it—I felt her capture before we attacked Waykemin, but to have the abduction confirmed? It is personal with Rekaré. She has vowed to kill Chatain herself, and Cenarth's death, even though it was through the influence of Chatain and not Chatain himself, just adds to her list of grievances against him. That he has also taken Witmara for whatever purpose...."

"The Kinslayer." His voice was bitter.

"It may take that to finish Chatain."

Unless Witmara strikes before Rekaré gets to him.

She allowed herself that much hope. If Witmara could get free somehow—if Staul worked through her—then she might well bring Chatain down.

"I suppose you will send Rekaré after Witmara?"

"As you said, she is the Kinslayer. Who would be better to bring Chatain down?"

"Indeed. But if she becomes Empress—" His face darkened. "A fell reward for all she has done."

"She has rejected that option at all turns," Katerin said. She wrenched her thoughts from Chatain and Daran. *It is not yet time—and there are more pressing matters closer to Heinmyets.* Time to change the subject. "And while we have won in Waykemin, I bring news of an even greater foe than Chatain. We cannot afford this anger, Heinmyets. Not with what lies ahead." She hesitated, thinking back across the past seven years. "I do not think Rekaré expects to survive the fight with Chatain. Do not hold her at arm's length. Please. She grieves as you and Linyet do, with the additional burden of guilt. They had grown close again before his death, and I think he planned to keep riding with her. She questions whether she should have allowed him to rejoin her, even though it made both of them happy."

She decided not to mention that Sesenth had been a third participant in the renewal of their relationship. Heinmyets didn't need to know, unless either Rekaré or Linyet decided to tell him.

He cast a sideways glance at her. "Is that Katerin Leader or Katerin Healer speaking?"

"In this case, both. I would sooner see her be mindful of what she does instead of going after Chatain in a blind rage—the Kinslayer rides her hard right now, as well as the Saubral *benghaalph*. I would prefer her to be able to have a few hours as Rekaré ea Miteal, the grieving spouse of Cenarth. Not Kinslayer or *benghaalph*." Katerin sighed. "She is more those than human these days."

"I—will try," he said. "That is all I can promise."

"Trying will be more than enough," she said. "Now. Let me tell you about what I learned in Waykemin. I do not exaggerate when I say we face a greater foe than Chatain."

AFTERMATH

Rekaré huddled on a campstool by one of the Mer Galad fires, watching the flames in the darkness as a slow drizzle more like Medvara's mists than Keldara in spring whispered down. An oilcloth slicker kept her dry but she was cold even next to the fire. Her body ached all over, knees throbbing, right shoulder tender, left ankle stiff. Tonight even the slightest old injury returned to plague her. Perhaps it was the damp, or perhaps she was just weary.

When does it end?

She sighed and buried her head in her hands, wanting to cry but not finding strength available for tears. Cenarth's funeral pyre and ceremonies had been uneventful, just long. Neither Kinslayer nor *benghaalph* rode her this evening, had not since Heinmyets acknowledged her as Cenarth's widow and the mother of the Two Nations' heir. A small mercy. Except for what that pyre had driven home, as she watched Heinmyets and Linyet lead the rites.

Only Linyet left.

She groaned and raised her head to stare into the fire again.

So much left to do. Gods, do I have the strength to face what lies ahead?

There had been a feast after Cenarth's pyre. She endured it as long as she could, then slipped out of the Leader's House to rejoin her riders in camp instead of spending the night in the room assigned her in the Leader's House. She couldn't stand the thought of sleeping there, even for one night. Not with the ghosts it could bring. After Medvara she didn't want to deal with ghosts—or shadows—even if they were only memories.

Sesenth had gone to bed. Basnen stood on the other side of the fire, head down, drowsing. Rekaré wanted to sit vigil alone with her daranval for a while, before the next phase of battle. Tomorrow they left for a fast trip to Medvara, and after that? Probably a swift ship to Daran, in pursuit of Toran—the young fool, to charge off with a minimum amount of support to rescue his beloved—and Witmara.

Daran.

She shuddered. Time to face her fate.

For years she had wondered about the land her ancestors came from. Had cursed it. Now she was going to see it—or however much of that cursed land that she needed to see before she got the chance to kill Chatain. Because that was the only reason she had to go to that damned place. She didn't want to rule it.

Rekaré poked at the fire with a long, twisted branch that had been dead long enough for the bark to fall off. She let the tip catch fire, then buried it in the drying dirt around the fire, repeating the process until the stick's tip formed a point sharp enough that she could have cooked with it.

Basnen raised her head, nostrils fluttering softly as she acknowledged someone's approach.

Probably Katerin, checking on me.

The Healer in her cousin still lurked under the Leader. Rekaré sighed and straightened up, prepared to dismiss Katerin as quickly as possible. She wanted to be alone and not fussed over. Senth was easily discouraged, but Katerin's persistence was a different thing.

To her surprise, the visitor was Heinmyets, wearing a herder's oilcloth slicker and broad-brimmed felt hat, his braid freshly shorn in mourning for both Inharise and Cenarth. He scratched Basnen's neck, the mare stretching out her head and wiggling her upper lip appreciatively. Then he grabbed another campstool and sat next to Rekaré.

"I did not expect you here," she said.

"I wanted to talk to you. I did not expect you to leave the Leader's House tonight."

"Too many memories." She stared into the fire. "Mother. Inharise. Cenarth. Others. I can't face any more shadows. Not tonight. Not without raising the Kinslayer, and I want to be free from her tonight, of all nights."

"I worried that you did not feel welcome." He rubbed his face. "I am sorry for my anger toward you earlier today, Rekaré."

"I've heard plenty on that subject from Linyet—and you were justified. Are justified."

"Linyet pled with me to make things right. That my son was happy with you at the end. That he held no anger toward you, as his father either had a vision that he would fall at Forsim or else intended to fall at Forsim."

She didn't know if that was soothing or if it made things worse. But it had been a thought that kept nagging at her.

"I have wondered about that myself," she said. She poked at the dirt. "I tried not to think it possible that he intended to fall. But he should have known better at the end. He was no magician. Not like me. Not like Katerin. We would have survived without him. But he couldn't...."

She jabbed harder at the dirt and the tip broke off. She put it back in the fire.

"He has always been putting himself into danger, especially

when protecting you." Heinmyets rested his hand on hers, stilling her fresh digging in the dirt. She shivered at the contact. Warm. Familiar. It brought back memories of running to him as a child. "It was his choice, not yours."

"Mine to allow him to come. That haunts me, just like the other kin-deaths of those too close to me."

Rekaré exhaled a choked, ragged breath. It was somehow easier to bear that Heinmyets was angry with her, even hated her. Not this remorseful old man with words of sympathy that scorched her heart.

"You cannot let yourself be haunted by these deaths," Heinmyets said.

"Who says I can't?" She gently slipped her hand free, to fiddle with the stick once more. "The Gods named me Sorrow at my birth. And now—I know sorrow. I live sorrow. I bring sorrow."

"Rekaré." She winced at the deep pain in his voice.

"It is true," she said quietly. "You can't deny it."

"I was there when the Gods named you. I remember it well. But you are more than just sorrow, Rekaré."

"Am I?"

Silence fell between them and they sat staring into the fire.

The wind changed and blew smoke into their faces. Heinmyets doubled over, coughing hard, standing up. It brought back memories of her mother's last years, winnowed down to nothing as she fought that persistent cough…. Rekaré dropped the stick and retrieved a waterskin. Heinmyets nodded thanks and drank deeply. She moved their stools out of the smoke. Hopefully it wouldn't change again soon.

"Thank you," he said. He wiped his mouth dry. "So. What now?"

"Medvara, to gather up who we may, and then to Daran," Rekaré said. "Confronting Chatain. Freeing Witmara. Gods, for all I know, crowning her Empress. I don't think Katerin's ready to admit it, but Witmara is not the Leader for Medvara. The land loves Katerin as it never did me—or Cenarth." She choked on his name. "And it loved him better than me," she whispered. "He did not kill his kin to rule it."

"After that?" Heinmyets' voice was soft. "After you face Chatain?"

She shook her head. "I do not know." She threw her head back, letting the cold drizzle bead up on her face. "Not even *benghaalph* shows me what happens after that. Whether I fall at last once I bring him down, or if I just find myself a nice little corner somewhere and fade into nothingness—I don't know."

Gods, both options sounded good.

I am tired of fighting.

"You would never fade into nothingness," he said. "Your mother noted that when you were young. Such a blazing young personality. The way your magic grew. Your boldness and skills."

A sardonic chuckle escaped her. "All to become the Kinslayer."

"You had eleven good years bringing Medvara back. You laid the foundation for Katerin."

"And she has done more in seven years than Cenarth and I ever did. Could do."

"Katerin built on what you and Cenarth did." He hesitated. "And in the past seven years, you have brought the Saubral from being a shadowy fear to allies. That was your doing, Rekaré."

"Because *benghaalph* took me. Because a young Shadowwalker-to-be saw that potential in me and somehow brought it out."

"Sesenth."

"Yes."

He exhaled long and hard. "You had a tripartite relationship with her and Cenarth for those few days, didn't you?"

Rekaré lowered her head and closed her eyes for a moment,

squeezing hard as somehow more dampness tried to work its way out to join the wet on her face.

"Nothing formal," she said finally. "Battlefield agreement. There was no need for anything more than that."

She wondered who had told him. Katerin or Linyet? Unlikely. Neither appeared inclined to tell Heinmyets.

"I watched Sesenth at the pyre. Both of you. I had not expected a Shadowwalker—even one in transformation—to shed tears for one of my kin. It was like watching Inharise during Alicira's pyre."

"I'm sorry."

"What is there to be sorry for?" He shrugged. "Both you and Cenarth saw the three of us as rulers, lovers, and friends as you grew up. It is not surprising that both of you have—had—hearts big enough to accept a third. My sorrow is that your reunion was much shorter than it should have been."

Rekaré buried her head in her hands. He pulled her to him as dry sobs wracked her body. Oh Gods, she hadn't done this since she was a child. The familiar scent of horses and the spicy musk akin to Cenarth's brought more tears.

"We are all that is left of them, Rekaré," he said softly. "Yes. I was angry at how he died. How could I not be? But if I let my anger rule me, then I lose the last of my love." He stroked her cowl. "Can I see what is underneath?"

She bit her lip and nodded, pulling back before she took off cap and cowl so that he could see her freshly shaved head. She had taken time to have Sesenth shear the remaining stubble before Cenarth's funeral.

He ran his head over her bare head. "Your hair used to be so beautiful. Your sorrow is so great that you cut all of it?"

She replaced the cap, then the cowl. "I cut my hair after killing Chiral. I have kept it cut ever since. It seemed right once I became Kinslayer."

"Oh Rekaré. Rekaré. My wild, strong, Heartsdaughter. To see

you become this breaks my heart. I would have spared you this anguish if I could have."

"Heartfather," she whispered, trembling, at last able to use the endearment, the acknowledgment of the man who had been her father in all but blood.

"Must it be like this?" he asked.

"I see no other clear path," she said. "Not since I left Medvara."

He wrapped both arms around her again, holding her tight. "Then we will say farewell tomorrow, perhaps forever in this life."

She nodded, unable to speak.

"Just promise me this, Heartsdaughter. If you can. If you see any path that brings you back to the Two Nations when you have exacted your vengeance on Chatain—please take it. I do not want to be the sole survivor of our family."

"You have Linyet."

"Linyet is the future. I am selfish, and want my Heartsdaughter nearby in my old age."

"I will try," she breathed.

But even as she promised she knew it would not happen. Not unless she were utterly broken.

FIRE, WRATH, AND DESTRUCTION.

Flames wrapped around her as voices screamed in terror. A red mist took form and reached for her, seeking to enfold her in its depths—

Witmara jolted awake, gasping for breath. She shot up. Darkness around her. Just a nightmare or more?

You must flee. Chatain seeks you.

The land pushed hard against her.

"Nereast, Petronin," she said softly.

"Wha?" Nereast startled up.

"Something's wrong. The land is warning me."

"Damn."

Flint and steel scratched as Nereast kindled a tiny spark on a long sliver of the grass-like wood, and lit one of the lamps. Petronin sat up.

"What's going on?"

"She says the land is warning her."

Petronin nodded. He picked up a stave—where had that come from? She hadn't noticed it last night—and slipped past the cloth curtain.

"I feel it too," Nereast said. "Damn, damn, damn. It's too early to get that donkey I wanted you to ride." She bustled about the hovel, gathering up their few scattered items and shoving them into bags.

Petronin returned. "Fire beyond the gate, and soldiers watch it. From the sounds of things, they're ransacking the neighborhood. We don't have much time."

"Goddess watch over us, because we need to flee." Nereast sighed. "Petronin. Can you take her on your back? I'll carry our goods."

"I can walk...."

"Not as fast as we need to go, woman! And not if you can't control the land's yearning for you yet. We don't have time for you to make that connection. We need to go. Now."

Petronin knelt by her cot, his back to her. "Climb on, my lady."

Gods, she hated to do this. It didn't feel right But if Chatain's soldiers were searching for her just beyond the gate—Witmara clambered onto Petronin's back and wrapped her arms around his neck. He took her legs and rose.

"Give me a moment." Nereast pulled back the curtain so they

could leave. Witmara heard water splashing and smelled smoke. Nereast burst out of the shelter, one of the lamps in her hand. Flame smoldered on the reed mats. Nereast dropped the curtain.

"Won't that attract attention?" she asked.

"Not until we're gone. And we don't dare leave any trace behind."

Nereast cupped the lamp in her hand and they set off down the path, plunging into the thicket. Witmara buried her face in Petronin's back to keep from getting smacked by vines and brush. Above and around them she heard hoots and calls from unfamiliar birds and animals disturbed by their passing.

She slipped into a trance-like state as she clung to Petronin and darkness grew lighter. Gods, it was hot and damp here. She had thought Medvara was miserable in the summers, but this was far worse—and it wasn't even summer here. Was this what the mainland would be like?

The sound of waves on a beach grew louder. Was that seagulls she heard, or something else? Then they burst out of the underbrush onto a white sandy beach.

"Gods be praised, at least this is going our way," Nereast said. "I feared it wouldn't still be here."

Witmara raised her head even though she couldn't see much in the dimness of the early morning light. They were in a small cove, protected from the larger ocean. A dock ran out into the cove, a small sailboat moored there—an ordinary sailboat with no feel of magic about it. Nereast marched onto the dock, Petronin following. He set Witmara down as Nereast put her bags into the boat, then helped Witmara aboard. He cast off the lines and jumped skillfully into the stern. They poled the boat into deeper water, and he raised the sail.

"Where are we going?" Witmara asked once the wind filled the sail and Nereast had collapsed on a seat in the bow

Nereast pointed toward a distant wedge of green on the

horizon. "We meet another ship on the Middle Island. Betsona's people will be expecting us there."

"And after that?"

"They will take us to Betsona, where you will have time to connect with your land in safety."

Was escape really to be this simple? As the sun rose behind them, the water seemed to sparkle and glow, waves lapping at the boat's hull in a joyful refrain.

Welcome, welcome, welcome.

But behind them an underlying rage mixed with fear surged stronger.

Chatain.

She almost wanted to turn and face him. Get things over with. But it was not yet time for her to challenge him. Not until she was stronger—and hopefully with the help of Daro and Toran. If they had survived. Witmara's hands tightened into fists. They must have survived. If they had fallen, wouldn't she feel their absence now that she was away from that cursed ship and her captors?

She hoped so.

Soon enough she would be in a safe place and could reach for them.

Nereast stretched and unwrapped her turban, shaking free her felted locks with bright ribbons twined within them.

"Ah, this is better. I feel more like myself." She rolled the cloth and set in in the bottom of the boat. "I feel my kinsman's presence. He will be here soon, Lady Witmara, and not alone." She smiled, her solemnness gone. "I no longer need to hide myself. Nereast was but a guise I used to follow Larien at my lady Betsona's request, the name and personality of another of her staff. I am Seijina, cousin of Sorcerer-Captain Setkin, and bondmate and Headwoman for the lady Betsona. I welcome you to Daran in Betsona's name, Lady Witmara. May you bring us the healing we seek."

Witmara stared at Ner—no, Seijina. "How did you manage to get on that ship?"

"We have our ways on the Islands. And if we can get you to Adalane, you will find support there."

"I—I am surprised."

"Betsona has been working toward this goal since Chatain became Emperor," Seijina said softly. "She cannot rule as Empress—it would consume her far too quickly, before she could fix our broken land. It would fall back into foul hands. We have been preparing to make things right for years, hoping that somehow one of our exiled kin would return. And now you have."

"I—see," Witmara said.

Seijina placed a hand on Witmara's shoulder. "Rest, Lady Witmara. You have quite the task ahead, and we still need to get you away from Chatain. Lie down so you cannot be seen. I will tell you when it is safe to sit up."

Should she trust this woman?

She had no other options. Witmara lay down. The waves chuckled against the boat's bottom. It hurt to stare up as the sky grew brighter, so she closed her eyes.

Lord Staul, protect me!

She fingered her necklace. At least that had been left to her.

The God did not answer, but she felt the presence of her father.

Was this how revolutions really began?

THE END

NEWSLETTER

Like this story and want to know what's coming out next, or what deals Joyce is offering on her book?

Check out Joyce's monthly newsletter at

https://joycespublishingnewsfromwideopenspaces.kit.com/a65eaa89cd

And get a free download snippet from the Martiniere Multiverse!

ABOUT THE AUTHOR

The work of Joyce Reynolds-Ward includes themes of high-stakes family and political conflict, digital sentience, personal agency and control, realistic strong women, and (whenever possible) horses. She is the author of *The Netwalk Sequence* series, the *Goddess's Honor* series, *The Martiniere Legacy* series, *The People of the Martiniere Legacy* series, and the recently published *The Cost of Power* trilogy as well as standalones *Klone's Stronghold, Alien Savvy, Beating the Apocalypse,* and *Federation Cowboy.* Joyce is a Self-Published Fantasy BlogOff Semifinalist, a Writers of the Future SemiFinalist, and an Anthology Builder Finalist. She is a member of the Science Fiction and Fantasy Writers Association and a member of Soroptimists International.

BOOKS AND PUBLICATIONS

Goddess's Honor

Beyond Honor and Other Stories: Goddess's Honor Book One
Pledges of Honor: Goddess's Honor Book Two
Challenges of Honor: Goddess's Honor Book Three
Choices of Honor: Goddess's Honor Book Four
Judgment of Honor: Goddess's Honor Book Five

The Cost of Power

Return
Snippet: Outtakes from Philip Martiniere
Crucible
Snippet: The Criminal Injustice Interview
Snippet: Sibling Warfare
Redemption
Omnibus Ebook Edition

The Martiniere Legacy

First Meetings: A Martiniere Legacy Short Story
Inheritance: The Martiniere Legacy Book One
Ascendant: The Martiniere Legacy Book Two

Realization: The Martiniere Legacy Book Three

A Belated Christmas Honeymoon: A Martiniere Legacy Short Story

The Enduring Legacy: The Martiniere Legacy Book Four

People of the Martiniere Legacy

The Heritage of Michael Martiniere: A Martiniere Legacy Novel

Broken Angel: The Lost Years of Gabriel Martiniere: A Martiniere Legacy Novel

Justine Fixes Everything: Reflections on Mortality

The Martiniere Multiverse

A Different Life: What If?

A Different Life: Now. Always. Forever.

A Very Multiversal Christmas Miracle

Netwalk Sequence Author Preferred 2022 Editions

Life in the Shadows: Book One

Netwalk: Book Two

Netwalker Uprising: Book Three

Netwalk's Children: Book Four

Learning in Space: Book Five

Netwalking Space: Book Six

Bright Star Fair Witches

Becoming Solo: A Bright Star Fair Witches Novella

Non-Series Titles currently available:

Alien Savvy: A Western SF Novella

Klone's Stronghold: Reeni

Beating the Apocalypse

Bearing Witness

Fabulist and Fantastical Worlds: A Short Story Collection

Federation Cowboy

Vision of Alliance

Vella Titles:

Falcon of the Martinieres (part of *Justine Fixes Everything*)
Bearing Witness
Beating the Apocalypse
A Different Life—What If? An Alternative Martiniere Legacy Novel
Becoming Solo
A Different Life—Linda's Story: An Alternative Martiniere Legacy Novel
Federation Cowboy

Audiobooks Available:

Alien Savvy: A Western SF Novella

Released from other publishers:

"Queen of the Snows," in *Once Upon A Winter: A Folk and Fairy Tale Anthology*, edited by H. L. Macfarlane

"My Man Left Me, My Dog Hates Me, and There Goes My Truck," in *Black-Eyed Peas on New Year's Day: An Anthology of Hope*, edited by Shannon Page

"Lost Loves," in *All Worlds Wayfarer*

"The Wisdom of Robins," in *Whimsical Beasts: A Campcon Anthology*, edited by Joyce Reynolds-Ward

"The Cow at the End of the World," in *Well...It's Your Cow*, edited by Frog Jones

"To Plant or Pull Up Stakes," in *Pulling Up Stakes: A Campcon Anthology*, edited by Joyce Reynolds-Ward

"The Notice," in *Children of a Different Sky*, edited by Alma Alexander

www.ingramcontent.com/pod-product-compliance
Lightning Source LLC
Chambersburg PA
CBHW031932110726
47902CB00001B/143